House
of
Iron

A MAGIC CITY STORY

T.K. THORNE

CAVEL
PRESS

Kenmore, WA

A Camel Press book published by Epicenter Press

Epicenter Press
6524 NE 181st St.
Suite 2
Kenmore, WA 98028

For more information go to:
www.Camelpress.com
www.Coffeetownpress.com
www.Epicenterpress.com
www.TKThorne.com

This is a work of fiction. Names, characters, places, brands, media, and incidents are either the product of the author's imagination or are used fictitiously.

Cover design by Scott Book
Design by Melissa Vail Coffman

House of Iron
Copyright © 2021 by T.K. Thorne

ISBN: 978-1-60381-797-4 (Trade Paper)
ISBN: 978-1-60381-798-1 (eBook)

Printed in the United States of America

*To Loraine Simons, cheerleader extraordinaire
and my mother's dear and devoted friend.*

Acknowledgements

The first person to read my work is always my husband, Roger. I'm grateful to him for his patience and keen eye as an editor and for his constant support. He is my rock. My family has always given the priceless gifts of their support and belief in me, especially my sister, Laura, who is my cheerleader and the queen of my Super Fan Club.

Thanks also to my literary agent and friend, Kimberley Cameron, and to everyone at Camel Press, especially Jennifer McCord and Mary E. Kelleher. Both Kimberly and Jennifer have kept me going with their belief and enthusiasm in the Magic City Stories, not to mention their wisdom and advice.

Appreciation to all my beta readers and to the professionals who offered technical assistance—Retired Birmingham Deputy Chief Henry Irby; retired Birmingham Deputy Chief Herman Hinton; Pat Curry, retired homicide detective and medical examiner investigator; Dr. D.P. Lyle, medical forensics expert; Sally Reilly, Esq., and David Brody, Esq; former Jefferson County District Attorney, Brandon Falls; Dan Katz, communications engineer at Johns Hopkins Applied Physics Lab, Jake Ray with Merrill Lynch, and Christopher Clay Gordon with Alfa Insurance.

Finally, I want to thank all the readers who love the story and the characters. I love Rose, Becca, and Aunt Alice too, and am grateful that they allow me to share their amazing stories.

Chapter One

I am the last witch of the House of Rose. I'm also a homicide detective in the Birmingham Police Department. Neither witch nor detective was on my future occupation wish list when I graduated from The University of Alabama less than two years ago. But back then I couldn't see the future. Nor did I know that witches and warlocks lived among the city's residents in three ancient Houses—Rose, Iron, and Stone. They arrived in the Magic City over a century ago to draw their powers from the abundant ores beneath and around Red Mountain.

It's not exactly true that I'm the last of my House. Though our enemies think her dead, my Great Aunt Alice is alive and kicking at a hundred-plus years. And I now have a daughter—that is, I *will* have a daughter. She's still technically a fetus, although close to her debut. My fellow detective in the Homicide Unit, Tracey Lohan, is her father. We aren't married or in a relationship.

It's complicated.

"Rose, we have a case," Tracey says, jerking me from my reverie.

Birmingham's Homicide Unit doesn't assign formal "partners," but Tracey and I team up on anything that's not routine.

"What is it?" I look up at him. Way up. Even when I'm not sitting, he towers over me. Standing, I'm five foot eight, and he has seven inches on me. It's not just his height. He's a bear of a man. If it weren't for the gentle glint in his gray eyes, he'd be intimidating.

"Guy fell seven stories off a construction site downtown," he says.

"Fell or was pushed?"

"That's what they're paying us to figure out." He sets his extra-large coffee mug that reads "Bad Cop, No Donut" on my desk to shrug into his jacket. It takes real cold for Tracey to be in a jacket, but this December qualifies, at least today. Tomorrow is unpredictable. There's not a lot of room in the cramped Homicide Unit offices where the desks are jammed into sterile little cubicles enlivened by family photos or children's art. Only two photos hang on my walls—one of my Great Aunt Alice in her mint garden with a floppy sun hat in one hand and clippers in the other, and one of my best friend Becca in red knee-high leather boots, a matching red turtleneck, and a colorful, trailing scarf, Becca's idea of casual. The six-year-old boy with burn scars at her side is Daniel. They're not related, but as far as either is concerned, they're siblings.

"Come on," Tracey says, "I'll fill you in on what I know in the car."

I refasten the tie that's straining to enforce my ponytail. I thought pregnancy made one's hair thinner, but mine has just gotten thicker, darker, and curlier. Trust me to be the outlier on the bell curve. I only keep it long because I'm afraid if I cut it short, I'll lose all possibility of control.

Trying not to grunt, I haul myself out of the chair, my once flat belly now a rounded mound preceding me. My feet hurt. My back hurts. Sleeping more than an hour at a time is wishful thinking. I need a bathroom pit stop every fifteen minutes.

Being pregnant is another something I never envisioned in my future. I like my life uncomplicated. Until Becca, I didn't even do friends. Until my ex-partner—now dead, thanks to me—I didn't do serious boyfriends. Now I have a *person* growing inside me, and I will be forever tied to her . . . not to mention diapers. *God, I am dreading the diapers.*

The homicide call takes us to the heart of midtown, an area popping with urban renaissance in the wake of the Railroad Park and a baseball park. A lucky angle through a gap in buildings might provide a glimpse of Vulcan, Birmingham's towering god of iron and steel who overlooks the city from the top of Red Mountain on his 123-foot-high pedestal. A little further north in downtown proper, ornate pre-WWII buildings have been renovated for offices, but here in Midtown, residential buildings are springing up, including the apartment complex in progress that looms above us. At the moment, it's a skeleton of steel bones.

Officers have cordoned off the block. Diagonally parked patrol cars claim the intersection, emergency lights blinking. Reporters press against the yellow crime scene tape. A barrage of shouted questions meets us. We wave the media off, duck under the yellow crime scene tape, and make our way toward the cluster of uniformed officers.

I'm not eager to look at a body that fell seven stories. In my first days as a rookie in the Patrol Bureau, which were only a little more than a year ago, one of the first things my fellow male officers did was to take me to the scene of a horrible, single-car accident. The deceased victim had either been high on drugs or fallen asleep at the wheel or had a heart attack. In any case, his vehicle rolled off the road, down a hillside, through a chain-link fence and right under a parked flatbed trailer. It almost decapitated him. The guys thought it would be grand fun to see how the female rookie handled the gruesome sight.

Horrified, but damned if I would let them see it, I found a way to mentally distance myself. To keep it together, I told myself it wasn't real, just a wax figure in a haunted house. It worked well enough that I walked back up the hill where a group waited, every eye on me, and simply said, "Looks pretty bad."

But I can still see that mutilated man in my mind's eye. Since then, I've seen plenty of dead bodies, but I don't particularly want to see something like that again. The damage done from falling seven stories will qualify as a gruesome sight, but I don't have the option of not looking. I stall by digging out a notebook from my purse.

"What's his name, Chris?" Tracey asks the young patrol officer standing nearby.

The officer's baby face confirms he is the Chris Lane I know from our martial arts class, my preferred partner because he is super patient and not as intimidating as Tracey. He's skillful on the mat, though he looks like a high school student with cinnamon hair in a military buzz cut and a splash of honest-to-God freckles.

Chris glances at the notebook in his hand. "Victim is Jim Jacobson." Reluctantly, I look down at the redheaded man sprawled before us. It would be easy just to think of him as a wax figure, like I did the decapitated man, but he's not. He was someone's husband, brother, or son. I'm hoping nothing triggers an upchuck—or worse, tears. Normally I'm not prone to either, but "normal" means BP, Before Pregnancy. Now, a whiff of perfume can make me nauseous, and I tear up at cute commercials. My whole personality is flipped. Who is this woman walking around in my skin? As bad as the decapitated man was, the only time I've ever been physically sick at the sight of a dead body was the night I had my first vision, a glimpse of the future that caused me to fire two bullets into a man's back. That little incident got me taken out of Patrol and snatched into the Detective Bureau to keep me out of the media's eye and out of trouble.

That didn't exactly work.

Tracey squats—a movement no longer a viable option for me. The man smashed onto the pavement face down. His front will have suffered the worst damage, head and face, which are mostly hidden from view. The blood is not as much as one would think either. When the heart stops pumping, blood thickens quickly. Paramedics apparently didn't have to turn him over to pronounce him DOS, dead on the scene, so they left him as they found him.

"Can't see anything obvious other than the fall that killed him," Tracey says from his position beside the body.

I rub my gritty eyes that are supposed to be green but were swimming in red the last time I checked a mirror. "I don't think it was the fall that killed him, more like the sudden stop."

Ignoring my lame attempt at humor, Tracey asks Chris, "The medical examiner been notified?"

"On the way," Chris says.

"What about an evidence tech?"

"Already been and gone. Took some photos and a blood sample." With a smile, Chris jerks his thumb up. "Said they don't pay him enough to dust for fingerprints up there."

My gaze follows his gesture to the naked steel beams high above us. A cold wind pushes at my back. I don't blame the tech.

"I understand," Tracey says. "Let's see what we've got before we worry about that."

Tracey rocks from his squat onto his knees, putting one foot forward to stand in the graceful manner that a Samurai from feudal Japan would rise—right knee first to allow the (hypothetical) drawing of a sword. I've seen him do it many times in class, but to anyone else, other than Chris, he is just a big man getting to his feet.

Tracey absently brushes off the areas where his knees contacted the ground and glances down at me. "We'll wait for the medical examiner's report to see if we've missed anything. His front side is going to be messed up. No point in moving him. Don't want to contaminate anything more than necessary."

I nod, grateful to avoid having to look at Jacobson's crushed face.

Although there's not officially a "training officer" position for a detective, I was assigned to Homicide with Tracey almost a year ago to learn from him. We've kept the arrangement. The entire police department is shorthanded, but the boom in gang violence, a nationwide trend, has hit the Homicide Unit particularly hard in terms of manpower. That's the only reason I, a rookie, got assigned to the elite unit.

"Any witnesses?" I ask.

"One." Chris motions over a middle-aged man in a yellow hardhat.

Tracey reaches out and shakes the witness' hand, introducing us to him. "Detectives Rose Brighton and Tracey Lohan."

I like that Tracey gives our first names. It's not something a patrol officer normally does. I guess that keeps a certain personal distance from the officer and the public. As a detective, I had to get used to giving my first name, but it seems to put people more at ease. Maybe it's a Southern thing.

"Zack Butler," the construction worker says. His gaze lands on my belly. Disconcerting, but better than having men stare at my breasts. Still, from Butler, it seems an accusation. He might as well be shouting, *You belong at home in the kitchen, not trying to play at being a man.*

I think Tracey may have picked up the same unspoken sentiment, because he loudly clears his throat for Butler's attention.

"Did you see what happened?" Tracey asks.

Butler shakes his head. "I was on the same level, but busy with a weld. Some guy below saw him falling and shouted out." He hesitates, looking up at the scaffolding rising above us, his voice distant, as if reliving the moment. "He never made a sound." Then, apparently jerking back to the present, his lower lip shoves out. "Jim was a good man. Had a golden arm."

"A golden arm?"

"It's a welder term. He knew his stuff."

"Did you know him well?" I ask.

"Not real well. We've had a few beers." He jams calloused thumbs into his belt.

He's hiding something.

"Married? Children?" Tracey asks.

"Yeah."

"Any problems there?"

At his belt, Butler's hands ball into fists. "You think he committed suicide?"

Butler is a beefy man, but Tracey is six foot three, all muscle, and wears a gun beneath his jacket. Unless Butler is a complete idiot, he will give up that testosterone stance quick. Even so, I take a small step to the side, ready to back my partner.

"Easy," Tracey says to Butler without a twitch of a muscle, as if he's talking to a frightened animal. "We don't think anything. We're just trying to figure out what happened."

Butler narrows his eyes, looking up at Tracey, lowering his voice to a confidential, if still growly, undertone. "Man commits suicide, the company insurance don't pay his family nuthin'."

"We don't work for the company." Tracey pulls aside his jacket so Butler can clearly see the badge fastened to his belt. "We're from the Police Department, homicide detectives, like I said. We just want the truth about what happened."

"What happened was an *accident*," Butler repeats. His voice is still tight, but he steps back and folds his arms over his chest.

"But you didn't see it," Tracey says.

"Don't have to see it to know it was an accident. Nobody was near him, and Jim's not a greenhorn. He's been a rigger a long time. He ain't gonna just step off the end of a beam."

"Shouldn't he have been tied to something?" I ask, remembering an old photograph I'd seen of a group of skyscraper workers casually having lunch on a beam of steel, their feet dangling over an abyss. They hadn't been tied to anything but looked as relaxed as if they were sitting on a picnic bench instead of a narrow piece of steel in the sky where a slight unbalance meant a terrifying death. But common sense would call for some kind of safety precaution, no matter how comfortable these insane people were with heights. Surely the company would require it for liability reasons, if nothing else.

Butler grimaces and his gaze shifts sideways. "Yeah. He should have been tied off. Maybe he was. Maybe his lanyard snapped."

"Is that unusual?" Tracey asks.

"Yeah, but falling is also unusual, especially for a man like Jim."

"Do we have your information?" Tracey asks. "We may want to reach you later."

Butler jabs his thumb toward Chris. "He's got it. Anything else? I gotta get back to work."

"We'll call you if we do," Tracey says.

With a grunt, Butler turns his back without looking at the body at our feet and strides off toward the lift that now sits on the ground, waiting.

"Where exactly was Jacobson when he fell?" I ask Chris. The officer cranes his neck back and points up. "Seventh floor right above us."

I follow his finger to the edge of the seventh floor, the framework of steel seeming to float on a sea of winter-blue sky. Before I can lower my gaze, a flood of golden warmth pushes through my feet, legs, and body, and the steel beams above seem to shiver. Color and sound leaches from the world. I'm rooted, unable to blink, much less move.

One of Alice's hypotheses is that this happens when an aberration in space-time causes another universe—possibly one created at the same moment as ours at the Big Bang—to intersect with ours. In that alternate universe, time moves in the opposite direction, and it's slightly out of phase with us.

When my "gift" engages, I "see" the past or sometimes the future. I think of it as the "witch" part of me twisting time. Whatever it is, when it happens, the space-time I'm in freezes. I'm unable to move or even breathe, which fortunately, I don't seem to need to do. In this instance, I am seeing the past because time appears to be moving backwards: Jacobson, face down and spread-eagle on the ground, floats upward past me, rising through the air all the way to the seventh floor until he is level with a horizontal steel beam. Then he tilts in an arc to the vertical, steps back onto the beam, his arms lowering to his sides, pauses, and then steps back onto what appears to be a platform with a railing around it. No one is near him.

As abruptly as it seized me, the vision releases me back into a world of color and focus and obedient forward-moving time. A familiar bolt of pain lances through my head, and I stagger. Tracey reflexively reaches out for me.

"You okay?"

I lean against the solid strength of his arm, holding on to it. Besides being a big man, he's also a warlock of House of Stone, which means he is even stronger and heavier than he looks. Trust me, you don't want Tracey Lohan stepping on your toes.

Deep breathing seems to be my best strategy against the assault of the severe headache that accompanies a vision.

Tracey watches me, giving me a minute to pull myself together.

When I release my grip on his arm, he asks quietly, "What is it? Did you 'see' something?"

I wince at a vicious stab of pain and nod.

Chapter Two

"What did you see?" Tracey asks when we are alone in his city car. I tell him.

"Sounds like a suicide," he says, rubbing his chin with one hand before placing it back on the steering wheel.

"It seemed to be." The pronouncement sits uneasily in my gut. "But—"

"But what?"

"That doesn't feel right."

"You think something happened that you didn't see in the vision?"

"I don't know, Lohan." The words come out sharper than I'd meant.

"Hey, don't jump on me." One side of his mouth twists in irritation. "And is there any possible way you could call me 'Tracey'? I am the father of your baby."

"That's immaterial."

It hits me how ridiculous that sounds, and he has the same reaction. The tension bursts into laughter that feeds off each other. Maybe it's a reflection of all that we have been through, the constant threat of death that hovers from a madman determined to kill me. All these months, there's been no release from it. Now it's apparently found its way out sideways.

Tracey fights it, then pulls the car to the side of the road and gives in.

"It's not funny," I say as soon as I can get control of myself.

He wipes at a tear in the corner of his eye. "Agreed. It's just so bizarre—"

"—I know. Don't say it. You'll start me off again."

I don't want to go down that horrible memory path where I sat handcuffed before a crazy man full of darkness. Not to mention the gun in my face. I put myself into that situation, and it haunts me in ways I'm not sure I understand. It's far better to laugh.

With a deep breath, Tracey puts the car into gear.

"Stop!" I blurt before we have gone more than a quarter of a block.

Stomping the brakes, he scans the visual field outside the car, looking for a threat, his right hand sliding under his jacket to rest on the gun in his shoulder holster.

"Sorry. I didn't mean to imply an emergency." Another giggle escapes.

"What is it?" His gaze goes to my expanded middle. "You're not ready to—are you?"

His concern is touching and sobers me. "No, I'm not."

"Did you have another vision?"

"No, not exactly."

His brow folds into concerned lines. "Then what?"

I clear my throat and point to the burger joint we just passed. "I'm hungry."

"We just had lunch two hours ago."

"Just ice cream. I really need ice cream. Now."

THE HOMICIDE UNIT IS LOCATED in the Police Administration building downtown. Tracey and I share a cubicle a few feet away from a small interview room. Lieutenant Barbara Faraday has the only "real" office. Faraday is a rectangular block of a woman with coffee skin and the ability to shoot a look like a shotgun blast, catching everyone within receiving distance. She suffers no nonsense.

Normally, a sense of camaraderie grows in a law enforcement group working together, but the general feeling about me in the unit is one of uneasy tolerance. I'm still considered a rookie who got a place in the elite Homicide Unit, not because of years of experience, but by a preemptive order from above, a whim of someone in the out-of-touch-with-reality administration. The other detectives at least try to be cordial, but to get to the lieutenant's office, we must pass Detective Frank Finkman's desk. Finkman makes no effort to hide his disdain for me as a rookie-who-doesn't-belong-in-the-Detective-Bureau-much-less-Homicide-Unit, or possibly as a woman in general. My pregnancy has only exacerbated his contempt. I don't talk about my personal life, but it's no secret that I'm single. The identity of the father definitely falls under the personal-and-private category, so naturally it's a subject of constant speculation. I can't exactly tell them that I got pregnant in order to save a race of witches and warlocks from extinction.

Today, fortunately, Finkman is not at his desk, and we make it unhindered to the lieutenant's office. Faraday has two inches of height and several pounds on me, even in my condition. Today, as most days, she's neck deep in paperwork. For a department in the digital age, there is paper everywhere. No one completely trusts computers. That means the machines supposed to make our lives simpler actually add to the workload. On the other hand, when you're searching for information, it's much more efficient to do a search on a computer than to sift through a mountain of paper. I'm not bad on computers, which don't give a whip that I am young, inexperienced, a woman, or pregnant.

Faraday looks up at us when we appear in her doorway. Her hawk gaze automatically goes to my belly, but her scrutiny is matter-of-fact, and I don't mind it. "Everything still okay?" she asks me.

"Fine."

"Remember, you've got a leave of absence whenever you need it."

"I know. Thanks."

"I've got plenty of paperwork duty I can put you on."

I must look horrified because she gives a snort that passes for her laugh. Then her mouth contracts into her normal scowling expression. "I'll not have you dropping that baby in my office."

"I'm good, Lieutenant, and I'll let you know when I need to be off."

She moves a piece of paper from one stack to the other. "Y'all went on the jumper call?"

"Yeah. Guy fell seven stories on a construction site downtown," Tracey says.

"What's the verdict?"

"Most likely suicide or accident, but we're not calling it until we get an autopsy report and see if anything happened before he made contact with the pavement."

"We're going to talk with his wife," I add. "See if there's an insurance angle or reason anyone might want to push him off a ledge."

"Or that he might step off on his own," Tracey adds.

"Sounds reasonable." She leans back in her chair, taking a deep breath. "Just don't spend too much time on it. We've got a gang war going on. You'll have plenty of real homicides to work if we can't impress on these kids that there's a better way than killing each other."

"You think there's any chance of that?" Tracey asks.

"A chance. The Task Force is working hard on it. Gang members are motivated by fear—fear of being seen as weak, fear of being shot themselves. It's a dirty cycle. We can promise to help, but we can't be there with them 24/7."

"But the street is," Tracey says.

She presses her lips together and looks away, maybe at a memory. "Yeah, the street is with them 24/7."

Chapter Three

Tracey and I head out of the office.

"Thanks for not dismissing my gut feeling," I say.

"Don't give me too much credit. Lieutenant would raise her eyebrows if we just brushed it off as suicide or accident without due diligence."

"Where to first?"

"Let's interview Jacobson's wife first and then his supervisor."

"Works for me. Your car?"

"Sure."

This is our normal mode of travel since I, as the most rookie detective, have a city car that spends more time in the shop than on the road. We head out the back door of the Administration Building, down a short flight of concrete steps into the police parking lot. Because of a newly renovated hotel, a doggie day care, and a loft development that all need parking spaces, parking for detectives has been relegated to the small area on the east side of the building. Overlooking the lot on that side of the building is an imposing mural of four boys, two white and two black, standing together beside the text of the Birmingham Pledge against racism.

Just as we reach Tracey's car, I notice a man approaching us. Even if I hadn't seen him coming, I would know who he was—Jason Blackwell, warlock of House of Iron. He is the negative to my positive or vice versa. My pulse does its skip-jump, hormones springing to attention. Even from an objective perspective he could engender that reaction—blonde, ice-blue eyes, chiseled features—and an effortless, worldly sophistication that turns heads and weakens knees. On top of that, the particular electricity between us is supernatural, and I don't mean in a fairytale sense.

Knowing that the attraction I feel when I am near Jason is most likely little magic-infused genes trying to survive doesn't calm my runaway pulse or my shallow breathing, any more than knowing that the release of oxytocin in the brain triggers motherly bonding. It is what it is.

I drop my hand from the door handle of Tracy's unmarked city car and cross my arms over my chest.

"Hello Jason."

He stops dead, taking in my condition. "Oh, *amore*, no wonder."

"No wonder what?"

My trust level for Jason Blackwell is in the negative zone. All roads lead to Rome. And Jason is Italian, or at least he spent a good part of his lifetime, or lifetimes, there. He's never told me his age.

But that is not why I don't trust him. He is House of Iron. The man who has tried to kill me at least three times in the past twelve months is also House of Iron.

Jason steps closer, putting his hands on my arms and setting off a cascade of reactions in my endocrine system. *Would the world really end if I just stepped into his arms and let his lips crush mine?*

He blinks hard, probably similarly assaulted by our demanding magics. Apparently, he's better than I am at controlling it. Part of me is disappointed.

"No wonder you are in great danger," he says, stepping closer, his gaze digging into mine.

"Tell me something I don't know." Desperate, I lift my chin in defiance of my body, which doesn't seem to be capable of backing away from him, and think about ice cream. *Chocolate peanut butter topped with rainbow sherbet.*

A very large man's hand plants itself on Jason's chest. The hand belongs to Tracey.

"Back off," Tracey says in a low growl.

Jason doesn't even look at him. His pupils are caverns edged with glacial blue and fixed on me.

"Remove your hand." Jason's tone is that of a man accustomed to being immediately obeyed. Not unusual, I'm sure, for a member of House of Iron. That's their power—manipulation. All it takes is a touch. He expects Tracey to drop his hand immediately.

But Tracey Lohan is House of Stone, immune to Jason's magic, as I am, and as Jason is to ours, other than the siren effect he and I have on each other.

"Release her now," Tracey says, "or I'm going to introduce the back of your head to the pavement."

I, for one, do not doubt this. Even if Tracey's magic is not called into play, the side effect of being House of Stone is enhanced muscle development. Additionally, he is an expert in at least two martial arts. His belt is black, but I don't even know exactly what his rank is. He said he trained in order to learn how *not* to hurt people.

Whatever Jason is, he's not an idiot, even with magic raging through his veins. He drops his hands from my arms and takes a step back, turning his attention to Tracey.

"Stone?" he asks.

"That's right."

Jason takes a breath. "That is good. She needs protection."

"From you," Tracey says.

"No, you idiot, not from me."

I can feel the tension pulsing in waves off Tracey.

"Who then?" I ask, unwilling to have Tracey pulverize Jason or do my defending. "Seems to me you are far from an innocent party since your 'chauffeur' and your 'boat pilot' both tried to kill me, not to mention kidnapping a little girl with cancer and threatening to wipe her mind like your uncle did with Becca." I welcome the rising anger that buffers the sexual storm.

"What are you are talking about?"

"Are you going to tell us you've been in Outer Mongolia for the past eight months?" Tracey's voice is a low growl.

"Europe, actually. On House business." He frowns. "But I suspect it was business manufactured to keep me away."

"Convenient," Tracey says.

Either Jason is an accomplished liar, or he truly doesn't know what has happened.

My hands go to my hips. "In case you haven't tried to take out your yacht lately, your pilot, Lawrence Anders, is in prison. He worked for Angola Simone, your 'chauffer,' who is still at large."

"Angola tried to kill you?" The grimness of Jason's mouth reveals he is not completely surprised. "I was promised you would be safe. It was Angola? You know this for certain?"

"That's right. He tried to kill both of us," Tracey says. "But since you've been out of the country and all, what made you decide Rose is suddenly in danger?"

"I returned a few days ago and overheard my uncle telling someone on the phone to 'Make it happen. It is time to end House of Rose.'"

I narrow my eyes. "I thought I killed your uncle."

"You did. One of them. Samuel is still very much alive."

I think of the short, jovial man who had shown off the secret rooms in the basement of the Simpson mansion. "Uncle Sam?"

"That is how he introduces himself. A nonsense name. Do not be fooled by his manner or size. He is as vicious and powerful as his brother."

"But aren't you head of the House now?"

"No. Samuel bears that title. He sent me on the extended mission in Europe." Jason looks at me intently, which makes my knees wobbly, damn him.

"I wish you had come with me, *amore*, or I had stayed to stop him."

"Could you have stopped him?" I think of Angola, his movements smooth and tight as a coiled serpent. "He was a Marine, wasn't he?"

"Yes, but very loyal to the House."

Tracey's shoulders tighten. As a former Marine himself, he hates that Angola is using skills he learned in the military to kill people, as much as we both hate police officers who betray their badge. Angola has his own hate issues. Insurgents captured him in Iraq, held him prisoner and tortured him. I know a thing or two about torture, but Angola's hell lasted a lot longer than mine. It twisted him. The Marines, his brothers in arms, failed to rescue him. But that doesn't excuse him. Again, I see Angola's gun an inch from my face, my friend's young sister at his mercy, taken from her bed at Children's Hospital. He was willing to kill her or wipe her mind. What kind of man would do that?

"Angola never spoke to me about what happened," Jason says. "I hired him to drive me while I was in town. Actually, that was Samuel's idea. I thought it silly, but it allowed me to take business calls without the distraction of driving."

"Iron has a lot of business," I mutter.

He ignores my sarcasm. "That is true, across the world."

I hear the quiet note of pride in his voice. I grew up in the military family of my adopted parents, but Jason cut his teeth on the primacy of family and House.

"Were you informed about your House being behind a scheme to keep a diabetes drug from market?" Tracey asks.

"Rose told me when we were last together. She said she was investigating a death, and that a pharmaceutical company owned in part by my family might have been involved. She mentioned Angola's alleged part, but there was no proof. Did you solve it?"

"We did. Angola *was* behind two murders and—" I tighten my lips as two detectives head to their cars not far away. I'm already branded by gossip. No point in handing them more on a plate. Besides, better to keep from saying too much in front of Jason. All his innocence routine could be a charade. The only thing I don't doubt is his loyalty to his House and his desire to get into my pants, which, unfortunately, is reciprocated . . . when he's near, anyway. Jason might be going straight back to Uncle Sam with everything we say. I never know with Jason Blackwell.

"Where is Angola?" Tracey asks. "There's an outstanding warrant for his arrest."

Jason huffs. "Arresting him would be a waste of time. He would simply touch a guard and suggest the man call a taxi and escort him to it." He stares at Tracey, considering. "If you want to protect our Rose, you will have to kill Angola and Uncle Samuel."

Chapter Four

Mary Ann Jacobson is a stout woman in her late forties. The bright copper of her hair is natural—apparent by the lack of dark roots and the matching brows that hover over moody sea-blue eyes. She stands in her doorway, a squealing infant in the crook of one arm, its tightly balled fists flailing the air. The little head is bald, but I suspect it might inherit its parents' red hair.

Tracey flips open his badge and introduces us. Like everyone, her attention lingers a moment on my belly, but it's an expert eye. "You're due soon, ain't ya?"

"Not for another three weeks."

"That baby ain't gonna wait three weeks."

"Great. I'm ready to have it now. Just knock me unconscious and wake me up when it's over."

"Don't you just wish," she says over the baby's wails. "Come on in."

Inside, the living room is chaos. It reminds me of my own house. Housekeeping is not exactly my forte. But most of this mess consists of baby stuff, toys, and toy parts.

Another child, about two years old, waddles in, diapers at half-mast. His flame curls and ruddy face leaves no doubt whose child he is.

"Ah, Jesus." Mary Ann shoves the crying baby from her arms into mine before I can protest. "Have a seat. I'll be back in a jiff." She grabs up the two-year-old and disappears down a hallway.

Tracey's mouth breaks into a grin. "You look like somebody just shot you."

I glance down at the scrunched red face in my arms. Terrified I will drop the squirming bundle, I've got both arms tight on him. At least

I'm assuming it's a boy from the blue blanket.

Moving aside a doll and a plastic motorcycle the size of his fist from the sofa, Tracey waves me to sit.

I scowl at the low sofa, envisioning having to get up. Sitting and standing have become operations involving creativity, maneuvering, and usually a hand or even two. How am I supposed to sit holding this baby?

My whole life changed when I decided not to take those "day after" pills. Everything would have been much simpler. But, apparently, I don't do simple.

According to Tracey's father, Dr. Orson Hobart—who also happens to be a city counselor and the head of House of Stone—all the Houses are dying out from genetic stagnation, infertility. Their only salvation is to mix their bloodlines with House of Rose, which is why eight and a half months ago, I lost my mind and initiated an "encounter" with Tracey.

Mary Ann finally emerges from the back room, the two-year-old clinging to her neck with a grubby hand.

"Jesus, you don't need a death grip on him," she says to me. "Loosen up." She gives me an appraising look. "This'll be your first, I reckon."

Since she doesn't seem available to rescue me, I try to follow her instructions, releasing one hand to grope for the sofa arm and lowering myself with the grace of an elephant onto the seat. That might not be fair to elephants, which are acrobatic despite their size. I am thinking seriously about hurting the man who did this to me. Even if it was my idea, he didn't have to go along with it.

"Now you look like you're about to *shoot* somebody," Tracey observes.

"I am," I whisper. "You."

"You're going to shoot someone?" Mary Ann asks with a scowl that says, *not in my house, you're not.*

"You have good ears." I force a smile to show her we're joking.

"Aye, good ears, which is amazing, I know, with all the racket. Here—" She produces a bottle and shoves it toward me. "I've checked it. The temp's right."

"How do I do this?" I ask, feeling as awkward as the day I first picked up a gun in the Police Academy.

"Just put the nipple against his mouth," she says. "He'll do the rest."

To my astonishment, he does, clamping onto the nipple as if he'd read the manual. Abruptly, his crying stops. The fiery red drains from his cheeks, and he turns big saucer eyes up at me. His gaze doesn't waver. I am the only entity in the universe, the source of everything good. I find myself staring back at him. Maybe I won't shoot my partner after all.

"How can I help you folks?" Mary Ann asks, settling herself into a worn chair. Stuffing has wormed out of a hole in the armrest.

Tracey responds for me because I'm absorbed by the tiny fingers that have a death grip around my pinky finger.

"We're very sorry about your husband's death," Tracey says.

She sighs. "He's got a hell of a sense of timing. I'll say that for the man."

"What do you mean?" Tracey asks.

She inclines her head at the baby I'm holding. "I mean that one ain't been out of the chute more than a couple of weeks. Now I got four others to take care of by myself."

I feel the color draining from my face at the thought.

"No family to help?" Tracey asks.

"Yeah, I suppose I'll have to pack up and go to my brother's, if he and his jerky wife will have me. Haven't talked about it yet."

"Will the company Jim worked for help any?" I ask.

"Hope so. They promise to if there's an accident."

But not if it's suicide. That's what Jacobson's co-worker said at the scene.

"We don't answer to the company," Tracey says. "Our job is to make sure it was an accident that didn't involve another person."

"You think somebody *killed* him?"

"Don't have any reason to think that at this point, but we're looking into it."

She frowns. "If somebody killed him on purpose, don't think the company would pay out."

"Mrs. Jacobson, did you love your husband?" I ask bluntly, taken aback by her matter-of-fact attitude.

She shrugs. "Guess so, but I got all these kids to think of now."

"Is there anyone that Jim might have had a serious disagreement with or any kind of problem?" Tracey asks.

She thinks for a minute. "Not really, unless you count a spat with Rick Victor. Jim and Rick had a fight a few weeks ago."

Tracey writes the name down in his notebook. "What did they fight about?"

"Jim drank and played poker with Rick and some other fellows. He came home one night with a busted nose and said he and Rick got into it over some cards."

I shift the emptying bottle to a steeper angle. The little guy is still going to town on the nipple.

"Did Rick work with him?" I ask, pulling my gaze from those unblinking saucer eyes.

"Oh yeah, all them boys that play cards together work for the company."

"Do you have a phone number for Rick?" Tracey asks.

"Somewhere," she says, "but I'll have to hunt for it." The child in her lap wriggles, and she sets him down. He stands beside the chair, one hand on the armrest, steadying his wobbly legs, considering us. A clump of hair, as red as his mother's, spikes in a pyramid on one side of his head. A fist plugs his mouth, reminding me of Daniel.

When his mother killed herself in Alice's house, the state took Daniel away. But his foster parents are good people. Becca visits him far more often than I. Just one item on the ever-present list of things to feel guilty about.

"That's okay," Tracey says. "Don't worry about trying to find the number. We'll get the info on Rick from the company."

"What about life insurance?" I ask. "Did your husband have any?"

"Nope. Not a dime."

Chapter Five

"You okay?" Tracey asks as we get into the car.

"What makes you ask?"

"The baby encounter."

I grunt. I do feel lightheaded, but I'll be damned if I'll admit that.

"My father would like to take us to dinner."

I twist to face him, trying to absorb the abrupt change of subject. "He what?"

"Dinner. Food. You know, that stuff you put in your mouth and chew."

"Lohan, I am not in the mood."

"It's just dinner. He wants to get to know you better. That's all."

I stare at him. "You're talking about the man who wanted you to smile, say hello, and jump in my pants to impregnate me?"

"There were mitigating circumstances, and that shouldn't even count, because I didn't do any such thing. You were the one—"

This time it is my turn to lift my palm toward him. "Stop. Don't even go there. I thought I was about to die."

"You're not very good for my ego."

"If I'd known I was going to live to endure the months of aches, pains, and wild emotional rollercoaster rides involved with the portage of a squirming bowling ball, I surely would not have made that impulsive decision."

"Why did you, by the way?"

I shift, seeking an angle to ease my back and uncomfortable with the question. Might as well be honest. "To purge my guilt of not trying to save an entire race of people."

"You wanted to dump your guilt without the risk of actually having a child."

"Bingo."

"That's all it was? You 'purging your guilt'?"

"Come on, Lohan. I told you up front it wasn't—"

"I know what it wasn't." He cuts me off, his mouth set in a stiff line. "But we all have to live with the consequences. And the fact is that she is my child too."

As a psychology major practicing without a license or education beyond a BS degree, I realize part of my grumpiness is fear.

"You're going to be a great mother," Tracey says as if reading my mind.

"Right. Like there's a handbook for having a daughter with the blood and magic of all three Houses."

My daughter will not just be a child of House of Rose. As an additional complication, since my unacknowledged grandfather was House of Iron and Tracey Lohan is House of Stone, she will be an unpredictable element, not to mention a target for those who have been attempting to destroy me for the very reason that they do not, under any circumstances, want the possibility of such a child to be born.

"My father's a good man, Rose. Do you want to deny our daughter a grandfather? Other than Alice, you have no family left."

Only Tracey and Becca know Alice is alive. She "died" to keep House of Iron from trying to kill her. To the world, she is Irene, an elderly woman who came to help me take care of my sick friend and stayed on.

I look out the window as we pass the suburban landscape where every house has a front porch. Tracey is right. All my family, except Alice, is dead, my birth family and my adoptive one. Do I have a right to keep my daughter from having a grandfather? I don't want her thinking that she wasn't planned. That translates in a child's mind to "not wanted." I was sixteen when I learned I was adopted. That is baggage a child should not have to carry, which leads me to the fact that her father won't be in the same house.

I eye Tracey critically. Is he daddy material? Do you have to love someone to live with them? I like Tracey. I respect him. Do I love him? I consult my body. No fireworks. Jason Blackwell makes me feel like an interior rocket is exploding every time he gets near. Is that love? Or just magic-infused hormones?

I lean my head against the headrest. "Lohan, I need some Rocky Road."

After an ice cream break, we head back to the construction site to talk to Jim's supervisor, Alan Gregory, and hopefully Rick Victor, our victim's card-playing friend.

The street is still barricaded to keep traffic and civilians out of the construction zone, though the crime scene tape has been removed. Tracey pulls up to the street barricade and speaks to an off-duty officer, a police officer paid by the construction firm to work in uniform. He waves us forward. We park in front of the iconic red neon Alabama Theatre sign. I've been meaning to visit, as it is supposed to be a grand 1920s restoration. Across the street sits another smaller restored theater, The Lyric. Becca, Alice, and I attended a chamber music performance there last month.

Both theaters have history. Prior to the 1960s, blacks were allowed at the Lyric, as long as they entered through a separate door and sat in a section in the upper area. A parade of famous Vaudeville stars played on the stage that is so intimate to the seats, you feel you can reach out and touch the actors. When that era passed, it had a seedier run, hosting an adult theater for a while before it was abandoned to time. Now, like its sister, Alabama Theatre, it's been restored to its original glory.

We exit the car, and I stretch my aching back, then fall in behind Tracey. A few yards inside the construction zone, a gum-chomping man in a hardhat and reflective vest stops us.

Tracey shows him his badge. "We want to speak to the supervisor."

Not missing a beat of chewing, the man eyes us. "This is a hard hat area. Got to have a hard hat. Don't matter who ya are. OSHA rules."

"Fine," Tracey says. "Give us two hats."

With a smirk and a pop of his gum, the man digs into a box and hands us what I'm certain are the two dirtiest, smelliest hats he has.

Tracey hands me one and holds his. "Okay, we got hats. Where can we find Alan Gregory?"

The man jerks a thumb over his shoulder. "In the trailer, most likely."

"Thanks."

Queasy at the reek emanating from the hat, I drop it on top of the nearest fifty-five-gallon drum. No way it's getting anywhere near my head.

Halfway across the open space that separates us from the trailer, a man wearing a blue flannel shirt meets us. "I'm Alan Gregory," he says. "I understand you're looking for me?"

"And I thought the rumor mill in the police department was fast," I say.

He holds up a walkie-talkie. "Nothing happens on my site I don't know about." He scowls at my head. "Didn't the guard give you a hat?"

"He did. It's there." I point to the drum.

I can see he wants to say something, but Tracey has his badge out. "We don't have to get any closer to the construction. Is there somewhere we can talk more privately?"

Gregory shrugs, turns, and leads us over to a white, nondescript trailer.

Inside is a metal desk whose surface has disappeared under various papers; a half-eaten sandwich; a landline phone; a compact refrigerator; and several metal folding chairs. Gregory offers us two of the chairs. "Water?"

"No, thanks," Tracey says.

I start to say yes and think about the filthy hat. "Only if it's bottled."

The water in the cool bottle he takes from the fridge settles my stomach, but now I will have to pee, as my bladder has been relegated to some tiny corner of my insides.

"This is about Jim, I suppose," Gregory says, sitting in one of the metal chairs. "How can I help you?"

"What kind of person was he?" Tracey asks.

Gregory shrugs. "I don't get close to my workers, so I don't know much personal info other than what I hear through the grapevine. He was a steady worker. Never showed up late. Did his job."

"What did you hear through the grapevine?" I ask.

"Well, a month or so ago, his wife had a baby, and I heard they were in a tight financial spot. The guys took up a collection for him, but I doubt it was much of a help. The company pays part of single health insurance, but not family coverage."

"Anybody he didn't get along with?" Tracey asks.

Gregory pats his shirt pocket, pulls out a toothpick and sticks it in the side of his mouth. "Guys get in disagreements all the time, but not up there." He jerks his head toward the building under construction.

"Shouldn't he have been secured to something?" I ask. "The lab said everything was working on his harness thing."

The toothpick rolls with some invisible action of lips and tongue. "We're 100% tie in."

At my confused look, he explains, "He was supposed to tie up with his cheater before he stepped out of the man-lift."

"His cheater?"

"His lanyard and carabiner."

Tracey interprets. "Straps and clip."

"Don't know what happened," Gregory says. "Whether he thought he tied up or slipped trying to do it." His level gaze focuses on Tracey. "As far as I'm concerned, Jim followed the safety rules. It was an accident."

Without saying it, he's telling us that ruling Jacobson's death anything but an accident will keep money out of his family's pocket. It doesn't jibe with what I saw in my vision, unless Jacobson was extremely distracted or thought there was another beam there, but his wife is alone with a newborn and the four other kids. Should we just let this go? Let it be an accident. Even if it was suicide, why take food out of his children's mouths?

Tracey hands Gregory a business card. "Anything comes up you think we should know about, call us." Then he consults his notebook. "You got a Rick Victor working here?"

Gregory nods.

"Can we see him?"

We wait while Gregory gets out the word he wants to see Victor. When the door opens, a heavyset man in a red flannel shirt, sleeves rolled to his elbows, and broad face dominated by a scrabbly, two-day beard, takes the first step on the metal rung at the trailer door. His gaze travels first over me, pausing at my middle that even the "pregnancy" top Becca helped me find doesn't hide.

"Victor, these detectives wanna talk to you," Gregory says.

Surprise lifts Victor's thick brows. He pauses mid-step and wobbles in indecision, then, without a word, turns and bolts back down the trailer steps and across the construction lot.

Tracey is after him, and I am hot on his heels for about ten steps. Disgusted, I stop, snatch the radio from my purse and call in Tracey's chase, giving the direction of travel and a description of Victor. "Suspect is just wanted for questioning," I add, to minimize the chance of anyone having a wreck chasing this yahoo. But he is running for a reason.

And I am not running for a reason. *What the hell good am I?*

Chapter Six

By the time I catch up to Tracey in the alcove outside the Lyric Theatre, Victor is cuffed. A police officer is with them. The graceful script of the theater's white neon marquee glows for an afternoon performance, and people stand in knotted clusters at a distance, gawking at the unfolding drama of a police chase.

"I think we'll have a conversation at my office," Tracey says to Victor. He turns to the uniformed officer. "Can you bring him?"

"Will do." The officer grasps Victor's arm. "Let's go pal and don't even think about rabbiting again."

Back in Tracey's car, we head back to headquarters.

"What's wrong?" he says into the silence.

"What makes you ask?"

"Don't know exactly." He smiles. "Maybe I got a little witch blood in the woodpile."

"Very funny."

"Give it up, Rose. Something has you upset. Did I do something?"

"Other than chase down that guy by yourself, no."

He opens his mouth and then closes it and doesn't speak for several moments. Then he says carefully, "So this is about you, not me."

"You don't have to step on eggshells, Lohan. I'm not going to break." My eyes fill with moisture. *Shit*.

"I'm an only child," he says, "and I've never been married, so I don't have personal experience with a pregnant woman. But I've read about this in books. It's just hormones. Don't be hard on yourself. I didn't need—"

"You didn't need what?" I interrupt. "You didn't *need* me? I'm supposed to be your backup. What if someone jumps on you?"

He scratches the top of his head. "I can handle myself in a fight, but I'm not very fast. If you hadn't called it in and patrol hadn't shown up and snagged him, I would've lost him."

"I am fast, or I was. Now I can't get out of the car without a crane. What kind of partner am I?"

"I think *I'm* the one who said you should take a break."

"You mean go home and *sit*?" My earlobes are on fire. *Amazing how fast "poor me" turns into "how dare you?"*

Tracey sighs. "I'm thinking I'll just bow out of this discussion."

IN THE INTERVIEW ROOM, Tracey uncuffs Victor and directs him to one of the three chairs in the space between four tight walls. There's nowhere to run now. Victor glances at the large two-way mirror, obviously no stranger to the fact that he is probably under observation, which he is not. Nobody has the time or inclination to observe anyone else's interview. Not with gang fights and shootings going on.

I am possibly as uncomfortable as the suspect. I don't like small spaces. Gritting my teeth, I concentrate on breathing and let Tracey handle the opening questions.

"Am I under arrest?" Victor asks.

A musky sweat smell drifts from him. *Fear?* There were no outstanding warrants on him, so why is he afraid?

"Should you be?" Tracey asks.

Victor crosses his arms over his chest. "What kind of answer is that? Either I am or I'm not, and if I'm not, I want out of here."

"You've been watching too much television. But we won't keep you long if you answer our questions."

"What questions?"

"Let's start with why you ran when your supervisor introduced us?"

He shrugs. "No reason."

"Really?" Tracey leans forward. "You aren't under arrest, but we are legally detaining you, and if you're not cooperative, we can detain you a long time."

"I know my rights."

"Fine, then I don't have to read them to you."

Victor taps the knuckles of his right hand nervously on the table. "I didn't do it."

"Be more specific," Tracey says.

Wetting his lips with his tongue, Victor shifts in his seat. "It wasn't my idea, okay?"

"Whose idea was it?"

"Look, a guy's got to make a living, you know? I got a wife and three kids. Construction work don't hack it."

"How did it start?" Tracey says.

I'm awash in admiration for my partner's interviewing skill because neither one of us has a clue what Victor is talking about. Tracey is pretending to know because Victor obviously thinks we do.

Victor shrugs. "This guy I met just told me how he was making a lot of money off the books as a kind of go between. This is a big betting town, you know? Everybody bets on the games, football especially."

Tracey leans forward slightly. "What part do you play?"

"I'm a small fish. I just collect the bets, that's all, and I pass 'em to my friend. He pays me a little percentage of the winnings. I think he sends them off-shore or something."

"Was Jim Jacobson involved?"

"Jim?" He looks surprised. "Well, he placed bets like the other guys in our poker game. He's a big Bama fan."

"Is that why you had a fight with him?"

"Wait a minute!" Victor pushes away from the table. "This ain't about bookie stuff, is it?"

"Maybe," Tracey says, unruffled. "Depends."

"On what?"

"On whether we think you're being straight with us, for one thing."

"I'm being straight."

"Did you have a fight with Jacobson?"

Victor rubs his chin. "Yeah, we got into it, but it was over a poker hand. Stupid. We'd both been drinking. I said something about his old lady or something. I don't even remember. We exchanged a couple of punches and got tangled up on the floor. The guys dragged us off. It was nothing. Next week, everybody's good."

"Did he owe you money?" I ask.

"Actually, I owed him fifty bucks. But I put it in the collection fund for his kids after he . . . fell, so I call it even."

"Had his behavior changed any recently?" Tracey asks.

"What do you mean?"

"Did he seem angry or down about anything?"

"He had money troubles. He didn't have enough for the ante, so we lowered it for everybody. It ain't no serious poker game. We just hang out and drink a beer or two."

"Did he have any enemies?"

"Jim? Not that I know about."

"Where were you when the accident happened?"

"I was up in the rigging doing a weld, but I had my back turned. I never saw it. The rumor is it happened after he stepped out of the man-lift, before he got his cheater tied off."

"You got anyone who can testify to where you were?" I ask.

"Uh, yeah, I think."

"And the names of the other poker players while you're at it," Tracey adds.

I write down the names he gives us.

"Anything else you can tell us about his death?"

"No, just that Jim's a good egg. The fight didn't mean nothin'. I hate what happened to him." He looks at Tracey, over to me, and back to Tracey. "That's it?

"We're not interested in the betting," Tracey says, "but if you hear anything that might be related to Jacobson, give us a call." He hands over a business card and adds, "As long as we believe you're not withholding any information, we won't hand you over to Vice."

Victor wipes his palms against his thighs. "You're not gonna arrest me for running from you?"

Tracey gives him a brief smile. "It's been a long time since P.O.P. was a good charge."

We escort him out and have the waiting patrolman drive him back to the construction site.

When he's gone, I turn to Tracey. "What kind of charge is 'P.O.P.'?" I ask, trying to make the connection with the criminal codes I studied in the Academy.

"Pissing off the po-lice."

Chapter Seven

I always stop by Alice's for a chat after work and the inevitable cup of tea. Her house mirrors the character of its fellows, tightly clustered one or two-story homes along narrow streets. Built in the 1920s and 30s, most display columned front porches dressed with the ubiquitous local russet-and-cinnamon stones. The residents are an eclectic mix by race, income, and education. A few blocks toward downtown, the homes yield to the sprawling domination of the red-brick campus that comprises the medical complex of the University of Alabama in Birmingham, known locally as "UAB." My modest house, just a block from Alice's, snugs up to Red Mountain, whose wooded slopes constitute the southern boundary of the Southside neighborhood. Only a piece of the winter mountain is visible from Alice's, a glimpse of green loblolly pines mottling the brown and gray of sleeping hardwood.

The "red" in the mountain's name derives from the rust-colored iron ore soil. Tunnels coil through the darkness beneath it, the legacy of years of mining that stopped in 1962 when alternative sources became cheaper. But the worming tunnels remain, invisible, hiding dangerous secrets, including the lairs of House of Iron.

It feels weird to knock on Alice's door after living there so many months. Today, I don't have to knock. The door opens before I can lift my knuckles.

"Welcome, dear," Alice says in her natural British accent. She is capable of a genuine Southern lilt when speaking to anyone except Becca or me. To complete her identity as "Irene" from Atlanta, Georgia, she's dyed her hair red and wears brown contact lenses to change the luminous witch-green eyes that mark the female members of House of Rose.

"Did you hear me come up the steps?" I ask Alice.

"No." Her mouth curves in a little cat smile of satisfaction that means her premonition kicked in. It's a random thing and nothing as detailed as my visions. Alice's primary talent is the one our House is known for, healing. She delights in her occasional premonitions. For me, they're disruptive and sometimes terrifying, but they have also saved my life more than once, so I'm not complaining.

"I've already set the water to boil," Alice says, stepping aside and beckoning me in.

From the doorway, I can see the teapot on the stove in Alice's domain, the familiar, comforting kitchen with its yellowing wallpaper pricked with small pink flowers that I vaguely remember from child-hood and cozy pots brimming with herbs on the windowsill. There's no dining room in her house, but the kitchen is large enough for a big oak table.

"Becca is gathering mint from the side porch," Alice says.

"Great." I tug off my jacket and toss it on the sofa. Alice grows mint year-round, either in the backyard or the enclosed porch off the kitchen during the winter. It's apparently very hardy, not to mention thriving under the influence of Alice's green thumb. All her plants, including the indoor ones that adorn every available windowsill, are a vibrant green, which I suspect has something to do with her being a witch. I missed that gene. Plants are allergic to me, so I try not to touch them. Alice makes all her teas with fresh mint. She grows more kinds than I can keep up with. A tea bag would not dare show its face in her house. I once asked her why she didn't just microwave the water to heat it. She looked as if I'd asked something scandalous. "Having tea is more than just drinking a beverage."

"How so?"

"It's about the whistle of the teapot," she'd said, "waiting for the leaves to stain the water, holding the warm cup, and most of all, taking a moment from the rush and bustle." Her hands on her hips, she practi-cally snorted, "Microwave, indeed."

At the moment, I welcome a reprieve from the "rush and bustle." It's been a long day. I dump my purse in a living room chair before heading into the kitchen, automatically stepping aside to avoid the toy truck that used to be parked at the juncture between rooms but is no longer there.

"The house is too neat," I observe.

Becca, her hands full of fresh mint, opens the back-porch door, entering the kitchen in time to catch my complaint. "Too neat? Says the Queen of Housekeeping?"

"Rose means she misses Daniel." Alice takes the mint from Becca and drops it into a colander to rinse. She's right. After the Ordeal—my name for the incident that still gives me nightmares—Daniel and his mother moved in with Alice, a catatonic Becca, and me. Toys sprinkled our living room, and it had looked almost like Mary Ann Jacobson's.

Becca gives me an appraising look. "Is it possible the quintessential loner actually misses people?"

"Not people, just Daniel."

"Doesn't he have a birthday coming up?" Becca asks, smoothing her silky hair that has never seen a tangle in its life as far as I can tell. "We have to get him a present."

"Not a toy," Alice says, gently patting the mint dry with a linen cloth. She doesn't believe in paper towels either. "Those foster people he lives with give him too many toys."

"You can't have too many toys, Alice," Becca says. "Don't you remember when you were a child?"

"Barely."

With over a century behind her, Alice is probably not exaggerating much.

Becca scoops Charlie, one of Alice's three cats, into her arms. I miss my own gray Angel not being here, but she is happier at our house without all the cat competition.

I settle into my spot at the oak kitchen table, a seat with my back to the cabinets where I can see into the living room and the front door. Sitting with your back to the wall is a paranoia that comes with the badge and gun.

"That reminds me," Becca says to Alice, stroking the seal point Siamese. "I've been meaning to ask you about witch history."

Alice's silver brows rise at the term.

The Houses call themselves witches and warlocks, tongue in cheek. To outsiders, we present ourselves as Families. If the world knew there were people with abilities among them. . . . History speaks for itself. Humanity doesn't have an outstanding reputation for tolerating "the other," a label that has too often resulted in torture, terror, burning at the stake . . . and in ovens.

"What do you want to know?" Alice asks, her face softening. This is Becca.

"Rose told me the warlocks followed House of Rose from England to Birmingham, but why did House of Rose come in the first place?"

Alice sets down china cups in front of the glass honey pot that lives on the table, along with a little ceramic jar of sugar lumps. Where do you even *find* sugar lumps?

"My mother came with us about 1870," Alice says, "when the city was founded. She wanted out of England and brought her family. I was a teenager, and my sister a grown woman, but mother was Head of the House, so we all came."

Becca sits in her own spot at the kitchen table across from me. Charlie makes a nest in her lap, resting his head on his chocolate paws. Bo, demure in his black-and-white tuxedo, weaves Alice's shins as if they were strands on a loom. The black demon, Alexander, appears from an unknown location and sits beside my chair, staring up at me with eyes as green as my own. I watch him suspiciously. I bear his scars.

"Did your mother choose Birmingham because of the coal here?" Becca asks.

Coal is the source of witches' power. Since it is the condensed matter of long-dead plants, we call it the living-green, even though it ceased being "living" several million years ago.

Alice inspects the mint to see if it is dry. Why she does this when she is about to pour more water over it has never made sense, but it is part of the ceremony of preparing tea. When she's satisfied the mint is dry, she distributes it into our cups.

"Yes, because of the coal, and the other Houses followed. It's a unique place, a 'Magic City.'" She smiles at the inside joke.

Birmingham's nickname of The Magic City reflects its explosion as a boom town in the late 1800s with the discovery of the same fact that drew the Houses—the close proximity of coal, limestone, and iron ore, the three elements required to make steel . . . and feed magic.

The little hand-painted teapot whistles. Alice picks it up, protecting her hand with a yellow dishtowel that matches the kitchen's wallpaper and brings it to the table. With care, she pours the steaming water over the mint in our cups. While we wait for the tea to steep, I "reach" deep into the ground below us, searching for the bright glow that indicates a pocket of coal, the living-green. There's not a lot directly under us.

To hit the rich deposits, I'd have to go under the iron ore seam beneath Red Mountain to the south or through downtown to the north, but I don't need much. $E=mc^2$. That means unlocking the energy in just an atom produces strong stuff.

As the flow of living-green floods up into me, I bask in its warmth for a moment and then reach across the narrow table to touch the place on Becca's chest beneath her shirt where the rose-stone, my family heirloom, hangs around her neck, filling the red diamond with honey-gold energy. This is the other reason I stop by every night—to keep her safe. As long as Becca is wearing the rose-stone, she's immune to House of Iron's manipulations.

Becca, now used to this "refueling" maneuver, ignores me, hooking her straight hair behind her ears to lean forward and blow on her tea. Like Alice, she wears brown contacts lens but not for the same reason. Without them, her eyes are an extraordinary pale blue. She pencils a light brown into her expressive ivory eyebrows, but lets her hair stay its natural hue. People assume it is ash blonde, but it is white, albino white.

"But why?" she asks Alice. "Why did your mother come here from England so long ago? Doesn't England have lots of coal?"

"We lived in Manchester," Alice says, as if that explains everything.

Becca props her elbows on the table, chin cupped in her hands. "I'm no expert on British history, but wasn't coal mined in Manchester?"

Alice reaches for the sugar bowl and drops three cubes into her tea. I've seen her use up to five when she is stressed. "Manchester was a hell on earth, dear."

"There is more family drama to it," I add. "Alice's older sister, my grandmother, had an affair with a man of House of Iron and was pregnant. You could say the family tried to separate my great grandmother from House of Iron by coming here."

"But House of Iron followed," Becca says with a sigh. "How romantic."

It's my turn to snort. "Romantic or a desire to kill off House of Rose, depending on who in that House you might have asked."

"'Whom' you might have asked," Alice corrects, "and no need to air the family's dirty laundry."

"Becca is family, as far as I am concerned," I say.

Alice folds her mouth into a prim pucker. "Seeing as we seem to be a bit short of members, perhaps that is just as well."

Becca beams her a smile, then asks, "How was Manchester a hell?"

"Well, for one thing, the smog from the factories was so thick, the sun was just a blur in the sky, no rays. You could look right at it in the middle of the day."

"Yuck."

"Yuck, indeed, but that was far from the worst of it. Children died left and right of rickets from not getting enough vitamin D, especially the ones in the mines. Wasn't unusual to see little ones humped over like old crones, their bones soft as clay." A ragged edge roughens her voice, and her eyes fill, as if she can still see those hunched children.

"Children *in* the mines?" Becca's front teeth capture her lower lip in distress.

"Children worked down in the mines, sometimes alone in the pitch dark if they operated the traps." At Becca's puzzled look, Alice adds, "The ventilation doors." Her gaze drops to the leaves in her teacup. "It was a terrible time. The average life span was less than twenty years for the poor. Not much longer for the gentry."

"That's awful." Becca frowns. "I can't imagine."

"And yes," Alice acknowledges with a sigh. "My mother was fleeing scandal as much as the city."

"Because of her daughter's pregnancy?" Becca asks.

Alice nods.

The Houses have forbidden intermarriage for a long time and with good reason. I am fruit, one generation removed, of such genetic mixing, which endowed powers that could take down a city block if I let them combine.

"It was pretty dismal here too, wasn't it?" I ask. "Freed slaves came to Birmingham looking for work and wound up arrested for petty crimes like loitering and forced into labor in the mines."

"That is a sad truth," Alice says. "The air was foul here too when we arrived. The price of coal. Plenty of people had Black Lung Disease from working in the mines, just like home. Sixty blast furnaces were going until the steel economy tanked."

"And the university rose from its ashes like a phoenix," Becca says, adding a sugar lump to her tea.

I go with the honey. Alice keeps both on the table and a bowl of fresh lemon and a tiny china pitcher of heavy cream in the refrigerator, ready for tea duty.

"Yes, but not right away. It took time. But before all that, my mother sent me back to England as soon as I was old enough. I was the youngest."

"Because of the air here?" I ask.

"That and the fact that this was a wild and woolly town in those days. She wanted me to have a proper upbringing."

"She sent you back to Manchester?" Becca's brows rise. "After leaving it because it was so horrible? That doesn't make sense."

"Oh, no. She sent me to a school for young ladies outside of London. London was its own hellhole. Mother worked hard here and sent the money to me to pay for it."

"Then what did you do?" Becca strokes Charlie, who arches his back under her hand.

"Eventually, I became a children's doctor and went back to Manchester on my own around the turn of the century."

I knew Alice had been a doctor in one of her "lifetimes." It seemed a natural fit for a healer, but I never wondered what it had been like for her. I tried to imagine the day-after-day illness and tragic wretchedness of those children, living beneath the swelter and choking smog where the sun was only a vague orb in a perpetually dirty sky.

"Why did you leave?" Becca asks.

"I came back to be with my family. My sister's child, Rose's mother, found a husband and had Rose . . . and another child. I wanted to be near her."

Becca's brows knit in sympathy. She turns to me. "Your sister Amber who died in the fire?"

I nod.

When Alice returned to this city, she chose this house, which was next door to her family, rather than move into the already crowded one that was home for me, my younger sister, my mother, father, and grandmother. When Theophalus Blackwell, then head of House of Iron, burned down that house and my family with it, I was only five. I survived by crawling through an open window and running to Alice's house, my only haven. I now live nearby in my own house. But this one is still my haven, I realize, because she and Becca are here.

Chapter Eight

"I'm not so sure this is a stellar idea," Tracey says, lifting his gym bag out of his trunk and eyeing my swollen middle. "You sure you don't just want to watch?"

"If I get uncomfortable, I'll sit and watch."

Shaking his head, he hoists the bag over his wide shoulder and closes the trunk.

I follow him inside to a room in the Trussville Sports complex that houses our dojo. Several rectangular mats pushed tightly together cover most of the floor. The inner mats are blue, and the outer ones are green. A ballet bar runs the length of one wall. Old pieces of exercise equipment are pushed into a back corner.

I greet the familiar group of people stretching on the mats and Sensei Richard Worthington, who is the only person I've ever seen Tracey's size. I've learned that every human, even a magically powerful one, has to stand and move within the parameters of having two legs. And off balance is off balance.

We bow onto the mat and join the stretchers for the remaining time before the official start of class. At a barked Japanese word, we line up by rank before Sensei Mark. I have moved from my spot at the far end of the line by a two places, reflecting new students and the youth. Tracey's position is at the other end with an assortment of green and brown belts between us in ranking order. I'm the only one in just a t-shirt and sweatpants, though I've earned a change in belt color. For the past month, I haven't even fit in the generous gi, the traditional uniform. I'm still the only female and the only pregnant person. Mark signals to Tracey, the highest-ranking student, and at Tracey's command, we all bow to Mark, then turn and bow to Richard.

What I can do on the mat is limited. My doctor has recommended against taking falls at this point. But I'll be damned if I'm going to sit and watch after being as useful as a sixth toe when Victor took off down the street at the construction site. God, I will be happy when this is over, and I can be myself again, instead of having my body hijacked by—

As if she heard me, my daughter gives an energetic kick, and I grunt.

Mark leads us in a series of warm-ups and light exercises. I skip the jumping jacks. Bouncing my breasts up and down has never been comfortable and now it is plain painful. And stretching is theoretical. My toes have been missing in action for months. I lost my waist and the week count of my pregnancy long ago, but Becca and Alice are keeping score. This is week thirty-seven. Forty is D-Day.

I can do the "walking" kata or form, which doesn't require engaging with anyone. I'm just now beginning to realize these forms are the foundation of everything else we do. When the rest of the class lines up and starts doing graceful forward rolls, I repeat what I did the first few classes months ago, lying on my back in a corner and rolling from side to side, practicing landing positions for a beached whale.

Chris Lane, the baby-faced officer who was the first to get to Jim Jacobson's smashed body, seeks me out to do the "release" kata. He's recently made black belt and could easily have worked with someone more at his level, but he gives me a bright grin and grabs my wrist. Without his police uniform, he looks even younger, and I wonder that anyone ever takes him seriously.

But someone did, because he is married with two children.

"How's the baby?" I ask as I try to execute moves that seemed much easier a few months ago.

"Good. We're just trying to keep Nathan from sticking his fingers into his mother's eyes. He thinks she's an interesting toy."

He gives me a leading pull, and I try to follow the direction of the force and use it to take him off balance.

"You're a real trooper to keep doing this being so . . . pregnant," Chris says.

"I don't feel like a trooper. I feel like a hippopotamus."

He grins. "I get it. Been there twice. I mean, not personally, but watching Carrie, it sort of feels that way. I feel guilty having another one so close to the first. We should have waited."

He pulls me in the opposite direction, and this time I manage to make him take a step. *Yes!*

"By the way," I ask, annoyed that I am getting breathy. "How were you the first officer on the scene the other day at the construction site? I thought you worked West Precinct."

"I do. I was running an errand at City Hall for the captain when the call went out." He shrugs. "I was close, so I took it." He shakes his head. "Nasty fall."

I CLIMB THE STEPS OF ALICE'S FRONT PORCH feeling tired, but in a pleasant way. The kitchen to my left is visible from the front door. As usual, water for tea is boiling, but tonight it's because I gave Alice a heads up on the way.

Becca jumps up from the living room couch, startling Alice's three cats from their positions adorning the furniture. She's practically dancing with excitement.

"What's up?" I ask, reaching out and feeding living-green into the rose-stone that hangs under her blouse at her chest. It's an instantaneous transfer, which is good because Becca is not in a mood to stand still for longer than a few seconds.

"I got a job," she says. "At a law firm!"

Before the Ordeal, Becca worked as a receptionist for a local law firm and moonlighted as a waitress to finance her studies. When her boss made inappropriate advances, she hit him between his legs with his golf club putter. She quit and was worried he would blacklist her in the legal community. But apparently, her ex-boss kept his mouth shut, as I suspected he would. Becca, slender to the point of frailty, looks anything but dangerous, but don't push her to the wall.

"It's a small firm," she says. "They just broke off from one of the big groups and formed a partnership, and they need a receptionist and get this—they'll pay part of the cost for me going through a law program at night! Can you believe that?"

"That is awesome!" We exchange high-fives. My eyes moisten. Only a few months ago, she was completely lost, her brain struggling to start over with a new personality. I took an awful risk to release her from the mental prison House of Iron's Theophalus Blackwell had constructed with a touch. It could have gone badly. She could have been lost forever. But here she is, excited about a new job.

"Oh my God," she says, distracted.

"What?"

"I have nothing to wear."

"What are you talking about? You have a closet of clothes. We brought everything from your apartment over when we moved you here."

Her face suddenly clouds. "I should move out, shouldn't I? Get my own place? I've been enough of a burden on you and especially on Alice."

"Don't even think such a thing." Alice bustles into the kitchen just before the teapot whistles. Hard to tell if she had a premonition, or she's just been boiling water for tea for over a hundred years.

"But I have," Becca insists. "You've taken care of me, but I can't stay now that I'm okay and I have a job."

"Nonsense. Come and have a cup of tea." Alice says.

Obediently, we both follow Alice back into the kitchen.

"I hope I don't smell bad," I say. "I need a shower."

Becca sniffs. "Not so bad. You can sit at the other end of the table." She points and then eyes my sweatpants. "But we have to get you a better outfit for that *Kung Fu* stuff."

I laugh. It's so good to have her back. "It's not *Kung Fu*."

"Whatever."

Chapter Nine

The next morning, Tracey looks over my shoulder as I open the interoffice mail envelope.

"What is it?" he asks.

I remove two pieces of paper and scan them. "Subpoenas. We're being called as witnesses in Lawrence Anders's trial."

Anders helped Angola kidnap a little girl from Children's Hospital and hold her hostage. He handcuffed me for Angola to kill. I'd rather that Angola was standing trial with him, but we have to catch him first, and he has disappeared.

"About time," Tracey says. "It's only been months."

"Eight and a half," I say, distractedly.

"Yeah, that's right."

I flush and yank my thoughts back to the case against Anders. It has wound its way through the system and is scheduled for a trial in circuit court. The prosecutor got a no-bond on him, so he has remained in jail over the months since his arrest. The fact that Anders is still in jail means he doesn't have House of Iron's manipulative powers. Angola may have used them to influence Anders, but my gut says Lawrence Anders just enjoyed being powerful and didn't require Angola's magic to make him a creep. If you've got a willing employee, why waste the time and energy of manipulating him?

Tracey and I faced disciplinary action for failing to report the incident before we intervened. We didn't contest it. Just did our time off. How could we explain why we didn't call in the troops or the TACT team on a hostage situation? Why I had to walk into my house where a killer waited. Why that was the only way to keep a little girl from dying

. . . or worse, from having her mind destroyed? Angola would not have hesitated to do either.

Jason's words from our encounter in the police parking lot echo—*you have to kill Angola and Samuel.*

"The subpoena is for Monday," Tracey says. "Let's get the rest of the Jim Jacobson case wrapped up today, if we can."

We split up to interview the two coworkers on our list who were working on the construction site when Jacobson tried to walk on air. My guy said he was only about twelve feet away and had eyes on Jacobson as he was coming up the man lift, a kind of open cage elevator. Then the witness got distracted by another worker, so he didn't see what happened after that, although he's sure Jacobson couldn't have simply stepped out of the man lift to his death. He would have had to move several feet forward first. This supports the still-unpalatable-to-me notion that he committed suicide.

Tracey's witness said he had also noticed Jacobson coming up in the man lift but had turned his back to drive in a bolt. Neither of them had seen Jacobson fall.

Dead end.

The poker player list yields the same. Everyone backs Victor's story that the fight was nothing unusual. They all knew Jacobson had some money issues and appeared subdued and down until the last week when he seemed more his normal, jovial self.

"That makes no sense," I say, when we meet back at the office. "Did deciding to kill himself make him happier?"

Tracey shrugs. "It's possible." He counts on his fingers: "(1) Money problems; (2) counting on his death being ruled an accident so the company would pay up; (3) no evidence of foul play or lines breaking or being cut; (4) he's an experienced rigger; and (5)"—he lowers his voice—"you 'saw' him just step off the edge. It's a clear-cut suicide, Rose."

"I know." *Why is that conclusion bugging me?*

I look up as Lieutenant Faraday approaches, frowning, as usual.

Tracey has seen her too. "I fear more dead bodies are in our future."

"Lohan, Brighton. Finkman's got a drive-by with multiple witnesses. He's asked for some help."

I don't voice the groan at having to help Finkman. He has had it in for me since I walked into the Homicide office.

Faraday hands Tracey a scrap of paper. "Address."

"Let's go," Tracey says.

We have to stop a block away because of the crowd. Chaos reigns. It looks like the entire West Precinct is on the scene, trying to secure it. Tracey approaches a patrol officer detouring traffic.

"Hey, Owen," Tracey says.

"Hi, Sarge," the officer replies without a break in his waving motion to the oncoming cars. "Haven't seen you in a while. What's it like up in the rarified castle air?"

"A lot of nosebleeds," Tracey says with a grin.

Cutting his eyes at me, the officer raises his brows in a question.

"My partner, Rose Brighton," Tracey says. "Rose, this is Owen Welling."

"Nice to meet you, Owen."

"The same. You're lucky to have Tracey Lohan at your back," he says. "Get him to tell you about pulling me out of a burning house. I bet he hasn't mentioned it."

"No, he hasn't."

"He got 'Officer of the Year' for that. He was the best sergeant our precinct ever had."

"I appreciate the kind words, O, but how about telling what you know about this shooting."

Owen shrugs. "Not much. Just that a kid is dead in the housing project and another wounded, and the crowd is all hyped up. They say it was a drive-by. Victim was just some young boy at a birthday party. Not involved. Sad."

I flinch. A boy at a birthday party and no doubt a devastated family.

"Thanks. We'll figure it out. Good to see you."

"Yea, come slum with us sometime."

"Will do."

We head into the densest knot of people. "You never told me you were 'Officer of the Year,'" I say.

"It hasn't come up."

I am privy to Tracey Lohan's secret and he to mine, but that does not make us truly know one another. Over the months in Patrol when Paul was my training officer, we talked for long hours into the night. We faced life and death together, depended on one another. It seemed so sudden, that moment in the hallway of my house when everything changed with a kiss, but it wasn't really sudden at all. It had been building and growing all those nights working together. Even so, the romance hadn't stuck. I was too selfish or screwed up to have a lasting relationship. I walked away.

I glance down at my baby's cocoon. I won't be able to walk away from her. Every aspect of being a parent terrifies me, from diapers to losing my freedom. She will be my world. At least for a while, I'll have to give up everything else about who I am. As we exit the car, I take a step away from my partner. The logical voice in my head protests—It was my idea to have sex with Tracey, an insane moment when I thought I was going to die in the next few hours. It's irrational to blame him. Deliberately, I unclench my fists and shoulders. My partner, unaware of the emotional storm that just surged by him, is focused on the here and now, which is where I should be.

We walk the block to the edge of the bleak, redbrick housing project. Despite the lack of trees, hardly a tuft of grass, even dead grass, emerges from the red clay yards, wet from the recent rains.

"There's Finkman." I point to the square shoulders hunched forward and the back of his sandy hair.

As we approach, Finkman turns, catching sight of Tracey first. "Tracey, hope you're here to help."

"We are." Tracey tilts his head to include me.

Finkman scowls. I have never figured out just why he hates me, and I don't particularly care. If I am living out the stereotype of women not belonging in police work, he is the dinosaur. Women have proved their worth in law enforcement over and over.

Nearby, a slender black woman sinks to her knees, sobbing.

"The victim's mother," Finkman says, his mouth a grim line.

"A patrolman said the boy was just at a birthday party?" Tracey makes it a question.

"Yeah, that's what it looks like. A drive-by gang shooting. Don't have all the facts yet, but so far looks like this kid was just in the wrong place at the wrong time."

"What can we do to help?"

"I got too much going on here. Can you canvass the neighbors and see if they saw anything?"

"Sure."

Tracey turns to me, his gaze drifting to my belly. "You okay splitting up?"

"Sure."

"Why don't you take the first few houses on that side and I'll take the other side?"

Making my way through the milling crowd, I garner several curious glances. I would flip open my badge and wear it, but it would be invisible on my waist, beneath the overhang of belly.

An older woman answers my knock on the first apartment door, a nondescript replica of every other apartment, except for the pots of dead flowers and a partially rusted metal chair on the concrete doorstep. I introduce myself, and she gives a nervous look over my shoulder at the ring of parked patrol cars, blue lights flashing.

"I heard that boy's dead," she says, shaking her head. Strands of wiry gray weave through her hair. "Such a bad business. I don't understand young folk these days."

"How do you know it was young folks?" I ask.

"'Cause they ain't got the sense God gave 'em, waving guns around and shooting people."

"We'd like to catch whoever did this and keep him from hurting anyone else."

"I didn't see nothing."

"Are you sure?"

She nods and then pauses.

"What?" I ask.

"Might not mean anything, but I did see a car cruising by the last couple of days."

"Can you describe it?"

"It was metallic blue. I noticed it 'cause they went real slow. Had a rusted patch over the wheel on my side, a big place, looked like the state of Florida."

"Front wheel or back?"

"Back."

"Could you see who was in the car?"

"Nope. Tinted windows. Them gang boys always tint their windows. Thinks it makes them scarier."

"This could be important information. Can I have your name?"

"I don't want to get involved." She shuts the door.

I scribble notes and go to the next two apartments to the end of the block. Nothing worthwhile comes from either of them.

Back at the scene, I find Tracey standing near the body. I have avoided looking, but I make myself, and tears sting my eyes. He is so young, about thirteen or fourteen. Nearby, his mother is still on her knees, sobbing, refusing to leave, despite the circle of people around her. I pull on the living-green, hoping to see something that will help.

Nothing will bring this young boy back to life, but justice might stop it from happening to another child. The rush of golden energy fills me. I open myself to it and wait.

Nothing.

Chapter Ten

Eyes closed in concentration, Alice runs her hand lightly over my belly, as if her fingers provide a sonogram view inside. I don't want to think about the dead boy I saw yesterday, so I think about Jim Jacobson, trying to figure out what keeps bugging me about his death. That's what happens when you work Homicide. You distract yourself from one murder by thinking about another. Suicide is the only answer that fits everything, but it just feels wrong.

We sit in Alice's living room, surrounded by the objects she has collected from around the world—sculptures of the Buddha, Japanese ginger jars, Russian nesting dolls, African and New Zealand art. Rooting plants in open Mason jars line any leftover space along the window shelves.

Dusting must be hell, but that is Becca's contribution. She actually likes cleaning, though Alice insists on watering her own plants. House of Rose witches can draw power from the living plants, but it is a poor source compared to the seams of coal that store concentrated energy. Under Alice's care everything that can flower seems to be constantly in bloom, and the greens are always vibrant and healthy. I stay away from them, because my thumb is apparently black. Maybe I suck their essence without meaning to.

In a rare moment, all three of Alice's cats are quiet, draping the furniture like elegant figurines. Alexander, my solid black nemesis and buddy, depending on where he is in his bipolar mind-state, is sitting in Alice's rocking chair examining his paw. Boo has curled his black-and-white self on a sofa pillow smaller than he is, tail tucked under his chin, and Charlie blends into the creamed-coffee pattern on the top edge of the same sofa, his tail draped down almost brushing Boo, his blue eyes watching us with lazy interest.

I am sitting in the big flower-patterned chair I sat in the first time I visited Alice. She has pulled over a kitchen chair in front of me to make her examination. I stopped by after work, as I usually do. Becca is working late at her new job, so tea is on hold.

I've learned to relax into the golden glow of warmth that accompanies Alice's "examinations." The experience is akin to someone scratching your back. You can salve the itch with a backscratcher, but it is not the same as someone else's nails. Same with a foot rub, and I am a regular for a pedicure now, just for the pleasure and relief of having my swollen feet massaged.

I watch Alice's face, taking comfort from her slight, self-absorbed smile that things are on course with my baby. She takes her time.

"Well?" I ask when she finally sits back.

"She is doing just fine and so are you."

I am always relieved to hear this, even though I visit my OB-GYN regularly. Alice can use her ability to "read" my body, sort of like an MRI or sonogram, but she can't heal me. I've learned from her that healing is actually about providing energy to the body in a precise manner to help it repair itself. Whatever it is, it is not, unfortunately, something I can do. I can't heal a paper cut. I can only see into time, manipulate minds, and blow things up.

Alice takes my hands. "Rose, when it is your time, I should be there. You need to make certain the doctors and hospital staff understand that, even if they have to do a procedure."

"I want you there, but what do you mean?"

"I can give an early warning if things don't go according to plan."

I feel the blood drain from my face. "I thought she was fine."

"She is. But right before birth, she has a little acrobatics to perform in the womb, so her head will come out first."

"What if she doesn't?"

"Well, if she doesn't or can't—"

"Can't?"

"Sometimes the cord gets tangled."

I can feel my heart rate accelerating.

"Don't worry," she says, apparently reading my panic. "If that happens, the doctor can do a Caesarean and take her out, but I must be present the entire time, and we should be on a ground floor, if possible."

I engage the breathing rhythms my pediatrician gave me. I don't relish anyone cutting me open with a knife, but the thought of something as large as a baby's head splitting me open at the "usual" exit is also disconcerting.

"There is something else," she says.

"What?"

"There's another reason I recommended a water birth."

Alice had strongly pushed that I go with a midwife and a water birth at home, since the hospitals here allowed water labor but not water birth, but I nixed that idea. I want doctors and drugs.

"If you don't have access to the living-green, the water can protect people. That's the safest option, although drugs can dampen your ability too."

Water somehow interferes with the use of House magic. No witch or warlock can use their gift over or through water, and distance from the ground also interferes with the ability to pull energy from the ores.

"I get that water would keep me from being able to pull the living-green, but why would I even be doing that?"

"It's instinctual when the pain comes."

"Will it help?"

She takes a breath. "Psychologically. But near the end that extreme pain will drive you to pull a great deal of it. I can help with the pain, if I can touch you and I'll stuff some coal in my purse, just in case."

I raise my eyebrows.

"After schlepping downstairs a few times at the hospital to draw living-green for Becca when she was in such bad shape, I kept a few lumps of coal in my car for emergencies. But if you have to have a surgical procedure, well, they frown on non-sterile objects in an operating room, so I would have to hide them."

"Why would I need lumps of coal?" Pulling the living-green is one thing I am good at.

"You can, of course, if you are close enough to the ground floor, but that is not guaranteed."

I recall the first time I connected with a seam of coal and drew the living-green. Alice made me sit on the ground in my backyard, "bum to the dirt," she'd said, because it was easier that way. And *safer*. Her words from that moment suddenly echo in my mind: *"We don't want to pull from the living. It would kill them."*

My breath catches. "Oh my God! It never occurred to me I would be dangerous *having* a baby. I mean, I'm terrified I will drop her or forget her or do something wrong—"

"Rose, you will be a good mother."

I look up at her, startled. "Are you out of your mind? I barely get how to be a friend, maybe a D+ for trying."

"I think Becca would disagree with you."

"Two broken, needy people hanging on to each other does not make me mother material."

"You listen to me," she says, leaning toward me. "We are all broken. All of us, witch or normal. We may walk around looking whole, but we all have wounds."

"Alice, I'm responsible for what happened to Becca. I let her go with me into that cave and into Theophalus Blackwell's hands. It's my fault Daniel got burned and nearly killed. And I let Deon Segal walk into a hostage situation and put his life at risk. I make terrible decisions."

Alice snorts and sits back. "It seems to me you are also responsible for bringing Becca back and saving Daniel's life, not to mention Mr. Segal's young sister."

"But I left my own family, Alice. I *abandoned* my little sister and parents."

"What are you talking about?"

"I knew something bad had happened, but I crawled out the window to save myself. I left them all inside and they . . . burned."

"Rose, you were not a police officer then. You were *five years old* and frightened."

"But I made the decision."

"You had no options. Think about it. What if Daniel had been in your situation?"

"What? It wasn't Daniel. It was me."

"Imagine it was him."

I look at her skeptically.

"Try," she insists.

I picture Daniel crouched in the bathroom tub in the middle of the night, hearing footsteps, muffled shots, padding to his room, the smell of gasoline burning his nose, seeing his little sister's Cinderella blanket soaked with blood, turning to the open window and billowing curtain.

"What if Daniel had crawled out of that window?" Alice asks softly.

I am miserable and embarrassed at the tears that flow down my face. *I don't cry.* I know it's because I'm pregnant. But knowing doesn't help.

Alice insists, "Would you forgive him?"

"Yes."

"Then why can't you forgive yourself?"

"I don't know," I choke out. More tears cascade. "I'm a mess."

Alice smiles gently and takes me into her arms. "It will be all right, dear. I promise."

Chapter Eleven

The next morning, I stare into the full-length mirror on my bedroom door. "I look like I swallowed the Great Pumpkin."

"That's 'cause you're pregnant," Becca says helpfully, chewing a mouthful of donut from her perch on my bed. She brought them and coffee over before work. She thinks nothing of getting up at the crack of dawn. It's all I can do to stumble into the bathroom. I think I own a coffee pot somewhere, but I never bothered to learn how to use it. I just grab a cup with a morning biscuit at a drive-through. Alice is constantly lecturing me about eating better, and I am trying. I keep a bag of carrots in the refrigerator.

Angel jumps lightly onto the bed and explores the open box of donuts, her dainty nostrils flaring. Becca flops back against a pillow.

"Be careful," I say. "Remember, I have a loaded gun under that striped one."

She shifts away. "I sleep with a stuffed teddy bear and my best friend sleeps with a piece of deadly steel."

I sigh. "Where did you say those donuts came from?"

Turning in disgust at the confections that are nothing even close to tuna fish, Angel curls into a gray ball against Becca's thigh.

"My office. A client brought them in yesterday, and my boss wanted them gone. He's on a diet."

"Not sure I want the calories either."

"That's ridiculous, Rose. You don't have enough extra weight. Didn't your OB-GYN tell you to gain a few pounds?"

"Yes, she mentioned it. And so did Alice. She wants me to eat vegetables."

"You say that like it's a dirty word. Well, are you?"

"I make them put lettuce and tomato on my hamburgers."

"Not sure that's what Alice had in mind." She sighs and pushes the box to me. I pick a frosted glaze one and take a bite.

"Whoa," I make a face. "Not used to all that sugar." I set it down on my dresser. "Rather have a bagel with cream cheese and a pickle."

"A pickle?"

I let her hang for a moment and then relent at her expression of disgust. "Just kidding. Although I could go for a scoop of butter pecan right now."

"Ice cream? For breakfast?"

"Yes, or mint chocolate chip."

She squints at me with the same disbelief that met my declaration that I didn't like shopping or being "gorgeous"—her word, not mine. I did lie about the pickle, but not the ice cream.

"O-kay," she says doubtfully.

I check the time. "How's everything going?"

She leans back and puts her hands behind her head. "I think I'm sore from shopping. Is that a thing?"

"I wouldn't know. But I meant your job."

"Great, so far." She licks the sugar crust from the edges of her mouth. "If you don't count that I have no clue what I'm doing."

"Give yourself time. It takes a couple of months before you get the hang of a new job. You should have seen me when they dumped me in the Burglary Unit. The important thing is that you like the people."

"I do. And my boss is super nice. Not like that creep I worked for before. What about you?"

"Me?"

"Yeah, you never talk about work."

"Umm. It's fine, I guess. I still feel weird being a detective with so little experience. Don't think the other folks in Homicide approve of me, especially Finkman."

"Finkman? You're kidding, right?"

"Nope, that's his name and his description."

"A jerk, huh? I bet you 'detective' rings around him."

I smile at her loyalty. "I don't think 'detective' is a verb."

"Whatever."

I rummage in the closet and pick out one of the maternity blouses Becca helped me find. It's fitted everywhere except the stomach where it's necessarily generous. Same for the blazer that goes with it.

"What about Tracey?" she asks.

"What about him?"

"Does he accept you?"

I start the buttoning process. "Yes, he always has. Even when I first went to Burglary, right after the shooting."

"I like him," she says.

"He's a good person."

"He's also very cute."

"Cute?" I smile at the description. "If you like bears."

"A cute hunk. And those gray eyes are wicked."

"Becca, are you trying to tell me something?"

"Yes."

"What? That you 'like' like him?"

"No, not me," she says. "Just want to make sure you have your eyes open."

"You are the biggest romantic I've ever seen. Tracey and I are *partners*."

"Right, but it's not every day that your detective partner is the father of your baby."

Pants are next. This has gotten to be a yoga exercise, standing on one foot and guiding the other leg without bending over. "I will give you that. But I am not ready for another relationship with a partner, even though everyone at the office thinks that's what's going on."

"Can't blame them. I mean, the first thing that jumps to mind is not exactly, 'Oh, she must have wanted to get pregnant with him just to save a race of witches and warlocks.'"

"It's nobody's business who the father is."

At that moment, I overbalance and have to grab for the counter, knocking over the full cup of coffee.

"Damn."

Becca hops off the bed. "I'll get a towel. You better change the blouse."

While I do that, she brings in two towels, one damp and one dry, and blots up my coffee.

"What about the baby?" she asks.

"What do you mean?"

"It might not be anyone's business who the sperm donor was, but does she get to have a father?"

I stop dressing. Tracey had asked the same question, but about his father being a grandfather. "I haven't thought about it."

Becca's arched brows rise halfway up her forehead, reminding me why I call them her "golden arches."

"Really?" she says. "Are you going to wait until you have her before you decide that?"

"I can't decide anything right now. I have to get to work and so do you."

I AM GETTING INTO MY CAR WHEN MY CELL GOES OFF with the ringtone for Tracey, "Dances with Wolves." I put it on speaker. "What's up?"

"There's a street fight going on in the neighborhood where that little boy was shot a couple of days ago."

"A street fight? Isn't that Patrol's purview?"

"Yeah, they're headed to the scene, but they're holding some folks involved at Finkman's request. He wants us to help interview them. Thinks the fight might be connected to the drive-by shooting of the birthday kid. Gang stuff."

"Want to meet me there?"

"Actually, I'm already headed your way, and I'm close. Why don't I just pick you up and we'll go together?"

"Sounds like a plan." I open the car door I just closed and swing my legs out just in time to see his car turn the corner. "I see you already."

We disconnect, and I get in his city car. "Have you even had your coffee?" I ask.

"No, why?"

"I'm not sure I want to be in the car with you until you've had your first cup. You're cranky."

"I am not." He gives me an indignant glance.

"Well, I am."

"I thought you just drank tea now."

"I do, except in the morning. Then I require coffee."

"How many months have we been working together, and I missed this?"

"Because I get it with my sausage and biscuit on the way to the office. You didn't think I *made* coffee, did you?"

He grins.

"Besides, I'm not supposed to have a lot of caffeine, and morning is when I need it. Becca brought some over, but I . . . didn't get a chance to drink it." Not exactly a lie. I don't see the priority in mentioning my clumsiness.

He pulls onto the entrance ramp of the interstate and turns on the emergency lights. "Maybe Santa Claus should bring you a k-cup machine."

"I'm perfectly happy getting my coffee handed to me at a drive-through window."

He shakes his head. "I'm glad your aunt is feeding you dinner. You'd probably eat pizza every night."

"What's wrong with pizza?" I ask crossly.

"Nothing. Should we get you breakfast and coffee before we get there?"

"I'm fine. But whoever heard of a street fight in the morning?"

"Before school, I guess."

The clock may say morning, but the day is overcast, bloated. Dark clouds and fog make it seem more like dusk. It's rained the last two days. We exit the highway, and he turns toward the neighborhood. A car going in the opposite direction passes us.

"Wait!" I shout.

Tracey immediately applies the breaks. "What?"

"Turn around and follow that car."

Emergency lights still on, Tracey makes a sharp U-turn and speeds up, trying to catch up with the car I saw. "What did he do?" he asks.

"Nothing, but he was coming from the direction of the fight, and there's a splotch of rust over the rear fender in the shape of Florida. That's the car a neighbor said had been slow-cruising the street where the shooting took place."

Tracey guns it, and I reach for the radio mike.

Chapter Twelve

I snatch the microphone and give my ID number. When the dispatcher responds, I add our location and direction of travel. "We're behind a metallic blue Chevy with a rust spot on the rear fender."

"Ten-four," she replies.

"Suspects may have been involved in a shooting two days ago," I add, as patrol cars chime in to take up the chase. I don't want anyone stopping the car without being aware the occupants could be armed. My gun is already in my lap.

Tracey pulls close behind the Chevrolet, which picks up speed. "They aren't pulling over."

Into the mike I say, "They're not stopping." I give her the code for a chase. "We're 10-100. They're getting on I-20 westbound."

A familiar voice comes over the radio. "I'm behind the detective car."

Tracey slows down and lets the marked patrol car move around us and take up position behind the Chevy.

"That's Chris Lane's unit," Tracey says.

Another patrol car gets on the interstate at the next entrance, sandwiching them. The suspect vehicle weaves through traffic, trying to shake us off. A West Precinct sergeant gets on the radio, asking what we've got. That's standard procedure. So many chases end in disaster, a supervisor has to approve one to continue.

"A suspect vehicle possibly involved in a homicide," I respond, hoping I am right. I'm making a presumption based on the description of the car by a neighbor and the fact that it was hauling butt from the gang fight.

"Ten-four," the sergeant replies, implicitly giving his okay to continue the chase.

I pull my gun from my purse and lay it on my lap.

Without warning, the suspect's car abruptly swerves and screeches down an exit ramp. The front patrol car has passed the exit, but Chris follows the suspect, and we do the same.

Knowing Chris is by himself and needs to concentrate on driving, I continue advising our location. "Turning south onto Avenue V."

I glance at Tracey, hating to distract him either, but I need him. "West Precinct is alien territory for me. If there's no street sign, can you help me out?"

He nods. "Left on Pike Road."

I repeat that into the mike, just as the suspect's Chevy jumps the curb into a grassy area, careens across the small park and into a tree. Behind it, Chris' patrol car stops, sliding on the slick grass.

"Suspect has hit a tree in a grassy area."

"Exchange Park," Tracey shouts, spitting dead grass and mud off our wheels as he slams on the brakes behind and to the right of the patrol car.

"Exchange Park," I echo into the mike.

Ahead of us, Chris' door opens. Before he can exit, the driver of the suspect's car jumps out, dashing behind the tree he crashed into. My focus is on the passenger and anyone else who might be hiding in the back seat.

Chris is out of his car, drawing his gun. Tracey bales from our car.

A *crack* and muted flash from the edge of a tree. *Gunshot.*

"Shots fired!" I say into the mike, trying unsuccessfully to keep my voice calm. I throw open my door, grab my portable radio with my free hand and exit my side. Tracey has angled the car to give me the protection of the engine block, but that has left him more vulnerable. He crouches behind his open car door. I go to one knee behind my door, using it and the front of the car as cover.

Tracey and the patrolman have a visual on the suspect's open driver door. I focus on the passenger side. His door opens.

"Suspect coming out!" I shout.

But he doesn't.

Instead, he disappears. *What the hell?*

"Tracey, watch out!"

The warning is just out of my mouth when another shot *cracks*. Focused on the passenger side of the vehicle, I'm not sure where the shot came from. I can't see Tracey or Chris from my angle.

"Officer down," I hear over my radio in my partner's voice, my heart sinking with the words.

Oh God, no!

"Lohan!" I yell.

"Stay back!" he shouts. "I'm okay!"

"*Double ought.*" The dispatcher's steady voice belies the panic churning in me. *"All units, double-ought at Exchange Park."*

I drop to the muddy ground, lying in a side position, the closest I can to flat on my stomach. I can only see the area beneath our car and the patrol car ahead of us and a piece of the fallen officer's torso, head, and neck. Blood pulses from the side of his throat. He will die in a matter of moments with that kind of loss.

Unaware I have pulled it, I feel the living-green coursing through me, but time doesn't stop. No shadow world descends over the real one. *I have to go to Chris.* Someone has to stop that bleeding. I start to crawl around the open passenger door of our car on hands and knees when another *crack* erupts a patch of dead grass in front of me.

The passenger. *Where is he?*

Dropping my left shoulder, I roll back behind the door. My body pulses with adrenaline and the heat of the living-green energy.

Before me is the muddy track through the brown winter grass the Chevy left. Its passenger door is still open. The second suspect jumps out, gun in hand, sprinting across the front of his car's engine block toward another tree. I don't have a clear shot. Vaguely, I'm aware of people on the other side of the small park, wandering out of their houses, gawking and pointing toward us.

"Go back in your houses!" Tracey shouts.

The radio is silent, the dispatcher—bless her—is holding all radio traffic, keeping the channel clear for us. No doubt she has started the paramedics and an ambulance, and I don't need to hear sirens to be certain that every car in the city is racing toward us. "Double-ought," officer down, is the one code no one ever wants to hear.

My heart is kicking my chest so hard, I think at first that it is my baby. Everything inside me wants to get to Chris, to help. I'm a witch of House Rose. What good is it to be of a line of healers if I can't fix anything?

Tracey's voice again on the radio—"Have units approach from Avenue Y and 22nd Street. Get the cars between citizens and the suspects. Two suspects behind trees in the park along 22nd Street. Can't see anyone else in the car. We're pinned down. Can't get to the shot officer."

The small park is roughly a right triangle and 22nd Street is the long bottom arm of the right angle. Tracey's call for patrol cars to station themselves there will protect the citizens wanting to see what is happening and trap the suspects between us and those marked patrol cars.

"Stay back, Rose!" Tracey yells again. "You can't get to him."

But he's dying.

A thud in my belly reminds me that putting myself in range of a bullet is not just about me.

"Amber," I whisper. "I won't let you get hurt."

Is that right? Wrong? My throat knots. It's the first time I've said her name, even to myself—my dead sister's name—the first time I have spoken it aloud since the night she died. *I left her behind too, to save myself.*

Seconds later, tires squeal behind us and on 22nd Street in front of us. Blue lights are suddenly everywhere.

Chapter Thirteen

I meet Becca for lunch at a Lebanese restaurant across the street from the building where she now works. Her hair, which had grown below her shoulders over the past months, is now trimmed in a stylish, asymmetrical cut.

"I'm glad to see you," she says. "I'm so sorry about that officer—?"

"Chris Lane." I close my eyes. *Blood spurts from the nicked artery in his neck.*

"You're feeling guilty about it, aren't you?"

"No."

"You're just saying that to keep from talking to me."

I look at her in exasperation, and she gives me a wan smile. "Best friends, remember?"

"You're impossible."

"Talk."

"Okay. Yes, I feel guilty. If I hadn't made Tracey turn the car around, that officer would still be alive and going home to his family. He has two children. One is a newborn."

"You did your job."

"I—"

"Those gang members killed a little boy at a birthday party. If you hadn't spotted them, they might have killed more kids. That's what the police spokesman said—that the killers had gone back to the scene looking for their original target."

"They were leaving when I saw them."

"But they would have gone back. After the police left. You're a hero for stopping them."

"I couldn't feel less like a hero."

"You didn't pull that trigger, Rose."

"Can we change the subject?"

"Yeah. Sure." She pauses. "Are you sure you don't want me to testify in court tomorrow?"

My mood has been so dark since Chris's death, I've given no thought to the upcoming trial of Anders for kidnapping and attempted murder of a police officer.

"We never told anyone you were even involved."

"But if you need me—you can't let that bastard go free. He kidnapped a little girl. He tried to kill you and that cute guy from UAB."

"Deon Segal."

"Yeah."

"Don't worry. Lawrence Anders has no chance of getting off the hook for what he did. I just wish we had Angola too."

"The guy with the ponytail?"

"Yep."

"I would testify against him too."

"You never saw him, Becca, so quit worrying about it. They don't need you to put him away."

Becca had been in her car up the street when Deon Segal and I went in to rescue Segal's little sister. Becca's job was to signal me by flicking on her headlights when Tracey confirmed the back door was clear, which she had done.

Angola had escaped. He's still a threat. Tracey and I agree we don't want him ever to learn Becca was involved. He's a killer and the primary reason she wears the rose-stone. Immunity to the power of House of Iron does not, however, stop a bullet or a knife, and Angola is an expert at both. "We got this, Becca."

She opens a pack of salad dressing and squeezes it on her salad. "Okay. I just want you to know that I am ready and willing to testify."

"Thanks."

"Speaking of cute guys," Becca says, leaning toward me. "I saw one in here yesterday. He noticed me, like big-time eye contact and a great smile."

"Who was he?" I take a bite of my lamb gyro.

"I have no idea, but we made a connection. I could feel it."

"Maybe he'll come back to see if you're here again."

"Yeah, but even if he doesn't, it felt good. And I didn't even smile back. I'm trying to learn to be hard to get."

I almost choke on my gyro, trying to imagine Becca playing hard to get with anything she wants.

She felt she had to try hard to win friends because she was different, a "freak." In the days of our developing friendship, she removed her contacts to show me her strange albino eyes. They seemed pink in the light. The aunt who raised her refused to let her get contact lenses. She was always last to be chosen for anything, and the other kids would scream and run to keep from touching her, calling her a demon. Like me, but for a different reason, she had few friends, at least until she was fifteen and allowed to have contact lenses.

"How is the baby doing?" she asks, peering over the edge of the table at my belly.

"Baby is fine from the strength of her kicks."

"It's so exciting! A little girl. I can't wait to dress her."

"Just no pink."

"Why not?"

I struggle for an answer and a brilliant bolt hits me—"Because I want to paint her room yellow. Pink and yellow are kind of yuck together, don't you think?"

Her thin brows furrow into thought. "Maybe—"

While she is pondering her color wheel, I dig into the tabbouleh. I prefer Pita Stop for Lebanese food, but it is much further away than this place, which is just across the street from the law firm where Becca now works as a receptionist.

"Have you registered for your law classes?" I ask.

"Yep, start in the spring semester."

"I'm proud of you for pursuing your dreams."

She beams. "I'm just glad my memory came back, at least of everything that happened before—you know."

She means before Theophalus Blackwell locked her sense of self into a prison inside her own brain. I'm glad she doesn't remember what happened. She has asked me over and over about that missing time, and I've been honest, but I don't volunteer anything about the Ordeal. It's got to be hard enough to deal with having a big blank space in your memory without with the trauma of what really happened. For me, it involved kidnapping and torture in an underground mine, courtesy of Theophalus Blackwell. For Becca, it is a dark hole of lost memory.

She leans forward, "What do you think?"

"About what?" I've been lost in my train of thought and have no clue what train hers is on.

"If the cute guy comes back in, should I say anything or play coy?"

"Are you sure he's someone you want to meet?"

"Rose, I can't make him take a polygraph just because he smiled at me."

"You don't know anything about him."

"I do. I told you, we had a connection." Her eyes slip out of focus. "I think we knew each other in a former life."

"Do you really believe that?" I ask.

"What?" She refocuses on me.

"That we've had former lives. Reincarnation."

"Of course."

She also believes aliens have visited the Earth, but who am I to say anything? If Becca wasn't Becca, she would never have believed in magic . . . or in me.

"You're such a fuddy-duddy," she says.

"Fuddy-duddy? Is that a word?"

"You know Tracey is in love with you, don't you?"

My earlobes burn. "I do not know any such thing, and that is an unfair U-turn."

"Well, it's obvious."

"How is it obvious?"

"The way he protects you."

"We're partners, we protect each other."

"It's not just that. It's the way he—I don't know. I just know."

"Why would you even say such a thing?"

"Because I'm your best friend."

"Just because we—" I shake my head. "There's no evidence that he feels anything more for me than friendship or as his partner. Or that people reincarnate, for that matter."

"What's that got to do with it?"

I clench my fork. "The next thing you'll tell me is—?"

"—What? That witches exist?" she asks with a sweet smile.

I glare at her and stab my tabbouleh.

Chapter Fourteen

It's snowing. The small flakes drift down to the plaintive, heart-heavy wail of bagpipes, clinging to the brown grass for only a moment, but dissolving instantly on the cold cement headstones of the cemetery. White-gloved officers from the Tactical Unit stand at crisp attention on either side of the flag-draped coffin. Chris Lane had served his country before he came home to serve it again as a police officer.

He died within feet of me. I should have saved him. I should have tried.

My experiments with healing others never went well, except once with Becca, and that was not a physical injury, but a magical one imposed by House of Iron. I followed the textbook and my training by not going to Chris while active fire threatened. And I kept my daughter safe. I did the safe thing.

Then why do I want to drop to my knees and weep? Why do those moments when Chris went down play over and over in my mind? Why do I wake every night since then in a sweat, dreaming I did something different . . . or did the same thing?

It's not my only nightmare, just the most recent. The only good thing is that the suspects are in jail. The young man who had been a passenger in the fleeing vehicle turned under Finkman's pressure and gave up the shooter, the man who shot Chris. And the neighbor confirmed what she had told me about seeing the car.

"His death was not for nothing," a speaker at the service said. "It stopped a gang war and saved lives."

That is what everyone is telling me, but I just see Chris Lane's blood seeping into the ground and now his wife, her baby son in her arms and a three-year-old at her side, standing at the graveside. He is not the first person who has died because of me. There is a list of them. Alice said I should forgive myself. I don't have the faintest idea how to do that.

Beside me, Tracey shifts, pressing lightly against my shoulder. Is he trying to tell me he shares what I am feeling? He was physically closer to Chris at the scene than I was, and he knew him personally at the school where we train, the dojo, for a lot longer. Tracey was the one who shouted at me to stay where I was. I am probably alive because of that. *But at a cost.*

Tracey has come in uniform. A strip of black tape covers his badge. It will be a common sight for days across the entire department, reminding everyone of their fallen brother.

Guys from the dojo are also here. After the ceremony, they come over to speak to us. I'm surprised to realize I've been crying, evidenced by the chilled trek of tears down my cheeks, the wind a bitter slap on wet skin.

On the way back to the car, I stop at the funeral home to use the restroom. Another "gift" from pregnancy—pressure on the bladder. Maybe Tracey is right, and it's time for me to go home and sit around and wait to have this baby. A pit of fear yawns before me with that thought. I *need* to be at work to keep that pit at bay.

Coming out of the women's restroom, the person I meet in the narrow hallway is the last person I want to see—Detective Frankel Finkman. I wait for him to step aside so I can pass, but he doesn't.

"I guess you think you're a hero," he says.

"Did you know Chris?"

"I did, and you didn't," he practically spits his anger. "You don't get to call him 'Chris.'"

Finkman is an ass, but this bitterness is beyond even his normal.

I meet his gaze. "I did know him, but what exactly is your problem with me, Finkman? It's just you and me. Spit it out."

"My problem with you is that you don't belong here." A tic jerks his left cheek. "The only way I figure you got into Homicide or the Detective Bureau is opening your legs, cause that is all you got going and that's going to get someone else killed."

The burn of anger replaces the ache in my chest.

He grins, but it's a mirthless expression. "You gonna file a sexual harassment complaint on me, *Officer* Brighton?"

"Why bother? You would lie about it."

"Why don't you just go home where you belong and stop being in everybody's way?"

That hits his target, but I'll be damned if I will let him see it. I am dying right now for a comeback that will hurt him equally, but I'm reduced to glaring.

"Get out of my way," I say.

"Or what?"

What I'd like to do is test out one of the moves I learned in martial arts class, but I am about skilled enough to get myself hurt. It also seems a dishonor to the principle of self-control that Akayama Ryu teaches just to kick him in the balls, as much as I would like to.

I fold my arms over my chest. "Well," I say, as brightly as I can, "I guess it's a stalemate then, since I am as much in your way as you are mine."

His jaw muscles tighten.

At that moment, Tracey appears. "Getting worried about you, Rose. Everything all right?"

Finkman's tension seems to evaporate. "She looks good to me," he says, turning to Tracey. "Healthy as a horse."

I flinch.

"The D.A.'s office called," Tracey says, addressing me and ignoring the comment. "They want us to stop by and answer a few questions for tomorrow's trial."

I hate it that Tracey is being so damn civil. I'd like to see him lift Finkman in the air by the chin and then accidentally drop him over a cliff. I sigh. That scenario will have to remain in my imagination. Tracey Lohan never loses his temper. He is a cool stone mountain. I am a bubbling volcano.

Finkman steps aside, opening a path for me, and waves his hand with a flourish. "I'd never keep a *lady* awaiting an important court trial."

Outside, Tracey reaches for my elbow as we descend the stairs. I jerk my arm away. "I'm perfectly able to walk down stairs, thank you."

"It's Finkman, isn't it?" Tracey says.

"Are you always so perceptive or is it my face?"

He snorts. "Both."

Chapter Fifteen

I dread what's coming. This is not like me, being early anywhere, but I'm sitting alone in one of the uncomfortable chairs in a small, bare room in the county courthouse with only one table connected to the wall. There's nothing on the table, not even a magazine. No art on the walls. It's basically a storage closet for witnesses waiting to be called before the court. I stare at the closed door, trying not to relive the encounter that Anders is standing trial for, although I am reminded every time I walk into my kitchen that he and Angola handcuffed me to my own chair. I need to give that chair away.

More nights than not, I wake up in a sweat from a nightmare. It's a tossup which one—the murders of my family when I was a child, the horrors of the Ordeal, Angola's gun leveled at my forehead, or Chris dying in a pool of blood just out of my reach.

Tracey enters the witness room, his dress shirt unbuttoned at the neck, his maroon tie too small for his broad chest. I frown. Becca is rubbing off on me. I'm hardly a fashion judge. Find me a tee shirt and jeans, or these days extra-large sweatpants, and I'm a happy camper, but Becca oversees my closet, so I imagine I look as presentable as a waddling penguin can look.

With Tracey is a young black man with long dreadlocks woven into a single braid down his back. I'm on my feet and engulfed in a bear hug before I can speak.

"Segal!" I manage.

He releases me. "Detective Brighton. It's good to see you."

"Rose," I correct. "You've earned that".

He smiles. "And you can call me Deon."

"I thought only Kaleshia got to call you by your first name."

"You've earned it."

I suppose we both have. Deon Segal and I walked into the lion's den together to save his little sister. Angola and Anders waited inside for us. Death came so intimately close, he whispered our names. Somehow, we escaped, but so did Angola. He's out there, biding his time. I still hesitate before walking out the front door and sometimes use the back door, but it's a useless exercise in caution. Angola has a rifle with a scope and has proved his proficiency. Tracey tried to get me to move into a House of Stone's safe house, but I don't think that would solve the problem. It would just expose Stone's location. It's not like Angola can't find me. He knows where I work. He could set up on the police parking lot and pick me off any time.

Segal eyes my belly. "Wow, I guess it's been a while since I've seen you. Congratulations!"

"It has," I say, skirting further questions with one of my own. "How is Kaleshia?"

"Doing well. Still in remission."

"That's wonderful." I sit down again, happy to be off my swollen feet.

His smile is wide. "It is. She's been so brave through all of this." Looking around, he asks, "Where do you get a cup of coffee around here? I had a late night."

"No coffee," Tracey says, "but there's a coke machine in the basement. I'm headed that way. Can I get you something?"

"Anything with caffeine."

"Rose?"

"No thanks."

When Tracey leaves, Segal and I are alone. "You're working late at UAB?" I ask. "Another drug study?"

"Nah. Working late on my . . . hobby."

I frown. Deon Segal's hobby, I would venture to guess, involves computer hacking. "I hope that 'hobby' doesn't get you in trouble."

He puts a hand on my shoulder. "Don't worry, sister. It's for the government."

"Really?"

"Yeah, where do you think they find the talent? They employ the best hackers to take out the bad dudes."

"That how you're paying off Kaleshia's medical bills?"

"Yep."

Tracey returns and hands a soft drink can to Segal.

Segal pops it open and takes a long swallow, then tilts his head toward the wall in the direction of the courtroom. "What's going on?"

Tracey shrugs. "We're witnesses, just like you. The defense attorney called a rule into play where we have to stay in seclusion, so other testimony doesn't influence us."

"When do we testify?"

Tracey grins. "Not that simple. All I can tell you is that the jury has been struck, so the attorneys will give opening arguments today. How long that lasts is anybody's guess, so we may have to come back if they don't get to us. The prosecution will put on their case first."

"I don't see how this guy can weasel out of this," Segal says. "I mean, he was in that house with the kidnapper, helping him."

Tracey tosses back his still steaming coffee. "The District Attorney has a solid case," Tracey says. "They expect to win it and put him away for a long while. I just wish we had Angola."

"Yeah," Segal says. "I'm still looking over my shoulder for that creepy guy. But I guess I don't have anything he wants now."

"Well, I want him," Tracey says, narrowing his eyes. "For murder, kidnapping Kaleshia, and attempted murder of Rose."

"Not to worry," Segal says. "If I see him, I got you and Rose on speed dial." He takes a tentative sip of the coffee. "If we're all witnesses, then we're not supposed to talk to each other about the case, right?"

"That's the idea," Tracey says.

"Then why put us all in the same room?"

"Honor system and not enough rooms, I guess." He turns to me. "Speaking of being in the same room, Councilor Orson Hobart is a witness too."

A subtle heads-up not to mention that Hobart is Tracey's father. Tracey had called on him to be part of our rescue operation of Segal's kidnapped little sister, Kaleshia. When Lieutenant Faraday learned we had involved a civilian, she went through the roof. But the fact that Hobart is a sitting city councilor probably saved our bacon from frying to a crisp. Fortunately, the media didn't hear of his involvement, and he asked the chief to keep it that way.

What to do with us was complicated. We were in trouble for not following procedure but simultaneously heroes for rescuing a kidnapped child. The chief compromised with a few days off without pay. It would have been a lot simpler if we could have handed everything over to the Tactical Unit. But we would have invited disaster to involve others. As an Iron warlock, Angola could touch an officer and command him to do anything, including shoot his fellow officers. And he could have wiped Kaleshia's mind in a moment with a touch as well.

Tracey and I have discussed how to respond should the defense bring up our deviation from police procedure. Our answer is that we felt we didn't have time to call in help. Lame, but Angola *had* threatened the child's life. Segal will say he was with us and insisted on going in too. Hopefully, we can skate by the fact that we had prep time. If we have to, we will lie about that. Segal is on board, as we told him we thought bringing in others would endanger his sister.

Regardless of that, evidence against Lawrence Anders is clear-cut. He was in the house with the kidnapped child. He put handcuffs on me at Angola's direction. The only thing unclear was whether Anders was acting on his own or "under" Angola's magical influence. I think Anders was just being paid. That pat down he gave me with lingering fingers did not feel like impersonal obedience under House of Iron manipulation.

Orson Hobart, head of House of Stone, arrives on cue. He's a sizeable man, only an inch or two shorter than Tracey with the same strong jaw and rich brown hair, except his is salted with steel gray at his temples and eyebrows. Despite the subdued but distinct curve of a belly, he carries an aura of power into the room.

"Councilor," Tracey says, offering his hand. Tracey keeps the father-son relationship with Hobart a secret, since Tracey was a product of a former life Hobart had left behind him. I wonder if Hobart faked his death as Alice had. These people have had life spans long enough to perfect the art of new identities.

This is the man who told his son to jump in my pants. I don't dispute it was for a "lofty" purpose, but I guess I don't hide emotions that well because Hobart turns to me after greeting Segal.

"Detective Brighton, good to see you again. I hope that scowl doesn't mean you want to do me bodily harm."

"It does."

Segal's brows lift, and he takes a step back.

"Well, I appreciate your restraint." Hobart sighs and turns to Tracey. "Do we have any idea what is going on? I have a lot of work to do today."

"Settle in," Tracey says. "This will take all day at the least."

"Not this time." A man in a dark business suit and sad blue eyes set in a nest of lines steps inside the doorway and introduces himself as Ted Danovitch, an assistant district attorney.

"What's up, Ted?" Tracey asks.

Segal frowns, "Did the son-of-a-bitch plead guilty?"

"Nope. The defense is calling for a dismissal of the case."

"What?" I am out of my chair faster than I've moved in the past six months.

"Calm down," Danovitch says. "The judge isn't granting a dismissal yet, but he is postponing the case."

"Why?" I ask, swallowing my fury.

"Seems our defendant is having a few mental issues."

I narrow my eyes. "He seemed just fine when he was holding a little girl with cancer hostage, not to mention her brother and myself."

"What kind of mental issues?" Tracey asks.

"Don't worry, he will be thoroughly evaluated at Taylor Hardin Secure Mental Facility. They're used to dealing with defendants faking mental incompetence. That's where they sent Bobby Frank Cherry."

"I don't understand," Segal says. "Who is Cherry?"

"Bobby Cherry," Danovitch says. "He was one of the Ku Klux Klansmen who bombed the Birmingham church in '63, killing four little girls. He tried to get out of it by faking dementia."

"Mental incompetence?" I am outraged. "What is he saying?"

"He's not saying anything. He's acting as if he doesn't know how to talk or feed himself or even walk on his own."

I take a stunned breath, images of Becca in a zombie state flickering through my mind.

Danovitch looks at me. "Sorry. We can't move forward until there's a hearing on his mental state."

Tracey, Hobart, and I exchange glances. We are all thinking the same thing.

Segal is not on our page. "That's BS," he says. "When did that happen?"

"Pretty suddenly. He pled not guilty at his arraignment, a few months ago, and we've heard nothing about mental issues until today, all of which makes it highly unlikely to be legitimate. Nobody at the jail thinks there's anything wrong with him. But he was pretty convincing in the courtroom, even urinated on himself right in front of the judge."

Segal steps forward, hands clenched. He has always appeared a gentle man, but anger has transformed him. "He doesn't get to do what he did to my little sister and get away with it."

I put my hand on his arm. "Segal."

He ignores me, glaring at Danovitch.

"Deon," I say.

He turns to me. "This is not right, man. Not right."

I have no way to explain to him that Lawrence Anders probably had a visitor who posed as his attorney or clergy, a visitor with a ponytail and the magic of House of Iron. And when that visitor walked out, he left behind a shell of a man. It is unlikely Angola had the skill or inclination to make it a temporary condition. He sacrificed Ander's mind to protect himself, or protect his House, or both. Taylor Hardin Secure Mental Facility will be Ander's "home" for the rest of his life. He is not Angola's first victim and unless we stop him, not his last.

Chapter Sixteen

"**D**ispatch has a hysterical woman at Mountain Lane Senior Living," Lieutenant Faraday says, glancing up at us from behind her desk in the Homicide Unit. "How about trotting over there and seeing what's going on?"

Tracey frowns. "Isn't that a Patrol call?"

"Patrol's on the scene, but there's a dead body involved, so go handle it."

I turn to follow Tracey out of the office.

"Hey Tracey," Detective Frank Finkman calls out before we can reach the door. "I hear your dog is gonna have puppies."

Tracey freezes and I almost plow into his back. His big hands knot into fists at his side.

A flush of blood burns my ears. I am frozen with anger and embarrassment, which is a good thing because, to my surprise, Faraday steps out of her office, brushes by us and marches to Finkman's desk. I would not like to meet Barbara Faraday in a dark alley. She is taller and heavier than I am, and not a bit of it is fat.

Smacking on a piece of gum, Finkman looks up at her and grins. "Yes, ma'am?" If he is rattled by her attention, he hides it well.

"What did you say?" she asks, her tone biting.

He shrugs. "I just heard Detective Lohan had a pregnant bitch, ma'am, a pedigree, and I was wondering if the pups might be for sale."

The entire room is still, watching the drama.

"You like working in Homicide, Finkman?" Faraday says tightly.

He shrugs again. "It's a job."

"What I heard sounds a lot like sexual harassment, and we don't tolerate that in this office."

"No ma'am," Finkman says, his eyes wide with feigned innocence. "Maybe I was misinformed about the canine situation. I do apologize to Detective Lohan."

Faraday can't push it. Making him apologize to me would mean acknowledging that my pregnancy was connected to Tracey. Rumors and innuendos have flown across the department like a stirred wasp nest ever since I began to show.

"I hear anything like that coming out of your mouth again," Faraday says, "and your 'job' will be on Ensley morning shift. That clear?"

Considering Ensley is the roughest precinct and morning shift refers to the wee hours between 11 pm and 7 am, that is a threat.

"Yes ma'am," he drawls, leaning back in his chair.

I grab Tracey's arm and pull, which is like pulling on a pickup truck. I've never seen him this angry.

"Lohan," I whisper, "drop it."

Tracey takes two long, deep breaths. "Let's get out of here before I smash a cockroach."

The silence on the way to the call hides a swirl of emotion, his and mine. I have never seen Tracey like this. I try to lighten it up.

"Finkman is an asshole, but I encountered worse in Patrol. I can handle him."

Tracey doesn't respond. Worry knots my stomach. "I don't want to have to work a homicide on Finkman. Nor do I want to be the cause of it, as lowlife as he is."

Still nothing.

"Talk to me, Lohan."

After a moment, he says. "I came so close." His words are quiet, almost too low to hear. "Right there in front of everyone. I almost walked over there and smashed a hole in his desk to let him know what was coming and then smashed in his head."

He pulls the car over into a convenience store parking lot and sits there, gripping the steering wheel. I suspect if he let go of it, his hands would tremble with adrenaline. I'm surprised he doesn't crush the steering wheel.

"Everything in me wanted to do that, Rose."

"I understand."

"I'm not sure you do."

He stares into the distance, silent.

Outside the window, a gust of wind blows a piece of paper across the lot. A car pulls up to the pump and a woman in heels opens the door. There's a car seat in the back seat facing backwards and a tow-headed baby screeching. I flinch at the sound. Before she exits, the woman twists in her seat and puts a plastic toy into his hand, which promptly goes into the child's mouth.

Neither of us says anything until Tracey speaks again. "All my life I've had to work to control this . . . rage inside me."

Rage? Tracey Lohan? He is the most even-tempered person I know.

"Sometimes it feels like something alive—I call it my *ryu*."

"*Ryu*? I thought that was the word for a school or style, like Akayama Ryu."

He takes a deep breath and then another one before answering. "It does when it's attached to a type of martial art, but the word also has Chinese roots that mean 'dragon.'"

Talking about it seems to help. His hands have relaxed their death grip on the steering wheel.

"Have you always had to battle your dragon?" I ask softly. Tracey has never talked much about himself or his childhood.

"Up until I was about twelve, no. I was a peaceful kid. I liked all the stuff most boys liked—baseball, fishing, teasing girls. But when I hit puberty, my *ryu* awoke. Fortunately, I didn't yet have access to my House inheritance, but I was still strong for my age. My parents had to move several times to keep me out of juvenile courts."

"Really?" This was hard to imagine—Tracey as a bad boy.

"My mother died, and that made it worse. My father made me take martial arts to learn discipline and help me keep in control."

I recall my tirade in Hobart's city council office. It never occurred to me that Tracey could have gone amok on me. "What about Hobart, your father?"

"No. Thankfully, it's a trait that skips generations. In ancient times we were the berserker warriors who went into a trance and killed every-one within reach."

My mind's eye sees a Norse Viking, soaked in blood, hair and axe flailing, mowing down anyone, friend or foe, who dared come near. This image is bad enough, but if that person had the kind of strength that belongs to House of Stone—

Tracey takes another deep breath. "I've never told this to anyone, not even other members of Stone."

"Why did you tell me?"

He turns to face me. "I don't want to have secrets from you."

I don't know how to respond. Somehow this shakes me more than the fact that a dragon lives inside my partner.

Chapter Seventeen

Mountain Lane Senior Living is a complex of biscuit-brick build-ings set back from the road among tall pine trees. I inhale the sharp scent of pine needles. Since the second trimester of my pregnancy, my sense of smell has sharpened.

We make our way to the front reception desk, show our badges and stand there while the receptionist summons the manager. The entrance hall, designed to portray elegance, includes several chairs that look too uncomfortable for actual sitting. Royal blues dominate. The foyer is empty, aside from a man and a woman in wheelchairs who sit facing each other, heads lolled to the side in sleep or unconsciousness. Neither looks capable of wheeling themselves, so I can only assume they are waiting for visitors, or someone has left them that way to encourage social contact, or perhaps they are props.

After a few minutes, a stout woman, well past childbearing age, arrives. A heavy perfume precedes her, masking a musky smell that worms its way through the saccharine. I take a step back, my sensitive stomach complaining. She holds out a meaty hand to Tracey. "Mary Densmore. Are you the detective?"

"Yes ma'am," he says shaking her hand. "Tracey Lohan, and this is my partner, Detective Rose Brighton."

Her penciled-on eyebrows lift in surprise. "Oh, she's with you?"

"She is." I extend my hand to grasp her moist palm from the furthest point I can stand and still reach her, forcing myself to ignore the nausea. I've had plenty of practice at that for the last several months.

Her gaze shifts to my belly.

Will I ever get used to that? Most men at least try not to talk to a woman's breasts, but I don't take it personally when their eyes wander. I have been known to notice a man's shoulders. We're all slaves to those little genes that turn our hormones on and off.

"What seems to be the problem?" Tracey asks.

"Oh, we can't talk here," she says. Her gaze flicks to the curious receptionist. "Come into my office."

She leads us into a small office off the foyer. Densmore retreats behind her pristine desk but doesn't sit or offer us the velvet blue chairs arrayed before it. I assume they are reserved for paying family members. Overlarge impressionist prints—Claude Monet's "Woman with a Parasol" and "Woman with a Parasol Facing Right" dominate the wall behind her desk, chosen for the blue tones, I suspect. I stay as close to the door as possible, trying not to breathe.

"It's Mrs. Zane's daughter," Densmore says. "She's been raising hell ever since she got here."

"Is Mrs. Zane the person who died?" I ask.

"Yes. This morning."

"Was she sick?"

"Cancer, multiple myeloma. She just went on hospice."

Tracey scratches his hairline. "The daughter is unhappy that her mother died. Is she still here?"

"She's in the room. Wouldn't leave or let us have the body removed until we called the police. Then an officer arrived, and now he's not leaving either." She throws her hands in the air. "Can you please talk to her? Her theatrics are disturbing other patients and the staff."

Her phone rings, and she picks it up, her voice changing to sweetness. "Yes, this is Mountain Lane."

Pause.

"Certainly. We'd love to have you visit us." She cradles the phone against her shoulder to free her right hand and scribbles a room number on a piece of paper, handing it to Tracey.

We find our own way down the hall, leaving Densmore cooing into the phone. Tracey knocks on room 316 and a uniformed officer opens the door.

"What have you got?" Tracey asks.

The officer steps outside and closes the door. I can hear a woman sobbing inside.

"This lady insists her mother was overdosed," he says. "I've tried to calm her down, but she's adamant."

"Did you call the medical examiner?" Tracey asks.

"Yep. He said he needs indication of foul play to take the body and do an autopsy."

"I see. Any kind of medical records we can look at?"

"Nobody gave me any."

Tracey sighs. "Okay. Guess we'll take it from here."

The officer brightens. "I can go?"

Tracey nods.

"Ten-four that!" he says and heads down the hall.

Inside the small apartment, we pass a compact kitchen on the right and enter a living room just large enough for the sofa, two chairs and a TV. Beige walls and matching beige carpet. A window in the top half of an exterior door presents a view of a small rectangular rose garden with bare stems cut back for the winter. In the chair closest to the back door sits a woman in her fifties, gray-streaked hair hanging straight over her shoulders and down the back of a sweater that matches the carpet. Long fingers that are still graceful, though the knuckles are knobby, clutch a handful of papers.

Awkwardly, I clear my throat. "Mrs. Zane?"

She looks up, her cheeks flushed and tear-stained.

"That's my mother," she says. "I'm Doris Jansen."

By some unspoken agreement, the sight of a crying woman catapults me to point-position for handling the situation. I don't try to shake her hand. Instead, I lower myself into the nearest chair. Tracey slips into the adjoining room, presumably the bedroom with the body.

"I'm Detective Rose Brighton, and my partner is Detective Tracey Lohan. We're from Homicide."

"Oh, thank goodness!" she says and breaks into tears again.

I hand her a nearby tissue, and she wipes under her eyes and then blows her nose softly.

"I'm sorry about your mother."

She nods but keeps her head down, obviously struggling for control.

"I understand she was sick. Can you tell us why you think she didn't die of natural causes?"

With a sniff, Jansen says. "Everyone has acted like I'm crazy. I'm not crazy. I know my mother. I come here every day, and she was fine yesterday. She was going to die at some point, but not yet. Neither of us was ready."

"Sometimes these things don't wait for us to be ready."

Jansen's mouth tightens. "Don't patronize me, please."

I guess I deserved that. "I didn't mean to. I was thinking about my sister. I lost her when she was very young."

Her mouth instantly collapses its defensive line. "I'm so sorry. That must have been terrible. I know Mother was old, and she didn't have much longer. But something wrong happened. I'm not crazy."

"Tell me."

"She's got a pain patch. I helped give her a bath yesterday, and I always check to make sure where it is and that they're not putting it in the same place."

"Are you sure?"

"I'm positive." She fumbles in her purse and brings out a small notebook. "I keep a record of exactly where they put it and when. It's supposed to be changed every three days. You have to watch these people, because they will forget, or a different person doesn't read the chart." She flips to a page at the end and hands me the notebook, pointing to the last entry. "See," she adds, "She had a new patch yesterday on the right shoulder blade and there's nothing there on her. Instead, there's one just above her *left* shoulder blade."

"I see. Could you have made a mistake about that?"

"No. I'm very careful with my records. Her skin is sensitive."

"Help me here—what would be the significance of someone moving the patch?"

"It's not moving it, it's putting a fresh one on before she's ready. It's a very powerful medicine, but it's time-released. I don't think it would kill her by itself, but if someone gave her morphine or something else on top of that. . . ."

"And what makes you suspect they may have done that?"

She blinks at me. "She was fine yesterday. I mean *fine*. I took her to dinner, and she was laughing and talking. I fell asleep in this chair. Sometimes I sleep on the couch, but I just crashed, and it was almost 4 a.m. when I woke up. I checked on her right before I left. Then I get a call this morning and . . . and she's dead!"

She breaks down again. I hand her more tissues.

Through her sobs, she says, "I just want to know what happened. I have to know. I want an autopsy."

"Let me go talk to my partner," I put a hand on her shoulder.

Tracey is in the bedroom with the dead woman. *Coward.* He is standing with his arms crossed, looking at her. The room smells like baby powder.

"Seems like she went peacefully," Tracey says. "I'm not sure I would fuss if my mother had cancer and died in her sleep."

"She says her mother was fine yesterday, and that someone put an unneeded pain patch on her." I hold up the little notebook.

He shrugs. "Maybe she was in pain."

"Let's at least look at her back and verify which side the patch is on."

Tracey snaps a few photos, just in case, and helps me turn the stiffening body onto her side. I pull down her gown. I've never seen a pain patch, but there is a square piece of gauze about the size of my palm stuck to her skin above her left shoulder blade, just as her daughter claimed. But it seems just as likely to me that Jansen wrote down the wrong side. Even so, it surely couldn't have killed her.

I pull the nightgown back onto Mrs. Zane's shoulder and roll her gently onto her back. She does look peaceful.

"Well," I say, "Mrs. Jansen wrote down that she placed it on the other shoulder, but I don't think that warrants an autopsy or homicide investigation—"

That was the last thing out of my mouth before it freezes, half-open, and a rush of unbidden warmth shoots into my feet and up my legs into my body. The room shifts into shimmering gray and black.

Chapter Eighteen

What little light illuminates the room comes from under an adjacent door. I can barely see the hazy figure that walks backward into the room, alerting me that I am seeing the past. By the general shape, I infer the person is a woman, but deep shadow and the wavering distortion hide her features. She holds something in each hand, a glass and a paper cup, I think, the kind nurses use to carry around medicine. Turning to Zane, who is sitting upright in the bed, she lifts the glass to the elderly woman's mouth. Water fills the glass from Zane's lips. The woman withdraws the full glass of water, holding it and then lifts the med cup to Zane's open mouth. Zane closes her mouth. Withdrawing the cup, the woman places both items on the nightstand.

As abruptly as I was wrenched into the gray and black world of the past, I'm released to reality, or what I think of as reality. I rock on my heels, dizzy.

Tracey steps forward, putting a hand on my arm to steady me. "Rose?"

"I'm okay." I press my hand to my head to stem the pain, a useless gesture. "Another vision."

"What happened?"

"A woman gave Mrs. Zane something. Pills, I think."

He shrugs. "Maybe that's normal."

"Maybe, but I think we should check it out. I just saw a little piece of what happened. She could have also given her another pain patch."

I return to the living room. "Ms. Jansen, do you have health proxy for your mother?"

"Yes, but what does that matter now?"

"We'd like to take a look at her medical charts and medications, but that's protected by law. As her personal representative, you can give that permission."

"Yes, of course. That's why I called. I want an investigation."

Tracey accompanies Jansen to request the information. Jansen returns first, and I sit with her while we wait for Tracey to return with copies of the charts and protocol on Mrs. Zane.

"How come you're not brushing me off like everyone else has?" she asks.

"We're just doing our job." I squint at her, trying to reduce the amount of light going to my brain and agitating my headache. "Tell me about your mother."

She looks up through teary eyes and glances to the window. "She loves . . . loved." Her voice catches. "I have to get used to the past tense, don't I?" She blows her nose. "Mom loved flowers, especially roses."

My thoughts skitter to the nearly black roses that have portended attempts on my life since I found the rose-stone. The first was left in my hospital room after someone tried to run me down in a car. The second was delivered to my house, and the third placed on Alice's doorstep.

"They let her plant those out back where she could see them." Jansen's voice snaps me back into the present. "They look bleak now, but when they bloom, they're gorgeous. Everybody here stops by the garden to see them." She waves absently at the door. "That's why they didn't move her to the assisted living area. This is the independent living section. She couldn't walk on her own anymore, but I took her out in the wheelchair to see her roses when they were blooming."

"Are you the only child?"

"I have a younger brother. He doesn't do sickness or anything difficult, even when he shows, which he hasn't for over a year. I have no idea where he is or even if he's still alive. So I get mother-duty. Not that I mind. It hasn't . . . hadn't gotten bad yet, you know? I understand Mom wasn't in a good place, but the doctor said she had at least a few months."

Someone robbed her of those months. That's an eternity when the days are the last ones with your family.

"I was going to come by this morning to take her to brunch. She goes—I keep using present tense." She takes a deep breath. "She went crazy for pecan waffles at the Pancake House in Five Points South. They put whipped cream on it for her."

"I know it well."

Tracey returns carrying paperwork and a frown. "Seems she has a prescription of morphine that she's not been using, but several of the pills are missing from her bottle." He turns to Jansen. "Mrs. Jansen, we will open the case and ask for an autopsy. We'll wait until an evidence technician gets here. I've also notified the medical examiner's office, and they're sending an investigator out. Can you wait for him? He'll want to talk to you too."

"Of course."

Tracey pulls out his badge case and takes a card from it, handing it to her. "Feel free to contact me if you think of something else, and we will get back to you after we see the results."

Tears leak again from her red eyes. "Thank you."

"THAT'S THE SECOND TIME IN A WEEK you've had a vision at a scene," Tracey says as we walk to the car.

A cold wind cuts across the trees, sending a crimson cascade of late leaves to the ground. I pull my jacket tighter. "I've noticed. They're the first ones in months, the first since I saw a vision of Angola attacking Devon Segal in the alley outside of The Edge of Chaos building."

"How many homicide scenes have we been to since then?"

"Too many. Why?"

He shrugs. "Just wondering what would trigger them now."

"I don't know."

"Do you think it has anything to do with—" He glances at my belly.

"Lohan, that makes no kind of sense. I've been pregnant all these months."

"But you're pretty close now, just a few weeks. How does that kind of magic work, anyway? Could hormones trigger it?"

He unlocks the car door and we both slide in . . . or he slides. I grab the overhead strap and lower myself.

"I don't think anyone alive understands that," I say. "My visions seem related to the place where I am at the time I have them . . . except once."

He glances at me expectantly

"Remember when we were on Jason's yacht last spring?"

"Not likely to forget Stonehenge in the middle of the woods in South Alabama."

It was a bizarre place, a kind of amusement park, but instead of rides, there were replicas of famous places and dinosaurs hidden in the woods around a bay near the coastline. Jason Blackwell had taken us there in his yacht, the *Iron Fist*.

"It was before we—before I got pregnant. I had a vision there."

"I remember you had a dizzy spell, but you never told me it was from a vision."

"I didn't know you were House of Stone then."

"What did you see?"

"I don't understand it exactly. At first, I thought it was the past, but everyone was moving forward, not in reverse, so I think I saw the future or a possible future."

He glances at me but doesn't say anything.

"I saw another set of stones superimposed on the faux ones and some people in robes. It was misty. A girl was on her knees and a person walked toward her and hung something around the girl's neck."

"What do you think it was?"

"I think it was the real Stonehenge."

"In England?"

"Yes."

"Have you ever even been there?" he asks.

"No."

"There are old stories related to the henges," he says vaguely. "Have you ever seen a vision of anything that far away?"

"No, never. Like I said, they've always happened in the same place where I physically am."

"What did it mean?" he asks.

"Maybe that I will be there in the future, but what if it's related to her?"

His thick brows furrow, and he glances over at me again. "Her?"

I rest a hand on my belly, and Tracey sucks in a breath.

"She is House of Rose too," I say.

"And House of Stone."

"And House of Iron." My other hand joins the first, clasping the mound that is home to my child, my daughter. "Maybe she is supposed to be there."

Chapter Nineteen

"Where is Becca?" I ask when I cross Alice's threshold that evening. "Her car is gone."

"Getting blue contact lenses," Alice says.

"Blue? I thought she wore brown."

Alice smiles. "She said she was ready for changes in her life."

"I don't like her not being here. We don't know how long the rose-stone can hold enough living-green to protect her."

"She was so excited."

I turn toward the door, trying to fight off thoughts of Angola laying his hands on Becca and turning her into a zombie again, this time with no hope of recovery, ever. I panic. "Where did she go? I'll try to find her."

Just then the door opens and Becca steps in, her cheeks and the tip of her nose flushed with the cold. "How do I look?" She spreads her mittened hands.

I exhale in relief and lower myself into the nearest chair, grateful for the footrest. I've had to buy shoes twice to keep up with the swelling.

"You didn't even notice, did you?" Becca says, plopping onto the sofa in the same spot Daniel's mother Nora had inhabited for weeks after the Ordeal. The burns Daniel suffered during that nightmare had healed, but something in his mother had not. Nora spent most of her days sitting on that sofa, her eyes following the movements on the television, her mind somewhere else. Somewhere dark. Not long afterward, she stepped into the bathtub and slashed her wrists.

I don't blame the judge for taking Daniel away from the place where he saw something that horrendous and putting him in a foster home.

I wouldn't want to grow up in the house where my family had burned to death.

"Rose?" Becca says. "Are you okay? Did you hear anything I said?"

"Yes, I'm fine. Why?"

"You look so sad."

I blink. "Blue looks beautiful on you."

"Really? You think? I have a date."

"You'll wow him. Who is it?"

"Remember me telling you about that cute guy at the place we had lunch?"

I wrinkle my forehead and then remember. "You mean the one that smiled at you?"

"The one." She looks smug. "And I didn't even have to do anything. He came up to me, and we had coffee. He likes to ski and read westerns. Now he's taking me to dinner at Oceans in Five Points."

"Nice. Have you picked out what you'll wear?"

"Does the cat have a meow?" She laughs. "A blue suit. Navy with a frilly blouse. Going out right after work, so it's a compromise."

Alexander, the schizophrenic of Alice's three cats, puts two front paws on my leg, probably trying to scope out possibilities on my non-existent lap. He is responsible for a scar on my leg, but now has taken a liking to me for unknown reasons. Jumping lightly onto the arm of the chair, he puts a tentative paw on my belly, testing to see if it will hold his weight. It probably looks like one of the sofa cushions.

"Would you mind handing me the rose-stone?" I ask Becca. "Once down, I stay."

"Sure." She loops the silver chain over her head and hands it to me.

I set it on the top of my belly. Alexander has apparently decided the armrest is more stable. His golden eyes follow the movement of the glittering chain. I look down at the red diamond pendant, lured, as always, into the intricate, endless crystal chambers.

"Why don't you see if there is any living-green still there?" Alice suggests, bringing me a steaming cup of tea.

I pull my attention from the stone with difficulty. "What?"

"You worried about the magic leaking out. Why don't you test how much remains by trying to pull some out instead of pushing more in?"

I blink. "I've never thought of that. Have you ever tried?"

She shakes her head. "You are the only one able to fill it. I wouldn't want to draw from it and leave Becca unprotected."

The more I learn about House magic, the more I realize how individual differences can shape its expression. I have visions but can't heal; Alice can probe what's going on inside someone and help them heal, but she only has occasional premonitions, not the kind of specific visions I have. Some in Iron are more skilled at mental manipulation than others. I imagine House of Stone members have the same kind of variations in what they can do.

I look back down at the stone, remembering the first time I touched it. It sent out a vibration alerting every member of the Houses. Tracey said it only did that when someone in a specific genetic line of House of Rose touched it.

The diamond has never "done" anything else. In the beginning, I used it as a focus-object to find the living-green. It's no longer necessary for that. Drawing that power is as natural as breathing, as long as coal is not too far away or covered by water.

I rub the surface of the stone. Red is the rarest of all diamonds, though sometimes I think I see a glimpse of purple, as if a blue lives deep behind the facets. "What is your purpose?" I ask it softly.

"What?" Becca says.

I smile. "Just talking to the rose-stone."

"Oh." Her face fills with wonder. "Did it answer?"

"Not that I'm aware."

Becca sighs. "My best friend is a witch, and I can't tell anyone. Bummer."

"Not if you wish to keep that new job," Alice says, bringing another cup of tea for Becca.

"I'm sorry, Alice." Becca jumps up. "You shouldn't have to wait on us. We can sit in the kitchen."

"Nonsense," Alice says, setting a platter of chocolate chip cookies on the coffee table. She's made them with pecans. I can't resist. I don't try. A little scoop of vanilla ice cream would be perfect, but not pushing it. Alice hasn't had ice cream in the house since Daniel left.

"How can a diamond hold magic, anyway?" Becca asks Alice.

"A diamond is among the least volatile substances known and the hardest, and it expands less on heating than any other material. Perfect to store magical energy."

"Any diamond?"

"An excellent question. We should set up an experiment, but look at Rose. She's worn out."

"But I'm not," Becca says. "Now you sit down, and I'll bring *your* tea."

"Well, that will be fine," Alice says and settles into the rose-patterned chair she favors.

We are momentarily alone.

I touch the diamond's face and "pull" gently. A tiny stream of invisible golden energy ripples through my finger and spreads gentle warmth throughout my body. The baby kicks.

I stop, suddenly afraid, and examine the rose-stone.

"What's wrong?" Alice asks.

"I pulled living-green from the stone, but it doesn't prove anything."

She cocks her head to the side. "It proves there is still residual magic inside it."

"No, it doesn't." I hold the stone up to the light and tilt it different ways, inspecting for any damage. "A diamond is carbon. Carbon that has undergone tremendous pressures but still carbon, the element in coal that we consume."

She taps her finger to her lip. "I think it would be quite a bit more difficult to pull energy from a diamond than from coal."

"Why?"

"Energy is released when matter changes form. A diamond, as you say, is pure carbon. That means the carbon bonds are one to one. It forms a tetrahedron shape, quite strong and stable. Much more stable than coal, which also contains oxygen, hydrogen, and nitrogen, if I recall my chemistry."

"And a little ash and sulfur," I say with a tired smile. I was a psychology major with an art minor and allergic to chemistry, but when I found out I was a witch who "ate" coal, I looked it up. According to the letter my mother left me, the rose-stone can hold all three of the Houses' magics simultaneously. I've never dreamed of testing that. The one time I managed to combine two of those elements, it created a conflagration that killed the most powerful warlock of House of Iron. No one could stand before a *Y Tair* that controlled all three. It is no wonder House of Iron is determined to prevent her.

"I wish I knew more about the history and use of the rose-stone," Alice says, "but I'm afraid I'm too young."

I almost choke. Fortunately, the tea is still very hot, and I only took a tiny sip. "What are you talking about? You're over a hundred—" I add, "Not that you look a day over ninety."

Oblivious at my attempt at humor, she sighs. "Whatever knowledge may have been passed down to your mother and grandmother is lost now." Old pain edges her voice.

I know that pain well. I have the same losses.

When I crawled out a bedroom window in the house that used to stand next door, I ran to the only person I knew, my Great Aunt Alice. She sent me away to protect me, but after I graduated from college, I returned. She insists I was answering the rose-stone's siren call, but if so, it's nothing I ever heard, not with my ears anyway. I wouldn't have believed anything so preposterous before I came to Birmingham, but now nothing seems preposterous, and mysteries have layers inside layers, like the red diamond between my fingers.

"Perhaps you should talk to Dr. Hobart," Alice says.

"What?"

"I've been digging around in some old letters I kept from my mother when I was in England, and she was here raising a family. She mentions a man of House of Stone as someone her mother knew under another name, but she said he was a Hobart now. Isn't that the name of Detective Lohan's father?"

I close my mouth because it has dropped open. "It is, but—"

"Then you should ask him about the rose-stone. I'm sure if he knows, he will tell you. You can ask him at dinner tomorrow night. I've invited him and his son."

"Alice!"

She sips her tea, her face placid with innocence.

Chapter Twenty

"I'm not going."

I step out of the shower and grab a towel. Through the dissipating steam, Angel watches me from her perch on the closed toilet seat lid. Her ear, the one with a piece missing, twitches.

"Don't look at me like that. Just because I took a shower doesn't mean I'm going. We'll fix some popcorn and watch movies tonight."

Angel lifts a paw and begins licking it. It seems like just yesterday that she moved in without consulting me, a non-cat person. Now I can't imagine life without her.

"How can Alice expect me to just sit down to dinner with Hobart?" I towel my hair, squeezing rather than roughing it to avoid the dreaded frizz and then applying a generous dollop of mousse in the curls. I rarely wear it down.

"He tried to use me like I was some kind of brood cow."

Angel takes the paw she has cleaned and smooths the fur on the side of her face.

"I don't care if he did it because he thinks he's saving House of Rose and all the families. That doesn't excuse him."

I can't believe I am talking to a cat.

I run my fingers through the wet curls.

Angel is watching me.

"I'm not going. I don't care if Alice is making chicken tetrazzini."

"I'm just here to keep from hurting your feelings," I say thirty minutes later when Alice opens her door.

She smiles. "How thoughtful."

"Are they here yet?" I peer over her shoulder into the living room. Both Tracey and his father are big men, not easily hidden from view, but I look anyway.

"Not yet. Would you like a glass of wine?" She glances at my belly. "Or some juice?"

"Wine. The doctor said a little won't hurt."

Becca enters the room with a swish of sky blue skirt and heels.

I'm wearing black pants and my white tailored work shirt with the silver earrings Becca gave me before the Ordeal.

She gives me a visual once over, turns on her heels and disappears.

Alice puts a glass of red wine in my hand. She's wearing a becoming red dress I suspect Becca selected for her, maybe even bought her with her first paycheck. I would have thought red would clash with Alice's dyed hair, but Becca found a shade that works.

Before I can take a much-needed swallow of wine, Becca reappears with a colorful silk scarf that she ties loosely around my neck. Then she unbuttons a second shirt button and fluffs my hair.

"There. Much better."

I take a generous swig of wine. My normal idea of dressing up is a clean tee shirt.

"I knew the chicken tetrazzini would get you here," she whispers.

I have to remind myself to loosen my death grip on the wine. If I had a drop of House of Stone blood, the glass would shatter.

"I can't believe she invited Hobart without asking me," I whisper back.

"Asking you what? It's her house."

I open my mouth but find I don't really have a reply to this. It *is* her house.

"Rose," Becca says, in a normal, but stern tone as she guides me to a chair, "Think about the baby. One day soon, she's going to come into the world and be a real person, a child, and she needs family."

I want to be angry, but I can't argue with her logic. I lower myself into the chair. "Tracey said the same thing, but what am I supposed to do, just overlook that Hobart is an ass?"

"What his father tried to do was disrespectful. He treated you like an object. I get what that feels like, but he didn't do it for himself and that makes a difference."

"Becca, you haven't even met him."

"I've met Tracey, and he's a good man. He must have a good father." She clears her throat. "Rose, you need to move forward."

"Why?"

"Because—well, think about South Africa. What happened there was awful, but they found a way for reconciliation. I don't mean to make light of anything, but frankly, in comparison. . . . I mean, lots of parents push their children to marry someone for money or social status. That's the way things used to be done."

"It's not the same thing. Everyone got something from those arrangements. Hobart just wanted Tracey to impregnate me, like I was livestock. And why are we talking about South Africa?"

"It's a project I had for my night law class. I got an 'A.'"

"I'm not a reconciliation project."

"The project part isn't important. It's about forgiveness."

I throw up my hands. "Are you saying I should just ignore what happened?"

"It's not about ignoring wrongs or excusing them. It's about not reducing justice to revenge."

"Revenge sounds good to me."

She lifts her arches at me. "You're being flippant."

"I'm a police officer, Becca. Justice is about finding the bad guy and sending him to prison."

"That's your *job*, but there are better ways to resolve things. And prison is a bit much for encouraging a liaison to save a race of people."

"I'll concede that, but what am I supposed to do? Every time I look at him, I get mad."

"Do you really want revenge?" She locks her now-blue eyes on me. "Or do you want justice?"

"Justice" seems a heavyweight word for my irritation at Hobart. I just don't like him. But Becca is talking about more than that. Does she mean justice for Amber? How many people have bothered to listen to Becca, really listen? I've lost count of the times she has piped up with an idea or observation right on target. When we first met, I dismissed her as a fashion-fixated bouncy blonde. I learned she was a faithful friend that would march into hell at my side. And she is so much more.

"Just what kind of justice are you talking about?" I ask, not ready to commit to anything, but listening.

"The kind that restores a community, not the kind that destroys it."

I take another swallow of wine. "I'm hardly a 'community.'"

"But the Houses are, aren't they? Families are. And besides, you *used* Tracey to get pregnant, didn't you? How is that different from Hobart wanting to use him to get you pregnant?"

Again, my mouth drops open. "Becca, you are going to be one hell of a lawyer."

She grins.

"What about the table?" I manage, needing time to work this out. "Shouldn't we help Alice get ready?" I can readily see that the kitchen table is already set with Alice's fine china.

"Done. You don't have to do anything. And everything is going to be fine. You'll see."

Still smiling at her coup de grâce, she leans over and pats my belly. "We need a name. We can't just keep calling her 'the baby.'"

She is trying to divert me, and at the moment, I welcome diversion. "Isn't it bad luck or something to name a baby before it's born?"

"That's superstitious nonsense," Alice says, emerging from the kitchen.

"Is this smart?" I ask Alice. "What if you slip up? You've worked so hard to be dead."

I haven't told her that Tracey has figured out who she is. Whatever I think about Dr. Hobart, he is not stupid. Even if Tracey hasn't told his father, Alice's secret is on tenuous ground.

Alice rubs her hands on an apron and unties it. "I'm willing to take that risk to give your baby a father and grandfather." She sniffs. "And Becca is right. You should give her a name."

"Where did that superstition come from anyway?" Becca asks.

Alice takes a breath. "At one time, an infant's survival of birth was no sure thing." She glances at me. "The mother's either. It was easier if the baby that died didn't have a name."

"That is morbid." Becca takes the glass of wine Alice offers.

"Amber," I say.

Becca's face lights up. "Oh, that's a beautiful name."

"It was my sister's." I feel tears well and take a generous swallow. All my adult life, I couldn't cry, but now I am a leaky faucet.

Becca lifts her glass. "To Amber."

Alice and I join her. "To Amber."

Though expected, the knock startles me. Is it trepidation at Hobart's presence, or am I nervous about something else? And why did I let Becca unbutton that button? Does she think I'm here because of Tracey? I'm not. That makes no sense. I see him every day.

Alice goes to the door and opens it, then stops dead. Hobart is similarly motionless. Their gazes lock. Behind Hobart, I can see Tracey, who has about two inches of height on his father. The frozen moment between Hobart and Alice extends. Puzzled, I frown. They both appear shocked. *Do they recognize each other from somewhere?*

"Irene, are you okay?" Becca asks Alice.

No answer.

Slowly, it dawns what is happening. I recognize the look in Hobart's eyes because I have seen it before. Jason's eyes devour me like that. Hobart is House of Stone; Alice is House of Rose. Whatever it is when the magics of two people of different Houses choose to entangle, this is it. I can't see it, but I imagine the dancing lights of two aurorae—northern light displays—clashing between them. This is why my grandfather and grandmother ignored the fear of abominations and the wrath of their families to be together; why my mother was born; and why I have the blood of House of Iron in my ancestry.

I take a deep breath. As far as Alice's secret, I'd say that cat just jumped out of the bag.

Chapter Twenty-One

Alice and Hobart remain facing each other, rooted in the doorway. Becca steps closer, focused on Alice. "What's wrong? What's going on?"

"It's okay." I haul myself out of the chair. "They gotta have some space." My struggle with resolving the philosophical issue of justice has just gotten trumped. Something has to be done regarding the two frozen people in the doorway, or we will never get to chicken tetrazzini. I move Becca aside and stand between Alice and Hobart, then I turn my back on Hobart and put both hands on Alice's shoulders.

"Back," I say.

She blinks. "What?"

"Step back."

She does.

"Again. . . . Again."

She takes a breath and puts a hand to her chest. "What in the name of The Three?"

"I didn't know you were a Catholic," Becca says.

"I'm not. It's an expression from my childhood."

Becca exhales in relief. "I thought you might be having a heart attack or something."

Dr. Hobart reaches out to steady himself on the doorframe. "What in the name of The Three is exactly what I would like to know!" He stares at Alice. "Who are you? What did you just do?"

Alice touches her flushed cheeks with the palms of her hands. "I could ask you the same."

Tracey moves his stunned father aside and steps into the room. "What's going on? Is something wrong?"

Frosty air, oblivious of the ongoing drama, seeps into the house. "Tracey, can you close the door, please? I think I can explain."

Hobart takes a step toward Alice. I put out my hand. "Stop."

He obeys, confusion clouding his face. I don't blame him. The first time I met Jason was in a bookstore downtown. It was only for a moment because he disappeared fast, probably as spooked as I was by the instant electrical connection between us. The second time was at the old Swann-Simpson mansion on Red Mountain, headquarters for House of Iron. The first time Jason put his hand on the bare skin between my shoulder blades, I thought he'd left a brand. House magic doesn't mess around.

I point a forefinger at each of them, now separated by about six feet. "You two stay apart for now."

"Am I ill?" Alice asks, blotting her forehead with the oven mitt still on her hand.

"Not exactly," I say. "Tracey, they stay put for now and no handshaking, but why don't you introduce your father?"

"This is nuts," Tracey says.

"Just trust me."

We exchange a look. I've lost count of the times we have trusted each other in ways that range from taking a lead in an interview to diving under bullets. He looks at Alice. "Irene, this is Orson Hobart."

"I don't think calling her Irene is necessary at this point," I say.

Hobart clears his throat. "Amazing. You must be Alice Rhodon."

"I am."

I guess having people "die" and appear again is not that unusual in the long-lived Houses. Then he bows, actually bows. "It is my great pleasure to meet you, madam, for a multitude of reasons."

Except for the absence of the color-leached, wavering, slow-motion-backwards thing, I would think I was seeing into the distant past.

Thankfully, Alice doesn't curtsy, only nods her head.

"I knew your sister here and your grandmother in England," Hobart says.

"Really?"

"Indeed. Both very bright and unusual women."

"I have only a few memories of my grandmother," Alice says. Her hands clasp together, her cheeks still bright rosebuds. "I would love to hear yours."

"This is weird," Becca says. "Can we stop pretending there is nothing strange about having to talk with someone at a distance?"

I eye the kitchen table, which is about seven feet long. "I think if we all sit down at the table, we can move into less weird territory. Dr. Hobart, if you will sit at the end?" I point to the seat farthest from the kitchen and from Alice's usual seat.

"Please call me Orson."

I nod just to get him to sit down. "Fine."

"Oh, the soup!" Alice says, and heads in the opposite direction.

I wave the others into the kitchen. Becca sits in her usual chair to Alice's left. I sit in mine, which is to Alice's right and faces the living room. It's no surprise that Tracey chooses the chair beside me to my right. No law enforcement person worth his salt wants his back to the door.

"Wine," Becca says, jumping back up and bringing the bottle. She pours a glass for Hobart and Tracey. Alice drinks nothing stronger than mint tea.

Alice returns and sits. "Well, I thought we would be in the living room for a bit, but this is fine."

Everyone looks at me.

"I believe that Dr. Hobart—Orson—has figured out what just happened."

"Well, please enlighten me, Orson," Alice says. "It was . . . disturbing."

Hobart's gaze moves to Becca.

"It's okay," I say in answer to his unspoken question. "Becca is privy to everything."

His brows, thick as Tracey's, but threaded with steely gray, furrow. "Is that wise?"

As head of Stone, I doubt he's accustomed to having House rules broken, and divulging information to a non-member is the number one no-no. I suspect had he not been a guest, he would have expressed disapproval in stronger terms. I don't blame him, or the rules behind his ire.

"Becca knows everything," I repeat. "Accept that or leave or don't talk, but that's not negotiable."

Hobart meets my gaze.

For once, Becca says nothing. I realize I have just spoken for Alice. We are in her home, and she is the eldest of our House, but she doesn't contradict me.

The invisible struggle between us lasts only a moment. Hobart lifts a hand. "Very well, but I prefer you do the explaining since you seem to be far more familiar with it than I."

I take a breath. "I think what happened at the doorway between Alice and you was a tangling of your magical 'fields.'"

"Magical fields," Alice says in a faraway tone. In her most recent "life," she was a physics professor, and I know that look. She taps her finger to her lip. "Like magnetic fields?"

"I guess," I say.

"I may not know how it works," Alice says, "but after my phone discussions with Orson, I think I understand why it happens."

"To bring the Houses' genetics together."

To my surprise, that statement came from Tracey.

"I've heard my father's theories more than once."

"It's rare," Hobart says.

The color drains from Alice's face. "This happened between my sister and that man from Iron?"

For a moment, I am catapulted back into the Ordeal, handcuffed to an iron chair in a mineshaft under Red Mountain, stinking in my own waste, my throat parched and raw from screaming. Fear, the absolute god of my body and mind. Beside me, a man in a wheelchair holds a modified cattle prod in his hand. Theophalus Blackwell was not the "man from Iron" Alice means—the man who had an affair with Alice's sister—but he told me about it and tortured me because of it.

I reach for the wineglass, pick it up and realize the liquid inside it is quivering. Tracey puts his big hand on my forearm, steadying it. I don't speak until I have emptied the glass.

"Yes, Alice," I say into the silence. "That is what my grandparents experienced."

"And how are you so certain that is what just happened between Alice and me?" Hobart asks.

"Because," I say, avoiding everyone's eyes, especially Tracey's, "it has also happened to me."

A lengthy silence follows my admission that I have experienced the same magic maelstrom that assaulted Alice and Hobart. Alice is the only person I have confided that to. Becca's mouth has formed a small, silent "o."

"It's Jason Blackwell, isn't it?" Tracey says quietly.

I nod, twisting the wine glass with my finger and thumb.

Alice's hand is at her throat. "You feel *that* with a man from House of Iron?"

"I can't believe you haven't told me," Becca says.

"It's something I have to deal with myself. Talking about it doesn't help anything. It just is."

"Does it get less . . . intense?" Hobart asks.

"No. But physical distance helps." I look from him to Alice. "But I've not remained close to him for an extended time."

The longest we'd been together had been last year on his boat, the *Iron Fist*, but the presence of water negated the magic. Even then, the memory of the feeling had been almost as intense as the real thing. The human brain is quite talented in the imagination area. My wandering mind still sometimes recalls a red satin bedspread in his yacht cabin and wonders what it would be like. . . . I clear my throat.

The unhappiness of everyone at the table is palpable.

"Well," Tracey says, lifting his glass. "I knew this might be a difficult night, but I didn't expect. . . . Um, anyway, I'd like to propose a toast to new beginnings."

I imagine he meant for the "new beginning" to be between his father and myself, but I'm grateful for a diversion from my revelation.

When the glasses return to the table, I turn to Tracey. "How do you feel about zoos?"

He looks bewildered at the abrupt change in the conversation's direction. "What?"

"Next Saturday is Daniel's birthday, and he doesn't want a toy. He wants Becca, Alice and me to take him to the zoo. Are you game to join us?"

"Sure."

"Becca?"

"For Daniel? You bet! Besides, I like the monkeys."

Chapter Twenty-Two

The following afternoon, a flower box arrives at my desk. There's no disguising the long package or the fact that a florist delivery man brought it. I catch a few snickers from the men in the office, Finkman's distinctive voice among them. I don't think he's aware of how close he came to annihilation when he made that "bitch" comment to Tracey. Since then, Tracey has avoided him. Far more than the insult itself, it upset my partner to discover how thin the edge of his self-control was.

I open the box, assaulted by the unmistakable scent of roses. But nestled in the crinkling green florist paper is only a single long-stemmed rose of such a deep red that one could almost call it black. A shiver runs up my spine. *Angola.*

"An admirer?" Tracey asks, his attention overtly on the same report he's been reading since the box was delivered.

"Hardly." No point telling him it is a promise of death, meant to remind me I am not safe even in the heart of the police administration building. I close the box lid. "Still good for Saturday and the zoo?"

"Yep." His mouth is tight, and he is still intent on the piece of paper he's holding.

"Damn it, Lohan, I didn't send this to myself."

"Not my business."

Men.

Fine. I chunk the rose back into the box and tilt the entire thing into the waste can.

"Take a look," Tracey says, breaking into my thoughts and offering me the papers in his hand. "Medical examiner's report on our most recent two homicides."

I don't take the papers. "Can you summarize, since you've been studying them so intently?"

If he catches my sarcasm, he ignores it.

"Our jumper, Jim Jacobson, showed injuries consistent with taking a fall from the height of several stories. No gunshot or stab wounds—in fact, no other wounds or injuries that would account for foul play unless someone smashed him in the front of his head before he fell on his face. No poison or drugs, other than blood pressure medication. In fact, he didn't even have a decent breakfast. Nothing in his system other than coffee and donuts."

I nod.

"I still think he just got tired of all his problems," Tracey says.

"Maybe, but—" I touch the tips of my fingers to my forehead in frustration.

Tracey waits, giving me the space to finish my thought, except I can't finish it. I have nothing to go after the 'but.'

"What about Mrs. Zane?" I ask.

"That is an entirely different story. Looks like your call was good. Fentanyl and morphine overdose."

"What's next?"

"You're the lead on this one. What do you suggest?"

I think about it. "What's the time of death on Zane?"

He consults the paperwork. "Sometime between 2 and 5 a.m."

I stand and grab my size extra-large coat from the back of the chair. "Then I'm headed to Mountain Lane Senior Living. You coming?"

AT MOUNTAIN LANE, WE HAVE TO WAIT AGAIN for the manager, Mary Densmore. I guess running a place like this is a busy endeavor. Despite the upscale decor, the place feels like a last waystation. At least the wheelchair people with the lolling heads are no longer positioned in the reception area. Tracey and I don't talk. Perhaps he is, like me, wondering if he will end up in a place like this, or worse—in a place like this, alone. We are both House, but we won't live forever. I wonder if Amber will come visit me when I'm old. I could have grandchildren. That thought is not nearly as frightening as having a child. Grandparents get a pass on diaper duties.

Densmore approaches with a sideways amble, perfume in her wake. I guess carrying her considerable weight that way is easier, but she makes only minimal forward progress and when she arrives, she is short of breath. If I am destined for a berth in this place, she will definitely not live long enough to be here. By the time I die, assuming natural causes—which might be a stretch considering the note that came with the long-stemmed rose—no one that I know will be alive. No one who isn't a member of a House, anyway. For the first time, it hits me that will include Becca. My chest clenches. Now that I have a real friend, a true friend, I don't want to lose her.

Longevity might be a gift, but there is a price for it.

Chapter Twenty-Three

I study the list of Mountain Lane Senior Living personnel that Densmore reluctantly gave me and the visitor lists. Tracey remains standing, his arms folded over his chest.

"I just find this hard to believe," Densmore says, shifting her bulk in her office chair, which creaks in protest. "Nothing like this has ever happened here before. Are you sure?" To my annoyance, she addresses her comments to Tracey, though the list was my request.

Tracey doesn't respond, forcing her to deal with me. I am reminded of how my training officer tested me during my last days on patrol, letting me handle situations. Maybe this is the graduation test for Homicide.

"I'll need this visitor list. Is there any possibility anyone came in or left without signing this log?"

"No. We lock the doors at 8:00 p.m. and after that you have to buzz out."

"Cameras?"

She sighs. "Yes, we have cameras on all the doors."

"We'd like to review the tapes, please."

Densmore frowns. "I'll have to call the security guard for that."

"That's fine. We'll wait."

She stabs an intercom on her desk. "Linda, have Mr. Miller come to my office."

"Yes ma'am."

Handing the list back to her, I say brightly, "Mark the night shift workers, please, and star the ones who were working that night. And I need copies of all the narcotics logs for the time period."

She frowns at the extra work. "This could take an hour or more."

She thinks she can get us out of her hair with threats of time. I smile politely. "I understand. We'll just take a look at the video recordings while you work on it."

"Really, it is going to take a while. Are you sure you don't want to come back later?"

"Ms. Densmore, we'll be happy to come back later, but it will be with a search warrant, and we will just take *all* the files and *all* the narcotics in your inventory."

I catch just the slightest twitch of Tracey's lips.

She straightens as what that would mean sinks in. "Oh, really? Well, that won't be necessary. I think I can cancel my other appointments and work on this for you myself."

The wait is not as long as threatened. As soon as we return from looking at the tapes, which showed no one entering the building after hours and only Doris Jansen leaving about 4 a.m. We have what we need in hand from Densmore.

"Thank you. Now perhaps someone can escort us to where you keep the narcotics."

She scowls. "We've already checked. There was nothing missing from Mrs. Zane's prescriptions."

"What about anyone else's?" I ask.

She sputters. "You have no idea—"

"I agree that taking everyone's medication and inventorying it somewhere else would be complicated. This is a murder investigation, and I'm sure you understand we must rule out that drugs could have been removed from your storage facility. You did say you wanted to cooperate with us? Because we are perfectly willing to get that search warrant—"

"No, I mean yes, we will cooperate in every way. I'll call in the head nurse. She can escort you and assist."

It takes two hours to inventory the medicines and determine that about thirty morphine pills of various strengths were missing, along with two fentanyl pain patches, each of which is up to a hundred times more potent than morphine. So, it's not just the pills from Mrs. Zane's bottle that are missing. Mountain Lane has a bigger problem.

Since, obviously, I can't testify about my vision of the night Zane was killed, we have to build a case without that. Finding medications missing doesn't prove the specific patch and morphine from Mountain

Lane were given to Mrs. Zane, but it supports the medical examiner's findings and the fact that the drugs could have come from Mountain Lane's supplies. At any rate, it opens them up to a lawsuit. Densmore will not be a happy camper.

We call an evidence tech who photographs the opened box of fentanyl patches and takes custody of the bottles with the missing pills in case we can get fingerprints. With the nurses' detailed notes and a signed statement, that should suffice.

We return to Densmore's office. As predicted, she is not happy with what we found and gives me a look that I'm sure is meant to be intimidating.

"I suggest you review your procedures regarding storage of pharmaceuticals," I say to her scowl. "And you'll need refills on these residents' prescriptions, because we're taking the bottles and the boxes."

As we leave, I stop at the doorway and turn, channeling the old TV detective, Columbo. "Just one more thing."

She looks up, clearly annoyed. "Yes?"

"Has anyone else asked for personnel information recently?"

She frowns. "No."

"What about anyone who might be in the office when you're not here?"

"That would have to be David Collins. He's the assistant manager and the only other person with access to those files."

"We need his contact information."

Eager to get us out of her office, Densmore pulls it up on the computer in a matter of seconds and prints off a sheet for me. "I hope that is all," she says, reaching across the desk to hand me the sheet.

"For now." I smile.

WHEN WE ARE BACK IN TRACEY'S CAR, I lean back in the seat. "What makes me think she's a bitch to everyone who works for her?"

"Oh, her personality. She didn't exactly charm you by wanting my attention, did she?"

"Oh, you noticed that?" I grit my teeth. "I guess she wanted to talk to a 'real' police officer."

He cocks his head. "I thought it was because I'm so devastatingly handsome."

"When I was on rotation to fill in for the desk officer at the precinct, I got that response from a woman. Even though I answered the phone as 'Officer Brighton,' she asked to talk to a 'real' police officer."

"Some people are living in the Dark Ages."

"It's still a man's world, Lohan."

"Could have fooled me."

A pain stabs my abdomen, and I double over with a muffled, "Ouch!"

"What is it? What's wrong?"

"Give me a minute," I gasp.

"I'll get you to the hospital. We can be there before an ambulance." He hits the blue lights.

"No. It's nothing."

"What do you mean nothing?" His voice rises. "You're obviously in pain."

"Just wait."

"For what? The baby to come in my car?"

"I'm not having the baby."

"How can you be sure?"

"Because this happens periodically. Probably gas or Amber practicing martial arts."

His shoulders relax. "How can you tell the difference?"

"If it keeps happening, then we do something. Remember, I've been seeing a doctor regularly, not to mention Alice's 'scans.' Everything is fine and on schedule."

"That's what they say about an airplane in a lightning storm until something goes wrong."

I straighten, alert for more pangs, but there aren't any.

"We're good," I report.

With the back of his hand, he wipes imaginary sweat from his forehead. "Okay. That was fun."

"Back to homicide investigation."

"What next?"

I hold up the personnel list. "We can eliminate the men on this list. The person I saw in the vision was a woman." I check off the males from the list. "It was too dark in the room to see a face or even get hair color, but she was medium build, about five foot six."

"That's pretty average. You couldn't see anything else?"

"Not in the dark and everything wavers in a vision."

"Wavers?"

"Yeah, like poor reception. Alice thinks it's because only partial data from that universe filters through, and my brain fills in details, similar to how the brain can read a sentence where the letters of each word are randomly scrambled, as long as the first and last letters of each word are right."

"Interesting, but that's going to make it hard to identify someone."

"Give me a minute."

I run the names through the NCIC database to check for outstanding warrants and then through the driver license system, getting height and weight info on the women.

"I think we can check off this very tall, skinny woman. That leaves two to focus on, regardless of what their logs say."

"I agree. What's your reasoning?"

I'm not sure if he is still testing me or just wants to see if we're on the same wavelength. "If someone intended to kill Zane or even made a mistake like that and realized what they'd done, they probably wouldn't write down they were there. Jansen was asleep in the chair, so she may have missed someone checking on her mother."

"True, and if she just looked in on her mother, she wouldn't know if Zane were dead or asleep."

"I think she'd assume she was sleeping."

"Can't figure out what the motive might have been. If Zane left money to her family, it would point to them. We can check her daughter's bank account, just to rule her out, but—"

"There's no way Doris Jansen killed her mother. She was heartbroken."

"I agree, but not because she was crying. I've seen killers cry before."

"Then why?"

"Because it makes no sense. All she had to do was keep her mouth shut and that would have been the end of it. She insisted on calling the police."

"So, we are back to staff."

"Or the brother."

"Jansen said he was the only other family left, and she's lost contact with him, but there's no written or video record of him visiting his mother, and he would have to have access to the cameras to alter the tapes . . . or magical transportation powers."

Tracey grins. "Now that's a possibility."

"Let's stick with the ladies on this list first. I don't want to give them a heads up we're coming. The first name is a Martha Patterson. They all work the night shift, so let's go wake her up."

Chapter Twenty-Four

"Is Martha Patterson home?" I ask the bear-like man who answers the door.

"She's sleeping," he says with a nasty scowl.

We wait several minutes before the door opens again. A woman in a pink bathrobe fingers her clumping brown hair. "Doug said you were cops? Wanting to talk to me?"

"Yes, ma'am." I show my badge and introduce us again. "Sorry to wake you. May we come in?"

She glances over her shoulder at the man—her husband, I assume, since she wears a ring. He sits in an overstuffed chair watching TV, beer in hand and two beers left of a six-pack on the stained carpet floor beside him.

"We can talk in the kitchen," she says, leading the way.

The kitchen feels old-fashioned with striped wallpaper and Formica tops. Alice's kitchen is definitely out of date, but in a comforting way. This room is forlorn.

A yellow cat with whorls sits on the counter observing us. She swipes him off. Landing with a *thump,* he leaves the room with an offended stalk. It's hard to remain ignorant of cat language with Angel and three other felines now in my life. Cats seem to have their dignity easily offended, although I might feel the same if I were abruptly swiped from my perch.

"Can I get you some coffee or something?" Martha asks, blinking bleary eyes, though the coffeepot on the counter is empty.

Tracey takes a seat where he can keep an eye on the husband. "No, thanks."

Martha and I join him at the table.

She yawns. "What is this about? Is it Doug? Is he in trouble?"

"No. It's about Mrs. Zane."

"Who?" She looks puzzled.

"At Mountain Lane," Tracey says.

"Oh, yeah, in 209. She died. Nice lady. Had trouble sleeping sometimes, and we would chat. She was really proud of her daughter."

I lay my arms on the table and lean toward her. "Was she in pain at night? Did she typically need morphine?"

"No, her pain patch was working fine so far. She just got it prescribed a week ago."

"Were you surprised that she died when she did?"

"To tell the truth, yeah, a little. She was doing well. She was on hospice, so they had stopped treatment, but I would have said she was still a good ways from death's door. I guess you never know."

I look at her carefully. She could have been the person I saw in my vision. Right height and build, but I can't say for sure.

"Did you give out any morphine that night?"

"I don't remember specifically, but usually I give one to Mrs. Weinstein. It should be on the Rx chart."

"It is." The chart supported that she gave a ten-milligram morphine pill to Weinstein in Room 229 at 2 a.m.

I consult the personnel list for the name of the other night staff. "Tell me about Miss Gates."

"Glenda? She's okay." She sighs. "Honestly? I have to cover for her napping. She works days on top of her shift at Mountain Lane. I feel for her, so I never say anything. Collins is a jerk. Almost as bad as Densmore."

"Jeffrey Collins, the night supervisor?"

"Yeah." She suddenly looks worried. "You're not interested in Glenda sleeping on the job, or the fact that I called Collins a jerk, are you?"

"Not in the least."

Her shoulders relax. "Well, what's the deal? People die at Mountain Lane at least once a month."

"Mrs. Zane died of a drug overdose."

She draws a breath through her clenched teeth. It makes a slight whistle through a gap between the front ones. "When?"

"On your shift." I give her the date.

"No way."

The bathrobe has slipped off her shoulder, revealing a bruise the size of a large thumb. She tugs it back quickly.

"You were working," I say. "You're a nurse, right? Don't you authorize any medications given out?"

Her faces pales. "Oh my God. Are you thinking—?"

I shrug. "We're not thinking anything at this point, just trying to gather information."

She hesitates and then says. "What do you want to know?"

"Did you talk to Mrs. Zane that night?"

"I don't remember. Really. The nights seem to blend—wait, that was a Sunday, wasn't it?"

"Yes." Tracey is still watching Mr. Patterson, who has lumbered out of his chair, leaving indentations in the cushion.

"Sunday nights *The Living Dead* comes on, and Mrs. Zane has to watch it, then she can't sleep, and she calls for me. Happens every Sunday, so yeah, I chatted with her. If she really has trouble getting to sleep, I can give her a sleeping pill, but most of the time, she just wants juice and a little attention to keep the zombies at bay."

"Was any staff there who weren't usually?"

"Not that I can recall. Her daughter was asleep in the chair. I didn't bother her."

Her back is to the living room and while she talks, Doug Patterson has ambled over to stand behind her. His tee shirt competes with the carpet for the most stains. He tosses an empty can in the sink. She jumped at the clatter.

"What do you pigs want with my wife?" he slurs.

"We're interviewing her on a murder case," Tracey says evenly, but I notice he has pulled his chair back from the table. He smells trouble. It's not difficult to smell. In fact, it stinks. Patterson's hands clench and release in a kind of spasm.

"I know my rights," he says.

His wife flinches. It doesn't require a great amount of imagination to figure out the cause of that blue-black circle on her shoulder. It's really a shame you can't arrest a person in their house for being a drunk.

"Doug," his wife says hesitantly.

"Shut up. I ain't talkin' to you."

I stand. "I think we're about through here, but we may want to talk to you again, Mrs. Patterson."

Tracey gives her a card. "Call us if you think of anything that might be useful, and if we need to speak again, we can do it at our office."

She takes the card, and I can see a tremor in her hand. When we leave, I suspect her hubby will take his ire out on her.

Tracey, perhaps sensing the same thing, steps around the table, standing where I have a clear path to the door. But before I can take it, Patterson swings. Surprisingly, it's not the punch of a drunk, although he is clearly intoxicated. It's a mean and powerful slug. Tracey blocks it and deflects the arm aside with a quick graceful motion I have seen in class.

Patterson stumbles to the side, off balance, his face darkening. "My house," he mutters.

"You're drunk," Tracey says. "We're leaving."

I'm itching to arrest this jerk, and we have a good charge of attempted assault on an officer, but it is rarely employed on a drunk when no harm is done. All's the pity.

In his stupor, he apparently transfers his rage at us to his wife, grabbing her arm and yanking her to her feet.

"There's no call for that," Tracey says.

I can see from the pinched look on her face his grip is hurting her. "Let her go," I say.

Still holding his wife's arm, he whirls on me. "Who knocked you up, bitch? Why aren't you at home where you belong?"

"That's enough," Tracey says.

Turning back, Patterson bellows, "Enough?"

I would have said it was impossible for his face to get any redder, but I was wrong. It's aflame with his rage.

"I say when it's enough in my own goddamn house!"

He shoves his wife into Tracey. She stumbles and Tracey grabs her, fighting to keep them both on their feet. Patterson, his back now to me, raises his hand for a backhand swipe to her head.

Without thinking, I lift a foot and come down hard on the back of his knee. He sinks to his own knees with a surprised grunt.

"Don't hurt him," his wife pleads, her fist in her mouth in a gesture that reminds me of little Daniel.

I let Tracey cuff him while I keep my eyes on her, having learned my lesson in Patrol that the victim in a domestic violence situation can do a sudden 180-degree turn in her sympathies when her batterer is arrested. He may beat her, but he's her family and often she is financially or psychologically dependent on him.

Tracey has no problem handcuffing him, despite his struggles. There's a definite advantage in having a partner who is of House of Stone.

Chapter Twenty-Five

Booking Doug Patterson in the city jail was a pleasure. He'll be behind bars for several hours before they allow him to bond out. A domestic violence charge, even an attempted DV, shares something unique in common with murder—the victim doesn't have to press charges. The prosecutor does that for the victim, regardless of whether she agrees. This is designed to protect her from retaliation by taking the choice out of her hands. Research and statistics have shown that jail is about the only persuasion that makes a dent in domestic violence.

Putting Patterson in jail and into the court system will also allow his wife access to resources, including a shelter and a range of services offered by non-profit organizations. It might even save her life. But if she refuses help, there's no guarantee Patterson won't take it out on her. Statistics are just that—numbers. Worst case, we could end up working a homicide. But we've done what we can. Like I told Becca, I'm a cop. My job is to stop the bad guys.

When we get back into the car, it's about 2 p.m. Plenty of time to check out the next person. I consult the personnel list from Mountain Lane Senior Living. "Glenda Gates. I did a little digging and discovered she works a second job at a doctor's office."

"What's the address?" Tracey asks, putting the car into reverse.

I give him the location, and we head to Springhill Health Center. Inside, I show my badge and ask for the manager.

"Yes ma'am." The receptionist snatches up the phone.

In a few minutes, a thin man with oval gold glasses and a tweed woolen vest appears and beckons us into the hallway. "How can I help you?" His posture and the set of his jaw radiate annoyance. I'm not sure whether it's because of the interruption or just our presence in his clinic.

I show him my badge and introduce us. Tracey is standing a foot behind me, continuing to let me handle the interviews.

"What does this have to do with me?" he asks, his lips as tight as his buttoned vest.

"It's not about you. We need to talk to one of your employees."

"Why?"

"An investigation," I meet his annoyed gaze.

"Who do you want to talk to?"

"Ms. Glenda Gates."

"I don't even—oh, yes, she's an aide. Hasn't worked here that long. We're really busy here. I can't afford to pay her while you talk with her. I suggest you interview her on her own time."

Sometimes I really wish I could hex people. "We need to talk with her now," I say, suspecting if Tracey were hovering over him or if I wasn't a woman—especially a pregnant woman—he might not be this annoying. It's amazing how my pregnancy seems to make people question my authority. Being pregnant is apparently the ultimate expression of womanhood and vulnerability.

Tracey doesn't offer to rescue me, which I appreciate.

"Okay," I say. "If you don't want to let us talk to her here, I guess we'll just take her downtown for the interview. I think it's about a twenty-minute drive each way, plus the time to get settled and talk to her. We'll have her back in a few hours."

He chews his bottom lip. "Wait. I can let you use the staff conference room."

"That's very generous of you."

GLENDA GATES IS A BRUNETTE, HER DARK HAIR streaked with auburn and striking light green eyes. Her high, wide cheekbones and strong nose would have made her easily identifiable, if it had not been for the dark, wavering environment in which I saw the person in Zane's room.

"Ms. Gates," I greet her when she walks into the tight room, filled with a table surrounded by folding chairs. "I'm Detective Rose Brighton and this Detective Tracey Lohan from Birmingham Homicide Unit."

Her face tightens. "What's going on?"

I put my arms on the table, palms up. "Sit down, please. We need a few minutes of your time."

Reluctantly, she sits in the chair nearest the door.

"It's about the death of Mrs. Jessie Zane."

"She had cancer. Why are you investigating that?"

"We have reason to believe she died of an overdose of opiates."

"Why are you talking to me?"

"You were working the night shift during the time of death."

"It wasn't just me." Her voice rises in pitch. "What about everybody else that works there?"

"We're talking to other people too."

"I didn't do anything." She tents her hands, pressing the tips of her fingers against her lips. "Look, I have to get back to work. They'll fire me, and I really need this job."

"We understand, but we need to ask you a few questions."

"Are you going to read me my rights?" Her eyes are wide. They're lighter than mine, the tea green of sea over a sandbar.

"Not unless you become a suspect. Right now, we're just gathering information."

"Should I get a lawyer?"

"We're not here to arrest you," I say. "We just want to ask some questions to help us narrow down the possibilities, but if you want a lawyer, we would need for you to come down to police administration."

"I don't have time for that," she says. "Okay. Ask me."

"Did you have any occasion to go to Mrs. Zane's room on this night?" I give her the date of the victim's death.

"I don't think so, but I'd have to look at my daily to be certain. Martha is the nurse on duty. If she was busy, she might have called me to help Mrs. Zane to the bathroom. She could still do that with a walker, but someone has to be with her. She's lost her balance before."

I show her the copy of the daily I got from Densmore.

"This is the right date?" she asks.

I nod.

She peruses the list and then leans back and takes a deep breath. "I didn't go to her room. I always write it down immediately."

"You're working a lot of hours. Is it possible you forgot?"

"No, that's why I always write it down, so I won't forget."

"You could have been tired and skipped this one time?"

"I didn't." Her eyes flash.

"What about medications? Do you have access to them?"

"No. Only Martha does. I'm not a nurse. I'm just an aide."

"We just talked to Martha. She's never given you the key?" I mean to imply that this is what Martha told us, watching for her reaction.

She flushes and shifts. "Maybe a couple of times when she's been really busy."

"We've done an inventory of medications and some morphine is missing."

She clasps her hands. "I don't know anything about that."

"You apparently need money. How come?"

"Student loan and my rent, and I help out my younger brother. He . . . got in some trouble."

"Like drugs?" I ask. I've already looked it up. Her brother is facing a narcotics possession charge.

She doesn't respond.

"You wouldn't be getting him a supply, would you?"

"No!" A tear trickles down her left cheek. "I would never do that. I'm paying to get him through rehab. You have no idea how hard it is to get help if you don't have money."

She wipes at the tear. "That's why I'm working two jobs. Martha knows. That's why she doesn't say anything if I fall asleep." She looks frightened. "You won't say anything about that, will you? If the night supervisor finds out I'm working this many hours, he'll dock me or fire me. Collins is almost as mean as Densmore."

"Who would want Mrs. Zane out of the way?"

"What?" She takes a moment to shift gears and absorb my question. "Nobody. She was a dear. No trouble really, compared to most of the people there. Always sweet. Loved her daughter, and it was obvious that her daughter loved her too. She spent a lot of time there, even stayed at night sometimes, just to be there in case her mom had nightmares."

"Really?"

She nods. "They were both very nice people. You don't see that often. A lot of people just don't even come visit, and it's a shame because a visit means a lot to those people. Even if they seem like they're not really there and can't acknowledge it, I think they know."

Chapter Twenty-Six

My exasperation at the hassle involved in coordinating an excursion with four other people dissolves when I see Daniel's excitement.

"Really?" he says when we pick him up from his foster parents' house. "We're really going to the zoo?"

"Yep," Becca says. "We're really going. All of us, and Mr. Lohan will meet us there."

"Mom promised we'd go." He stares out the window. An early morning rain slicks the street. "But we didn't go."

Silence descends in Becca's car. She bites her lip. I close my eyes, seeing Daniel's mother, as I last saw her, as Daniel last saw her—fully clothed in a tub of water stained with her own blood.

"What do you remember best about your mother?" Alice asks.

I admire Alice's bravery in going there.

Daniel is matter-of-fact. "My favorite is going to the Railroad Park. We saw a train, and she bought me a hotdog."

"That's a good memory," Alice says. "Hang on to your good memories."

Daniel nods solemnly. He has grown at least two inches since I first met him and his mother. The fading white patches on his skin from the grafts are the only physical scars he bears. Considering what he has been through—being caught in the conflagration I generated by combining the magics of iron with the living-green—it's amazing he's even alive. Something he owes to Paul, my ex-partner, who shielded him as best as he could, sacrificing his own life to do so, and to Alice's remarkable skills.

"Are you still liking first grade?" Becca asks.

"Yep," he says, "except for play period."

"What happens in play period?"

"Boys hit me."

Becca and I exchange worried glances.

"Why?" she asks.

Daniel shrugs. "I look different."

"Do you hit them back?" an indignant Alice asks.

"Alice!" Becca says.

Alice crosses her arms across her chest. "Well, he has a right to defend himself."

"Mrs. B says I shouldn't hit people, that I should run away and tell the teacher."

I feel the stirrings of panic. My instinct would be to tell him to fight back too, but what if that isn't right? The complications of raising a child balloon from diapers to first-grade advice. And what about dating, and men, and career choices? My fingers tighten around the door handle.

"Do they have ice cream at the zoo?" I ask.

"Yeah!" Daniel says. "Do they?"

TRACEY IS WAITING FOR US AT THE ENTRANCE. Alice insists on paying for all our tickets. When we make it through that hurdle, we step out to a beautifully landscaped area with a pool and elegant pink flamingos standing on one leg or grooming themselves or just hanging around being admired. Becca is entranced. "They are born gray and turn pink because of what they eat!" she says, reading the plaque.

"They eat pink stuff?" Daniel asks.

"No, they eat shrimp and blue algae."

"Then why don't they turn blue?"

"That does make better sense, dear," Alice says, "but life is like that sometimes. Now, what shall we see first?"

"Elephants," Daniel says without hesitation.

"Elephants it is." Alice takes one of his hands, and Becca takes the other. They lead the parade. Tracey and I hang back a few steps.

"How are things going between Alice and Hobart?" I ask him.

"Slowly. I think he's taking her out to dinner one day this week."

I can't help thinking of the first time I had a dinner date with Jason—how he lightly stroked the inside of my wrist with his thumb, and I about choked on my wine. I shiver. "I wish her good luck."

"I understand you don't think very highly of him, but—."

"—That wasn't a comment on your father's character."

"What then?"

"I just know how difficult it is to do something normal, like have a meal, with all that magic zapping around."

For a few steps, Tracey says nothing. Then, "Do you have feelings for Jason Blackwell?"

That is a loaded question. "Too many feelings."

"What does that mean?"

Tracey has a poker face for victims and suspects, but in the past months, I've become attuned to him. The tension in his shoulders and stance gives him away more than facial or voice changes. I want to say it is none of his business what I feel or don't feel about Jason Blackwell, but I don't.

"Right now, I am a basket case of feelings," I say instead, putting it off on my pregnancy.

The tightness in his body doesn't dissipate. Maybe he reads me as well as I do him. What can I tell him? Thanks to my dinner table admission at Alice's house, I can't pretend Jason doesn't jack my temperature through the roof. Being near him is as difficult as being with Tracey is easy.

I change the subject. "The lab results came back on the bottles of morphine from the Zane case."

"And?"

"No luck. There were no readable latent prints on the bottles."

"That was a long shot, anyway. Too many people handling them, or they were wearing gloves."

We turn the corner, greeted by the sight of several elephants in a large naturalized area. Daniel breaks loose from Becca and Alice and runs forward, getting as close as the fencing allows.

"I'm glad to see that," Tracey says.

"What? The elephants?"

"I haven't been here since I was young. Back then the elephants had a tiny area, and there was only one female. Her longtime companion died. She paced around and around in a cement stall. Her feet were eaten up with sores. Even as a kid, I could tell she was miserable."

I frown, imagining a huge creature in a confined space, missing her friend. "Why didn't they send her to a rescue park?"

"There was a big controversy about it. A lot of people wanted to send her, but the zoo vet said she was too old for the trip."

I step forward to read the plaque on the fence. "These are all male elephants."

"Bachelors," Tracey nods. "With a lot more room than that old girl ever had."

"But still," my gaze sweeps the enclosure, "compared to their natural habitat, this is terribly confining."

The elephants seem contented enough, blowing dust onto their backs, tails occasionally switching. A cluster of them are eating what appears to be hay.

Daniel has none of our reservations, dancing from one foot to the other in his excitement. The day is warm for December, and the sun decides to make an appearance, warming it even more. I take off my jacket, tying it around my waist, or the narrowest part of my torso, which is no longer my waist.

We ride the carousel, see the monkey exhibit, and let Daniel ride a camel. Then we walk, with Daniel running rings around us, to the pavilion for lunch. Daniel ponders between a hot dog and chicken tenders. He settles on a hot dog with fries and a promise of ice cream later.

"Can't we eat by the elephants?" he asks.

"We can't," Becca says. "We need a table for our food, and these tables are bolted down."

"Oh."

"But you can pick which table we sit at."

He brightens.

I am delighted at how much little things matter to him, like getting to choose which table on the outside patio to spread our feast on and who sits by him—Becca on one side and Alice on the other—and how much ketchup goes on his fries, ketchup that is quickly transferred to both sides of his mouth and somehow his forehead. Maybe kids are not so terrifying.

Daniel insists on Alice and Becca going back into the restaurant with him to get more ketchup. I turn to Tracey and catch a frown creasing his forehead. "What's wrong?"

"Nothing, just bothered about our case." He pitches his voice low, though the crowd is much thinner than I'm sure it is in the summer, and no one is sitting close to us.

"Which one?"

"Mrs. Zane."

"What about her?"

"Just recapping in my head. Trying to come up with something new out of old data."

"Well recap out loud."

He leans back. "We have your vision, and we have facts—she was overdosed with a combo of morphine and her pain patch meds, and the time of death puts it sometime between midnight and 5 a.m. Whoever gave her the meds, it was someone she was familiar with. Which narrows us again down to the night staff."

"And Collins is a man and way too big to be mistaken for a woman."

"But that is a thought. Are there any men working that shift who could be mistaken for a woman?"

"No. I checked. Martha Patterson is still number one on my list."

"Because—?"

"She admitted to talking with Mrs. Zane that night. But why kill her? Why would anyone kill her? It didn't benefit Mountain Lane. They were making money on her being alive and staying there. Nothing unusual in the business bank account or Mrs. Densmore's."

"There's no motive," Tracey agrees. "And that's bugging the hell out of me. There's only one person we haven't talked to."

"Who?"

"Jansen's brother."

I digest this.

"We know he didn't do it directly, but what if he stood to gain from her death?"

I take a bite of my hotdog. "Jansen said she didn't know where he was. He's just dropped off the map."

We tried everything either of us could think of to locate him, including a couple of tricks from the lieutenant but came up empty. "He hasn't been at his last known address for over a year. Not even a credit card trail, nada."

"So, either some spy agency is covering his tracks, or he's living in the under-the-table cash culture."

Daniel, Becca, and Alice return with handfuls of ketchup packets. Tracey reaches for one. Behind him, near the edge of the pavilion, a man with stringy blonde hair and a backpack catches my attention. He stops, his gaze tracking over the people at the tables. A rush of golden warmth shoots through me. Color and sound leach from the world, painting everything in it a wavering gray and black, as if we have suddenly plunged deep underwater.

Chapter Twenty-Seven

My thoughts are the only things that can move. I can't blink. I can't shift my gaze. I can only watch, frozen to my chair at the zoo pavilion where Daniel, Becca, Alice, Tracey and I were eating lunch.

A shadow version peels off the stringy-haired man at the pavilion's edge. He stands in the exact posture as his flesh-and-blood doppelgänger, staring directly at me. Slowly, the shadow man shrugs one arm out of his backpack and shifts it around in front of him, digging his hand inside. When he pulls it out, it holds a gun. By the shape, I think it is a small semi-automatic. He drops the bag and points the weapon in my direction. I hear nothing, but the gun jerks in his hand, and shadow-bullets race in slow motion toward us.

Abruptly, I am thrown back in the normal time-flow of my world. The man is still staring at me. His arm moves to lower the backpack.

"Gun!" I shout, pointing at him. "Get down!"

Tracey surges, not down, but to his feet, picking up the heavy table in the same motion, ripping it from its moorings and turning it on its edge as a shield before us. French fries and drinks fly. I grab Daniel and hit the ground behind the table with him beneath me. He cries out in muffled protest and fear. I barely feel the lancing pain in my head that follows a vision.

Above us, gunshots, loud, relentless.

"Down!" I yell again, and Becca and Alice join us on the ground behind the table. Are they hit? I roll to my side, putting my back between Daniel and the gunfire, curling around him to protect him and my head.

Screams. People shouting, running. More gunfire right above us. From Tracey? My mind scrambles. *Where is my purse?* I left it hanging on the edge of my chair, but the chair is toppled over, too far away to reach it and the gun inside without exposing Daniel.

He is quiet, his breathing ragged gasps. Terrified. He's not the only one.

And then it is over. The quiet is almost surreal.

Tracey squats beside us. "Anyone hurt?"

I'm not bleeding anywhere, though my head is pounding with a familiar pain. A bullet would have had to go through me to get to Daniel, but I check him over, anyway. Alice and Becca say they are all right.

"Stay down," Tracey says, his gun still aimed in the shooter's direction.

"It's okay," I whisper in Daniel's ear, still holding him close against me. Stretching out, I peer around the table, exposing myself only enough to see. Tracey moves around the table, focused on the body sprawled a few yards away. The man is motionless—dead, unconscious, or faking being unconscious? I can't see his hand, but I'm betting the gun is still clinched in it.

Tracey kicks it away, then kneels, pressing his fingers against the man's throat. After a moment, he looks up and gives me a nod. *Threat neutralized.*

Tracey returns to us, gun still in his hand, but when his gaze falls on Daniel, he quickly puts it back in the shoulder holster he wears beneath his jacket.

"What happened?" Becca asks, her voice higher than normal.

"A shooter. He's dead." Sitting abruptly in the only chair that remains upright, he pulls out his cell phone and calls it in.

In the distance, a siren wails. Somebody must have already called 911.

Rolling to my knees, I check Daniel again. Other than a few scratches on his face and hands where I knocked him onto the ground, he is okay, but he's crying.

Becca scrambles to her feet, then helps Alice and me to ours.

Alice takes Daniel into her arms.

Several holes dent the upturned table's surface. Thankfully, none of the bullets got through. If the surface had been thinner or the rounds higher velocity—I don't want to think about it.

Voices intrude on the silence: children crying, people speaking. A few are rising from the ground, visibly shaken. Others must have headed into the closest building, the restaurant, when the shooting started because they are now starting to ease out.

I've been shot at on duty and off, more than once. This is different. It's a zoo, a family place. A safe place. This is not supposed to happen here.

THE MEDIA ARRIVE NOT LONG AFTER the police and paramedics. Spotting cameras, I call Daniel's foster parents to tell them we are all okay, trying to spare them finding out from TV or social media. I wish I could send Daniel home, but police have shut down the zoo. Nobody comes in; nobody leaves until someone has questioned them, adults and children.

All kinds of law enforcement superior officers, including the chief, the mayor, the FBI and our boss, Lieutenant Faraday, have come to the scene, but the patrol officers don't need them. Without direction, they run crime scene tape, establish a perimeter and round up witnesses. Two evidence technicians arrive to process the scene—photographs from every angle, the suspect's gun, backpack, clothing, and his cell phone. One tech works the bullets from the table and anywhere else they may have landed. As soon as possible, investigators will get a search warrant and execute it at the suspect's house, confiscate his computer and peruse his emails. Detectives will search for accomplices and a motive. If they find evidence the motive is political and the suspect is not a US citizen, the FBI will have jurisdiction. If he's "just" crazy or he "just" wanted to kill someone for personal reasons, it's Birmingham's homicide case.

The suspect's family will live a confused nightmare for a long time.

Faraday assigns a homicide detective, thankfully not Finkman, to work the case. Allen Harper has never been involved in any of Finkman's ugly harassments. He checks my gun to verify I didn't fire it and returns it, but he takes possession of Tracey's for processing. I'm sure they will determine that bullets from it killed the suspect—a good thing in my opinion, and, hopefully, in the minds of all the people who were present when string-head started firing, but until a determination is made, this is a homicide case.

An Internal Affairs officer joins the medley. She will do a parallel investigation to make sure the shooting violated no department policy. When a Birmingham officer is involved in a fatal shooting, on duty or off, the chief also wants an independent, outside inquiry, and a state investigator steps in alongside the homicide detective. Then there's the medical examiner and his investigator crawling around.

Even if terrorism is ruled out, there is always the possibility of a federal case against Tracey for violating the suspect's civil liberties. Everyone will question every move, every decision, and that's before the public weighs in.

I know the drill. Not long ago I was in Tracey's shoes. I shot a man in the back after seeing a future, seconds away, in which he killed my partner. It was my first vision, the first time anything like that had ever happened to me, and I thought I had lost my mind. As a rookie patrol officer on the last night of my three-month field training, I was still on probation. A lie saved my job. Alice saved my sanity, although it teetered for a while.

National media will turn their attention here for a moment, amid the growing list of insane mass shootings. Everyone, not just law enforcement, will wonder if this was an act of terrorism or just a lone crazy man. I am wondering the same thing, along with another possibility. That man had locked his gaze on *me* before reaching into his bag. He didn't look like a gun for hire. I don't remember ever seeing him before. But it felt personal, which means either he is someone I have arrested or who felt I wronged him in some way . . . or someone sent him. What did he believe about me that would make him try to shoot me in a public place like this? I don't know, but I have a good idea who might have put that belief in his head.

Chapter Twenty-Eight

To get to the desk of Detective Allen Harper—the homicide detective working Tracey's shooting—I have to pass Finkman. He crosses his arms over his chest and looks me up and down.

"Never thought a pregnant chick would be hot." With raised eyebrows, he leans sideways, looking past me and encountering—I assume from the direction of his lean—Lieutenant Faraday's scowl. With a faux smile, he amends the statement to, "That is . . . would be such a lovely lady."

I snort and keep going.

Faraday is still frowning as I pass her office, but that doesn't mean she heard Finkman. Her mouth is permanently fixed in a down-turned horseshoe.

I am without a partner for however long it takes for Tracey to be cleared. He's on administrative leave, which is standard when an officer is involved in a shooting. We haven't had a chance to talk much to each other, having both been formally interviewed at least three times, not to mention having to brief the chief, the mayor and Faraday.

That was perhaps the worst interview. Faraday had asked sardonically if we had a target on our backs, referring to the fact that months ago, someone—probably Angola—had shot at us at Vulcan Park, and, more recently, Angola had tried to kill me at the YMCA swimming pool. We have no proof Angola was behind the shooter at the zoo or Vulcan, but we have one warrant out on him for attempted murder of a police officer (me at the pool) and another for kidnapping and attempted murder in a different case (me at my house)—the messy business that ended with Angola's escape and the arrest of his employee,

Lawrence Anders. Most unfortunate for Anders, who won't even get his day in court. A mind-wipe is not a pretty thing.

Detective Harper looks up. He's about two decades my senior with hair gone gray and heavy black-rimmed glasses. "What's up, Rose?"

I sit opposite him. "Can we go have coffee or something?"

He rubs his chin. "Yeah, why not?"

As we pass Finkman, I hear him mumble under his breath. "Fickle, ain't we?"

"Don't mind him," Harper says. "He's just jealous."

Of Lohan? I highly doubt this, despite Finkman's "hot" comment. It is clear he said it to annoy me. It's equally clear that the only thing he feels toward me is disdain.

We ride the elevator down with two people arguing over where to go for lunch. They're still arguing when the doors open to deposit us on the first floor. We walk across the street to the coffee shop.

When we enter, I ask, "What will you have?"

"I'll get it," he says.

"No. I asked you here."

"Okay. Black with sugar."

I pay for the coffee and a tea and bring them to the table in the rear corner, the one Tracey and I prefer because we can both have our backs to the wall and speak without being overheard. For that reason, the table is in high demand, but today it's open.

Settling down with my hot water and tea bag, I ask him how the investigation on the zoo shooting is going.

"Like molasses," he says. "Everyone and his brother have to be in on every step."

"Is the FBI involved?"

"Not as the lead agency. It's our baby. They're just working with us, in case we suddenly find out he's a Russian spy."

"Are they sharing anything?"

He laughs. "That ain't the way that goes, hon."

I smile. "Remember, I'm still a rookie. I've never worked with the FBI."

He leans forward. "Let me clue you in then. With the feds, information flow goes one way—to them."

"Even when you're working on the same case?"

He touches the coffee to his lips, then pulls it back and blows on it, setting it back down.

"They'll share, eventually. Then again, maybe the sun will come up in the west, and they'll offer me everything they have tomorrow, and I'll be wrong." One corner of his lips twitch. "It's been known to happen a few times."

"Will you tell me what we know so far?"

He considers. "Not supposed to, but for a cup of coffee and a few minutes with a beautiful woman?"

I lean back, tensing.

"Lighten up. Just teasing."

I take a deep breath and let it out. His goading is on the other side of the rainbow from Finkman's jabs, which are designed to injure.

I sip my tea, though it still tastes like hot water. "Then pay up for your privilege."

He grins at my repartee. "I probably shouldn't be telling you this, but the investigation is done as far as I'm concerned. The witnesses were all over the map with what happened. What you'd expect in chaos like that. But the surveillance cameras back your statements."

"That's a relief."

"But it was kind of weird for a while."

"What do you mean?"

"Two cameras caught the action from different perspectives. At first it looked like you both reacted inhumanely fast. Then we realized the clocks had to be off, 'cause according to the timestamps, you were reacting *before* the shooter pulled his weapon."

I stiffen, but he moves on.

"We've ID'ed the zoo shooter as Yancey Lancer, twenty-six, lived with his mother, worked in a tattoo parlor. Bought his first gun a week ago. The only thing we have for a motive is that Lancer's girlfriend 'done him wrong,' and he was upset about it. Vowed to kill her and the man she ran off with."

"That's it?"

"That's all we've found so far, and we've dissected his social media posts, talked to family, friends, even his girlfriend. He's apparently one of those quiet-until-he-explodes types. He just stepped off the edge."

"Then why target families at the zoo?"

Harper takes a breath. "We don't think it was just about the zoo."

"What then?"

"Lancer spent all his bullets on one target—your table."

I look down at the tea slowly staining the water in my white cup.

"Is there anything you're not telling us, Rose?" Harper asks gently.

There is so much I am not telling him. But he would believe none of it and consider it his duty to report that I'm a fruitcake who shouldn't wear a badge or carry a gun.

Calmly, I meet his gaze. "As I have repeatedly said, I've never seen that guy before in my life. Do you need me to take a polygraph?"

He shakes his head. "I believe you, and there's nothing we've found that contradicts your story or Tracey's. Lancer talked to his mother about going to the zoo with his ex-girlfriend when they were together and how much she loved the giraffes, so possibly he went hunting her. Our best theory, or mine anyway, is that he lost his marbles and decided you were his ex, or you represented her in some way. She does have dark curly hair."

"You think my pregnancy had something to do with it?" I ask, purposefully feeding him the idea.

"What do you mean?"

I shrug. "If he lost it over jealousy and thought I was her and saw I was pregnant and with another man—?" I leave the thought hanging.

"Never thought of that," he says. "Jealously can be a powerful motive."

"Speaking of which, what did you mean that Finkman might be jealous of Tracey?"

Harper grins. "You don't know?"

"What?"

"Finkman is gay. He's had his eye on Tracey Lohan ever since he walked in the Homicide door."

Chapter Twenty-Nine

That evening, Tracey and I are early to class and sit outside the dojo, our backs to the wall.

"It wasn't random," Tracey says.

I don't have to ask to confirm he's talking about the zoo shooting. It's already dark. I feel vulnerable, although we've chosen a spot at a distance from the overhead lights.

I wrap my arms around my knees to get warm. The weather has decided to be winter for December. It may or may not stay there. People in Birmingham rarely bother to switch their closets to winter clothes until mid-December or even January.

Tracey twists the thick, woven black belt in his hands. We're both still in civilian clothes, but he's pulled a length of the belt from his bag. I notice it's frayed from use. His gaze continually sweeps the parking lot and street beyond the grassy bank before us.

"You think it was Angola?" he asks.

"Yes, I do. I talked to Harper today, and they haven't found anything except Yancey Lancer had a spat with his ex-girlfriend who left him for another man. He's never even owned a gun before. Besides, he looked right at me and *then* pulled out his gun."

Without saying it, we both understand that Angola did not pull the trigger, not on the gun anyway. He pulled some kind of trigger in the mind of the guy who held the gun. That's the power of House of Iron.

Amber kicks the walls of my uterus, and I'm reminded that she will have the power of all three Houses. Diapers and dating may be the least of my worries. I am having a child who could wreak havoc in the world. It's no wonder that children of the Houses come into puberty and their abilities late. Otherwise, a temper-tantrum could leave someone a walking zombie, or suck the carbon out of any nearby human, or crush someone's skull. Jason told me that children born of mixed House blood are abominations. I reject that, but with the power of House of Rose and House of Iron, I am a ticking bomb. Mixing those magics creates an uncontrollable inferno. Not for the first time, I wonder if I am doing the right thing, bringing such a child into the world. Maybe the right choice was to let the Houses die. Maybe we are too dangerous to exist.

"Yeah. He could have. I imagine they have cameras, at least at the entrance."

"Lots of people going in and out of that zoo," Tracey says, "even this time of year, but you can bet the investigators pored through the images."

"Yeah, but Angola would have been aware of the cameras. My guess is that he didn't come inside. Just met with Lancer in the parking lot or somewhere nearby. There are places at the far end of the parking that are in the woods."

"Well, all we can do right now is try to figure out what happened. I'm guessing Yancey Lancer was already unstable and maybe primed to hurt his girlfriend. Angola could have pushed him further in that direction. He could have made Lancer believe I was his girlfriend."

Tracey shakes his head. "Bizarre."

"Not really." I rub my chilled hands together. "Think about all the things we do because of one tweak to what we believe: A business owner convinces himself that cheating on his taxes isn't stealing because it's not taking from another person, just from the amorphous 'government.' We believe in not killing each other, but if we call something 'war,' then the act we supposedly abhor—killing another human being—becomes not only okay, but heroic."

"I see your point." He turns to look at me. "Have you ever used Iron's power?"

I take a breath and let the air out slowly before answering. Tracey has told me he didn't want to lie to me no matter how difficult the situation, and I don't want to lie to him.

"Yes."

He says nothing, giving me the space to tell him more or be silent.

"Once to make a nurse let Alice into critical care at the hospital to heal Daniel's burns, and once to make Deon Segal go to a hotel to keep him out of Angola's grasp."

After a moment, Tracey stares back at the roadway beyond the hill. "I've put a witness in jail before to keep him safe."

"But you didn't mess with his *mind*."

A wry smile crosses his face. "Oh yeah, I think it did mess with his mind."

"I appreciate your efforts, Lohan, but it's not the same."

"Okay. Fair enough. Something else is bugging me, though."

"What?"

"How did he know where we were?" Tracey says.

"Angola?"

"Yeah. I can imagine Angola had that guy, Lancer, primed to kill, but he had to have a location on us and foreknowledge that we were going to the zoo."

So many questions have peppered my mind, I can't believe I haven't even thought of this. "That is an excellent question."

We look at each other.

"Tracker?" I ask.

"Got to be. That or he is somehow monitoring our conversations."

"Jeez." I dump out my purse and paw through the items, then check every compartment twice. Nothing.

"More likely a tracker or a bug in the car," Tracey says. "We'll get both our vehicles checked. The Technology Unit will have some kind of device that can pick it up."

I nod.

"I'll talk to them tomorrow," he says.

"You're not supposed to be working."

"I'm not working. Just talking."

At that moment Sensei Richard arrives, unlocks the door, and we follow him inside. The *thunk* of the heavy metal shutting behind us is reassuring. It's the first time we've been to class since Chris was killed. When we line up to bow to sensei, the person who usually stood beside Chris makes a space for him. The hole is an unspoken tribute, and no one tries to move into it.

After the formal bowing, warm-ups and movement *kata,* all of which I can do, Sensei Mark skips the falling stuff today. Instead, he has us practice what to do if we are pushed against a wall.

Psychologically, it's intimidating to have a strong man push you against a cement wall, but there are principles that, to my delight, work. One technique involves applying pressure to the outer elbow of one arm and the inner elbow of the other with a hip turn. Suddenly the attacking person is the one smashed into the wall.

It works even with someone as strong as Tracey, although he could easily lift me off my feet. I ask sensei about this and we veer off into other interesting avenues of responses, including the debilitating effects of a knee kick to the bladder.

As usual, the time passes quickly. I'm overwhelmed by the interesting principles governing the human body—balance, timing, physics, and the limitations of joint movements. I suppose if you look at it all a different way, it can also be viewed as energy flow and management or intention, what the Japanese call "*ki.*" I now understand Tracey's determination to channel his dragon, his *ryu,* within this discipline. Everything we do requires control, including attacking each other and the response. It requires all of my attention.

I stop for a swallow of water and watch the other students and teachers on the mat. Two are young children, about eight and eleven years old, but anyone who tries to barge in here and start trouble would regret that decision. *Oh God*—my mind flashes to Lancer reaching into his backpack—*unless he has a gun.* No one in here can leap aside or apply martial arts principles to a bullet. An unlocked steel door won't stop anyone. If Angola is tracking our vehicles, he knows we are here. My heart freezes.

Nowhere is safe from him.

I beckon Tracey off the mat. "We have to leave now."

"What are you talking about?"

I wave at the door. "What is stopping Angola from forcing some other depressed or confused person to walk in here and shoot everyone?"

His face pales. "You're right. We may be putting everyone in danger." He goes to the mat and asks for a word with Richard.

"Sensei, can we lock this door and explain why to you afterward?"

Aware that we are both police officers, he doesn't hesitate. When he's locked the door, he asks, "What's going on?"

"You heard about that shooting at the zoo the other day?" Tracey says quietly.

He nods.

"We were there."

"Really? The news said only the shooter was hurt. What happened?"

"Pretty much what they said. A guy just walked up and started shooting."

Shaking his head, Richard says, "More and more of that happening."

"They don't have a motive yet," Tracey says, "but one or both of us may have being targeted."

"I thought the shooter was killed?"

"He was, but again, we aren't certain that he was a loner. Just on the off chance—" He looks towards the kids wrestling on the mat. "We don't want to risk it."

"Okay. What do you want to do? Cancel the rest of class?"

"Wait. I'll call in a 'suspicious person,'" Tracey says, "and get a patrol unit over here to be present while everyone gets to their car. We can leave last. I'm sorry we didn't think about this earlier. It's probably just paranoia on our part."

"Will you be here next week?"

Tracey sighs. "No. Not until we figure out if there is really any threat. Until then—" He shrugs and gives me a grin. "We'll practice on our own."

Chapter Thirty

It's a chilly Saturday evening. The day has spun out while I painted the walls of the extra bedroom a sunny yellow for the nursery. I plan to stretch whatever artistic talents I have to create a mural with an *Alice in Wonderland* theme to honor Alice, who has gone berserk on being a great-great-aunt and sent boxes of toys, clothes, books, and assorted who-knows-what. It's all piled in the hallway along with the crib and rocking chair from Tracey and his father. To get to the bathroom while the paint dries, I have to suck in my belly, which doesn't suck in to a noticeable degree, and edge around the stuff.

Pleasantly tired, but pleased with the transformed room, not to mention a day's work that didn't involve dead people, I curl up on the couch in my 2x sweatpants and a sweatshirt that reads, "Gravity, It's the Law." I own three sets of overlarge sweats, along with the "appropriate" maternity outfits for work a la Becca. I rub a swollen foot. Thankfully, Becca has given up the campaign for heels, a temporary reprieve I expect will last only as long as my pregnancy.

I settle on the couch, relishing the quiet. Angel curls into a warm gray fluff ball against me, her little heart beating against my ribs. We're perfectly content with a bowl of popcorn and *People Will Talk*, a 1951 movie with Cary Grant and Jeanne Crain. The film knocked the first chink in the strict morality rules that governed Hollywood from 1930 to the late 1960s. Among other things, if a woman became pregnant outside of marriage in a movie script, the code demanded that she had to suffer for it in the film. No happy ending for the morally fallen. I rest the popcorn bowl on the unsteady table of my belly, thinking of the irony. Today, it's fairly acceptable to have a baby out of wedlock. I pause. Interesting word—wedlock.

"Sounds like prison, doesn't it?" I ask Angel.

One moment she is vibrating contentedly against me, the next, she explodes to her feet. Her back arches, hairs stiff. I feel a prickle of something as well, like a faint wave of electricity lifting the hairs on my arm.

A knock on the door confirms Angel's warning.

I pause the TV, put the popcorn on the coffee table and get to my feet in a practiced roll maneuver. Pulling back the window curtain gives me a view of the front door. The porch light shines on a man's back. My pulse jumps.

Jason Blackwell.

Instantly, my palms break into a cold sweat, and I wipe them down the sides of my pants. Angel jumps off the couch and disappears.

I run through my options. I could ignore him. Eventually he would have to go away, right?

My cell rings with "Purple Rain." I dig it out of my purse and stare at it for a long moment before answering it. "What?"

"I'm standing at your door," Jason says.

"I'm aware. Why?"

"I need to talk to you."

"About?"

"Do we have to do this? I won't bite, I promise."

I hang up and stare at his back through the window. He doesn't leave. *Damn it.*

Steeling myself for the hormonal storm about to be unleashed, I grab my oversized jacket and purse and yank open the door. "You're not coming in my house."

"Fine. Can we talk on the porch? I'm getting used to that."

"No."

"Take a walk?"

I step out. "Just around the block."

He smiles. On a normal human, it would be a nice smile. On Jason Blackwell, it is deadly. My knees wobble and, not for the first time, I think of the movie *Meet Joe Black*, where Brad Pitt plays the mouth-watering Death who falls in love with a mortal woman.

We step down the front porch stairs and onto the short walkway. At the sidewalk, he takes a right turn.

"Not that way," I say, shifting my purse strap across my chest. The last thing I want is for Alice to look out her window and see us.

He turns on his heel in the opposite direction. I keep as far from him as the sidewalk allows and walk fast, trying to deal with the seductive tendrils of magic snaking around us, pulling us closer and closer. My ears are burning and that is not the only location on fire.

"You're a fast walker," Jason says, his voice tinged with amusement.

Reluctantly, I slow. "Okay, we're walking. Now what?"

He puts his hand on my arm and the spike of it goes straight to the pit of my stomach . . . and the elsewhere that is burning.

"I can't sleep," he says.

"They make pills for that."

"Not for getting you out of my mind."

I sigh. "Neither of us asked for this, I know."

"It's not just the magic," he says. "That happens when I am near you, but I can't stop thinking about you no matter where I am."

I don't respond.

A neighborhood dog barks, and he releases me. We walk on. Above, the moon carves a white sickle into the inky sky. Wind buffets my jacket, tangling my loose hair, but I'm unaffected by the chill. Magic boils my blood at Jason's presence. I resist the urge to draw the living-green as a defense. The last time I tried that, I learned better. It's complicit in this assault and just makes it worse.

Jason looks up at the thumbnail of moon. "I took my uncle's assignment to Europe in part to get away from you, but it only made this pull stronger. I fear I am consumed. And, I will admit," he brings his gaze back on me with a slight smile, "no woman I have wanted has ever denied me as you do."

"You want me to go to bed with you to extinguish this desire so you can sleep?"

He laughs. "You have an amazing way of putting things. I love that about you."

This is the first time the "L-word" has been used and panic joins the swirl of emotions. When he turns to me, his winter-blue eyes catch the streetlight. Despite his light air about it, I believe him that few women, if any, have turned him away, even without a touch of Iron magic to convince them.

"Rose." He steps close and strokes bent fingers lightly along my cheekbone.

Not fair. My throat tightens. A tendril of magic serpentines my calf and up my thigh.

"Nothing can come between us, Rose. Nothing can stop this."

I eye the grass behind us and wonder if I can pull him down right here in the moonlight. Pregnancy be damned. *Let the fire burn—*

Amber twists, kicking the walls of my abdomen. Does she feel it too? Is she agitated? Or is it a warning?

Breathing heavily, I step back and shake my head, trying to clear it. "Back. Step back, now."

"I'm not sure I can."

"Then don't move." With great difficulty, I put space between us, slowing the thundering of my heart. How on earth did my grandmother survive this? No wonder the Houses pulled them apart. No wonder, as well, that my mother was conceived.

"Don't move," I say, my shaking voice in sync with the rest of my body. "I'm sorry, but I can't. I won't—" Words fail me.

My legs almost fail me, as well, but I make it across the neighbor's yard, up the stairs to my house. Despite the release every step brings, I don't breathe until I am inside with a door between me and the night, the man outside, and a desire that will drown me.

Chapter Thirty-One

After work the following day, I climb the steps to Alice's house. It feels strange to knock on her door after living there for many months, but I do it, even though I still have the key. Can't expect people to respect my boundaries if I don't respect theirs.

A gust of wind rattles the oak leaves along the sidewalk behind me. The skeletal trees loom, bare branches glistening in the streetlights from the afternoon rain. I look over my shoulder, scanning the street in both directions, reminded of the day a year ago that I left Alice's house and a car bore down on me. Somehow, I came away from that encounter with only a few broken bones. It was the first confirmation of Alice's warning that House of Iron wanted me dead. I thought other attempts would stop with the death of the head of House of Iron, but Angola has stepped into the position of "Angel of Death" with an unchanged agenda.

Becca opens the door. "Hey. You okay?"

"I'm fine." I reach out in the daily ritual to refuel the rose-stone, no longer even having to think about calling the living-green or where the pendant lies beneath her orange and navy blouse.

I am not fine. I have been plagued all day by the frustration of not knowing when Angola will strike next or having any idea where to go on the two unsolved murders—Jim Jacobson and Jessie Zane. Not to mention the memory of Jason Blackwell lifting the back of his knuckles to stroke my cheek and the concurrent stab of hot, panting lust, the memory of which still strikes when I allow my mind to wander. Other than that entertainment and the fact that the Technical Unit guys found two trackers and hidden microphone transmitters on our cars, it has been a day of mostly paperwork.

"How was your day?" I ask Becca.

She smiles. "Perfect."

"Yeah?"

"Yep."

I stop and regard her. "You're not keeping something from your best friend, are you?"

Her smile widens. "I went on that date last night."

I hesitate. "Terrific . . . I think. The guy from the restaurant across the street from your office?"

"Yep."

"Tell me about him."

"Well, *Mom*, he's taller than I am and good-looking in a rugged sort of way, and he likes cinnamon in his coffee."

"Okay. Where does he work? What do you know about his past?"

She laughs. "I didn't realize having a police detective for a best friend means I need a checklist for any man who smiles at me."

"Smiling is not dating. Dating is dating."

"Are you saying you need to do a background check before I can go out on a date?"

"Sorry." I toss my coat on a chair. "I don't get to say who you go out with. I'm just a little paranoid."

"A little?"

I shrug.

She shutters, wrapping her arms around herself. "I get it, Rose. I was messed up some after the zoo thing too."

"Oh, Becca, I've been so busy at work, I should have—"

"No, I'm not a baby. I'm okay. I just worry about Daniel. He's had so much craziness in his life."

"You're right."

"Alice and I are going to go see him tomorrow, take him a pizza. You want to come?"

"No," I say quickly, too quickly.

She looks hurt.

"I have to stay away from him, Becca. If I was the target at the zoo, I don't want Angola or anyone from House of Iron putting together that Daniel might be a way to get to me."

She nods slowly. "Yeah, that makes sense. Like when Angola kidnapped Kaleshia to get to her brother."

"Exactly." I change the subject. "And congrats on the date. I'm glad someone has seen how wonderful you are."

"I think it's my amazing blue eyes." She bats her eyes in a wicked imitation of femme fatale.

I laugh.

"Oh, that sounds good," she says. "I haven't heard you laugh in a while."

"Not too much to laugh about, I guess."

"Any breaks in your cases?"

"Nope. Nothing. We've hit a solid wall."

I should confide to her about Jason's visit, but it feels like such a tangle. Becca would say that was the point of having a best friend—to talk about confusing things to a willing ear. Maybe she's right. Maybe I should try. I open my mouth—

"Becca?" Alice calls from the kitchen. "Is that Rose?"

"It is," I answer, a part of me relieved that I don't have to verbalize my confusion, another part disappointed.

"Come into the kitchen," Alice says. "We have a guest for tea."

I step deeper into the living room where there is a view into the kitchen.

"Do come join us," Alice says, beckoning me.

She sits at one end of the table and Hobart sits at the other. Across the expanse, they are staring intimately into each other's eyes. It is obvious that this is not the first time they have seen each other since they discovered the magic fireworks between them.

"I take it the dinner date went well," I say stiffly.

Alice breaks the contact and smiles at me. "Come on. Sit. At this distance, nothing dangerous is sizzling between Orson and me."

Although I am all sorts of uncomfortable, I can't help another laugh, this one sort of choked out. Walking around her, I take my seat. A cup with mint is already at my place and Becca's. In the center of the table, Alice's porcelain teapot sits on a ceramic tile with a hand-painted red rose.

Looking from one to the other, I ask, "How do you do that?"

"What, dear?"

"Be . . . together."

"Well," Alice says, "it's difficult to reach anything if we're alone, but as long as someone is in the middle to pass things, we do quite nicely."

Like Tracey, Hobart is a large, powerfully built man. He nods and lifts the delicate teacup, pinching the handle between his thumb and forefinger as if he were having tea with a child's set of china.

"So we do," he says.

I stare at him, feeling like I have stepped through Alice's looking glass into Wonderland. If he'd put on a top hat, grown rabbit ears and said, *Down with the bloody Red Queen*, I don't think it would surprise me.

Chapter Thirty-Two

For two weeks, Tracey has been on administrative leave, but we've stayed in touch with phone calls and coffee breaks, and a few times, he has set up surveillance on my house, hoping to watch the watcher, to no avail. Homicide and Internal Affairs have finally cleared him, though the FBI and the state are taking their time about it. Anyway, today he is back.

Frustrated, I drum my pen on the surface of the desk until Tracey gives me an annoyed look.

"You need an ice cream break?"

"God, yes." I do my best impression of jumping up.

I can feel Finkman's gaze boring into my back as we walk out, and I dearly want to call him out as having a crush on Tracey or whatever, but I don't. That would sink me to his level, and I have enough problems of my own.

"Anything in particular bothering you?" Tracey asks as we take the stairs.

"You mean besides Angola trying to kill me and two unsolved murders?"

"I thought we decided Jim Jacobson's death was an accident or suicide."

I grind my teeth. "At the risk of sounding like a scratched DVD, it doesn't feel right. There's something we're missing about it."

He sighs. "We've been over this a hundred times."

I have nothing to say to argue my case, which is based solely on—what? My gut? I switch to the other unsolved murder. "What about Jessie Zane? Even though she had cancer, that doesn't give someone the right to kill her."

"Agreed. Somebody's lying. Too bad we can't use your vision as evidence. We could see if those staff members will take a polygraph."

His phone dings as we're getting into the car.

"Lohan," he answers. "Yes, ma'am. We're available."

I wait while he listens and then says, "We're on it."

"That's got to be Faraday," I say when he clicks off.

"Can you hear that well or is this a magic trick?"

"I can tell by your tone, the way you say 'ma'am.'"

"I say that to other people."

"You do, but not with the same respect. With others, it's just being polite."

"Since when did you become my shrink?"

"Since I've worked with you every day for the past eight plus months."

"That, um, reminds me," he says.

"Of what?"

He clears his throat. "I'd like to be there when you have the baby, when Amber is born." The words come out in a rush, as though he's practiced them.

I'm not sure why, but my throat catches on a lump. *Damn it.* I clamp hard on the lump, forcing it down and engaging my rational mind. He has a right, sort of, to be there. Amber is his biological child. But how do I feel about him being present at her birth?

"I think . . . I'd like that," I say.

A smile spreads across his face. "You wouldn't believe how hard it was to ask that."

"Why?"

"You're kind of prickly about the pregnancy."

I decide not to go there. "What did Lieutenant Faraday want?"

"She's sending us a case. Check the screen, will you?"

I sigh. "Does this mean no chocolate-chip mint?"

THE CALL IS TO AN AREA EAST OF THE CITY in a section called Crestwood. The modest houses clustered on compact lots have the feel of an older generation that made it to the lowest rung of middle class. At the front door of a brick house with forest green shutters, an officer meets us. I've never seen him before. My few months in patrol were spent in the South Precinct, and this is East Precinct territory. The officer's nametag says McCrory.

"What have you got?" Tracey asks him.

"White female in her forties. Killed in the kitchen. Her throat was cut. I'd say execution style. We found her on her stomach, but the medics rolled her over."

Tracey pulls out the little notebook he prefers over a digital tablet. "Who called it in?"

"A neighbor. Said she'd been keeping the victim's dog for her, and when the victim never came by to get it, the neighbor checked on her."

"You got a name?"

"Neighbor's name is Simpson," McCrory says. "Lives next door." He consults a driver's license in his hand. "The victim is Doris Jessie Jansen."

I snatch an audible breath, and both men turn to me.

"That means something to you?" McCrory asks.

The light goes on in Tracey's eyes. "It does," he says.

Doris Jansen is Mrs. Zane's daughter. This can't be a coincidence, but the meaning of it eludes me.

"Technician's already been here," McCrory says. "Happened to be around the corner dusting for prints on a burglary. She's gone back to that, but says to call her if you see anything she missed that needs to be collected."

Tracey nods.

If the evidence tech's already taken photos and canvased the scene, then we don't have to worry about disturbing the evidence. Still, we walk down the hall with care and stop when it opens into the kitchen. Nothing seems amiss, aside from the woman's body lying face up in a large pool of blood. No chairs overturned, nothing out of place.

Tracey steps closer and squats beside her body, eyeing the white palms of her hands, which face upward. "No defensive cuts on her hands." He uses his pen to move aside the long, sticky strands of hair that cover her neck, and I close my eyes, fighting nausea. The sight is not nearly as gruesome as the man whose car rolled under a flatbed truck, but I wasn't pregnant when I saw that.

"It's a professional job," Tracey says flatly. "Severed trachea and carotid."

He looks up to see my face. "Rose? You okay?"

"I think I need to sit down," I say weakly.

He rises and guides me to the nearest chair, making me put my head as close to my knees as possible over my belly. After a few minutes, I mutter, "I'm better."

"Sit up slowly," he advises.

I do, and to my relief, I'm okay.

Tracey steps back over the body and yanks open a cabinet, getting a glass and filling it with water from the sink. He hands it to me. I drink.

"Sorry," I say.

He shakes his head.

"It's bad enough when it's a stranger's body. You spent time talking with her."

I lift the glass toward my mouth again, my gaze drifting to the body on the green kitchen tiles. I don't want to look, but I make myself. Without warning, my hand freezes halfway to my mouth. Color leaches from the floor tiles. Doris Jansen's yellow blouse fades to a light shade of gray. A wavering shadow version of her lies face down, superimposed on the one lying face up. Slowly, she rises from that position to one on her knees, her head dropped against her chest. Her head lifts. A man's gloved hand rests on her shoulder. The other holds a blade that slices right to left. I can see only part of the man's back.

Abruptly, I am back in the present timeline. The floor is green, the blouse yellow, the blood a dark crimson. I gasp.

Tracey grabs the glass of water out of my hands and shoves my head back down.

"No." I push his hand aside. "It's not that."

He releases my head, and I look up at him through the jabs of pain at my temples. "I know who did this."

Chapter Thirty-Three

I stare at the body of Doris Jansen lying on her kitchen floor, my mind whirling through the jagged thrusts of pain a vision engenders.

"You know who killed her?" Tracey asks. He leans toward me.

"Yes."

"Did you have a vision?" This question he whispers, afraid a patrolman might be in the hallway within earshot.

I nod. My mouth is dry, and I take a swallow from the glass of water still in my hand.

"Did you see who it was?" he asks.

"No, I could just see hands and part of a man's back."

"Then how—?"

"It has to be connected to her mother's death, to Mrs. Zane."

"I think the same thing, but how?"

I look into his eyes. "Let's get out of here."

He understands at once.

When we step out onto the small porch, Tracey asks Officer McCrory, "Is the neighbor who found her at home?"

"Yes, she said she would stay until someone came to talk to her. I know I was supposed to keep her here until you arrived, but it's just next door, and she was pretty upset."

"I imagine," Tracey says. "It's okay. We need to discuss something, and then we'll go talk to her. You can go ahead and call the medical examiner's office."

"Will do."

Once we are in his car, Tracey rests an elbow on the steering wheel and twists toward me. "Spill it."

"It's Angola."

"Angola?"

"Yes. I'm almost sure."

"Why?"

"It has to be."

He shuts his eyes. "Is this another 'hunch?'"

"No, not exactly."

He sighs. "Rose, I need better than that."

"The man in my vision was left handed."

"Angola is left handed?"

"Yes. At least he held the gun in his left hand when he pointed it at my head."

"Okay, so is about ten percent of the world."

"It's not just that. It hit me that every time I have a vision, it's had something to do with House magic, or I've been in the vicinity of a member of a House."

He rubs his chin, thinking about it. "You're sure?"

"I've been over every instance before Jacobson."

"You think House of Iron was involved in Jim Jacobson jumping off a crossbeam?"

"I do."

"Angola was not up on that beam, pushing him," he says reasonably.

"No, but he could have been in his head pushing him. Like he did with the zoo shooter."

"And Mrs. Zane?"

"Angola could have been manipulating the person who killed her."

The ramifications of what I'm saying seem to sink in. "Holy crap," he whispers. "You think Angola got into Jacobson's head and made him step off the seventh floor?"

"I do."

Tracy's gaze drifts out the window toward Doris Jansen's front door. Tracey Lohan is not stupid. He is putting it all together. I can almost see his mind buzzing with the ramifications. He scratches at his jaw.

"Iron magic does wears thin with time," I remind him. "Unless the wielder re-ups it regularly or creates a *tabula rasa*, just completely wiping the mind, like Angola did to his 'friend' in jail, Lawrence Anders."

"What about what Theophalus Blackwell did to Becca? That didn't just wear off."

"That was a *rasa*. It's much more complicated. A *rasa* walls off the personality. He probably did that to Becca for practice, because he intended to kill us. It's questionable whether Angola is capable of doing something that sophisticated. According to Jason, it takes a high level of skill to accomplish a *rasa*. Wiping a mind completely, however, is apparently a simple matter."

Something I could do.

I shudder. I have the power of House of Iron. I could do that to a human being. Not for the first time, I promise myself I will never again use it.

"If Angola manipulated someone to kill Ms. Zane, that someone would eventually remember what she did and who 'persuaded' her to do it. Angola would have to take care of that witness. And that would mean that—"

I finish his thought. "That Doris Jansen killed her own mother. And now that Angola has killed her, she can never 'recall' that she did it or that he influenced her." I lean my head back onto the headrest. The pain is subsiding a little. "At least Doris never found out she overdosed her mother. That would be a horrible thing to live with."

"This is crazy."

"No crazier than Angola's previous murder to keep witnesses quiet and protect House of Iron's financial interests. I suspect he made Dana Jansen believe she was easing her mother's pain and then told her to forget what she did."

"And killed her before his influence wore off and she remembered."

"Yes." I'm having a difficult time not "seeing" that knife sliding across her neck. Another scenario to add to my nightmares. . . .

"So, now we think we know what happened, but we have no idea why Iron would want Jacobson or Zane dead or what the connection is between them." He looks sideways at me. "Or do we?"

"No. No idea."

He takes a deep breath and expels it slowly with a little whistle. "We have to find out. Whatever the reason is, there might be more people on that to-be-murdered list."

I squeeze my eyes shut, wanting to blank out that thought—a list of targets, people, that Angola is planning to kill, as coldly as he sliced that knife across Doris Jansen's throat or whispered in Jacobson's ear that he could fly or that stepping off the scaffolding was the way to protect his family or whatever he told him. My fists clench. "What do we do now?"

"When you have a new perspective, you go back over everything you've done and look at it again from the new angle."

"That something you learned in detective school?" I am still rankled that I have never been officially trained to be a detective.

"No, I learned it from an old detective."

I quirk my brow. "Who?"

"My father."

"Hobart?"

"That wasn't his name then. He was an Army man long ago. Military police."

"Is he why you became a police officer?"

"Probably," he says. "What's your excuse for signing up for this exciting life?"

I shrug. "I thought it was just a coincidence. I was looking for a job here and saw the opening, but my whole concept of 'coincidence' has been jostled."

"What brought you back to Birmingham in the first place?"

"I thought it was unresolved family business, but Alice says it was the rose-stone."

"Your pendant?"

"Yeah. The way she tells it, it has a mind of its own."

"Literally?" He sounds worried.

"No. I don't literally think the stone has a mind, but like I said, reality isn't what I have always thought it was. Alice has a theory about me, or witches of my 'line,' the rose-stone, and genetic entwinement."

He frowns. "Entwinement? Like in quantum·physics?"

"Yeah, like that."

"That's what Einstein called 'spooky action at a distance,'" Tracey says slowly. "I never heard of it being linked to genetics, but I guess atoms make up everything, including genes."

"You're familiar with quantum mechanics?"

"Not really, I mean, just what I've read about it. I try to keep up with science news. Just a hobby."

"Well, I had to look it up. Alice has all kinds of theories about House magic. That's why she went and got a doctorate in physics to add to her MD."

"An advantage to living more than one 'life.' I look forward to that, to being able to have the time to learn new things."

"Is this your first 'go round?'" I've never asked about his real age.

His mouth twitches. "Yeah. I'm thirty-two in 'real' years and this is my first 'lifetime.'"

"Do you have any secret siblings?"

"No, unfortunately. I'm an only child. I suspect my father may have tweaked something in a petri dish to make me viable."

"Is that something that could help repopulate the Houses?"

"Maybe one day, but he said I was attempt number 220, and he hasn't been able to replicate it. So, we are back to mixing the bloodlines with House of Rose as the only solution."

He hesitates. "That doesn't justify him trying to, um, push us together, but he did it to try and save us all."

"I'm not a brood mare." A flush burns my earlobes.

"I said it didn't justify anything."

"But you implied it."

"I just said I believed his motivations." His jaw sets.

"That's the same thing." I want to hit him. I want to hit his father. And I don't want to think about anything Becca said about trying to get me to change my mind about being mad. I want to be mad.

Tracey opens his door. "You are impossible lately, you know that?"

Tears spring to my eyes. I sniff. "I know. I'm—"

He shuts the door without getting out and turns back toward me, his voice softening. "It's okay, Rose. I guess there's a battlefield of hormones going on in there."

This makes me angry again. "I am not a battlefield of hormones. I'm just . . . confused."

He takes a deep breath. "While you're sorting it out, let's go interview Jansen's neighbor. We have three homicides to solve, and we'd better do it fast if we don't want more on our hands."

I sniff again, this time indignantly, set my lips and open my car door.

Chapter Thirty-Four

If I am a battlefield of hormones, Doris Jansen's neighbor is ground zero. A middle-aged woman wearing too-short sweatpants and a pink turtleneck that only emphasizes the teary red of her eyes. It takes fifteen minutes and a cup of coffee before she is able to speak.

The act of making and putting Tracey's coffee in front of him seems to distract her. I passed on the coffee and she didn't offer tea. We all sit at her dining room table.

"Why don't you tell us what happened?" Tracey suggests in a calm, comforting voice with just a hint of firmness to try to keep her from going off again.

"I . . . I went over to Doris' to take Corky back, and that's when I found her." She sniffs. "There was so much blood—" Tears begin again, tracking deeper ruts through her makeup.

"Corky is Mrs. Jansen's dog?" I ask.

"Yes." She looks down at the Welsh corgi lying at her feet. "I keep him when she's away."

Corky waves a short, feathered tail at her attention and the mention of his name.

"She was away a lot taking care of her mother at—I can't ever remember the name."

"Mountain Lane Senior Living," I say.

"That's it. She spent a lot of time there until her mother died. It was sudden. I mean, she was sick, but Doris thought she was doing really well and that they would have more time together." She stops for a tissue and blows her nose. "Poor Doris. Why did this happen? She was such a nice person. She brought me these Christmas cookies yesterday." She pushes a plate of red-and-green sprinkled star-shaped cookies toward us.

Tracey plucks up one with red sprinkles. "We plan on finding out what happened and who did it. Meanwhile, you could play a very important part in helping us."

She sits up a little straighter and blows her nose again. "What can I do?"

In this case, the crying woman is responding more to Tracey than to me, so I let him carry the lead.

"Did you see anything out of the ordinary in the past few weeks?" he asks, taking a bite of the cookie.

"No. Not really."

"Anyone come to see Ms. Jansen?"

"I'm not the nosy type," she says and leans toward Tracey. "But there was a motorcycle that parked in her driveway once, and a man got off and went to the door. I've never seen him before, but she let him in, so I assumed she knew him. He didn't stay long."

"What did this man look like?" Tracey asks.

"He was a well-built man, but not big like you." She nods at Tracey. "He wasn't black, but his skin was kind of brownish, and his hair was dark. He could have been Hispanic, I guess, or maybe Middle Eastern."

Tracey takes a sip of his coffee. "How long was his hair?"

My shoulders tense, waiting for her answer.

She shrugs. "I didn't notice. It wasn't particularly short or long."

But it has to be Angola.

"What about his motorcycle?" Tracey asks.

Her forehead wrinkles. "I can't tell one from another. Black. Dark anyway, I think."

"Chopper? Cruiser?"

She shrugs again. "Sorry."

"When did you see this man?" Tracey asks.

"About a week ago." She gives us a weak smile. "I'm just no good with time, you know."

"Did you see anything out of the ordinary today?" I ask.

"No. I was watching my TV shows. Me and Corky. He likes to curl up on the couch with me. Doris asked me to watch him while she attended to some business about her mother's estate."

"Will you be keeping him?" I ask. "He seems happy with you."

"I will unless some family member wants him. Doris has . . . *had* a brother. To my knowledge he was all that was left of her family, but he didn't even show up to help take care of their mother, so I'm pretty sure he won't be wanting the responsibility of a dog."

"I'm sure he'll be grateful that you want him," Tracey assures her.

"DOESN'T PROVE ANYTHING," Tracey says as we walk away from her house. "It could have been anyone Doris Jansen knew or even her brother."

"Or it could have been Angola," I insist. "He could have had his ponytail tucked into his collar."

"Or he could have cut it off. He knows law enforcement is looking for him."

"Nothing else makes any sense," I say.

"Until we figure out why House of Iron would target a construction worker and an elderly woman already dying of cancer, none of this makes any sense."

"What's next?"

"I want to search Jansen's house."

"What are we looking for?"

"No idea. Hoping something will pop up."

At the car, we divide, Tracey going to the driver's side and me to the passenger side. I stop before opening the door and look over the top of the car at him.

"I apologize," I say.

His thick brows rise. "For what?"

I can tell that he is suspicious of following the conversation, afraid I may go off in an erratic emotional direction, but—inspired by the encounter we've just had with drama—I've decided not to be emotional. I'll look at everything rationally.

"I am sorry I let my anger at your father direct to you. That's not fair."

"Okay." He opens his door.

"What about you?" I ask before he can get in.

He freezes. "What do you mean?"

"Aren't you going to apologize too?"

"Sure." He looks blank. "What do I apologize for?"

Anger surges back as if it has never really dissipated, just simmered. "For implying I am an irrational woman battered by hormones!"

"Oh, okay, I'm sorry I said that."

"You don't mean it."

"How do you know that?"

"I can tell."

He rolls his eyes, which further infuriates me. "I think you just want a fight."

"A lot of good that would do me. It'd be like beating on a stone wall."

We glare at each other, tension crackling between us like unseen electricity. Then, suddenly, it breaks. We laugh. Not the utter hilarity that caught us up before, thankfully, as we are still at a homicide scene.

"But I'm not going to apologize again," I say.

"Good. Me either."

Chapter Thirty-Five

While Tracey is getting a search warrant for Doris Jansen's house, I employ the advice of the best detective I know—*When you have a new perspective, you go back over everything you've done and look at it again from the new angle.*

I want to talk alone with Mary Ann Jacobson, the wife of our "jumper." I told Tracey I thought I might get something more from her woman to woman.

At her door, I pull my jacket tighter as a gust of December wind rattles the branches against a window, and I knock again. Has Mary Ann already moved to be with her family? To my relief, the door opens.

She takes up most of the doorway, sleeping baby in the crook of her ample arm, her face sweaty despite the cold.

"You again?" she says, a wooden spoon in her free hand.

"Yes. I'm sorry to bother you, but I need to ask you some more questions."

She scowls. "The company says it was an accident, and that the police closed the case."

"We did, but something new has come up, and I need to talk with you."

Her knuckles whiten on the spoon handle, her stout body blocking the doorway. "They gonna take the check back? I already spent part of it."

"No, I promise. I just need your help to figure something out."

"Don't know anything."

"Please, Mrs. Jacobson. I won't take up much of your time."

With a sigh, she uses the grip end of the spoon to brush aside a lank strand of strawberry hair that has fallen over her eye.

"Come on in then." She steps aside and shakes her head. "Still say you're gonna pop any minute now."

"I assure you I feel that way, but my doctor says not yet."

She squints at me. "Your doctor ever had a baby?"

I grin. "Don't think so. He would be a miracle man."

She snorts. "Well, I've had five." She leads the way into the kitchen. "Boys are playing in the living room, and I got something on the stove. You mind the kitchen?"

"Not at all."

Before I can sit at the kitchen table, she shoves the baby at me. "You want to hold him?"

I don't, but it seems rude not to. "I'm afraid I'll drop him or something."

"You get over that pretty quick." She transfers the child into my arms. "This is your first, ain't it? Bet you never even changed a diaper."

I'm certain the look I give her is one of terror.

She laughs. "Thought so. Well, enjoy your life, 'cause it's about to change forever."

My stomach does a flop. "Is it really so awful?"

She starts to say something and then has pity on me. "Sometimes, yeah, but then—" Her gaze falls on the sleeping baby in my arms. "Sometimes it's all worth it."

She sighs. "But I wish my man were here. Not just for the money and the help." Her eyes glisten, and she shrugs, as if rejecting sentimentality. "I come from a strong family. I'll manage."

"I'm glad the company gave you the money," I say.

"It helped. Jim came up with some cash too before he died, so with the company money, we'll be all right for a while."

"Some cash?"

"Yeah."

"Um, where did he get it?"

She rolls her head back, looking up at the ceiling. "Now there's God's sense of humor. Jim sold his life insurance and then he went and died not a month later. Cost us, that did, but we'll survive. They say workman's comp is coming too."

"Wait a minute. You said he *sold* his life insurance?"

"Yeah, he saw an ad on the TV about it."

"I didn't realize you could do that."

"Seemed kind of odd to me too, but he did it. They gave him about ten thousand more than he could have cashed it in for, but if we'd known he was gonna fall to his death, we'd have kept it. Too bad we couldn't see the future."

I flinch. "Who did he sell it to?"

"No idea . . . Well, maybe I do. He wrote it down while we were watching the show, so it might still be in the drawer. That's where he puts all his papers to keep them out of the children's paws."

"Could I see it?"

She holds up a wooden spoon. "I'll go look for it if you can stir this for me."

That means baby in one arm. "What if he wakes up and starts crying or something?"

She gives a guffaw, one hand on her stout hip. "He came into the world screaming his little lungs out and keeps up the practice every day. It ain't going to kill him . . . or you."

I stand, the arm holding the baby braced on the ledge of my belly and take the spoon from her hand.

"Now keep stirring," she says, "and don't let it boil."

I can't believe I am doing the two things that do not exist in my skill set—at the same time. "What do I do if it starts to boil?" I ask, trying not to panic.

She looks at me as if I have grown rabbit ears. "You turn down the flame."

The baby stirs in my arm. I give his mother a weak smile. "Hurry, please."

With a shake of her head, she leaves me. The baby makes a squeaking sound, and I try to rock him. "Go back to sleep," I say in the most soothing voice I can muster. "Your mom will be right back."

He opens his eyes and stares at me, realizing immediately that I am not his mother. The pudgy face pinches up, and he lets out a howl.

"Hush, hush." I rock harder. He screams louder. The white liquid in the pan starts to bubble.

"Shit."

Chapter Thirty-Six

I am back at my office desk on the computer when Tracey arrives.

"I got the search warrant for Jansen's house," he says. "Told the judge we were looking for evidence of a financial motive in a dead woman's possessions. She has no expectation of privacy herself, but there is a son, and the house might have gone to him. Anyway, I asked the judge to make the warrant parameters as broad as possible."

Although we had the constitutional right to a limited sweep for evidence the day her body was found, we need to do a thorough search, and a warrant that lets us do that and makes whatever we find admissible in court.

"Good," I say. "I called Mountain Lane. They had boxed up all Zane's possessions and sent them to her daughter, so everything should be at Dana Jansen's house."

Tracey sits. "What about you? Any luck?"

"Maybe." My fingers dance over the keyboard.

"Wanna share?"

I stop typing. "Ever heard of selling your life insurance policy?"

"*Selling* it?"

"Yep."

"No. I thought there were rules about who you could take out a policy on, like it had to be a family member or someone in business that you depended on."

"That's right, but there are no restrictions on who can *buy* your policy."

"But—"

"Yep, that means the buyer, a third party with no other connection with you, will benefit on your death."

"Why would anyone sell their life insurance?"

I shrug. "Same reason they might surrender their policy to the insurance company, cash it in—they need the money. But if they sell the policy instead, they get several times what the insurance company would give them."

"That's nuts. Is this related to your interview with Mrs. Jacobson?"

I reach into a manila envelope on my desk and wave it at him. "This contains a copy of a cleared check for $60,000. Mary Ann—Mrs. Jacobson—says it was for her husband's life insurance policy. They were in financial straits after she had the last baby."

He takes the check and examines it. "How does one go about doing this?"

"There's a front company, a marketing company set up to screen applicants. They advertise on television, and they have a website." I turn the screen so he can see it. "You have to fill out a form. They don't want just anyone or any amount of insurance. They start at $100,000. Has to be worth their while."

"Then what happens?"

"If you are a lucrative prospect, then a life settlement broker steps in and arranges the deal between the buyer and seller. The brokers can also package a bunch of settlement policies and sell them that way too. As far as I can tell, there are no regulations in our state on who can broker that kind of deal."

"I'm still trying to wrap my head around being able to buy someone's life insurance policy."

"That's because you're a homicide detective. You see a motive for murder; other folks see a financial deal that helps them out of a difficult situation."

"How come I never heard of it?"

"It's been around a while, but it became popular in the 1970s and 80s with the AIDS epidemic. The medicines AIDS patients needed were very expensive. People had a choice—find money to pay for treatment and buy a little time or just die. It was the perfect scenario for the buyers. AIDS was a guaranteed fatal disease, so they just sat on the policy and paid the premiums for a while. If the guy ran out of money to pay for treatment, the buyer just collected sooner."

"How is that legal?"

"It went to the Supreme Court in 1911 when a guy sold his policy to his doctor in exchange for treatment. The family sued, but the

Court ruled life policies were property, and the owner had a right to sell them."

"Wow." He's quiet for a moment, processing. "Let me think through this. The buyer has to keep paying the premiums, right?"

"Right."

"The longer the insured lives, the more it costs the buyer."

"Exactly."

He rubs the side of his chin. "Damn. Jacobson got $60,000 from his policy? How much was the death benefit?"

"About $150,000. I imagine he thought it was a good deal. Helped him out of a bad spot. Could explain why his poker buddies said he was depressed and then brightened up."

"Then he wasn't a suicide. No medical condition that he was trying to escape or anything?"

"According to his wife, he was healthy and in good shape. I imagine he didn't expect to die anytime soon, so it looked like the thing to do from his perspective."

"The buyer of his policy would have had to keep paying premiums until he died of natural causes. That would eat into their profit."

I lower my voice. Even though we appear to be alone in the Homicide Unit, I'm not taking chances with someone overhearing us talk about magic. Wouldn't that make Finkman's day?

"Unless," I add, "he didn't die of natural causes."

"And that's where Angola comes in."

"Specialty: making deaths look like accidents or natural causes. Use a little 'House influence' to make someone forget his safety tie off and step off a steel beam."

"But Doris Jansen didn't have an accident," Tracey says. "Her throat was slit."

"What if it was Doris' mother who sold her policy, not Doris?"

"If that's true, it wouldn't matter to the life insurance buyer when or how Doris died, just when her mother died."

"Right."

"But why not wait? She was on hospice. She'd have died soon."

"Soon is relative, I guess. For Mrs. Zane, there was a motivation. When I called Mountain Lane, I learned she had stopped paying her bill two months ago. They were about to evict her. She couldn't wait, and I imagine Mrs. Zane didn't want to tell her daughter or burden her. Sure enough, she suddenly paid off the bill a week before she was killed."

"What about the purchaser of the policy? Why not wait until she kicked the bucket on her own?"

"For one thing, they have to pick up the premium, so the longer they waited for her to die, the more it would cut into their profits. And people have been known to stay on hospice for a while or even go into remission. Maybe the premium was high, or maybe Angola just got a hit list and went down the line."

"Wow."

"It's just a theory."

"It's good work, detective."

I can't help preening under his praise. He doesn't give it lightly. But my pleasure is short lived. "Now what?"

"Now," he says, holding up a piece of paper, "we go serve this search warrant and see if we can find anything about a life insurance policy on Mrs. Zane."

I check the time. "Tomorrow. Tonight is Becca's birthday, and I promised to take her out."

"HAPPY BIRTHDAY, BECCA." I lift my wineglass, and she reciprocates. We are at Oceans, an upscale seafood restaurant in Five Points South.

"I could never have afforded this," she says. "Are you sure you can?"

"I can on your birthday." I lean back. "If I were rich, I'd buy you a shopping cart of clothes."

She giggles. "I hope you'd let me pick them out."

"Certainly. A gift card. That's what I'd do."

"That's very generous," she says, "but you know what I'd really like?" Her eyes shine.

"Name it. I'm feeling generous on the verge of solving two murders."

"Congratulations!"

"Well," I admit, "they aren't exactly ready for arrest warrants, and, if the suspect is who I think it is, he already has a warrant out on him. But I think we've had a breakthrough on the cases."

She lifts her glass of wine. "Let's drink to that."

We do.

"You were saying what you really want for your birthday?" I prompt.

She settles her glass on the white tablecloth and cocks her head at me. "I want you and Tracey to double date with me and Jon."

"Jon?"

"The guy I met in the restaurant, remember?"

"Ah, the one with the nice smile. That's still going on?"

"Oh yeah. Heating up, I'd say."

"As long as he is treating you right."

"A gentleman, but a hot gentleman, if you know what I mean."

"I do." I'm thinking of Jason. *Damn it.*

She dives her fork into the butter-wine covered scallops. "What about it?"

Thinking of Jason has dislodged me from the conversation track. "What about what?"

"What about you and Tracey going out with us?"

My mouth opens. "Tracey is my partner, not my boyfriend."

The golden arches rise.

"Yes, he's the father of my baby too."

"And he's pretty hot himself."

"Tracey?" I recall him stripping off his shirt at the dojo and my earlobes burn.

"You're blushing!" Becca says.

"It's the wine."

"Right."

I take another long swallow.

"What about it?" she prods. "It would be fun, and I really want you to meet him, and he wants to meet you."

"Okay," I say impulsively. "If Tracey is okay with it, we'll do it."

"Promise?"

"I have to promise?"

"Yes."

I sigh. "I promise then. It'll be cheaper than taking you shopping."

Chapter Thirty-Seven

Technically, Doris Jansen's house belongs to her estate, but when I tracked down her attorney, I learned her slippery brother, Ted Zane, has taken up residence. Good. If he's there, we'll kill two birds with one stone. We arrive in the morning as soon as I have had my once-a-day coffee fix. Two uniformed police officers accompany us to serve the search warrant.

Zane opens the door at our knock. He is a short, skinny man with a growth of dark stubble on his chin and an uneven spattering of hairs on his cheeks, lips fixed in a sour twist. "I live here," he says when one of the officers explains our purpose and shows him the warrant. "I don't have to let you come in."

"Yes sir, you do. We have a search warrant that says you do." The older officer's voice sounds bored and matter-of-fact.

Zane examines the document, keeping his lanky frame in the doorway. "I want to talk to my lawyer."

"Well, you just go right ahead, sir, but we're coming in to search the premises for the items listed."

"Why?"

"Mr. Zane," Tracey says, stepping forward, "I'm Detective Tracey Lohan, and this is Detective Rose Brighton with Birmingham Homicide. We're investigating your sister's murder."

"You're too late. I already had the blood cleaned up," he says.

"We're not here for that kind of evidence."

"Then what do you want?"

"We're looking for the belongings of your mother, including paperwork."

He scowls. "What kind of paperwork?"

"It's all listed on the warrant you have in your hand," the officer says. "Now step aside, sir."

"Or what?"

The officer grins. "Or you'll be interfering with the execution of a lawful warrant, and we'll arrest your little ass."

"You can't talk to me like that!"

"Like what?" the officer asks.

Zane puffs out his chest. For a moment, I think he is going to take on the officers. Doris said he never bothered to come help take care of his mother. I won't shed any tears for him if he goes to jail.

"Since I don't have a choice—" he says, stepping to the side. "But I'm making a complaint about this."

"Knock yourself out," the officer grumbles and brushes by him.

His partner follows, and they pat Zane down for weapons. We enter last.

"Mr. Zane," Tracey says, "we have a few questions we need to ask you. Are you willing to stick around for that?"

He rubs his nose. "I got someplace to be, matter of fact."

"Well, you need to cancel it and wait here, or I'll have one of these officers take you to the office to wait for us there."

He gives the first officer a nervous glance. "Alright. I'll wait. You said you were looking for my mother's papers. Her boxes are all in the study. Last room down the hall."

In the two days since his sister's death, Zane appears to have made his nest in Doris's bedroom. We give the room a cursory look. Clothes are scattered about. Smelly clothes. I am not one to win any Betsy Housekeeper awards myself, but the bathroom is nasty, and that is one place I am fastidious about keeping clean.

"Let's save this room for last," I say.

Tracey nods. "We'll check the study first."

It's chaos in the study too, but not the smelly kind. Piled beside the far wall are several boxes, most of them unopened.

"I'm guessing these are Mom's stuff." I take out the heavy-duty scissors I brought. "I'll start on these."

Tracey moves to the desk. "Let's see what we can find in here."

Two hours and countless boxes later, we have what we're looking for—a bank receipt for a deposit of $200,000 with "sale of life policy" on it.

"You were right, Rose," Tracey says.

"That might be my favorite phrase, other than 'Good job, detective.'" He grins.

I take the receipt from his hand and study it. "The date on this jibes with when Mrs. Zane paid off her bills at Mountain Lane and probably went toward payments for medical treatment. I'm betting she never told her daughter."

"The question is, did her Ted Zane think his mother still had a life insurance policy?" Tracy rubs his chin. "We know he didn't kill his mother himself, but what if he was in cahoots with one of the staff at Mountain Lane, and had her killed and—?"

"—And," I finish his sentence, "killed his sister to be the only one to inherit."

"He looks like he is living hand to mouth, and he showed up out of nowhere fast. If his sister didn't have his contact info, how did he find out his mother was dead?"

"Those are good questions, but here's another one—how would he be connected to Jim Jacobson?" I wave the receipt at him.

"I don't have a clue, yet. I know you believe Angola's behind this, but we can't rule out Ted Zane."

"I'm with you. At least we know where he is."

The heavyset officer steps into the room. "You guys need a hand in here?"

Tracey waves the deposit slip. "We believe we found what we needed."

"I'm sure Mr. Zane will be happy," I say.

"Oh, I don't think so," the officer says, leaning against the doorframe.

"What do you mean?" Tracey asks.

The officer runs his tongue along the inside of his lower lip. "He ain't been too happy for the last couple of hours."

Tracey arches an eyebrow.

"Found some contraband in plain view in a dresser drawer when we were looking for papers. Mr. Zane's been sitting in handcuffs in a chair for a while. If you guys are finished looking, we'll just take him on down to the jail and book him."

"What did you find?" I ask.

"Looks like heroin to me. A stash of needles and a tie-off next to it."

"Jesus," I say. "No wonder he didn't want us to come in." I look at Tracey. "What now?"

"Let's see what Mr. Zane has to say."

An hour later we are back in the car, and Ted Zane is heading to jail on a drug possession charge. Not murder. On the night his mother died, he had an air-tight alibi, having been in jail in a small town in Texas. In fact, he'd served six months there for another drug charge and DUI and had just gotten out. After spending every cent he had on the heroin and a bus ticket, he headed home to mamma, unaware until he got there that she had been in Mountain Lane or that his sister was dead. He had just gotten the key from under the flowerpot where his sister kept it and gone inside. Dana Jansen's attorney sent an appraiser to the house and discovered him, and that's how Zane came into legal possession of it.

After the first ten minutes of the interview, it was clear to Tracey and me that he didn't have enough brain cells left to plot a complex murder from a jail cell three states away. Besides that, he drank the water we gave him with his right hand.

We are back to Angola. I am more certain than ever we are dealing with House of Iron.

"Now what?" I ask.

"Now we've eliminated a suspect, and we have a motive."

I lean back into the headrest. The euphoria of finding the receipt and ruling out Zane has melted off. "Lohan, I am not sure what we've really gained."

"I'm expecting it to lead back to the same brokerage company as that check to Jim Jacobson."

"And?"

"And we'll get the info on who bought the insurance policies. We've got enough to subpoena that."

"And let's say we're able to trace a link to House of Iron." That could involve a lot of digging, as I learned in a previous case, but surely it can be done with patience and some luck.

"Then we'll have confirmation that your theory is right," Tracey says.

"But we won't have a case. All we'll have is the coincidence of two people dying after they sold their policies. How do we link Angola to Jacobson? It's not like he pushed him. He got in his mind. Same with Doris Jensen. Our supposition is that she was murdered to keep her from 'recalling' who told her to overdose her mother. I can't even imagine trying to explain that to Faraday."

He sighs, crossing his arms over his chest. "So, where are we?"

"I hate to say it, but nowhere."

He bangs his fist into the heavy plastic console, leaving a dent. Considering what he is capable of, it was a very tempered blow, but it speaks to his frustration level.

"We're not 'nowhere,'" he says after a minute. "We have a crime scene. With some luck Angola left a hair or skin cell on her body and we'll at least have him for that."

"What good is pinning that on him going to do? We already have a warrant out for him for attempted murder. Even if we find him and arrest him, a prison can't hold him, and any officer who tries to arrest him is going to have a big problem. We've been over this before."

Tracey's grip tightens on the steering wheel. "How to bring in Angola is not the only thing we have to worry about," he says darkly.

"What are you thinking?"

"Jacobson and Zane may not be the only people in Birmingham who have sold their insurance policies." His knuckles are white on the wheel.

"We can get a list of names, but how can we predict which one is next? We need to find Angola before he plucks off another victim."

I lay a hand on his arm, feeling the tension in the steel-cable muscles. "Lohan, killing the car isn't going to help anything."

He takes a steadying breath. "You're right."

I stare out the window, giving him a moment to tame his *ryu* dragon.

"Maybe we're wrong about this," he says finally.

"We're not wrong. I can't believe I'm saying this, but . . . I think Jason was right."

"What are you talking about?"

"We have to kill Angola." I say it quietly.

He stares at me, his gray eyes hard. "That makes us the same as they are, just killing people to solve problems."

"It's not the same."

"Yes, it is. I've spent a career going after the bad guys. Some of them walk out of jail. Some of them walk out of the courtroom. I don't like that, but I live with it. My job is to put them there."

"I can't see how we have a choice."

"There're always choices."

"This is House business. We can't risk officers' lives to arrest him."

"Police officers risk their lives every day making arrests. That's their choice."

"I get that. But this is different. They wouldn't have any idea what they were up against. And again, how could a prison ever hold him?"

"That's a damn slippery slope, Rose. We become vigilantes, and it gets easier and easier to take the law into our hands."

"What are you saying? We just drop it? Let Angola kill whoever's on his list with impunity? Let him kill me?" A hand drifts to cover my belly.

"No, of course not."

"Could we take him somewhere?"

"Where?"

"Find a cabin in the wilderness. Would your House hold him?"

"You're talking about a war between the Houses."

"You told me House of Stone would protect me."

He turns to me. "We will. I will."

"You'll talk to your father?"

"Yes. It's a desperate idea, but—"

"It only works if we can find him alone."

"I'm sure my father will agree if it is the only way to protect you. We'll have a place ready, but until we absolutely have no choice, we do this legally. We make a case. Trace who is buying those policies. We may find another way to stop him."

I close my eyes, seeing guns pointed at me—Angola's as he stood on the pool's edge, the guy at the zoo pulling his out of a bag and lifting it toward me. I see other bodies in pools of blood, people I don't know. People I do. I see Becca staring mindlessly into nothing. The odds of us finding Angola and being able to kidnap him are very slim.

"Okay," I say. But I leave my next thought unspoken—*I'm going to have to kill him by myself.*

Chapter Thirty-Eight

The moon, brushed with a touch of crimson, sits low on the horizon. Becca and I lean over the top of the metal fencing on the walkway bridge at Railroad Park, peering down at the waterfall below us. Illuminated by colored lights, it falls in a beaded curtain of blue strands into the pristine lake that meanders through the rolling grass hills of the four-city-blocks park. Behind us runs a railroad track, and behind that the cluster of downtown's signature buildings stand like stiff sentries against the night sky. The sides of the Harbert Center gleam with its traditional green holiday wreath and tree against a background of white lighting.

The air is bitterly cold. I'm determined not to think about homicide cases or Angola or House of Iron. I promised Becca we would have a fun night and meet her new boyfriend.

Beside me, Becca pulls her furry coat tighter. I've never understood how she walks in those heeled red leather boots, but they do look good. Her eyes are sparkling in anticipation of showing off her boyfriend.

"A strange choice for a meeting place," I say, grumpy from the chill wind. The cold is appropriate for the season. It's just the back-and-forth temperature swings that make it difficult to adjust. Last week, I almost got out my tee shirts before I remembered they don't fit anymore. Or it's the pregnancy. I'm usually oblivious to cold.

"This is our special place." Becca's breath crystalizes into mist.

I raise my brows. "Special place?"

"First kiss."

"Ah."

From the height of the bridge, I look out about eye level at the temporary raised ice rink set up on the other side of the lake. Strings of white lights canopy it like suspended stars. Several wobbly skaters make their way around the ice. Alabama is not best known for this sport. The crowd is thick around the park, so this elevated spot is a smart place to find someone. We are the only ones here on the bridge.

"I have everything planned," Becca says, bouncing a little on her toes. "When Jon gets here, we'll all go to the Wine Loft. Have you ever been there?"

"Nope, but I like the wine part."

"It's really upscale and sophisticated. That's what Jon likes. Yummy food, and it's quiet with candlelight and comfortable sofas so Tracey won't be scrunched up in a little chair."

I hate loud bars, so this sounds nice. "Tracey should be here soon." I sip from the steaming hot chocolate I purchased from the park vendor before we made our way to this perch. Becca looks terribly pleased with herself.

"What?" I demand.

"Nothing, just glad you're finally going out with Tracey."

"It's not really a date—"

"Oh, stop grumbling about it. That guy is crazy about you."

"Becca—"

A man in his twenties with a snippet of mustache approaches us from the path. After the zoo incident, I check out anyone who even remotely seems to look my way. He catches my gaze and gives a friendly grin.

"Hey there. What are two beautiful women doing up here by themselves?"

"Waiting for our dates," Becca says, lifting her spiced apple cider in salute.

A *tsk-tsk* accompanies his headshake. "My bad luck. Crazy guys to keep you two waiting." He points down to the crowd under the covered pavilion to the right of the skating ring. "If they don't show, come find me and my friend, and we'll see what the elves are up to for Christmas."

"Thanks," Becca says.

I look away, though I keep him in my periphery.

"Oh, an ice princess." He moves closer. "Perhaps a little Irish coffee could melt some of that cold?"

"Not a chance," I say, this time meeting his gaze directly.

"Can't blame a guy for trying."

As he walks away down the path, Becca watches his back and then turns to me. "No wonder you need my help."

"I don't need your help. I'm fine."

"Right, Ice Princess."

"Tell me more about Jon," I say to divert her, "besides that he likes cinnamon in his coffee."

"Well, he's muscular, but not a bear like Tracy. Dark, piercing eyes. A couple of inches taller than you."

"Not what he looks like. What he's *like*."

A dreamy smile spreads across her face. "He is so polite. I mean, a real gentleman." One brow arches mischievously. "Most of the time."

I laugh. "What else?"

"He isn't all 'about him,' like some guys are. He wants to learn about me, what I like and don't like, and he asks about my friends. It was his idea to meet you."

"That's unusual."

"Yeah, he is unusual. And to think it was just happenstance that he looked up and smiled at me in that restaurant—"

"I doubt that was happenstance, Becca. He saw something that interested him, and he went after it."

"Yeah, but most guys are put off by me once they meet me. I'm too much. I push too hard."

We've had this conversation before. "Stop it. You're perfect just the way you are."

She puts her mittened hand on mine. "I'm so lucky to have you as my best friend."

Yeah, lucky. Lucky enough that you almost got your mind perma-nently wiped. I don't say this aloud. No sense reminding her of that nightmare. I feel my eyebrows knitting. Something else besides bad memories is bothering me.

Before I can fathom what, the bulky figure of a large man approaches from the same direction as the previous visitor. To my surprise, my pulse gives a little jump at the sight of his broad shoulders. Silly. I see him every day. I'm just happy it's not another stray man wanting to flirt or a deranged killer wanting to shoot me.

"Hi," Tracey says when he steps onto the bridge. "Sorry I'm a little late. My father wanted to get together."

I frown—my habitual response at the mention of Hobart—and

change the subject. "Did you have any luck getting info from the insurance brokers?"

"Got it, but it doesn't have addresses or other personal info. We'll need to go through all the names and prioritize them on the theory that Angola will target people from this area first."

"Then what?"

"Then we see how many people we are dealing with."

"We could start with the ones who had the highest amount of life insurance."

"That's as good a way as any. If we're not out too late, I'll start on that tonight. Send you half to start looking up. We may not have much time."

"Work," Becca says with an exaggerated sigh. "Can't you two talk about something besides murder?"

"Okay," Tracey says. "We do need a break. So, where's this mystery man of yours?"

"He'll be here," Becca says. "I'm always late, so he probably told me earlier, so I'd be on time."

Tracey snorts. "That's cheating."

I move over to let him between us.

"Don't think I've ever been here at night," he says, looking below us at the luminous pearl strands of falling water. From our position directly above the waterfall, each droplet, now purple, seems suspended in time—

Time. Is that connected to what's making me anxious? It's as though I'm trying to have a vision, but I can't, because . . . because I'm over water. Water buffers House magic, and we are standing in one of the few places in the city that is over water. Is that a coincidence?

Behind us, a train roars by, parallel with the park's northern edge.

"I think we should get off this bridge," I shout, trying to be heard over the train.

"Why?" Becca protests. "This is where Jon wants to meet us."

Because this is where he first kissed Becca. Is that a little odd? Why would he make us stand out in the cold to meet him? I'm suddenly not liking this guy.

I shift my weight, uncomfortably aware in a muted way that my gift wants to express itself but can't. Like an itch I can't locate. Was someone killed here? Or is it something that will happen here in the future?

"Where are we going from here?" Tracey asks as soon as the train passes. "You're not getting ice skates on me."

Becca giggles. "Don't tell me the police detective is clumsy."

"As a bull in a china shop, but the truth is I'd probably break through the ice."

I'm feeling physically sick now. "Guys, something's not right." I turn toward the walkway's end, wanting earth beneath me, wanting the living-green.

Becca leans forward to look at me across Tracey's bulk. "You're pale as a ghost. What's wrong?"

A waft of cinnamon from her cider floats into my nostrils.

Cinnamon.

Suddenly, I am remembering walking into my kitchen to confront Angola, the ironic place he chose to hold his kidnapped prisoner and kill me. I was terrified, but there was something oddly out of place. What was it? Nothing I saw. It was . . . a smell—the homey smell of *cinnamon*. Angola was sitting at the table, a cup of steaming coffee before him.

"Oh my God!" I shout. "Off the bridge. Now!"

Becca's hand tightens on the rail. "What?"

Panicked, I face Tracey. "Now, Lohan. Get her off the bridge now!"

Without questioning, Tracey scoops Becca by the waist, tearing free her grip on the railing. Snatching me under the other arm in a grip that takes my breath, he sprints off the bridge. I reach for the living-green, but light and thunder crack the world apart, and a blow against my back lifts me into the air.

Chapter Thirty-Nine

I am mist, unfocused, diffused, until my shattered sense of self gathers like broken glass reassembling.

Acrid smoke clogs my throat. A cough ignites pain everywhere. I can't identify which part is hurting, but more importantly, I can't breathe. Not from the smoke, but from pressure. Something heavy is compressing me into the ground.

"Roll him off her. Easy now."

The pressure lifts.

Amber!

My arms jerk toward my belly, but something keeps them from moving. I'm trapped.

"Easy, be still. Paramedics are on the way." The unfamiliar voice is somewhere above me. A man's voice.

My eyes blink open, confused at the blurry images. Faces? Thin lines cut through them. No. Grass. Long blades of grass. I remember the clumps of long grasses planted in the park. Railroad Park.

"Becca? Tracey?" My mouth moves to form their names, but the sound that emerges is a muffled groan.

Sirens howl.

"What happened?" I croak.

"An explosion. A bomb."

"My baby?"

"Be still. Help is coming."

"My friends? Are they—?"

"Help is coming."

I WAKE AGAIN IN THE HOSPITAL, remembering a jumble of sounds and pains as hands disentangled me from debris and bodies. *Jesus.* My mind shies. No one has told me about Becca and Tracey that I remember. My hand gropes toward my belly, afraid of finding it flat. A tube trails my hand. Comforted by the hard, round surface of my abdomen, I weep silently. *Please be okay, Amber.*

"Rose?"

I turn my head, eyes still closed, at the familiar deep voice. A voice like layers of velvet—

"You drifted off. I envy you that. I don't think I could ever fall asleep with you this close."

A light touch wipes the tears from my cheek. From somewhere far away, my pulse gives a twitch, as if to a remembered stimulus. Slowly, my eyes open a crack, but it takes several moments before the shape beside me resolves. I struggle with naming the emotions that tangle in my mind and then give up.

"Do you want some water?" Jason asks.

A straw approaches me. I want it. I focus on staying awake to get my cracked lips around it, but then I am gone again.

When I open my eyes, I remember only the straw and the promise of water. After a moment, it is there again. This time, I drink.

Cool liquid salves my mouth and throat. A gentle damp cloth clears crud from my eyes.

"My baby?" I ask.

"I haven't seen a doctor come by yet, but your nurse says the baby is okay." Responding to the question he must see in my eyes, he adds, "And the other people with you, that big detective and your friend, Becca, are alive. But I won't lie to you. Becca is in critical condition. They're not sure she will survive."

A pain lances through my chest that has nothing to do with my injuries. It is my fault. I should have gotten them off the bridge sooner. I should have known not to stand there.

"Alice . . . Alice can heal Becca." I mutter, trying to form a coherent thought.

"Rose, your great aunt is dead."

No, she can't be dead. She wasn't on the bridge. My breath is coming in gasps. I can't breathe—

Something cool and wet presses against my forehead. "Be still," he says. "It will be all right."

It's not all right. It's not.

"She's agitated," Jason says to someone else.

And then I am pulled back under.

WARMTH PLAYS ACROSS MY FACE, and I blink my eyes open to see Jason at the window, pulling back the curtain. The medley of corrosives that batter my heightened sense of smell is unmistakable. I am in a hospital. In front of me is a Renoir print I'm too familiar with, *The Grands Boulevards*, an impressionist scene of a rainy city street. I must have been in this same room after being hit by a car months ago because I remember this painting, having had only that to look at for hours on end. Or the same artwork could be in all the rooms. With my eyes, because I am not sure I can move anything else, I follow the plastic tube in my arm up to a stand with a two bags hanging from it. Someone has hung a piece of tinsel over the top. A sad Christmas tree.

Jason turns toward me. "Good morning."

I swallow, my throat dry again, but find I can talk. "What are you doing here?"

He lifts an eyebrow. "Taking care of you."

"Why?"

A clipped laugh. "Because I love you."

I cough, an action that stabs acute pain throughout my body, and he moves to the bed, pressing something out of my line of sight that makes the bed lift me into a sitting position. I can't process what he has said, so I ignore it. "Becca?" I croak.

"Amazingly, she is, as you say, 'hanging in there.'"

"Is—is anyone with her?"

"That woman you hired to be her nursemaid when Becca was, uh, under my uncle's influence."

I try to recall Alice's cover name. "Irene?"

"Yes, I think so."

My shoulders relax. If anyone can help her now, it's Alice.

"She has come by to check on you. She says the doctors think Becca can handle surgery now. They weren't expecting she would."

"And Tracey?"

"Your detective friend?"

"Yes."

"I popped in to take a look because I knew you would ask. Porcupine-ish with all the tubes and monitors, but they say he has an excellent chance of recovering."

I reach for the water beside my bed, happy just to be able to do that on my own. After long swallows, I replace the empty cup with a shaky hand.

"How long have you been here?" I ask.

"Since I heard what happened on the news."

"How long?"

"That was two days ago."

I'm startled. It doesn't feel as if I could have lost two entire days. "And you've been here the whole time?"

He looks down at himself. "Can't you tell?"

If I look closely, he does look a little wrinkled. "I just never pictured you as a . . . caretaker."

"Well, you're right. I'm not much good at it, but I'm not bad at my other job."

"Which is?"

"Protector."

I stare at him. Jason Blackwell is either the last person on Earth to protect me or the best person. I don't know which. I never have.

"What happened?" I ask.

"Someone planted a bomb under the bridge at Railroad Park. A terrorist, according to the media."

I meet his eyes, not drowning in them for the first time, a happenstance I suspect I owe the drugs in my system. A single word comes out of my mouth—"Angola."

"That is an appropriate guess. I've tried to stop him. I thought I had succeeded, but—"

"—You failed," a man standing in the doorway completes Jason's sentence.

Jason's head snaps toward the source of the voice, and he tenses. I follow his gaze, fighting the dizziness invoked by moving my head suddenly.

A short, balding man stands with both hands resting on a black cane with a silver handle. Despite his short stature, he dominates the doorway and the room. I recognize him from my visit to the headquarters of House of Iron a little over a year ago: Jason's other uncle and the head of House of Iron, Samuel Blackwell.

Chapter Forty

Samuel Blackwell, who introduced himself to me when we first met as "Uncle Sam," is the most unimposing man I've ever seen. He exudes a warm charm, a smile dimpling his jowly cheeks.

But the man who steps into view behind him sends a shiver down my spine—Angola Simone, minus his ponytail with a short beard and goatee, his face chiseled stone. He enters the room and then steps to the side where he can see the door and the room without turning. Standing with his legs slightly apart, arms at his side, his gaze is in constant motion—from me to Jason to the door. A coiled serpent, waiting for a word to deal death.

My attention shifts to Samuel. Cane clicking on the hospital floor, he moves to my bedside.

"You are a difficult person to kill, Ms. Brighton," he says, almost jovially.

"What do you want?" Jason's voice is tight, his hand squeezing the side rail near the base of my bed.

"Why, just visiting. I heard what happened and thought I would stop by and pay my respects."

"You are well aware that Angola was behind this," Jason says with a glaring glance at Angola, who remains silent, a backup for his true master.

Samuel's expression remains neutral. "Yes, he was."

I'm following this conversation with a growing unease. Why is he admitting to knowing about an attempted murder? The only reason he would do that is that he has no fear of consequences, and that is definitely not a good sign.

"That makes what happened our House's responsibility," Jason says.

"So it does." Samuel lifts the cane and points it at Jason. "What are you doing here, anyway?"

The air between them seems to crackle with invisible arcs of energy. There's some longstanding animosity here.

My heart is racing overtime. I'm hooked to a monitor. Why doesn't a nurse come check on me? Stupid wish, I realize. If one shows up, Samuel or Angola will simply touch her and suggest everything is fine.

"The question," Jason says to Samuel, "is what are *you* doing here?"

"I go where I wish."

"Likewise."

"I see."

"Did you come to try to kill her yourself?" Jason asks.

"Perhaps. Why shouldn't I?"

"Why would you?" I croak, entering the conversation for the first time.

He considers me. "The nurse says the baby you are carrying is well. I can't risk that you will bear another in the line of House of Rose or, God forbid, the mother-to-be of the *Y Tair*, herself."

Y Tair, a child of all three House bloodlines, with the powers of all of them. My hand slides to my belly under the sheets. Only Tracey, Hobart, Alice, and Becca know this child does carry the blood of all three Houses.

"Why not wait until she has the baby?" Jason asks. "An infant should be easy to do away with." His tone is heavy with sarcasm, but I start at his bluntness. My throat tightens. Things do not look good here. I can barely move. Tracey is incapacitated. No one stands between this madman and me, except Jason, who is sworn to obey the madman.

"No, no." Samuel shakes his head, his mouth pulled into a sad frown. "I'm afraid there has been too much ineptness." He turns to me. "We were quite shocked to find you were alive. That was clumsy of us."

Ice. My chest is frozen. How can my heart beat so fast in a frozen chest?

"My brother Theophalus was wrong. Even after we learned you were alive, he wanted to flush out the rose-stone before killing you, but the stone is not a threat without a *Y Tair* to wield it."

His hand slides into his pocket and emerges with a syringe. "The happy news is that you will just slip away peacefully, my dear, and it will be assumed you died of your injuries."

I want to scream. Surely someone will come in if I do, but if they see something they shouldn't, I'll be condemning another innocent to death. House of Iron has a thousand ways to kill someone. I have followed their trail of bodies.

"Why?" I manage. I need to stall him, to think, but my mind is sluggish. I hear his words, but there's a delay in my brain to make sense of them. He plans to inject me with something. I try to get up, to defend myself, but I can't seem to get my body to obey.

"It's nothing personal," Samuel says. "In fact, I rather admire you. But, you see, my Family has built an empire over the years, employing methods frowned upon by the other Houses, especially yours, which just kept meddling."

"Don't deny it," he says when I open my mouth. "You have been just as meddlesome as your forebears."

"You fear a *Y Tair* would control you," I say.

He considers me. "I fear she would try. But there is another reason. A *Y Tair* is dangerous. Far more dangerous than you can imagine. Not just because she could control the Families. She could bring devastation to us all, to humanity, for that matter."

It feels like fluid is filling my chest, making it difficult to breathe. "So, you're trying to save the world?"

"Actually, yes."

"Without House of Rose, your Family will become extinct."

"I am aware."

Jason's face remains neutral.

"You're willing to let all the Families die out," I croak, "to keep the status quo?"

"Considering the alternative, yes. And we have the finest medical brains working on a solution. I'm sure they will find one. What did you imagine the financial projects were for? Merely playthings for the wealthy?"

Jason moves closer to Samuel. Angola hasn't moved from his post at the door.

Desperate, I reach for the living-green, but because we are several floors high or because the drugs have dulled my senses, I can't find it.

My gaze falls on the needle securely strapped into the vein on top of my left hand. Samuel doesn't even need to stick me with a needle. All he has to do is inject whatever is in that needle into the port on the line, and it will go straight into my veins.

I have to rip out that needle.

My other hand jerks toward it, and an explosion of pain in that shoulder makes me almost faint. Everything fogs and for a moment, nothing matters. Then I am back, my breath coming in quick, shallow pants. Samuel reaches for the port on the line, just below the bag that hangs on a pole beside my bed.

Abruptly, Jason puts a hand on Samuel's wrist. "Wait," he says.

Samuel cocks his head. "For?"

"What if the baby is a boy?"

He shrugs his hand loose. "What if it is?"

"Rose bears a child with the blood of House of Iron. The boy would be of our House."

"That is a rumor that has never been substantiated." His cheerful face is now a flat stone. "Release me."

"Listen to me," Jason says. "Uncle, by the laws of House Iron, I claim an audience."

Samuel sighs and drops his hand. "Very well. You have one minute."

I eye the needle in my forearm again. If I rip it out, could I use it as a weapon? I lick perspiration from my upper lip. If by some miracle I'm able to rip out the needle, there's no way I could fight off Angola and Samuel to keep them from just injecting me with whatever poison he has. The heart line on my monitor is tracing jagged peaks against the screen.

"How long has it been since a child was born to our House?" Jason asks.

Samuel shakes his head. "The risk is too great."

"Let me make my case. How long?"

"A long time."

"She could be carrying a boy," Jason says.

"I didn't want to know." I mumble the lie, not sure where Jason is going, but wherever it is, he is my only chance, Amber's only chance.

"If it is a girl," Jason says, "you can always 'take care' of it later, but if she bears a boy-child—"

"It's never been confirmed that she carries any Iron blood in her line."

I start to say I can prove it, but I realize that I can't. If I can't reach the living-green here, which is now as natural as breathing, I won't be able to pull from iron in the ground either. I don't have the strength to try to rip the chemical bonds of the steel bedframe, not to mention how dangerous that would be. Steel contains iron and carbon. If I let those magics combine, at least everyone on this floor could be ashes.

"This baby has Iron blood," Jason says again.

"How can you claim such a thing?" Samuel raps the cane onto the steel frame of my bed with impatience.

"Because Rose bears *my* child."

Samuel pales, and I feel my eyes widen.

"Why do you think I am here?" Jason asks calmly, a calm belied by the tiny beads of sweat along his chin line, but he holds Samuel's gaze.

A rush of blood flushes Samuel's rotund face.

"How could you do such a thing? To lie with a woman of House of Rose is forbidden." He punches his cane, this time onto the floor.

"So I have always thought, but my research says that is mostly nonsense."

"Research? What do you mean?" His voice is scoffing. "Did you look it up online?"

"Books, Uncle. The ancient books and scrolls in—" He glances at me. "In our Britain home."

"Books?"

"I surprise you?"

"You do. And what have you uncovered from this 'research'?"

Months ago, I had asked Jason to find anything he could to help me restore Becca's mind. He did, researching it in an ancient House library in England. When he returned, what he told me enabled me to bring Becca back. I owe him for that. And now I think he is trying to save my life, so I keep my mouth shut. But I am tired. So tired. Maybe it would be better if whatever is in that syringe stops me, stops the *Y Tair*. Sampson is wrong about one thing—I understand the danger she might bring. Am I making the right decision to protect her? Am I saving the Families at the cost of releasing destruction onto the world?

"I learned," Jason says, "that the fear of an abomination is a tool used by Iron to keep a *Y Tair* from coming into being."

"Fool. One burned down my village when I was a boy. My mother and youngest brother died." Samuel yanks up the sleeve on his right arm, displaying a patch of white skin.

My stomach clenches. I'm familiar with what leaves that kind of scar—grafted skin from what must have been a deep burn.

Jason leans toward Samuel.

Angola tenses, one hand sliding under his jacket to the back of his waistband. I doubt Jason misses the implied threat, but he doesn't flinch, his words clipped and distinct, as if he is stabbing them through Samuel's painful memories.

"Uncle, I remind you if our child is a boy, he cannot be *Y Tair*. Only a girl child could be that. He will be the first child born to our House in—as you say—a very long time. Are you willing to take that chance and kill him in the womb?"

For moments that seem to suspend time, they say nothing, staring at one another.

"I could have you exiled." Samuel finally sputters.

"You could, but then you would lose any children I might produce. Perhaps I would start my own House."

Samuel lifts a hand in dismissal. "What makes you think you can have children?"

With debonair casualness, Jason turns his own hand on edge, aimed in my direction, saying everything with the gesture—here she is, proof of my virility.

Samuel considers me for a long moment. His voice is tight. "As you say, if her spawn is female, we can handle that later."

Chapter Forty-One

The breath I exhale when Samuel Blackwell and Angola leave my hospital room becomes a short pant.

"Are you all right?" Jason asks, putting his hands on my shoulders. "You are trembling, *amore*."

Terror and its release compete with the throbbing energy that emanates from Jason. At this moment, terror has my attention.

"Are they gone?"

"Yes, gone. For now."

He takes my hand and closes his eyes, feeling, I assume, a keener jolt at the touch than I, buffered by drugs and pain. I have just brushed the blade edge of death for the second time in a matter of days, yet, absurdly, what rushes into my mind is Hobart and Alice sitting at either end of her kitchen table, and Alice saying, *"It's difficult to reach anything if we're alone, but as long as someone is in the middle to pass things, we do quite nicely."*

A slightly hysterical laugh bursts from my mouth.

Jason looks confused. Even after two days sleeping in a chair and the harsh glare of the hospital room lights, he appears merely a little tousled, the unshaved cheeks just adding a rugged GQ fashion model appeal. "What—?"

"You saved my life," I say. "Why?"

"I told you—I love you."

It occurs to me that the smart thing to say at this point is, "I love you too."

"That's crazy," I say.

"It has happened before across Houses."

"That's not why it's crazy."

He's staring at me in the way that men do right before they kiss you. I admit my heart is thumping, and I've no doubt that the touch of his lips on mine would set off a cascade of hormones and chemicals that might even overwhelm the drugs in my system. But would the magic be the "true love" kind of magic in the fairy tale books, the kind that can break the spell of the evil queen? Or just the magic of whatever controls my hormones?

How would I know the difference?

He leans closer.

"Why is it crazy?" he asks in a low, husky voice. I can feel his breath on my lips.

I try to answer, but I seem to have lost my ability to speak, and once his lips touch mine, my predictions materialize. *Can you burn alive in a kiss?*

I'm not sure we could have pulled away had someone not knocked, and Jason, possibly still on alert for Samuel or Angola, turns to the door.

Alice clears her throat.

Jason straightens and steps from my side. I feel it as a withdrawal, something ripping from me, and stifle the urge to grab him and pull him back, hell, to pull him down into the hospital bed with me. My hand lifts toward him until a stab of pain from my shoulder reminds me I'm in a hospital for a reason.

Jason takes another step back. He looks disoriented. Part of me wants to laugh in satisfaction. I doubt a kiss has ever disoriented Jason Blackwell before.

"I thought you might want a report on Becca," Alice says in her adopted Southern accent.

I can't imagine Jason would ever recognize Alice. In addition to the accent, red hair, and brown contacts that cover her witch-green eyes, her entire posture is different, her shoulders slightly hunched. If I didn't know she was the same person as the crisp, silver-haired, perfect-posture-at-all-times woman with an endearing British accent that is my great aunt, I would never make the connection.

"It's Irene," she says, presumably to keep me from slipping up and calling her Alice.

"Becca?" I ask. Saying her name sobers me from the fireworks kiss.

"She's out of surgery and in recovery, doing well."

I take a deep breath of relief. "Thank you for being with her." I glance at Jason. "Can we have a few minutes alone, please?"

"I'll be in the hall," he says, and leaves us.

Alice closes the distance to my bedside and leans close. She takes my hand.

"Amber?" I ask.

With a professional firmness, she lays a hand on my belly, and I hold my breath until she smiles.

"Amber is still doing just fine," she whispers. "I've checked on her several times."

"That's what the doctor said, but I am more relieved to hear it from you." Then I notice the dark shadows under her eyes and how pale she is. "You've stayed at Becca's side this whole time, haven't you?"

"I had to go to the first floor periodically to reach the living-green, when the coal in my purse petered out, but other than that and checking on you and your partner on occasion, yes." Her brows furrow in apology. "You seemed stable, and I can't heal you or Tracey. Becca needed everything I could muster to keep her alive."

I squeeze her hand. "You made the right choice."

"But I was so worried about you." She keeps her voice pitched low, but she's slipped back into her native British accent, a sign of her exhaustion.

"I'll be okay. You've got to have some rest. Why don't you go home and sleep?"

"How can I sleep?"

"You're completely drained. Go home."

"What if something happens while I am gone?"

"Alice," I whisper, "it doesn't take a vision to see you'll collapse if you don't get some sleep. And then you won't be able to do anything."

"But I can't protect you."

I smile. "I don't think you could protect a fly at the moment." Better not to tell her of my brush with Samuel and Angola right now. "Besides, I don't think they have any more interest in Becca. I was the real target, and Jason is staying with me."

For a moment, color rushes back into her face. "That is the fox guarding the henhouse!" Her words are a fierce hiss.

"But the fox wants me alive, and that will have to do for now."

The moment of anger sustaining her passes, and she looks even more drained.

"Please go home."

"All right." Her shoulders slump more than her disguise calls for. "But here," she takes my purse out of a bag. "I took custody of it when they brought you in."

The leather looks like a big dog chewed on it, but a quick check assures me my gun is still inside, as well as my phone and a charger cord. "Thank you. What about the rose-stone?"

"Not to worry. They let me have custody of that too, and I put it on Becca as soon as they brought her back from surgery."

I tuck my purse beside me under the covers, feeling better. If Uncle Sam decides to return and stab me with a syringe, he'll have to do it with a couple of holes in him.

Alice looks as if she is going to collapse. "Do you think you can make it home?"

"Truthfully, no, but I can call a taxi or that Uber thing. Becca showed me how last week when my car was in the shop, and I wanted to go to my yoga class."

"That's smarter. Promise you will not try to drive yourself."

"I promise."

"A hot shower, food, and sleep, then you can come back and help Becca."

"Oh, that sounds lovely."

"I wish I could go with you" I eye the walls and the tubes that crawl like tentacles from my skin.

"They say you have fractured ribs, a mild concussion, a torn muscle in your shoulder and some internal bruising. It's a good thing we heal quickly and that your spleen was removed when you were in that car accident last year, or it would have probably ruptured like Becca's."

"Her spleen ruptured?"

"Yes. She had severe internal bleeding, one of the most difficult things to try to heal. It kept breaking through, but I was able to stabilize her enough for surgery."

"She would have died without you."

"Yes."

I grab her hand. "Thank you."

She straightens her shoulders. "I care about her too, you know."

"Don't get huffy. What about Tracey?"

"He had a serious concussion and some bruises. If he wasn't a House man, he would probably be dead. I'm sure he did his best to shield you and Becca."

"Was anyone else hurt?" I'm embarrassed not to have asked this before.

"I don't think so, other than superficial injuries. At least that's the word down in the ER."

I raise my eyebrows at her.

"Well, that is the quickest way to the first floor from here. And if you just walk as if you belong, no one asks questions. I just happened to overhear a pair of nurses. It seems that is all the entire city is talking about."

"Great. If the police discover who it was, it could be an even bigger mess."

"It was Iron, was it not?"

Nothing I say would dissuade her from believing that, so I just nod. "I think so."

"And you think the power of the magic between you and that Iron man is enough to break the bonds of House that bind him?"

"Jason. His name is Jason."

She sniffs.

"I don't know," I admit. Then I pull the only trick I think will work. "But I'm really tired myself, so please go home."

She sets her mouth.

"And be nice to Jason so he doesn't suspect you're a witch."

That gets me a tiny smile. We both remember how much I protested the term "witch" when she first tried to tell me who and what I was.

She leans over and gives me a peck on the forehead. "And don't think I didn't see that Iron man taking advantage of you. He should recognize that your resistance is compromised. He's no gentleman."

"I can handle him."

She sniffs again.

"What I can't handle," I say, "is you passing out and hitting your head and joining the three of us here."

"Very well. I shall leave you in the care of the devil, but only for a while."

Chapter Forty-Two

The next time I open my eyes, Alice has returned. I'm suspicious that she never went home and rested, but she looks much better, so she must have gotten some sleep. We are alone in the hospital room.

"Becca is doing well," she says, answering the question before I can ask it.

"And Tracey?"

"He's fussing about getting up, now that he is awake."

"He's been unconscious all this time?"

"Actually, they induced a coma and kept his body temperature down."

"That sounds bad."

"It's the appropriate treatment for a brain trauma. The cold decreases the possibility of swelling and lets the brain rest. Any exertion could quicken brain damage."

"Brain damage? He has brain damage?" I am numb, unable to even begin to process this possibility.

"He recovered very quickly, of course. The doctors are amazed. He says to tell you not to worry, that he has a hard head."

I let out a long breath. "He does."

"I checked you again while you slept. Amber is fine, and your ribs are already knitted."

I raise up on my elbows and do some experimental shifting. "Yes, much better."

Alice opens her purse and brings out a small cloth bag decorated with flowers. "I brought you a little something. This should make you feel better and help even more. Soft tissue is more difficult, because the healing process involves inflammation."

I eye the bag. "What is it?"

Without answering, she presses it into my hand. There's no mystery now what is inside. Lumps of coal. I suck the living-green from it like a diver starving for air. Warm energy courses through me.

"Thank you. I haven't been able to draw any since I woke up."

"You're still so weak, and we are on the fifth floor."

"Where is Jason?" I ask.

"I convinced him to take a break to get something to eat."

Though we are alone, she keeps her Southern accent for the benefit of any staff that might pop in.

"I want to go see Becca and Tracey."

She frowns. "Are you ready for that? Maybe you are pushing yourself—"

"I want to see them." I feel my mouth set into a stubborn line.

"I know that look." With a sigh, she helps me move the stand holding my tubes into position and adjusts the hospital gown to make sure my bottom is not exposed. At my direction, she puts the purse strap across my chest. The shoulder is better, but still sore. My steps are shaky, but as I shuffle forward, I feel a little surer of myself. My first stop is the bathroom, and then we head out. A nurse comes in just as we are exiting.

"Oh," she says, surprised. "You're up."

"Going for a walk."

"That's great. Don't push yourself this first time. I'll get your vitals later."

"Yes ma'am, but I want this needle out of my arm."

Samuel may have agreed to keep me alive, but I don't trust him or Angola. One touch from either and a nurse could come in and finish the job Samuel was about to do.

"I can't take your needle out without an okay."

"Well," I say, "find someone who can or when I get back, I'll just pull it out myself."

She studies my face for a moment. "I'll see what I can do."

"Thank you."

Our progress down the hall is slow. Alice has my hand tucked under her arm. I lean on her. At age one hundred and I forget what exactly, she is amazingly solid. My purse hangs from my other shoulder. I'm not about to be separated from my gun or the little flowered bag.

Becca is our first stop. When I see her, I tell myself she's an albino; she always looks pale.

Her eyes open, blink, and then focus. Without her contact lenses, the light turns them pink for a moment, and then they are back to the lightest shade of blue possible, almost clear.

"Hey," I say, reaching down and pouring the remainder of energy from the bag of coal into the rose-stone hidden under her hospital gown.

"Rose. I'm so glad you're really okay."

"Same."

"I thought Al—I mean, Irene, was just saying that to keep me calm. But you look good. If anyone can be said to look good in this nasty faded hospital gown."

Becca talking about fashion—all is right with the world.

"What happened?" she asks.

"A bomb went off."

"Well duh, but why? Was it a terrorist?"

"It most certainly was," Alice says.

"At Railroad Park?"

I open my mouth, but nothing comes out. How do I tell her that her "boyfriend" set us all up? Set *her* up?

"Does Jon know what happened?" she asks.

"The whole city knows," Alice says. "In fact, it was on the national news."

Becca frowns. "I don't understand why he hasn't come by."

That gets to me. She is going to be miserable either way, but at least telling her will be quick. Painful, but better than wondering every day why she's been abandoned.

"He's hurt, isn't he?" she asks before I have a chance to figure out how to tell her. "Why else would he not come?"

I clear my throat.

"Or is he dead?"

"Becca—"

"You have to tell me."

The pulse line on her monitor is rising.

"No," I say. "He's not dead."

"How can you be sure?"

"Because I saw him."

"He came? While I was unconscious?" Her tone is now hopeful.

I look to Alice. She can heal wounds, but not hearts. I will find no help there.

"No, he didn't come to see you." I make myself meet her eager gaze.

"I don't understand."

Without makeup, her brows are the same pale white as her hair. They dive into a puzzled "V."

"Becca, Jon was not who you thought he was."

"What do you mean? You never got to meet him."

"I already knew him."

Shadows pool in her clear eyes. Her voice turns brittle. "How do you know him?"

"Not like that. And I didn't know I knew him. I just figured it out when we were standing on the bridge."

"You're not making any sense."

"Just—think about it. All the places in the city we could meet him, and he chose a spot that is over water."

"I told you, that's our special place where—"

"—I remember. But water blocks magic."

She stares at me. "You think *Jon* put a bomb under the bridge? That's crazy."

"I think Angola did."

"That makes no sense—wait. Are you saying you think Jon and Angola are the same person?"

I nod, miserable.

"I don't believe it." She curls her lips over her teeth, something she does when she's in distress.

Taking a deep breath, I manage to say the rest. "Angola came to my hospital room right after we got here. He's cut off his ponytail and grown a little goatee beard."

Becca goes still, not even blinking. Alice, too, has her full attention on me. I haven't had a chance to tell her what happened either. I didn't want her freaking out that House of Iron came into my room, afraid she would refuse to leave me and get the rest she'd needed so badly.

"Why?" Becca asks in almost a whisper.

Does she mean why did he come to my room or is her "why?" just a wounded cry?

"He came with Samuel Blackwell, who brought a syringe of poison."

She gasps. Alice's eyes widen with horror.

"He didn't intend to let me or my baby live," I say.

"But—what did you do?" Becca asks, torn from her personal pain by fear for me.

"I didn't do anything. I could barely move at that point. Jason was there. He saved my life."

For once Alice does not disparage Jason. "How?" she asks.

"Apparently, Hobart was right, and children are a rare commodity in the Houses."

"Without House of Rose, that's true," she says.

"Jason told Samuel that the child was his and convinced him that if it was a boy, he should let him live to add to Iron's family stockpile."

"But it's not a boy," Alice says. "I'm certain."

"Jon has a goatee," Becca says, her mind on a different track. "And a mustache that meets it."

I give a quick nod, giving her time to accept it.

It doesn't take her long. Her eyes glisten. "He . . . he set it up from the beginning—that restaurant. It's right across the street from my job. He knew I'd go there eventually." She looks up at me, tears escaping. "It was never about me. He never cared at all. He just used me to try and kill you."

Chapter Forty-Three

I feel physically sick for Becca. The rose-stone protects her from magic, but not a shattered heart. Angola is a total, warped creep, not to mention a cold-blooded serial killer. He used her. He was willing to sacrifice her life to kill me.

By the time we get to Tracey's room, I have to sit, worn out by the walk and my anger. Hobart is there and gets up, giving me his chair. Tracey is asleep.

"I just found out you and Tracey were the victims of that bombing," he says, retreating across the room to keep distance between himself and Alice.

I nod, determined to stay civil and too tired to pick a fight.

Tracey stirs and opens his eyes, focusing on me. Bruised circles ring them. I imagine I look pretty horrible too.

"Hey," he says hoarsely.

"Hey."

"You okay?"

"Yeah."

His gaze goes to my belly. "And our—the baby? Amber?"

"She's fine. A doctor has checked us out and so has Alice."

His eyes have not left my abdomen, and I push myself out of the chair and go to his bedside, lift his hand and place it on my belly. An expression of wonder suffuses his face, his voice almost a whisper.

"I feel her!"

"Yeah, she's been testing her boundaries."

"I was so afraid—"

"Me too, but she's okay. We both are, thanks to you."

He clears his throat. "We're alive because of *you*. You figured out what was going on and got us off that bridge."

"Almost too late." I go back to the chair and sink gratefully into it.

"'Almost' is the key word. Those seconds you bought us are the only reason we're having this conversation."

"Hmm, well, you don't sound brain damaged to me. I don't want you using that as an excuse not to solve cases."

He grins. "Faraday said something along the same lines."

"She came to see you?"

"Yeah, she checked on you too. Said you were sleeping."

"She'll probably cuss us out as soon as we get back to the office."

"No doubt."

He closes his eyes for a moment and then opens them again. "How did you know we had to get off the bridge? Does your gift work over water now?"

"No, but that was the clue that triggered me wondering why Becca's boyfriend had arranged to have us standing right there. That and cinnamon."

"Cinnamon?" His brows furrow. "Maybe you're the one with brain damage."

"Becca had mentioned that her boyfriend liked cinnamon in his coffee, but I didn't put it together until I was standing on the bridge and smelled the cinnamon from her hot apple cider. Then I suddenly recalled Angola at my kitchen table with a cup of coffee that smelled of cinnamon and thinking how incongruent such a warm, comforting smell was on top of the terror I was feeling."

"Wow. That's impressive work, detective."

"If I'd put it together sooner—"

"Stop doing that."

"What?"

"That blaming yourself thing. Just stop it."

My mouth opens and then closes. I've never thought of that as a "thing" I did.

"How did you know there was a bomb?" he asks.

"I didn't. My first thought was Angola in an apartment above the park with us in his rifle sights. All I knew when I realized Becca's Jon might be Angola was that he wanted us right there, and we needed to not be there."

"Oh, Rose," Alice says. "I am so sorry."

"Sorry? You didn't have anything to do with it."

"But I did. I should have taken you away from this city when you were a child. We could have run away somewhere on the other side of the world where Iron couldn't find you."

I rub my head where a vein throbs. "I don't think there's any place safe from House of Iron. They have tentacles across the globe."

"I should have tried." Her hands twist together.

Tracey reaches for the plastic cup near his bed. "Now I see where you get that self-blaming thing. It runs in your family."

His gaze jerks over my shoulder, and I twist to see Jason in the doorway.

Hobart is instantly alert and on his feet, the ex-military cop pushing through all the years . . . and maybe lifetimes.

"Rose," Jason says. "When I didn't see you in your room, I was afraid—"

"I'm fine." I hold my palm toward him. "Please stay over there. I'm too tired to deal with overwhelming lust."

Tracey's mouth flattens, but he zeroes in on what Jason said. "What do you mean you were afraid?" Then he turns his attention to me, narrowing his eyes in a look of suspicion I know well. "Rose, what's happened that you aren't telling me?"

Jason looks to me, giving me the floor to respond.

"What?" Tracey says. "Spill it, Rose."

My instinct is not to tell him. Worrying about me will add stress he shouldn't have to deal with while he's trying to get well. But it's not fair to keep it from him. He's vulnerable up here too, and Hobart needs to be watchful.

I tell them about Samuel and Angola's visit to my room and how Jason intervened.

"That was quick thinking," Tracey says grudgingly to Jason. "Thank you."

"It was not exactly 'quick.'" Jason folds his arms over his chest. "I've been arguing with my uncle over this insanity ever since Rose convinced me my family was behind murders and attempts to kill her."

He takes another step into the room but keeps his distance from me. "The morals of my House may sometimes be questionable, but murder is beyond the pale."

Hobart is now leaning against the far wall, but the tension in his body belies the relaxed posture. "I will have someone come stay with you in your room."

"That won't be necessary," Jason says. "I'm the best protection she can have, and I will be with her."

"That's not enough," Hobart says.

"It will have to be. If my . . . relatives discover one of your family is guarding her, my entire ruse crumbles, and I assure you that is the only thing protecting her. Any nurse could walk in and put something in her IV line or give her the wrong pill or any number of things."

Tracey scowls, but says nothing.

A sudden wave of exhaustion washes over me. Trying to ignore it, I force my shoulders back and sit up. "When Angola tried to kill me at the YMCA pool last year, he told me that honor drove him. He said I would never understand." I look at Tracey. "But he said that you might."

"What do you have in common with him?" Hobart asks.

"Nothing, I hope," Tracey says and then, "except we were both Marines."

I rub an aching spot on my forehead. "On another occasion when Angola had a gun pointed at my head, he told me that when he was a prisoner in the Gulf War, Samuel saved him, walked into the enemy camp and took him out." I look at Jason.

"That," he says with a frown, "would explain Angola's loyalty to him." He crosses his arms over his chest. "I've never considered myself naïve, but all these years, what I thought was Angola's dedication to me was actually for Samuel."

"Angola made a point," I say, "to emphasize it wasn't the Marines who rescued him. Samuel did what Angola thought his buddies should have done. I'm thinking loyalty to House and to Samuel, in particular, took the place of the Marine brotherhood in his mind."

"The Marine's motto is *Semper Fi*," Tracey says grimly. "'Always faithful.' In boot camp, they break down everything you thought you were and then rebuild you as a Marine. When bullets and grenades are flying, you don't fight for ideologies or even your country. You fight for your buddies. You believe in them. Angola's brothers let him down."

I ask a question that has bothered me. "Why couldn't Angola have used House magic to manipulate a guard and get out on his own?"

"I was twenty-five before I came into my powers," Jason says. "Angola joined the Marines at eighteen or nineteen. He may not have acquired his 'abilities' yet."

That makes sense. I didn't find out I was a witch and could see bits of the future or past until I was twenty-two. Apparently magical puberty hits later than the hormonal kind.

"Okay, but I have a difficult time imagining Uncle Sam walking into an Iraqi war camp."

"Appearances can be deceiving," Jason says. "My uncle seized power after his brother died. He appears disarming. But, as you have seen, he is ruthless. And he is determined to kill you and your child if it is a girl."

None of us trust Jason enough to tell him that I am carrying a female child, not to mention one that has the blood of all three Houses and is perhaps to be the *Y Tair*. As soon as Samuel learns that, I will have a death sentence back on my head, as will my baby.

Chapter Forty-Four

I spend another restless night in the hospital, but I refuse to wait around for my baby to come and then have Samuel and Angola show up when I am even weaker than this. I can't wait around like a victim, too scared to do anything. It's time to face my demons.

Tracey and Becca are not in any shape to help. Alice has to make certain both of them stay on the road to recovery, and Hobart needs to protect Tracey. I asked him if another member of his House could stay in Becca's room. He agreed and was as good as his word. When I check on her one last time a young man who looks as if he eats nails for breakfast is sitting with her. He flashes me a bright smile.

"This is Jamal," Becca says. "You remember him?"

I do. He's House of Stone, a man Tracey trusted to watch our house when he and I were trying to track down Angola.

"He's promised to read to me," Becca says.

"That's great. Good to see you again, Jamal."

From the rosy flush on Becca's cheeks, I am thinking Jamal's attentions might be better medicine than anything the hospital or even Alice can produce.

"How are you feeling?" I ask her, moving to the clear side of the bed and reaching down to touch her chest. I made Jason take me downstairs before visiting Becca to draw the living-green myself. I can hold way more than I could get from the bag of coal Alice brought me.

She smiles at the familiar gesture. "Better. I'm over the hurt thing, by the way. Now I'm angry."

I release living-green into the rose-stone. Alice made sure Becca had the pendant back around her neck as soon as they returned her to her room after surgery.

Becca hooks a strand of cream-white hair around an ear. "Irene went home to get some rest."

"Well deserved."

"Yeah, no kidding."

I nod at Jamal. "I see that you're in good hands. I'm a little tired too, so I'm going to call it a day."

Becca's forehead wrinkles. "You've pushed yourself too hard, Rose."

"Maybe you're right. Night."

Jason had followed me to her room, but remained outside, leaning against the wall. When I pass him, he pushes off and falls in beside me, leaving distance between us as a buffer for the magic. I can still feel it, but I can manage not to jump into his arms. My lips still burn from that kiss. As always, female nurses' heads, and a couple of male ones, turn when he goes by. Even after several nights sleeping on a couch in my hospital room, he still has that power, but he ignores them.

"Every woman in here is salivating over you."

"And every man over you, although. . . ." He examines my face. "Perhaps you are not at your best."

I give a strangled laugh. "'Perhaps' is right."

"Speaking of right, Becca is."

"Right? About what?"

"That you push yourself. Not only have you survived an explosion, but you are very . . . pregnant."

"This is supposed to be news?"

"Why did we have to go downstairs and outside into the cold before you saw Becca?"

"I wanted to breathe some fresh air."

"You were pulling your magic. What does your House call it? The living-green?"

I squint at him.

"Seriously, you must rest, Rose. Using magic to keep going has a cost."

"And let you guard me?"

He looks surprised. "Yes. I won't let anyone hurt you."

As if to prove his point, when we come to the closed door of my room, he stops me. I step back. He pushes open the door, stepping inside first and checking the bathroom. I've left the closet door open, so it only requires a quick visual scan. He beckons me, and I follow him into the room.

"Just how," I ask, "do you think you will stop Angola if he decides to kill me, either before or after this baby is born?"

"I am not as incompetent as you seem to think."

I climb into my bed. "How are you planning on stopping them?"

"I don't know. I am working on it."

"Are you armed?"

"Of course."

I scrutinize him. No visible sign of a gun. "Ankle holster?"

He nods. "Yes. Now will you relax a little?"

"I can't."

"Why not?"

"I'm hungry."

"You ate dinner three hours ago."

"That was three hours ago. I'm eating for two."

"Your appetite has always amazed me."

"I want a hamburger."

"I'll see what I can get from the cafeteria."

I smile. "And chocolate-chip mint ice cream."

"I don't think they have that in the cafeteria."

"Probably not, but I really want some. You owe me that for your relatives trying to kill me."

He snorts. "I don't like leaving you that long."

I hold up my purse. "A bullet from mine is just as good as one from yours."

He hesitates.

"I can't sleep when I'm hungry."

With a sigh, he leaves.

As soon as he leaves, I am up, digging through the bag of clothes Alice brought. The FBI confiscated the scorched and torn clothes I wore to the ER, no doubt hoping to glean clues from them about the explosives used. I have a vague memory of talking to a special agent in the ER. But the feds are as helpless as the police against the magic of House of Iron. Best case, if anyone got close enough to Angola or Samuel, all thoughts of pursuit would be directed elsewhere. Eventually, they would recall, but it would be too late. Worst case—I don't even want to go there.

Happy to be in my jeans, an oversized sweatshirt, and jacket, I am out the door less than five minutes later.

My night nurse looks up from the desk. The staff has seen me walking around with my purse and a bathrobe Alice brought me, but not in clothes. "Where's the smoking deck?" I ask.

"You're a smoker?"

I shrug and try to look guilty.

"We don't really have one." She looks down the hall to make sure no one can overhear her. "But I'll tell you where I go if you don't rat on me."

She gives me directions, and I head that way. Around the corner, I call for a taxi on my cell and take the stairs to avoid the possibility of the elevator door opening on the cafeteria floor and a chance meeting with Jason.

Chapter Forty-Five

As I descend the hospital stairs, Amber does a kick-twist combo I've never felt before. Panic stabs me. What if she decides to be born while I'm trying to kill people?

My hand grips the banister, and I stop. *I don't want to kill anyone. I'm not a murderer.*

Should I go to an ATM, head to the airport and get on a plane as far away as I can afford? *Run.*

I'm frozen on the steps of the stairwell for several long moments considering this strategy. It didn't occur to me while I was thinking about what to do. Maybe that's because running is not in my DNA. But this is about Amber. It's my responsibility to protect her. Can we disappear? Alice sent me away all those years ago, and I had a happy childhood, if you don't count scarcity of friends and the isolation of always being the new kid in town. I could do the same, hide Amber, let her grow up like a normal child, if anything about being a *Y Tair* can be normal. I don't have a clue what that will entail.

But I don't think I can pull off faking my death like Alice did. She had a coconspirator at the medical examiner's office and a house full of actually dead people—my family—as cover. Even so, Alice's attempt to fake my death only worked for a while. They figured it out. Alice thought she'd hidden me, but she made one tiny mistake, and they were watching.

When House of Iron first realized I hadn't been killed in that fire, they let Alice live to be custodian of the rose-stone so I would return to Birmingham. They didn't want me wandering around the world outside their control, having children, rebuilding House of Rose.

The fact is that there is nowhere to run. The same conclusion Alice must have come to when I was a child. If she and I had just "disappeared," they would have followed us. Iron's fingers are all over the world, and their power makes any information trail, like taking a plane, easily obtainable. Jason has told me as much. I could ask for protection with House of Stone, but Amber and I could never leave the prison of that protection. Besides, Angola is apparently an explosives expert. If I hole up at Hobart's or that cabin in the woods I asked for, I would put others at risk. House of Stone can't protect me, and Alice can't. I would simply be putting her in harm's way too.

The circle of my reasoning swings back to the place it started. There is only one answer—if Angola and Samuel are dead, we will be safe. I am the only one who can do it. And I have to do it before I am incapacitated and vulnerable giving birth. If I don't, Amber will not have a chance at life. My baby has only me.

I take a deep breath, refusing to think about it anymore. The time for thinking is over. I must act. The words of Yoda, the Jedi from Star Wars, settles into my mind. *Do. Or do not. There is no try.*

On shaky legs, I descend the stairs and walk as quickly as I can without appearing like a fugitive, down the hallway and into the women's wing section of the hospital, again to avoid a possible encounter with Jason. The taxi I called for is waiting.

I get out at Railroad Park. I planned to go straight to where I parked my car, but I'm drawn to the lake. The walkway over the water is gone. Much of the debris has been cleared away. Construction tape and cones have replaced what was surely crime scene tape. The ice-skating rink is also gone. The beautiful waterfall is no more.

I stare at the hole in the landscape.

Becca, Tracey, Amber and I almost died there.

People of all stripes are still enjoying the park, even on a winter day, walking, playing on the winter grass, and buying hot drinks. A little spark of pride ignites. Birmingham has a history of enduring. Its people will not be cowed.

I will not be cowed either. Deliberately, I turn my back on what is broken and go to where I parked my car the night I met Becca and Tracey and waited for Becca's supposed boyfriend. Thankfully, the car hasn't been towed. I stick the parking ticket in the glove box. Next stop is home. Alice says she put food and water out for Angel, but I want to see my cat. Who would have ever believed I would need a cat?

When I walk up the front steps, my heart drops. No Angel. But when I push the door open, she darts out of nowhere between my legs and into the living room. How do cats hide in plain sight? I close the door and fall onto the sofa. My eyes close. Just for a minute. . . .

Angel's paws kneading my side wakes me. I glance at the clock. Twenty minutes have passed! I can't afford to do that. Jason is probably back at the hospital room with my hamburger and ice cream soon and discovered I'm not in Becca's room or Tracey's. He will figure out what I am doing, and this will be his first stop. And I only have about an hour left of daylight. I can't afford to collapse.

I take a moment anyway to stroke Angel. "I have to go again. I'm sorry, but I'll leave your window open."

Angel meows. It is a demanding, plaintive sound that only a cat can produce. There is no doubt what she wants. Alice has laid out dry cat food, but Angel is a tuna fish girl. I grab a can from the stack I keep in the cabinet while she twines figure eights through my legs and *meows*. This is a different sound, more anticipation than complaint. Not only do I need my cat, I now speak cat.

She wastes no time when I put it into her dish. While she is chowing down, I rinse out her water bowl and push the kitchen window open enough for her to get in and out, wincing at the stab of pain in my shoulder. Alice has a key to the house. If she comes by, she will notice the open window and know I've been here.

I glance longingly at the shower, but I don't have time now and just tape my handcuff keys to the front and back elastic bands of my underwear, a daily habit since my last encounter with Angola. You never know when you might need a handcuff key. In the bathroom, I grab the mouthwash to ease the wicked taste in my mouth. Does fear have a taste?

The image in the mirror has a face still swollen and purple above her right cheekbone; the same eye is red with blood. But besides the pasty white skin everywhere else, she's fine. She's good. She's ready to take on Angola.

The image in the mirror doesn't move, but I could swear it said I was a lousy liar.

Chapter Forty-Six

I take a moment to watch my cat as she devours her tuna fish. "Aunt Alice left a big bowl of cat food on the front porch. I'll be back as soon as I can." I take a deep breath. "I'm going hunting." A cat would understand that, right? I lean down to stroke her, which doesn't distract her from the consumption of tuna fish, but a soft vibration warms my hand as she arches her back into it.

Hunting. The word echoes in my head as I strap on an ankle knife and tuck it into my boot. Messages have popped up on my cell phone, one from Becca and three from Jason. I ignore them, keeping the phone setting on vibrate and sticking it into my back pocket. The last thing I do is pull on my patrol utility belt. I have to adjust it and it rides more on my hips, under my belly, than on my waist. It holds my holster, an extra ammunition magazine, a flashlight, and a pair of handcuffs. Retrieving my gun from my purse, I slide it into the holster. It is not the best weapon for an assassination, but it's all I have.

At the door, Angel, finished with her food, lifts onto her back paws, resting her front ones on my leg, and bumps her nose against my extended hand—her way of reminding me I belong to her. Ordinarily, I would walk the few blocks from my house to the back entrance of the Vulcan Trail at the bottom of Red Mountain, but my daylight is disappearing fast, and I have to conserve my strength. I was not exactly released from the hospital.

I park the car a half block from my destination and pull on gloves and jacket. The sleeves are rolled. To find a jacket that would cover my belly, I had to go up a two sizes, and without the roll, the sleeves hang down past my fingertips.

For a moment, I stand facing the slope ahead. The wood-edged path leads to the end of the Vulcan Trail that runs along the north side of Red Mountain. This is either beyond stupid and ends up a fruitless endeavor or beyond stupid and ends up in tragedy. The odds of success are small, probably minuscule, but fortunately, I have no way to calculate them. I would be happier to have Tracey beside me, but I can't wait for him to get well. I have to do this before I go into labor, which means now, and therefore, I have to do it alone.

Enough self-talk. I start up the hill and very shortly have left the Southside residential neighborhood for the woods. Old hardwood trees, barren of leaves, reach for the sky on either side. Scattered bits of black iron ore lay exposed along the sides of the trail, the dribbling remains of long-ago mining, I assume, blasted from the mountain by dynamite. Overhead, the sky hangs low and dark, heavy with rain or snow. The temperature feels right at that iffy point. I reach for the living-green, for the comfort of its presence and for the energy. This mountain's underground riches are primarily iron ore, but coal is nearby, close enough to draw.

The living-green I draw gives me enough strength to reach a point about halfway to the endpoint of Vulcan Trail. I lean against a tree, afraid to sit on the steep slope. Getting up from a seated position on the ground with the weight of Amber and my gun belt would be tricky. Can't risk a fall. At this rate, it is going to take much of the day to reach my goal. Spying a broken branch, I grab it, stripping off the small limbs for a staff. It holds, and it helps, but like a caffeine junky, I have to pull more of the living-green just for the energy to keep going.

At the trailhead, I veer off, taking the older path behind the Vulcan Trail. About twenty minutes in, I sit on a fallen log at the trail's edge for another break. My back is aching with a fierce intensity. Without my conscious draw, living-green courses on its own through me, freezing me in time. Wavering gray and black shadows patina the world. To say I'm getting used to this would be a lie. My heart ceases to beat. I feel wedged, squeezed—between universes? Between time?

From a higher point on the trail, a shadow-man walks backward down the path, a dark and round object tucked under his left arm. A few feet before he reaches me, he puts the round object, now identifiable as a motorcycle helmet, on his head, then continues backward to the edge of the trail across from me and into the woods about ten feet near a large rotten stump. He moves aside several dead pine branches, reaches down and pulls a motorcycle upright. It's impossible to tell the color, but it is dark, possibly black. Backing it out of the brush onto the trail, he mounts, turns the key, and rides the cycle backwards down the trail I just walked.

When the vision releases me, I shiver, pulling my jacket collar up and pressing my fingers against my skull, an unsuccessful attempt to counter the headache left in the vision's wake. I suspect I'm shivering for a reason other than being cold. Faces are difficult to recognize in the shadow world, and I never saw his, but I didn't need to. I would recognize Angola anywhere, if nothing else by his tight, controlled walk.

What I just saw happened in the past and this time of year, judging from the leafless trees, but was it years in the past or fifteen minutes ago?

Nine months ago, after we got a warrant for Angola's arrest, Tracey and I searched House of Iron's mansion. Twice. We found nothing. I couldn't tell the officers with us that there was a secret door at the end of one of the basement corridors leading into a reinforced old tunnel, or that the tunnel ended up in an abandoned mine entrance hidden on the side of this mountain, the one that is not too far above me now. But Tracey and I checked that too and came up with nothing.

For weeks, we staked out the house, rotating with other officers on the Fugitive Detail. Those officers had orders not to approach him, but to call us no matter what time of night it was. Not once did anyone see Angola stepping foot onto the property. Either he was not there, or he had some other way into and out of the house.

That hunch was on target. Angola is entering the house through the tunnel, a long-distance route, to be sure, but one safe from surveillance eyes. He could come up the back road from Southside or he could take a more circuitous route down the Vulcan Trail from 20th Street and cut a sharp left when it ends.

I had a lot of time to think about it, lying in that hospital bed, and I believe he must be coming and going through the old mine entrance and tunnel. What I have just seen confirms it. Since time flowed backward in the vision, it means I was witnessing the past. If it was a recent past, Angola is just ahead of me. That gives me an advantage, however slight. I know where he is, but he doesn't know that I am on his trail.

In my mind, I leap up off the log to follow him. In reality, it takes a kind of rolling maneuver, aided by the staff, to keep my displaced center of gravity over my legs. The duty belt just adds to the difficulty. I'm an off-balance, walking incubator. God, I will be glad to have my body back!

Chapter Forty-Seven

Winter has made trekking through the woods a much easier task, but brambles do not shed their thorns, and I am grateful for the thick denim of my jeans. The place I'm seeking lies off the trail. The brush, even denuded of most of the leaves, covers the entrance to the mine from casual sight. Perhaps Vulcan, looming somewhere overhead, can see it, but I can't. If it were not for the vague pull of massive amounts of iron, I would never find it again. But I follow that pull until it becomes a discernible tingle in my feet. I wonder if Amber can feel it too.

When the sensation starts up my legs, I know I'm close. What if Angola is aware I'm following him? I've not exactly been quiet, cracking branches and cursing at the embrace of thorns. What if he is waiting for me inside the cave entrance?

I slip my gun from the holster, the wooden stock and weight a comfort in my hand, a familiar hard steel against my fear. I hold it close to my body, aimed ahead, and try to place my feet where there are no leaves to crunch or twigs to snap, but it is impossible. The ground is dry and frozen. A bloated gray sky hovers overhead. Chance of snow. Kids will be hoping for the rare white Christmas. Snow might soften my footfalls, but I can't sit out here and wait for it.

I swallow and move forward, catching sight of a familiar tangle of vines and brambles that shield the mine entrance from the casual eye. Red Mountain is riddled with old mines where men chipped and hauled away pieces of its heavy seams of iron ore.

The first time I stumbled upon the entrance, a pull on my Iron blood drew me to it. The second time, Becca and I came seeking answers, and I had a vision of Theophalus Blackwell from two decades ago—the night he had killed my family and burned down our house. He had seemingly stepped out of the inside wall of the mine entrance.

Trying to lessen my breathing, I stop just to the side of the opening, listening for the almost imperceptible clues of an occupied space. I pick up no sound or sign that Angola or anything else is in there, but I move with caution. Angola is a trained Marine who doesn't hesitate to kill. He will understand why I am here, why the hunted is hunting.

Shifting aside the thick tangle of leafless vines, I let the subdued afternoon light into the dark mine entrance and give my eyes time to adjust, aware that a rattler or copperhead might be wintering in a hole inside, curled and sleepy, almost as dangerous as Angola. Nothing moves, though it's possible the boulder-sized rock that must have fallen from the roof long ago could hide a crouching person. I step inside and work my way slowly around it, my nerves on a trigger.

Nothing.

My knees buckle and I lean against the stone rock, taking deep breaths and letting my body recover from its exertions. I can still pull living-green, but a bomb, a steep path, and being very pregnant takes a bit out of one.

What in the hell am I doing?

A bubble of hysterical laughter threatens, but I strangle it back. Angola could be close by. I lay the gun in my lap and contemplate the solid wall before me. Even knowing there is a door there, my eye can't find its edges. Behind it is a damp corridor that leads, eventually, to another fake door in the basement of House of Iron. That is my plan, such as it is—to enter the basement and hide in one of the rooms there until the wee hours of night. Then I simply go up the stairs. I have done that before. I know the quiet of that house with only the steady ticks of a grandfather clock. I know where Jason sleeps and where his Aunt Stefanie's bedroom lies. One of the other rooms on that floor must be Samuel's. I can get him to tell me where Angola's lair is before I shoot him. *I can shoot him, can't I?* I banish that. I have to or I will die, and Amber will die. I will do what I have to do to protect her.

But to get to the house, I must go past the grotto where Theophalus Blackwell held me prisoner, torturing me with a modified electric prod. He wanted the rose-stone. He wanted to eradicate House of Rose.

I remind myself he is dead. But that is no comfort, as his brother, Samuel Blackwell, wants the same thing—the assurance that the power of House of Iron will never be challenged, that a *Y-Tair* will never arise. That my daughter, my Amber, will never live.

Here, in the mine entrance, the presence of iron is a sensation in my body, but once I am in the mine itself, iron will be so strong, I won't be able to reach around it for the living-green. This is the last fueling stop before the desert.

Closing my eyes, I send my senses down into the earth in a zigzagging course around seams of iron ore, seeking the snippets of coal I can reach and pulling its energy like a near-drowning man sucks air into his lungs. The flush of living-green shoots up from my legs through the rest of me, even into my fingers. It feels wonderful. I don't want to stop. Would it keep me alive if I just sat here and drank the living-green? Or am I just using it as an excuse to delay doing what I must do, what I came here to do?

Reluctantly, I stop pulling. I feel light with energy. I can hold it for a while, far longer than Alice can, which is why she had to trek up and down in the hospital to save Becca.

Becca and Alice will have figured out by now that I left the hospital. They will be furious and worried, as will Tracey, but it is my responsibility to do this. I may not be successful. I may die. Amber may die. But at least it won't be because I sat around on my butt waiting to be a victim.

I push off the rock boulder supporting me, the aches in my back and feet drowned in the temporary glow of the living-green. Then I turn and face the wall with the hidden door. I know which stone I have to pull to open it.

Chapter Forty-Eight

I pull on a protruding stone in the mine's wall, and a section of the wall swings out easily and quietly, just as it did when Becca and I found it. Flashlight in one hand and gun in the other, I step into the damp tunnel. Behind me, the door swings closed on its own with a *snicking* sound.

With my next step, lights blink on, triggered, I assume, by a motion detector. That is new. In their cool glare, the red rock and clay walls gleam, slick with moisture. I slide the unneeded flashlight into its holder on my utility belt.

The sensation of descent is subtle, but the iron seam that the mine tunnel slices through is thick and abruptly cuts off my connection with the living-green. A prickly sensation grows along the slope of my spine. I feel watched, but I don't see any cameras. Despite the cool temperature, my hands grow sweaty, and I pass the gun to my left hand to wipe the right against my jeans.

Down, down into the black maw of Iron. Flashes of the past— Becca seems to be behind me, swatting at unseen spiders hanging from unseen webs. Twice I whirl to catch the presence I am certain is really there, masquerading as a memory.

But there is nothing. No one following. No companion, other than my own fear breathing onto the back of my neck. *I can still go back.* I want to stay huddled under the covers, because somehow it is safer there than looking under the bed where the monsters lurk.

Stop it. Just keep walking.

I do. One step after another, losing all sense of time. I check my cell phone, which has no signal but still tracks the time. It's surprising that almost an hour has gone by. At some point, the tunnel levels out, although I can't pinpoint when it happened. Another sensation grows. One I will never forget. I don't want to think about it, but not thinking about it is an impossible task. The image it provokes slithers into my mind—a silvery-gray rock carved into a chair. It is solid iron, and it pulls me toward it.

I have no doubt when I have come to the section of wall behind which it hides. The door itself, like the one at the mine entrance, is not visible when closed, made of the same rock and stone as the wall. But this time, it is slightly ajar. I stop. My body is a hollow drum filled with heartbeats. Inside is a room with the iron chair where I was shackled for days without food or water, where I was tortured with an electric prod that knotted and twisted every muscle in my body into spasms of unending agony. I remember wanting to die, to slide away from the pain and misery into cool darkness. It was light that brought the pain, light that brought Theophalus.

I don't have to open that door. I am searching for Angola. I can't imagine he would be in an empty dark room sitting on a chair. But the door is already open. I have to look. I have come too far not to make sure, and I know better than to move beyond an uncleared room.

A phrase taken from medieval maps warning of uncharted areas comes to mind: *Here be dragons.*

The dragons are just my memories of what happened in there, but they are as palpable as real dragons. Every nerve in my body warns against stepping foot inside.

It's just a chair in a room.

My sweaty hand trembles over the embedded stone that will widen the gap of the door. I press my gun hand against my hip to steady it. The throb of my pulse is so hard I can feel it in my lips.

Abruptly, I push the door, lifting my gun to face whatever is inside.

Light stabs the room. It is just as I remembered it, except the stench is only in my mind. It's empty, save for the iron formed into a chair in the room's center. I step inside.

Drawn to the chair, I move forward and holster my gun. No matter what fears ricochet in my mind, a hunk of iron is not going to succumb to a bullet. Power thrums around it. Months ago, sitting there as Theophalus Blackwell's prisoner, I opened the conduit to draw on iron's magic, mixing it with the carbon wrenched from the carbon steel handcuffs that held me and creating an inferno that killed two people.

I stand before it, my pulse now a muted staccato, my hand reaching out of its own volition.

Nothing happens. I draw a little iron magic into me, but even this solid block of iron doesn't feed me energy like the living-green. Perhaps because only a quarter of my blood is House Iron, or perhaps because I am a witch and a woman, not a warlock.

"It's difficult not to sit there, isn't it?" asks a familiar voice.

I whirl, hand going to my holstered gun.

"That, as well, I do not advise," Angola says, a semi-automatic in his hand aimed at me, finger on the trigger. He stands in a different threshold than the one I just crossed, a doorway that had appeared as a rough stone-and-dirt wall just a moment ago. Behind him is a lit room.

"I left you in a hospital bed," he says. "I wasn't expecting to see you so soon. You keep surprising me, Rose Brighton."

My mouth is dry. I feel empty. I have failed.

"You do look pale, however. I think you'd best come in and lie down."

I don't move.

"Don't be difficult." The gun in his hand adjusts slightly, followed by an almost imperceptible squeeze of his finger on the trigger.

An explosion of sound, magnified by the rocky walls, vibrates my chest. A puff of dust rises at my feet.

"The next one goes directly into your heart."

"You would kill the baby. Samuel wants it alive." I can't believe I'm talking calmly, rationally to a crazy man.

Without altering the aim of the gun, he leans sideways and pulls a large hunting knife from his boot. "I said I would put a bullet in your heart. I don't miss. I've killed animals to eat. I am skilled at slitting one open."

I shiver. He is capable of doing that. And then when he sees Amber is a girl-child, he will cut her tiny throat just as quickly and professionally.

"Now, remove your gun belt slowly and leave it on the throne. You make any move to touch anything except leather and I will shoot."

I follow his instructions, exhaustion making me dizzy. As I approach him, he steps aside, careful not to let me too close. A professional.

Not that I have the strength to offer a threat. I doubt I could make the kind of conflagration that killed Theophalus Blackwell, even if I could draw carbon through the mass of iron around me, which I can't. There's steel in my gun, but it's too hard to wrench chemically bonded carbon atoms without touching it, and I have no doubt I would be dead before I could do that. If he weren't a member of a House, I could suck the carbon from his body and kill him where he stands. But he is House of Iron, and my magic can't affect him any more than his can affect me. I step inside, and he pushes the door shut with his foot.

Chapter Forty-Nine

Perhaps to make up for the darkness surrounding us, the spacious room is well lit, illuminating a bed made with sharp military square corners, a nightstand, a chest of drawers, and a desk. I've never understood why people make a bed they are just going to mess up again. One wall has a two-by-two-foot safe embedded into it. Several potted plants hang from nails driven into the red clay between the rocks in the walls. A tropical-looking palm grows in a large barrel-sized pot.

"I wouldn't have pegged you as a plant guy," I say.

He shrugs. "Takes away the taste of the desert."

Before I can respond, a strange, buzzing noise distracts me. Taking a step toward the chair, I shake my head to dislodge the static, but it only grows louder. My legs buckle. Vaguely, I'm aware of Angola catching me and cradling me in his arms. *Not right. He's the bad guy.*

My next visual input is the grid of heavy wooden beams supporting rock and stone. I blink, trying to orient myself, and realize I am lying on my back, so my view must be of a ceiling. This is not the hospital ceiling. Nor is it the ceiling of my room. I turn my head to see Angola sitting in a chair watching me. Memory returns. The only thing I can't remember is why on earth I thought coming after him in his own lair was a good idea.

"You are an interesting woman."

I blink again to bring him into focus. Unless he has his gun stuck in the waistline of his pants at his back, he appears unarmed, but my thoughts are still too woolly to evaluate my options. I lick dry lips. "Water?"

He stands. "I wouldn't try to get up. I think you must have been using your 'living-green' to make it this far."

"I wouldn't have needed to if you hadn't tried to blow me up."

A twitch of his lips. "But I didn't succeed at that, did I? Or at my other attempts to kill you."

I try to get up, sitting and swinging my legs over the edge of the bed. Neither movement was a good idea. The room spins, and I lay promptly back down on my side, gripping the cover to keep from sliding off as the world tilts sideways.

"Stubborn," Angola says. "Not a surprise. A weakness that is a strength."

I concentrate on not fainting and wishing away the nausea.

When he brings the water, I'm not able to sit up to drink it, but the cool cloth he puts on my forehead helps.

"You think me a monster," he says.

"Aren't you?" I mutter.

He is silent.

I close my eyes. If he kills me, he kills me. There is nothing I can do at the moment, except vomit on him. But the nausea and spinning eases.

"Relying on outside energy sources only works temporarily," he says. "Then you suffer the consequences."

He sounds as if he speaks from personal knowledge. I wonder if there are any iron deposits under the Iraq desert and if he drew on them to survive when he was wounded and alone there, but then I remember that Jason said he probably hadn't yet come into his powers when he was assigned there.

Tentatively, I prop on my elbow and grope for the glass he placed on the nightstand. Miraculously, it comes to me. I study the fingers wrapped around it. Although the nails are clipped and clean, they are not a dandy's fingers. Calloused, a nest of scars on his right hand. From the torture when he was a prisoner? Angola's other hand supports my shoulder to steady me. *How do you kill a man who brings you water?*

I shove away the thought. I have to kill him. My daughter's life is at stake. There is a knife in my boot. My left hand crawls down my thigh toward that goal before I realize my boots have been removed. Exhaustion sweeps over me like a desert wind. Eyelids close over my dry, gritty eyes, shutting out the light. My boots may be gone, but Angola has one in his.

Tomorrow, I will get it. I will kill him tomorrow....

When I wake, I wonder if it is tomorrow or the same day. How does one tell underground? Angola is not in the room. I sit up tentatively, but the dizziness and nausea seem to have abated. A tray with one of those circular metal covers used in hotels for room service sits on the desk. My cell phone is in plain sight on the nightstand. I snatch it, frowning at the "No service" notice. No surprise, but I try a text anyway and receive a "Not sent" message. Better to turn it off and save the battery.

No calls for help and no Internet, unless the room has a wireless connection somewhere. I check that with my phone. Dead end. I stand on wobbly legs, intent on escaping, but my body demands another activity. There are two regular looking doors in the room's far corner. If Angola lives here, one of them must be a bathroom.

The door to my left opens easily enough into a kitchen with a small stove and plain counter. I jerk open the drawers, looking for a knife or anything I can use as a weapon. Unless plastic spoons qualify, I'm out of luck.

I return to the bedroom and try the other door. The bathroom is neat and squeaky clean, something I would expect from a man who makes square corner tucks on his bed. No razors or metal objects that could be used as a weapon. The man is thorough. There's a tub and shower and a cabinet of towels. I look at it longingly. But first things first.

When I emerge, my stomach growls, and Amber gives a fierce kick to my side—in protest of what must to her be the loud noise of my stomach, or perhaps she's putting in her two cents on food. Ignoring stomach and fetus, I find the area of the wall that opened, or at least that I think opened. I wasn't in great condition at the time I stepped through. On the other side of that wall are a chair, a "throne" of iron, and my gun belt, unless Angola has moved it. Somehow, I don't believe he has. It's hard to articulate why I think that—some hint in the things he has said or not said that make me think he is a man driven to walk the edge, to play the game. It would appeal to him to leave my weapon just out of reach . . . unless I figure out how to get to it.

Chapter Fifty

Alone in what appears to be Angola's room in an underground cavern, I first look for my boots. They are gone. I'm barefoot. Barefoot and pregnant. I snort. Then I examine the section of wall where the hidden door must be. It's well concealed. My eye can't find a seam. Stepping closer, I run my fingers over the surface. They telegraph dirt and stone, no gaps.

Closing my eyes, I reach out with my "witch" senses, searching for the extraordinary dense mass of the iron chair. I move slowly along this wall, but the spot where I feel the strongest draw is right behind the bed's headboard. Angola is sneaky enough to have moved the bed while I was out to confuse me, but there's just not enough room to do that. The bed was to my right. The door has to be there.

When I pass the desk, my stomach knots at the teasing scents of cooked food. With a sigh, I stop and sit, lifting the pewter cover that is meant to keep the food beneath warm. A gush of steam confirms it has done its job.

The sight of the thick bacon-wrapped piece of meat, accompanied by green beans and mashed potatoes with a pad of butter melted in the center and a sprig of parsley beside it prompts saliva. Hardly prisoner fare, but dare I eat it? What if it's laced with poison or a knockout drug?

Stupid. If they wanted me dead, Angola would have slit my throat while I slept or shot me when he first opened the door. I'm living on borrowed time until they discovered my baby is a female, but I might as well eat on that time. It's hard to plot murder and escape when you are fainting from hunger.

The meat is so tender that I have no problem cutting it with the plastic knife and fork. My stomach and Amber unanimously approve of my decision.

When I finish, I feel stronger and examine the pewter metal cover, considering it as a weapon. Whacking it against a person's temple might do the job or at least knock them down. But it's too big to conceal. I doubt Angola will let me sneak up behind him with it. Perhaps I could discus throw the plate into his temple? I heft it. Such a feat would require practice. Unfortunately, the plate is china. It would break on my first attempt, not to mention earning me disfavor from Stephanie.

My first meeting with Jason's Aunt Stephanie was at the gathering of House of Iron's party on All Hallows Eve. I thought I detected some sympathy behind her sophisticated coolness. Does she have any idea I am here and what Samuel is planning? Is there any way to get word to her? My gaze flies around the room at the bare furnishings and rock-studded walls. Can pigs fly?

I go back to the puzzle of the door. How would Sherlock Holmes solve this? He would have recalled every detail of the moment when he walked through the door. Unfortunately, I was on the verge of passing out and can't remember much. But it's worth a try.

I move to the wall and turn my back to it, leaning against it. Closing my eyes again, I take several deep breaths. Alice once told me that her sister spoke about a meditation exercise of "watching the rock grow." It never made sense to me, but for some reason the concept, along with staring at the rose-stone, helped me make that first connection to the living-green. Becca has the rose-stone, but it doesn't matter. Surrounded by the thick iron seams, I can't reach the living-green here, anyway.

Before meeting Alice, I rolled my eyes at what I considered nonsense New Age stuff. But reality turned upside down the first time I touched the rose-stone and the power that resided in the eons-old carbon transformed from green life to stone. Life is energy in different forms. I am energy temporarily expressed as matter. I get that now. That's not hocus-pocus; that's reality.

At the moment, however, I'm not looking for magic, more something closer to self-hypnosis. I need to put myself back in time, not via a vision, just to find the memory of exactly where that door is.

Pressing my back against the cold, stony wall, I focus on breathing, staring into the cut diamond facets of the rose-stone suspended in my mind, not trying to recall anything, just watching. Not thinking.

Not thinking morphs to thinking about what is going to happen to Amber when she is born.

Damn it! Where is the ability to relax when you need it?

I hear Aunt Alice chortling in my inner ear. *"Patience, dear. Have patience."*

I am not a patient person.

I can do this. I can be patient. What else can I do?

With a sigh, I try again.

This time I'm distracted by Amber doing what feels like a somersault. This is stupid. I should give up.

I don't do giving up.

Yet again, I bring my focus to the mental picture of the rose-stone, but this time when an image of Angola's knife sliding across a bloody infant's throat arises, I don't fight it or flee from it. I face it, accept it and all the emotions that go with it. I can feel the tears tracking down my face, but I don't let myself turn away. It is the frantic desire to escape this image that makes it so difficult to clear my mind and concentrate.

Not easy. I make myself do it in the same way I play out mental police scenarios approaching a scene: *What happens if the burglary suspect is hiding behind a door or in the attic? Or the beam of my flashlight in a dark warehouse finds a rotting corpse? Or a prisoner goes for a gun at his waistband?* All these possibilities must play out to various conclusions to pluck the best response and tuck it away in the toolbox of my subconscious. Some have no answers but death, but accepting death is not just the way of the samurai; it's the way of cops.

When I can "see" the knife, the thin line of blood trailing the blade, "hear" my baby's last gurgle, accept the unacceptable, the horror and sorrow, I turn my mind's eye to the glitter and refraction of the diamond's heart, the pattern within a pattern that forms a stylized crystal rose. . . .

Only when I feel perfectly still, do I let my mind drift back to the moment I looked up and saw Angola standing in a doorway that had not been there, recreating every detail I can.

I took off my gun belt and laid it on the iron chair as instructed and walked toward him, stepped up and into the room beyond, saw the room even as dizziness grabbed me. The chair at the desk seemed nearest, the bed too far to my right to reach—

My eyes open with a little thrill, and I shuffle sideways until the distance to the bed and chair seems right, then I turn and face the wall again, stepping back and sweeping my gaze over where the outline should be. When I entered, the door opened *into* the room. So there has to be something that could be pulled. The only possibility is a stone that protrudes a bit, enough to get fingers around it, perhaps?

With a rush of satisfaction, I reach for the stone and pull. Nothing happens. But it has to be here, right here. It has to be. I pull harder. It doesn't budge. I need something with leverage.

The biggest wooden spoon in the kitchen will serve. I snatch it out of a drawer and come back to the door, working the spoon under the rock.

"Damn," I mutter. "I need a fulcrum." How much time do I have? Angola will return soon.

A stab of pain in my abdomen sends me to my knees. Was the food poisoned after all? No, that makes no sense. A labor spasm? "God, not now!"

Desperate, my gaze sweeps over the room. Something has to go under the spoon for leverage. I have to get out of here. A pen would work. I go to the desk and yank open drawers. A letter opener would be nice too. It could double as a weapon. No pens. I remember the opening of a spy novel where the main character killed a man with a pen. Angola must have read the same book. No pens.

Another pain lances through me, like the worst menstrual cramp I've ever had, and I've had some doozies. I have to stop and lay on the floor in a fetal position until it passes. There's something about how close these pains come together. They're always yelling about that in the movies when a woman is giving birth. How long ago did the first one hit me? Never mind. It doesn't matter.

Frantic now, I heave myself up and stagger back into the kitchen, snatching up a spatula with a thick plastic end.

Back at the wall, I work the end under my spoon and press as hard as I can on the end of the spoon. The lever does its job, but instead of the door opening, the spoon cracks. I step back.

That is where I am, spatula in one hand and a broken spoon in the other, when the door opens.

Chapter Fifty-One

The door to my prison swings open. I get little satisfaction from the fact that it is right where I predicted it would be. Angola and Samuel regard me. Samuel frowns. Angola smiles and drops something into his pocket.

My angle prevents me from seeing the iron chair and whether my gun belt is still there.

"You were right twice," Samuel cocks his round head at Angola and taps his silver-tipped cane twice on the ground.

Angola steps up into the room, followed by Samuel. It doesn't seem like the best time to dive for the knife in his boot. I highly doubt he will give me that opportunity.

"Angola predicted you would return here, hunting us, though not this soon," Samuel says. "I thought that would be extraordinarily foolish on your part." He lifts a hand. "But here you are."

"What was Angola's second prediction?"

"That you would bear watching even in this escape-proof environment."

"Well, it is spoon-proof." I drop the broken spoon and spatula onto the floor.

Taking a step back, I claim the desk chair. Since it is the only one in the room, they will have to sit on the bed or stand. A small victory compared to being held prisoner, but I'll take what I can get.

"You'll forgive me if I am not much of a hostess," I say. "I think there is water in the kitchen sink."

Again, Samuel frowns, and I catch a quirk at the corner of Angola's lips. Amusing him is not my intent. My enemies stand before me, no weapons visible. If I had mine, would I gun them down in cold blood? That is why I came. They will do the same to me once they see Amber is not a male child. I can't forget, no matter how congenial Samuel appears, his sausage-plump hand held a deadly syringe he would have used if Jason had not intervened.

"Does Jason know I'm here?"

Samuel hesitates, as if considering whether truth or lie will serve him.

"I see no need to tell him," he says after a moment. "He's aware only that you disappeared from the hospital, and he suspects we had a hand in that. He is not aware of this room, and I suppose he can't imagine that you would willingly walk into our hands."

"That wasn't exactly my plan."

He smiles. "It was very generous of you to save us the trouble of bringing you here."

They had planned to bring me here, perhaps to have my baby. That explains why the room is devoid of anything I could use as a weapon. I start to ask about Becca and Tracey, but I don't want my concern for them to give Samuel or Angola any additional leverage.

"How long are you planning on keeping me here?"

"Only as long as it takes for you to have the baby. And after that—" Samuel shrugs. "It depends."

I can only imagine he means if I produce a boy, he might keep me around for a while until he can work out a way to feed him. I feel sick. All I have done is save them the trouble of kidnapping me.

"You're going to risk me having a baby down here alone?" My throat catches on the question. I planned on being in the hospital with drugs for pain, my doctor and staff ready to address anything that might go wrong, and Alice beside me, "seeing" inside me with her gift to make sure we both came through this and feeding me living-green from a bag stuffed with lumps of coal. Why didn't I bring some? Note to self: Never go hunting for bad guys in an iron cave without a bag of coal.

This is all my fault. I have put myself in an impossible situation. Obviously, I should have taken another path. I should have let Hobart and House of Stone protect me until I could figure out what to do. Instead, I worried about being *their* prisoner. Were those my only choices—whose "captive" I would be? If so, I made the wrong one. With House of Stone, at least Amber and I would have survived the birth, assuming they could get me somewhere Angola couldn't find us. And

Tracey would get well and would have helped me. I can't believe my stupidity, thinking I could handle this myself. I need to work on leaning on other people. I promise, Amber, if we get out of this alive—

Samuel interrupts my internal barrage of self-blame.

"Perhaps we should let the child be born on the iron throne, as in ancient tales." His tone is sardonic.

Angola's dark brows rise. "Isn't the *Y Tair* what we strive to prevent?"

He shrugs. "If it's female, it won't have a chance of growing into the *Y Tair*."

It. Indignation replaces my self-incrimination. Have women with power always been a threat to men? Instead of getting into that, I go for information.

"What's so special about that chair in there, anyway?"

"Chair?" Samuel rises to my bait. "The iron throne?"

"Why do you call it that? It's obviously not made of iron."

Even blind, I couldn't miss the iron pull of it, but let them believe I don't have a drop of the blood of their House. It is the only play I might have in this game.

"Why do you say that?" Samuel asks.

I shrug. "It's gray. Iron is black."

"Ah, I see. The material you are familiar with is wrought iron or cast-iron. Both are alloys contains differing amounts of carbon. Pure iron is a silvery gray. It doesn't even exist naturally on Earth."

"The last time I checked, we were on planet Earth. Did you import the chair from Mars or something?"

"Cheeky, aren't we?" Samuel says.

I glare at him.

To my surprise, Angola, who has hardly spoken, says, "Pure iron is only found on Earth as meteorites."

"Meteorites? I thought those were small."

"Most are, but there is one almost twice this size in Africa."

"But not pure," Samuel says quickly. Then he turns to me. "This one has been on Earth perhaps for billions of years, but only in our family a few thousand."

"You brought it here—to Birmingham?"

"Certainly. It belongs with the head of the House."

WHEN SAMUEL LEAVES, ANGOLA SHUTS THE DOOR without giving me an opportunity or excuse to see if my gun still lies on the iron chair.

From the corner of my eye, I note Angola again slips a hand in his pocket. Locking the door with some kind of remote?

"Well," he says, consulting his watch, "it's 1600."

Tea time for Alice, although she waited until Becca and I got off work. They must be frantic by now. And Tracey, what was he doing? Was he still in the hospital? Would he think about this place and try to get in the mine entrance?

"You left the mine entrance unsecured for me, didn't you?" I say.

Angola has started for the safe in the far wall, but he stops and turns toward me at my question.

"Yes. After you found it and somehow killed Theophalus, we had all the entrances secured. But I left the mine one unlocked. I figured you would find it again."

"And you left the door to the iron chair room open?"

"Yes."

This confirms they don't believe I have any blood of House Iron and would not have found it on my own.

"I just walked right into your trap, didn't I?"

For a moment Angola regards me with eyes as dark as the black roses he has left for me. "Make no mistake, Rose. I know you are dangerous and that you came to kill me. I would have done the same."

I return his steady gaze. He has, in fact, tried to kill me on multiple occasions. It is a strange and somehow intimate connection between us.

"And will you kill me?" I ask.

"Even if you bear a boy-child of House of Iron, Samuel will not allow you to live."

"And if it is a girl? You have no problem killing an innocent baby?"

"There are no innocents in this world."

"Even a baby?"

"If Samuel orders it."

"You'd do anything Samuel orders?"

His dark eyes do not waver from mine.

"Yes."

Chapter Fifty-Two

I watch Angola's back as he strides to the safe embedded in the wall. He's a killer. He's made that clear, and he's loyal to Samuel. Something in me can't help but admire that clear, uncompromised devotion. I don't think I have that to anything. I swore to "protect and serve," but I'm ready to commit murder. I thought I knew who I was, but that keeps shifting. Which "me" is real?

Angola stands between me and the safe. I can't see what's exposed inside when he opens the door, but he removes an object and reopens the door to the iron chair room, closing it behind him. I check the door to make sure he hasn't been careless, though I doubt Angola is ever careless.

It is, of course, locked.

I'm unprepared for the unmistakable sound that leaks in from the adjoining room—the reverberation of violin strings being tuned. The sound seems to come through a place high on the wall over the bed. I climb onto the mattress to get as close as I can. Just above me is a small opening the size of my hand, an air vent, I guess, cleverly concealed to match the stone and dirt wall. Through it, beautiful music is now pouring.

I stop worrying, stop thinking, and sink into the sound. It's not any piece of music I'm familiar with. It's something modern that seems to incorporate Middle Eastern motifs, but I am lost in it. I'm not a very good artist, but when I'm moved to paint, it comes from some raw place beyond the reach of words. Angola's music touches this place. *Can the same person who draws a knife across a throat, draw a bow across strings with the delicacy required to make such sounds?*

I lean against the cold wall, unmoving while he plays. For some reason, my mind drifts to the Holocaust of World War II, where musicians were forced to play while their friends and family marched to their deaths. It is said they could not pray, but that their violins prayed for them. I wonder, all those months while Angola was a prisoner in Iraq, if he played music in his mind to stay sane.

If you can call a man who can do what he does, sane.

When Angola finally emerges, I sink into a squat on the bed and stare at him.

He ignores me, returning the violin and bow to the safe. Then he turns to face me.

"I heard through the vent," I point overhead.

No response other than a twitch under his eye. I don't think he normally lets people hear him play.

"It was beautiful. I don't understand how you can play like that and be so immune to feeling, to be such a—"

"Monster?" he finishes.

"Yes."

"We are all monsters. If you think you have escaped that, you are deluding yourself."

Alice's words echo—"*We are all broken.*"

"Everyone?" I ask.

"You cannot honestly look at the world, at the people who rape, who take, who kill without compunction, ignore without the burden of guilt and pretend innocence, and not realize such is everywhere, in all of us."

He is right. I came here to kill him.

"But so is good." I struggle not to fall into the despair he paints.

"An illusion, a desperate attempt to keep from acknowledging the darkness."

"I want a shower."

He nods toward the bathroom. "Help yourself."

THERE IS NO LOCK ON THE DOOR IN THE BATHROOM. The stall has clear glass walls. Naked, I feel even more vulnerable, but I want that shower. Setting the temperature as hot as I can stand, I turn my face into the beating droplets. I need to be clean, to wash away the lies, or maybe the hard truths.

When I turn to let the water access to my back, I notice, to my surprise, a small plastic basket with a brand of shampoo, conditioner and liquid soap that I would not expect to see in a man's shower. The more masculine products on the shelf, I assume, are his. The basket's presence is evidence of a female visitor or confirmation that I was expected. I suspect the latter, since they are unopened. Their presence confirms that if I hadn't come under my own power, they intended to kidnap me and bring me here to have my baby, a plan that must have been formed after Samuel agreed to wait and see the baby's sex before killing us both.

I lather my hair and rinse it twice, something I haven't done since Academy days when I felt overwhelmed by the haranguing and physical stress. Then I soap everywhere else, lingering on the blue-veined curve of my belly.

As if Amber reacts to my caress, a sharp pain laces my abdomen, doubling me over. Another spasm follows, dropping me to my knees with a loud moan.

Angola pushes open the door.

Bent over, my head touching my knees, I struggle to breathe through the pain. *Is this normal? Is it time?*

Angola yanks open the shower and reaches down without bothering to turn off the water. With an easy strength, he lifts me, still curled into a ball, into his arms, pressing me against his chest. In a few strides, he places me gently on his bed, yanks open a drawer and covers me with a blanket.

The pressure on my lower back and rippling spasms ease, but if this level of pain is any indication of how the rest of this is going to go, I'm ready to call it all off. Unfortunately, that's not an option.

"What can I get you?" Angola asks.

"Towels."

He brings two large ones. I wrap one around my head and use the other to dry off under the blanket.

"What else?"

"How do I know? I've never done this before. Have you?"

"No."

"I planned to have a doctor around and a medical staff. What if I have a boy and you lose him? Do you think Samuel will be happy about that?"

He frowns.

"I thought you planned everything. Did you think I was just going to drop a baby on your bed with no mess or fuss?"

"You are in the early stages. This can last 8 to 12 hours."

"I'm glad to see that you've looked up the information. What are you going to do if my body doesn't comply with your time schedule?

The first contractions are supposed to be mild, and I would hardly call what I just felt 'mild.'"

"Perhaps not."

And without another word, he leaves me alone. That only fuels my fears. I roll over to my side and tears leak onto the already wet towel.

Chapter Fifty-Three

I almost don't recognize the woman who enters the room. The last time I saw Stephanie Blackwell, she was wearing black slacks and a white tailored shirt with a striking diamond pin. Today, she is wearing sweats and sneakers, her obedient blonde hair hanging straight down her back in a ponytail.

Angola must have caught her during a workout, although I would have imagined her wearing stylish leggings, at the least. Perhaps she knew what she was getting into and didn't want to ruin any of her good clothes. She glances at me, still curled on my side, and then turns her attention back to the doorway where Angola lifts a rolling cart over the threshold. The sight of him dispels the notion that just bloomed in my mind of overpowering Stephanie and making an escape.

Then she surprises me, yet again, by waving him from the room. "Stay away," she says. "Have the guard deliver dinner."

Angola nods and leaves us alone. The door seals shut behind him.

Stephanie turns to me. "I told you once you were a fool. I see my pronouncement was correct. You've gotten yourself knocked up by Jason, I'm told."

I sniff.

"It's a bit late for regrets." She takes towels and folded white sheets off the cart.

I am not about to tell her the truth. Let her think I am having her grandnephew or grandniece.

"Up," she says, waving a hand.

I stand, holding the rough blanket against me. My hair is still wet and falls in ringlets around my shoulders and down my back.

"My only regret is having my baby in a hole in the ground at the hands of crazy people."

"Hmm. Not my first choice either." She hands me a dry towel and rummages in the pile of things in a box on the rolling tray, bringing out two large cotton nightgowns. "These were my aunt's. She was rather large, so I think it will be comfortable."

While I dry off, she lays several layers of sheets on the bed. Then she removes a notebook and pen from the cart's bottom tray and writes on it.

"What are you doing?"

"Preparing to note the length of your labor pains. And how far apart they come. That and measuring your dilation will indicate where we are."

"Are you aware," I say, letting the towel fall to put on the nightgown, "if this baby is a girl, they're planning on murdering—?"

A ripple of pain steals the words from my mouth, and I crawl back onto the bed, getting on my hands and knees with my bottom in the air, a position that helps relieve bad menstrual cramps.

Out of my eye's corner, I see Stephanie consult a diamond watch on her thin wrist. Despite her business-like manner, her face has paled.

"They didn't divulge that, but I'm not surprised."

"You once assured me that children were rare and not at risk," I say when the cramps subside. "When did that stop being true?"

"Since Theophalus died. Samuel has made no secret of his desire to eradicate your House."

"And that's just okay with you?"

"It's not about me," she says, and I can almost taste the bitterness in her voice. "It's about the men. They are House of Iron. The women are merely adornments and brood stock. We have no opinions, and are of no consequence, save in those roles."

"You will help them murder me and my baby?"

She considers me, her face expressionless. "I suspect you are not ignorant of the power of Iron. They can compel me to do whatever they wish, but I'm not here because of that."

"What are you here for?"

"To help deliver this baby—for their purposes, of course. But I won't harm your baby on my own. That I can assure you."

"You seem like the last person to deliver a baby."

"Appearances can be deceiving. I was a nurse in England when I met my husband—Samuel's son."

"Where is your husband?"

"He's in Europe taking care of business while Jason is here."

"Is Jason part of this?" I'm surprised how important this is to me.

She takes a deep breath. "I'd like to say no, but he hardly speaks to me. He's gone so much, and we don't . . . talk easily."

I watch her.

She settles her shoulders. "The truth is, I haven't asked him. I've learned to keep my nose out of House business."

For some reason I believe her.

"Now," she says, snatching a cloth and a pot off the cart. "Let's get started."

I watch her puttering around and something eases a bit in me. She seems competent. "Did you deliver babies as a nurse?"

"No. I worked in critical care in hospital."

The ease dissolves, replaced with a knot of tension.

"Then this is your first delivery?"

"Yes, other than my own. I did a rotation there years ago, but it is absurd that I should be doing it, except if they brought a doctor down here to help, they'd have to kill her or him, and I don't want that blood on my hands too." She stops and stares into the distance at something unseen behind the wall. "There's been enough of that."

"Will you help me?" I ask her.

"That's why I'm here."

"I mean, will you help me escape?"

She laughs, a bitter, short laugh. "How would you propose I do that?"

"You have a remote for the door, don't you?"

"No, and there's a guard on the other side."

"Angola?"

"I doubt it. He has little patience for that kind of duty."

I prop myself on an elbow. "Then I can take care of the guard."

She arches one of her carefully shaped eyebrows and looks at my distended belly. "I highly doubt that, but even if you could, then what?"

"I can get out and call for help."

Cramps seize my abdomen and back, and for the duration of their grip, I can't speak. Stephanie makes a notation. When it passes, she says, "Let's have a look." Peeling back the blanket, she scowls. "Not enough light." She drags over a standing lamp. "There, that will work."

I feel exposed having her examining me, but Angola is not present.

"You had better put escape plans on hold, dear. You're already over three centimeters."

I've heard that things happen depending on centimeters, but I never paid attention. I expected the doctor would measure other things.

"It is my understanding," Stephanie says, her hand on my knee, "that each birth is unique. There's no actual prediction of how long labor will go on. But you can't go traipsing down a tunnel in your condition, and I wouldn't help you do it, even if I could."

At that point a particularly painful spasm hits, and I shut my eyes and scream.

Between my screams and pants, I register an exclamation from Stephanie—"Good God!"

I open my eyes to see her face pale, her hand to her mouth.

"What?" I mutter, trying to breathe deeply. "What is it?"

When she doesn't answer, I follow her gaze around the room and gasp. Every plant in the room is dead.

For the first time I remember Alice's warning: *"That pain will drive you to pull the living-green. You need me and a ready source because pulling it from the living . . . would kill them."*

Unconsciously, I sucked the living-green from the living plants. The next time such a pain hits, there won't be any plants in the room—only Stephanie.

Chapter Fifty-Four

Without thinking, I snatch Stephanie's hand. In the same breath, I draw from the riches of iron around me and let it flow into her.

Her attention snaps to me. The horror at seeing the dead plants melts from her expression. I wonder if she really understood the significance of that. It doesn't matter. I may be ready to kill Angola and Samuel to save Amber, but I'm not ready to wreak collateral damage on innocents nearby.

"Stephanie, listen to me."

Her gaze obediently lifts to mine, which pierces me with a pang of guilt. How many times has her will been subjugated to a man of House Iron? She is hostage to their slightest whim. Not so long ago, most women were culturally obliged to obey their fathers until handed off to their husbands. I swore I would never do this again. I hate doing it, maybe because deep underneath, I feel the pull of it, the thrill of having that kind of power over others. Is that part of all human beings' hardwiring?

We are all broken. We are all monsters.

We may be, but I have to do what I have to do. "Do you have a remote for the door?" I ask.

"No,"

Damn.

"Listen to everything I say before you act on it."

How much time do I have before the next spasm hits, and I suck all the carbon out of Stephanie's body?

She is still. I keep my hand on hers.

"As soon as I release you, start banging on the wall and shouting until the guard opens the door. Convince him you must have some vital piece of equipment you don't have. Then go find Jason. Tell him I am here against my will and having the—having his baby and where I am. Then hide. Stay away from me and this room and don't let Angola or Samuel find you."

I take my hand from hers.

Instead of jumping up to follow my instructions, she blinks at me. "What about you?"

"Hurry. We don't have time to discuss it."

She takes a step toward the door, then pauses, and I marvel at her ability to fight the magic of Iron. I guess she's been subjected to it so many times, she is practiced at how to slip around the constraints without violating them. "I'm going," she says. Then she digs in her pocket and chunks several pieces of folded paper at me. "I hadn't planned to let you see I had this—"

Just after Stephanie leaves, the door opens. A man steps in. Not Jason. I've never seen him before. I note the sidearm and a pair of handcuffs. His gaze sweeps over the room in a professional manner. This is not an "innocent." This is a collaborator, holding a kidnapped woman hostage.

I reach out deliberately to pull the carbon from him, recklessly thinking perhaps I can control it enough to just debilitate him. I am that desperate, but he doesn't even notice. He must be House of Iron.

"Okay," he says to someone out of my line of sight.

Another man in a starched white linen shirt enters, carrying a tray similar to the previous one. He sits it down on the desk. "Broth and toast, madam. Mrs. Blackwell gave orders for it earlier."

This man is a servant. It would do no good to kill him. He has no clue how much danger he is in. *Please wait*, I send a silent plea to Amber and my uterus. I am terrified I will suck the carbon from him in unconscious reaction to the pain.

With a slight, surreal bow, the servant leaves, as does the guard. Apparently, neither appears to be aware that Stephanie is supposed to be with me. Angola strikes me as the type to say little to anyone about his business.

Broth and toast. Amazingly, I am not the slightest bit hungry, possibly a first in my life. Too nervous.

I'm will get you—get us—out of here, Amber. I promise.

As soon as I am alone again, I inventory everything on the cart. A pair of scissors emerges, unfortunately the medical kind with blunted ends and, of all things, a pair of silk shoestrings. My first thought is the possibility of using it to garrote the guard. Then it hits me that I am going to being having a baby by myself. I consult the papers Stephanie threw at me—birth instructions! Reading quickly through the steps, I realize the shoestrings are to tie off the umbilical cord. Both the string and the scissors have to be sterilized.

Didn't I see Stephanie disappear into the kitchen alcove with a pot in hand? I waddle in there with scissors and string. A pot full of water sits on the stove, but the stove eye is not on. Not sure when I'll need it, but when I need it, I don't want to wait for a pot of water to boil. That is one of my few culinary skills, and boiling water always takes longer than it should. I dump in the scissors, rip open the shoestring packet and add those into the water, setting the stove eye on the lowest setting and placing a clean towel on the counter.

Mystery finally solved—why the first thing any prairie woman calls for in attending a birth is boiling water. The next thing I want is a mirror. Angola has an extendable magnifying mirror in the bathroom, I assume for shaving. Perfect, except it is screwed into the wall. Digging into the bowels of the medicine cabinet and then a shallow drawer, I find a pair of tweezers and use the end as a screwdriver. Relishing the tiny triumph of accomplishment, I take the mirror back to the bed and examine myself.

Stephanie said I was three centimeters. The metric system is second nature for a British woman, but I have to figure out how that translates into inches. I know a kilo of cocaine weighs 2.2 pounds, my bullets are 9 mm, and a bottle of soda is two liters. None of those factoids is helpful for this application. According to the information sheet, at ten centimeters, the baby is ready to be born, so I spread my hands about the size of a baby's head to work backwards—that is a mistake. My gut tightens at the realization that my delicate parts have to stretch that far. Is that even possible? I check the sheet again to verify.

After the next contraction, I take the mirror and instructions into the bathroom, clean the tub with disinfectant I found in the cabinet, turn on the water in the tub and climb in, leaving on my nightgown, the last shred of dignity I suspect I will have in this procedure. Then I look more closely at the papers Stephanie had tossed onto the bed. It looks like something printed out from the Internet on how to have a baby at home. They aren't instructions for a water birth, but there's no reason Stephanie would have known that is what I must do. If some non-House servant walks in, I don't want to kill them. Women in House of Iron or House of Stone, for that matter, are normal people who aren't capable of sucking elements from bystanders.

But these pages I have are all I have, plus whatever I can remember that Alice told me when she was recommending a water birth. The pages tremble in my hands, but I make myself study it. Midway through the third read, another set of labor pains interrupts. I lie back and ride it out, clinging to the knowledge that it will not last forever and imagining that Tracey is on one side and Alice on the other. Becca is . . . out buying more baby clothes to add to the collection she started. Alice is telling me to breathe slowly and deeply. My friends; my family. They will help me get through this.

Women gave birth in the rice fields once. They just squatted and had the baby, strapped it on their backs and went back to work. I read that somewhere, didn't I? Whether it's true or not, I'm going to believe it is, and if they could do that, I can do this.

God, where is Jason? What if he is in this with Angola and Samuel? What if he doesn't come?

Time passes slowly, way too slowly during the cramping. At first, I get up and pace between waves of labor and try to keep up with the duration of the pain and time between, but I give it up. The time is shortening; the pain getting worse. I stop looking, although I'm not supposed to push until I am ten centimeters. Surely, I will be aware without looking when such an abnormal thing happens. I drain the tub when it gets cool and add more warm water.

With every spasm, my body scrabbles futilely for the living-green beyond the walls enclosing me. Nothing. The iron walls or the water when I am in the tub blocks my access.

Where the hell is Jason? What if he isn't at the mansion? Would Stephanie call his cell? I didn't tell her specifically to do that, but I did tell her to find him. What if he is still at the hospital? *I hate him.* While I am at it, I hate men altogether.

This time when the pain comes, I scream. Loudly.

The guard either can't hear me in here or has been told to ignore me.

Something is wrong. It can't possibly be supposed to hurt this much.

Chapter Fifty-Five

When the bathroom door opens, I'm panting and barely care that it is Jason who enters. I am in the tub again, driven by pain and the hope of assistance against gravity.

"My God, Rose!" Jason rushes to my side and kneels beside the tub. "I'll get a doctor."

"No, too late."

"What do I do?"

I struggle to get out instructions. "Tell me to breathe."

"What?"

"Breathe!" I scream at him.

"Breathe," he says.

"Do you see it? The baby's head?"

He bends over to view the most private part of my body.

"I see something, I think. It's hard to tell through the water."

"Get the mirror."

He hands it to me, his face tight with worry. "Won't the baby drown?"

"No. Not as long as she's born completely underwater. She won't try to take a breath until air hits her face."

"I guess that makes sense. A baby is in fluid in the womb and not breathing."

I groan. "More hot water."

He turns on the spigot and drains some water at the same time.

"I assume your body temperature would be right."

I nod and groan again. My skin is asked to do the impossible. Surely it's ripping apart. When he puts the mirror in place, I look, certain I'll see a bloody mess of my own delicate tissue. All I can see is my inner thigh.

"Move it over. Left. Tilt it up."

When he adjusts the mirror, I gasp. I am not torn into shreds yet, and the baby's head is just visible. *Dear God*, that means the awful pain has not finished and worse is coming.

"Do you know how big a centimeter is?" I ask.

"Of course."

"How many centimeters open am I?"

"I'd say about ten."

It is time to push. I bear down.

"Talk to me, damn it," I say between pants and then scream at the wave of agony that grips my abdomen and back. Screaming is my only release. Oddly, it helps. The louder the better.

"It moved a little," he says.

"Wash your hands. Quick."

While he is doing that, another spasm and the overwhelming need to push and scream. Then he is back.

"What do I do?"

"Papers on the floor. Read it fast."

He grabs the instructions and skims down. "Looks like you are already here."

"Hurry," I beg.

"Hang on." His attention is on the page. "Breathe," he says absently.

I want to throw something at him, but the only thing in my reach is the mirror, and I don't want to break it.

"Okay, I have it. I will read the rest later about the cord."

I nod. Tears of relief spilling onto my cheeks. I don't have to do this alone anymore.

Jason frowns. "I think we should drain the water and try to get it cleaner for the baby."

I nod, push again, and scream. My total focus is on getting this enormous object out of me.

"Okay, that's better. Filling it up again."

I couldn't care less. My entire world is *pushing*.

"Here it comes," he says. "It's bloody and some white stuff. Is that normal?"

I scream. It is a weapon I turn on him, on whoever or whatever came up with this sucky method of procreation.

"Okay," Jason says, consulting the paper, "I'm turning the head to align with the neck. My God, you're doing it. The head is out!"

Unbelievable relief.

"Don't stop," he says. "Push. Push, damn it!"

I push.

"We've got a shoulder. Well done."

I hate him.

"Push again."

"Can't you pull?" I plead.

"The instructions say nothing about pulling."

"Is the cord—?" I have a nightmare vision of the cord wrapped around Amber's neck. It's a real nightmare that has woken me multiple times in the last few weeks.

"I don't see it. It's not around the neck. You're close! *Push*, Rose. We're almost there."

"*We?*"

He laughs. Unbelievably, I laugh too, a little hysterically, hiccup, and push again.

"That's it!" he says, pulling her up to the surface and lifting her from the water. "Cord attached. Other end, still in you somewhere."

"Clean nose, mouth," I pant.

"Already ahead of you."

"Breathing?"

"Not sure."

Oh God, my baby is dead. She can't be. Not after all this, but how could she live through all that pressure?

"Is she breathing now?" I pant. "Pat her feet."

"Yes, she is breathing. But she's covered in whitish mucus. They're always pink and clean on a television birth. Should I try to get it off?"

"No! Just wrap her and hand her to me."

I can't believe the tiny bundle he presses into my arms. I could have sworn she was three times this size. The tiny fingers and ears mesmerize me.

Jason is reading the rest of the instructions.

"I want to get on the bed."

He helps me stand on wobbly legs and strips off the wet nightgown, wrapping me with a large towel. At his touch, I realize the sexual jolt has been missing. Apparently, the mixing of our different magics ignites it and cutting off my access to the living-green douses the reaction. I'm grateful. Sex is at the top of my don't-ever-do-again list at the moment, and I prefer it stay there.

He dries me off as if I will shatter at the slightest pressure and puts on the second nightgown Stephanie had brought before easing me onto the bed. I relax for a moment, everything in me wanting to drift away into badly needed sleep, but Amber twists in my arms, and I realize both my breasts are leaking. The second loose gown Stephanie brought me easily slips off a shoulder, and I hold Amber to the worst one, the left. It was always the first offender and leaked at the regular meetings with the Crimes Against Persons captain. I have no idea what it was about him that triggered it, but it got so bad, I started putting pads in my bra.

I press Amber's tiny, perfect lips to my enlarged nipple, hoping her instincts will take over. Alice had me roughing the nipple to prepare, but nothing prepared me for the feeling of her latching on and drinking hungrily. Her dark blue eyes blink and then close in contentment.

I am smitten. I know intellectually it's hormones, but it doesn't matter. This is my baby, and I will protect her with everything in me.

While she is nursing, I push out the placenta. The instructions say to bring it to a doctor or hospital, but that is the last thing on my mind.

"How long do you think we have?" I ask Jason.

"Not long. The guard will report that you stopped screaming soon. They'll want to come see if you had a boy or girl."

I don't dare scream and make Amber cry.

While we're talking, Jason is tying off the placenta with the sterilized silk strings. "Do you think that is tight enough?" he asks.

"I don't have any idea. I can't feel it."

"It says not too tight, but tight enough. How am I to know what that means?"

"Can you tell them it's a boy? Buy us time?"

"Okay, here goes." I hear the snip of the scissors. "Yes, not leaking on either end. That's good."

"Wrap the stump in a little towel."

"I'm capable of reading the instructions, Rose."

"We have to get out of here."

"You need to rest."

"I can't rest. This isn't over. They will kill her."

"I know."

Chapter Fifty-Six

"We have to get out of here!" I am near hysteria. Adrenaline kicks in, countering the exhaustion.

Jason sits on the bed beside me. "You are amazing. You just gave birth in a cave."

"Here." I shove Amber into his arms.

"What are you doing?"

"Getting dressed." I stumble to the bathroom and put on the clothes I came in wearing, checking to make sure the handcuff keys are still taped to the front and back of my underwear and cursing Angola because he took my boots.

"We must talk," he says from the other side of the door.

"Have you lost your mind? There's no time to 'talk.'"

I tighten my belt to hold up the jeans, but despite the pounds I've shed in the past few hours, my stomach still has a pouch. I frown. That's something I've never had to deal with.

I yank open the bathroom door. "Angola is walking death and neither of us can stop him."

"I understand that very well. That is why we have to leave the country."

"What?"

"Angola will never rest until he has fulfilled Samuel's wishes. You will be looking over your shoulder every moment. Life will be hell . . . if you survive."

I take a deep breath. "I can just take one step at a time right now."

"No, we can do more than that. I have been thinking about this for weeks, ever since I heard my uncle's plans to eradicate House of Rose. We must leave quickly, with no trail."

"How do you propose doing something like that? Iron has tendrils everywhere. You told me that yourself."

"I did, and it does. But I have money in a bank in the Cayman Islands that is not traceable to me. More than enough. Once there, we can get fake passports, go anywhere, disappear."

I stare at him. "What about your family, your House?"

"That is the past. You are my future."

A slightly hysterical laugh slips out of my lips. "That's very sweet. Just considering it for the moment, what makes you think we could get to the Cayman Islands undetected? You have to get on a plane, and that leaves a pretty clear damn trail."

"No plane." He smiles. "You forget, I have a boat."

The *Iron Fist,* a sweet, not so little yacht parked at a boat slip in the Intracoastal Waterway, just a few hours away in south Alabama. Becca, Daniel, Tracey and I spent a day on her, back when Becca was struggling to recover from the mental damage Theophalus Blackwell had left in his wake. Daniel had fallen overboard. Tracey heroically leaped in after him, only to sink like a rock, and I had to save Tracey. It had been a terrifying but, in other ways, lovely day. We had sailed east on the Waterway into Wolf Bay and a succession of other bays, right out into the Gulf of Mexico. And the last time I looked at a map, the Gulf of Mexico connected to the Caribbean. And the Cayman Islands were in the Caribbean.

Escape. Safety. Anonymity. My mind whirls.

"I need to think." I hold Amber tighter. "No matter what, the first thing is to get out of here."

"That, I'm afraid, I did not plan for. But I have a car waiting in an innocuous spot, if we can get to it. I planned to drive it to the hospital when you were released."

Ball back in my court. "The guard is the first obstacle."

"And the second?"

I look hard at him. "Can you hot-wire a motorcycle?"

He grins. "Perhaps surprisingly, I can."

"You can tell me later how you acquired that skill."

He rises, snatches the blunt-nosed scissors he used to cut the umbilical cord, and then yanks the lamp from the wall outlet.

"What are you doing?"

"Obtaining a piece of electrical wire."

While he is engaged in that, I go to the desk and remove the plate cover. Despite the cover, the soup has long gone cold, but I don't care. I sit, shifting a sleeping Amber to my lap and pick up the bowl with my other hand. I'm starving, and what's ahead is not likely to be pretty. It might even involve running, despite the fact that a sixteen-wheeler truck has just rammed itself over and through my body, and there are still unhealed bruises and sore muscles from the explosion at Railroad Park.

"Got the wire," Jason says as I down the soup. "Any ideas about handling the guard?"

I jam the toast and my cell phone into my pockets and hand him the heavy pewter plate cover.

Jason calls for the guard to open the door. The door obliges, but the guard does not.

"Nate," Jason calls, "come in and take the first look at my son. House of Iron has a baby!"

"Congratulations!" Nate says, stepping inside. "*By the Three*, that's a miracle."

The Three. The *Y Tair*. My baby. He used the term without thought of its history or meaning as easily as we say "Holy Cow" without thought that it refers to a holy bovine in the Hindu religion on the other side of the world.

Nate turns to me. I'm sitting on the bed facing him and have deliberately woken Amber and put her at the other exposed breast, making no effort to cover any part of my swollen breast. His eyes widen. I have his attention. From behind him, Jason takes a hard swing with the heavy food warmer. The man crumples.

"Sorry," Jason murmurs.

"Get his gun," I say.

"And the remote from his pocket. We may need it to open doors."

When we step into its room, the iron throne vibrates its soundless song. The sight of my gun belt on the seat gives my heart a jolt of hope. I lay Amber down beside it, pick it up and adjust the hook buckle in a few notches. Then I swing it around my hips, leaning forward to keep the weight on my back while I fasten it.

"Close the door," I say. "It may buy us a little time if they think we're still in there."

When I turn to pick up Amber, I hesitate. She has gone perfectly and unnaturally still, her dark blue eyes wide and fixed.

Chapter Fifty-Seven

Too late, Samuel's words echo—

"Perhaps we should let the child be born on the iron throne, as in the ancient tales."

I snatch Amber into my arms, checking her from head to her tiny still-blue toes. My nightmares were about leaving her at the grocery store, not setting her on a magic iron chair. Fortunately, she seems unhurt, a bubble of spit forming in the corner of her mouth. I wipe it aside with the sheet and blanket wrapping her.

"I doubt communication devices work well down here," Jason says, "but I imagine Angola will be checking soon. Are you ready? Do you need me to carry you?"

"What I need is a sling."

"I do not have one handy."

"Here—" I hand him Amber and work the sheet out from around her, tying it into a secure knot. I consider putting her on my back, but if anyone chases us and there is shooting involved, she'll be vulnerable. I take her back and tuck her into the homemade sling, tying the long loose ends of the sheet around her again to make sure she is snug against my breast. Now my hands are free.

"Impressive."

I draw my gun, happy to feel the familiar heft of it in my hand. "Let's go."

I motion him to the other side of the door that opens into the corridor. It doesn't respond to my push but opens with the remote we lifted from the guard's pocket. Jason peers out into the dark corridor. At his movement, the overhead lights flick on.

"Looks clear," he says.

"To the left. It's about a mile."

"Where does it come out?"

"On the side of Red Mountain, past Vulcan."

I want to ask him why the family kept secrets from him, but I don't want to talk in the tunnel where even the softest sound travels. He told me once that he didn't get along with his father or his uncles, and they kept him traveling on family business.

The adrenaline burst drains quickly, and I am fighting to keep my feet. Exhausted, barefoot, with sweat dripping from me in what seems like pools, I can only manage a walk, punctuated with a periodic slow jog. Again, I try drawing from the iron around me for energy. Nothing. I let it dissipate.

The gun belt I was so happy to have around my waist becomes weight I want to drop and finally do. The battery on my radio is dead. The hell with the handcuffs. I stuff my extra magazine in my back pocket with the toast, hold my gun, and let everything else drop.

"I can carry you," Jason says again.

"Not for long." I lean against the wall. If my knees buckle, I won't be able to get up. "Just a few seconds rest."

Voices raise behind us. We look at each other. *They know we're gone.*

Fear gifts me with another spurt of adrenaline. I don't have time to be exhausted. There were dozens of times running miles in the Academy when I felt this way, that I was at the very end of my strength. Somehow, I kept going. That was the point of those runs, to teach us there is more in us than we can imagine, that if the worst happens—if we're injured, even shot—we don't stop, that there is a place deep down from which we can draw. Even before the Academy, my adoptive father taught me there was such a place in me. "Keep going, Rose," he would say when we ran together. "Focus. One foot and then the other. Dig. Find it inside you. Pull it up!"

I call on that place.

"Look," Jason says about ten minutes later.

I drag my gaze from the ground to follow his pointing finger. It's the end of the tunnel, the door into the mine entrance, but something is wrong. I can't get my brain to figure out what it is until we are closer, and then I realize it is broken, hanging crippled from its hinges.

As I stumble out, barely in control of my legs, a flood of warmth and energy embraces me. The living-green! I gulp it in with every breath of the rich, oxygenated exhale of the woods about us.

"You okay?" Jason says. "I can't believe you are still on your feet." His hand on my arm sends a spike of desire into my body. I am, for once, happy to feel it. It means iron no longer blocks me from the living-green.

"I'm okay." I may pay for it later, but right now I am a junkie calling on my fix.

"Where's that motorcycle?"

Throughout the wild ride down the mountain, I worry about Amber. She has not uttered a single cry. My arms are wrapped around Jason's chest, my back arched to keep from crushing her between us, but I'm not able to cushion the jars and bumps of the rough dirt path. She doesn't complain. That doesn't seem normal. Babies cry, don't they? Did I do something to her by putting her on House Iron's throne chair? I cling to the fact that she didn't cry coming out of the womb either. But either way, there is nothing I can do now but hang on.

Jason can't go too fast or risk spilling us, and I can't hear much over the roar of the motorcycle engine—that is, until the unmistakable *crack* of gunfire from behind us. Splinters from a nearby pine tree fly into my face.

The sharp turn that deposits our wheels onto a paved surface protects us temporarily from more fire.

"My car is down the next street!" I yell in his ear, a fresh burst of adrenaline and terror subduing my attention to the magic entangling us, but he ignores me, taking random turns to shake off any followers. We have a small gift of time. Unless Angola has another motorcycle hidden in the woods, pursuers from the mansion will have to go the long way around the mountain, and we will be long gone . . . as long as we don't wreck. Jason has throttled down on the speed, obeying stop signs and traffic lights. He has given me the helmet, so a patrol unit could stop us for his failure to have one, and the baby is definitely not in an appropriate carrier, but no blue lights appear behind us.

Conversation is impossible as we roar toward wherever Jason has stashed his car. It's not until we hit the Airport Highway, an older back road to the airport that I realize his destination. The airport parking deck is a smart choice. Leaving a car over a long period of time wouldn't draw attention.

We find his car on a mid-level of the long-term parking section, a black sedan. It is stocked with a pillow and blankets on the back seat, a bag of snack food and even an infant car seat. I settle the sleeping Amber, strap her in, tuck a blanket over her, and then fall into the passenger seat, wrapping another blanket around my shaking body.

Jason straps in and starts us down the parking deck toward the exit. I hunch as close to the passenger door as possible. The distance between us isn't enough to counter the sexual tension, though something, a flood of hormones or sheer exhaustion, has reduced it to a muted throb. I can't believe with what it has just been through, my body could even consider sex ever again. Just behind my desire for oblivion is thirst. I open one of the bottled waters in the bag on the passenger floorboard and drain half of it at one time.

"You want one?" I ask.

"Not now." He hands cash to the manned parking attendant. "The *Iron Fist* is less than five hours from here."

I've been so focused on getting away, it takes a moment to remember what he is talking about—boat, Cayman Islands. My thoughts dance wildly.

It sounds crazy, but it might work. I'd be looking over my shoulder the rest of my life, but Amber might have a chance to grow up. *Without Alice or Becca. Without her family.* I know what that is like, always wondering who they were, what they were like. Alice put her life in danger to protect me. She sent me away. Should I do the same? Send Amber away? The ache inside me at that thought is stunning. How could I love this child I didn't plan so much, so quickly? I reach back to rest my hand on her chest, to feel her tiny heart beating.

As my thoughts tumble down the chain of possible unintended consequences, I close my eyes, suddenly dizzy and nauseous. I want to open my lids, but I can't. I can't move.

As if my eyes are open, shadows of gray and black resolve into a crystal clear image—it is Amber, suspended in the air against a moonlit sea. My heart has frozen mid-beat, but my mind spins. She must be falling!

With a painful wrench, I am cast back in my time or my universe in the car with Jason. I've never had a vision of anything other than something associated with the physical place I inhabited, other than that one time among the pseudo-stones of Bama Henge where I saw a ceremony that I now believe involved the *Y Tair*, my grown daughter.

My daughter.

My hand on Amber's chest is tingling. Was the vision I just had mine or . . . hers?

Regardless, I am not about to let it come to be. I can change the future, choose a different path. I must.

"No," I say aloud, fighting dizziness that seems more intense than the normal residue of a vision. "Jason, stop. We're not going to the Cayman Islands with you." *I'm not going anywhere near water with my child.*

That is the last thing I remember before waking up on a rocking boat.

Chapter Fifty-Eight

Asound I somehow realize is important punctuates the silence, but I can't identify it. Gradually, I drift upward into consciousness. The first thing I recognize is not the noise, but the overpowering scent of roses in a cloistered space. Then I realize the sound is screaming, a baby, *my* baby—proving she has lungs and the capacity to use them.

My eyes open next, but it takes time to orient myself in space. I am, I decide, lying down. Spread out under me like a crimson tundra is a shiny expanse. A bed?

Where is Amber? I don't see her, but the sound is so close. I lift up on one elbow and fall back, dizzy. The screaming intensifies. It's behind me.

The sweet pull of oblivion beckons. I could close my eyes again and drift there. Instead, I force myself to roll over until I am eye level with a red-faced Amber. She's balled her little fists tight, and she is kicking in displeasure.

My mouth is too dry to make a sound or form a word, but I pull her toward me and fumble with my shirt and my leaky breasts. Some women don't produce milk right away, Alice warned me, but that is not a problem here. Amber latches on immediately. A sharp cramp twists my abdomen but fades after a moment. I lie still with her cradled against me and drift away again.

THE NEXT TIME I OPEN MY eyes, Amber has fallen asleep, milk on her lips and chin. My other breast feels tight, but I'll have to wait. I look around. The first thing I see is a crystal vase on a mirrored dresser holding what must be two-dozen red roses. I take in the luxurious, thick carpet and golden pine paneling and realize I am in the place of my fantasies—on the red satin spread in Jason's bedroom on the *Iron Fist*.

Anger churns. The last thing I remember is telling him I was not going with him. I was exhausted, but I couldn't possibly have fallen asleep that deeply for that long. Could I?

My waking body alerts me that I have neglected it for a long time, and I roll away from Amber, careful not to disturb her, to find the bathroom. I feel like I've been ripped open. The soreness from birth makes it hard to walk. I would kill to sit in a tub of ice.

As I remembered, the bathroom is luxurious. After relieving myself, I drink cold water from the tap, splash it on my face and eye the multi-headed shower. But first, I have to figure out where we are, and give Mr. Blackwell a piece of my most unhappy mind.

Back in the bedroom, I press the ornate lever on the door that leads up to the deck. It's jammed. No, it's locked. Who has a lock on the *outside* of a bedroom? Was this part of Jason's preparations for "saving" me?

I am still too groggy to be waking from a normal sleep, and I don't remember anything after getting into Jason's car. He must have drugged me. But I ate nothing from the time I had that soup in Angola's underground room—drank nothing but a bottle of water from a supply bag in Jason's car. I can't remember if I broke a seal or just twisted it open. There was a lot on my mind at the time.

I bang on the door. "Jason! Let me out!"

Not surprisingly, my gun, ammo, and cell phone are missing.

"Damn it, Jason!"

Amber whimpers.

"Shit. Sorry Amber," I croon. "Go back to sleep."

A sudden jerk throws me a step toward the bed. We are moving. That means we weren't moving before, so we're probably still at The Wharf's docks. People might be around. I stagger to the window port and yank aside the curtain. The window normally cranks open but is locked, apparently with a key, which is not in the lock. I pound on the thick glass, hoping to break it, but it's too thick. I can't imagine my screams will attract attention, either. It's misty and rainy outside, and I can't see a soul on the pier. Nevertheless, I give it a try, which only wakes Amber.

I pace, trying to figure out something to do. Amber twists in agitation but refuses my breast, and I finally figure out she has to be changed.

Where did the diaper she has on come from? The last thing I remember, she was wrapped in a sheet and a blanket.

I spy a large bag in the corner and dump it out on the bed. A box of diapers, baby powder, a pad, some plastic bags and other baby accessories, and a small stuffed bear. Jason playing Daddy. My hands shake with anger. On top of that, this is my first diaper ever in my life, and I'm spatially challenged. She is so tiny. Why didn't I take diaper classes? I undo the one on her and dump it in one of the plastic bags and try to reconstruct it with the clean one, at least approximately.

I'm terrified for her, but I can't put my finger on why. Then my fuzzy brain remembers the vision in the car and why I don't want her anywhere near the ocean. *Too late.* I tried to stop that path from happening, but I failed.

Damn you, Jason.

I pound on the door again. He's keeping me locked in here until we are too far away from shore for me to do anything about it. I squelch the urge to throw the vase of roses into the door. The noise might frighten Amber. Frustrated and still groggy, I finally give up and crawl back on the bed, scooting Amber close. I look at her and can't believe just hours ago she was in my body, a part of me.

I should have given birth in the hospital with Alice beside me, feeding me living-green. Alice and Becca would have been fighting over who got to hold her and change her. I was counting on them to be there to help me. Now, I'm on my own with this mother stuff, trapped on a boat with an obsessed, crazy man.

And I totally failed at the plan to kill Angola and Samuel.

Jason can't intend to keep me down here the whole trip to the Cayman Islands? But if I keep Amber in the room until we get there, she can't fall into the sea, right? And then I will escape and find somewhere to call for help. I don't want Amber anywhere around water. Tracey will find a way. I know he will, like I know my own bones will hold me upright. I frown. If he thinks I need him, he will be out of that hospital bed no matter what condition he's in. What did he do when he discovered I left the hospital?

At that moment, the sound of a key in the door's lock makes me sit up. Hastily, I make sure my shirt covers my breasts, brace myself for the attack of sexual energy, and ready my verbal barrage for Jason.

The door opens and my planned accusations exhale with my breath as Angola Simone steps into the bedroom.

Chapter Fifty-Nine

Everything I thought I knew about my situation fragments. I stare at Angola, trying to reconstruct the pieces. The only way anything makes sense is that Jason betrayed me. But that makes no sense either. Why go through the farce of rescuing me when I was already at the mercy of Angola and Samuel? If the goal was to get me on this boat, they could have just as easily drugged me in Angola's room and brought me here.

"I see you have questions," Angola says calmly.

"A few."

He pulls up a chair and straddles it. "Ask them."

"Where's Jason?"

"On the deck."

"How—? Did he bring me here to you?"

"Not deliberately."

"How did you know?"

"Everything said in my apartment was recorded. When you escaped, we played it back."

"So, you knew Jason planned to come to the yacht."

"We arrived before you."

I recall Jason's invitation last year to bring me here via a personal plane.

"You didn't drug me?"

"Can't take credit for that."

The bottled water. Jason acted against my wishes, but he hasn't betrayed me to House of Iron. I can still hope for his help.

"Is that the only question you wish to ask?"

I stall with questions I already know the answer to. "You killed all those people using Iron magic, didn't you?"

"Which people?"

"You killed two people to cover up your attempts to fail a diabetes drug trial."

He cocks his head at me. "Yes."

My stomach clenches. A man who admits to murder so easily is not planning on leaving a witness to his confession. But I might as well hear it all. He can only kill me once.

"How did you make that guy at the zoo think he had to kill me?"

"You would be surprised how many people walk a thin edge of sanity. All they need is a little push."

I tuck away this little horrifying piece of perspective to think about later . . . assuming I have a "later." Right now, I need to stay focused.

"You convinced Jacobson and Zane to sell their life insurance policies, and House of Iron purchased them under a corporate cover."

"I told Samuel you were too smart. You are correct, except it was not necessary to convince anyone to sell their life insurance. A company advertises it on television. We only had to buy the policies that were offered for sale."

"You mean you just got a list of whose insurance you owned?"

He nods.

"Then you made Jim Jacobson step into air and fall to his death, and Doris Zane Jansen give her mother an overdose of morphine so Samuel could collect the insurance money from the policies he purchased."

"Only a very partial list of my sins."

"Did you give Doris Jansen the morphine and patch?"

"I did."

"Then you killed her. You slit her throat, so she wouldn't remember that you made her kill her own mother."

"That was a kindness, do you not think?"

"I was right in the first place. You are a monster."

"I never denied it."

Why do I want to see something else in him? Why does his music haunt me?

"You sent the black roses, didn't you?"

"Yes."

"Was that something Theophalus or Samuel ordered?"

"No."

"Then why?"

"I thought you deserved the warning."

I bite my lower lip.

"Those, however," he glances at the vase with the dozen true red roses, "are not from me. I imagine Jason ordered them in preparation for you."

"How thoughtful."

His mouth quirks. "No more questions?"

"Who else is on this boat?"

"Samuel, two of our men, and your detective friend."

"Tracey?" My heart stammers. "He's here? Is he hurt?"

"Nothing permanent."

"Why did you go after him? He has nothing you want."

Angola leans back in the chair. "That is true, and we did not 'go after him.' He came to us."

"What do you mean?"

"He literally tore down the old mine entrance to the tunnels."

I recall seeing the damaged door when Jason and I fled. Tracey had done that trying to find me. He must have figured out I had gone looking for my enemy and knew I was in trouble. He is House of Stone. A door, no matter how strong, would not have held him for long.

"Our new alarm system picked him up when he entered the tunnel," Angola says without waiting for my question. "As they did when you entered."

"And you took him prisoner too."

"It wasn't easy. He is a strong and determined man. We have had to keep him sedated."

"Where is he?"

"Cuffed in the engine room below."

I'm silent for a moment. "Why are you answering all my questions?"

"Because you deserve answers. You have earned them."

I'm not sure what he means, but if he's talking, I intend to get as many answers as I can. "What do you intend to do with us?"

"It is not my intentions that matter."

"Samuel's?"

He doesn't acknowledge that. He doesn't need to.

"Is he going to make us walk the plank?" I meant the question sarcastically. But when he says nothing, I feel the blood drain from my face and look down at my sleeping child. "All of us?" My voice is a hoarse whisper.

"Yes."

"When?"

"Tonight, after we are out of sight of the land."

I take a breath and meet his dark gaze, recalling the violin's exquisite voice in his hands and the fact that he left my gun belt on the iron chair, as if to say—if you are smart enough, arm yourself and come after me.

"You don't want to kill me, do you?"

He hesitates. "No, I do not."

"Will you go against Samuel's orders?" Hope beats butterfly wings in my sore chest.

"No."

There is no hesitation, only, perhaps, a regret. His will might as well have been subject to Iron's magic, except he's a member of the House and immune to it.

I swallow, my throat dry sand. "It means that much that Samuel saved you from the Iraqi camp?"

"Yes. I owe him more than my life—I owe him my sanity."

"What about your soul?"

Silence.

"I see." My gaze drifts to his boots.

"Would you have really cut out my baby?"

"Only if I had to kill you."

Out the thick glass porthole, I can see no land. That and the movement of the boat means we have spilled out into the Gulf of Mexico. The sun is a crimson globe dipping toward the horizon. Darkness will follow soon. Instead of panic, I feel a strange calm.

"I think it's customary to have a last request granted," I say.

"What is it?"

"I want to see Tracey."

He considers it for a moment and then nods.

I put a hand on Amber's blanket. "If I leave my child here, do you swear no one will take her while I am gone?"

One dark brow lifts. "You would trust your baby's life on a monster's word?"

I hesitate. "I would." It makes no sense, but I do. Angola is a cold killer, but I trust his word.

He stands and takes the key from his pocket. "I will lock the door behind us."

Afraid Amber might somehow fall off the bed or suffocate herself in pillows, I lay her on a blanket on the floor and follow Angola. Outside the room, the temperature is oddly mild, though the metal rungs of the stairs are cold against my bare feet. It will be cooler on the deck, especially when the sun disappears.

Outside, the briny smell of the sea is a welcome relief from the cloying roses. The stairway to our left leads to the deck, but he motions me ahead of him and to the right, down another set of stairs. I recall it leads to the kitchen and another bedroom, but we take yet another short flight down to the servants' quarters and a smaller galley. I work one hand surreptitiously into the front of my jeans and the inside elastic of my underpants.

At the boat's aft, we come to the engine room. Diesel tinges the air. The room is clean, the metal parts gleaming, but cramped and uncomfortably warm. Despite the chill outside, I immediately break a sweat. Tracey squats in front of a thick steel pipe, his arms behind him. His face is swollen with bruises and shadowed with the stubbles of a beard a darker shade than his hair.

Seeing us, he pushes his back against the slick metal surface to stand, the sound of metal against metal confirming that he's handcuffed to the pipe. Normally, he would could snap the cuffs or the pipe, but we are over water. No magic augments his strength, and he looks drugged. I step close.

"Rose," he slurs. "I was hoping you weren't here."

I look up into his gray eyes. The pupils are contracted under the influence of opiates. Tears swim in them.

"There's something I need to tell you," I say, standing on my tiptoes. He bows his head so I can touch his rough cheek to mine and whisper in his ear. "I'm sorry."

"For what?"

"For using you to make a child. That wasn't right. I'm sorry."

"I'm not," he says thickly.

I take a ragged breath. "I had the baby. Our baby."

"She's okay?"

"She's perfect."

Silence connects us. I don't break it. Let him hold that joy for a moment. The answer to his next question will shatter it.

Angola doesn't rush us. He stands nearby, watching, but giving us space.

Finally, Tracey quietly asks, "When?"

"Tonight. We just entered the Gulf. We'll be far out to sea."

The tears held in his eyes spill, rolling down his cheek. I've never seen him cry.

"I'm the one who is sorry," he says. "I messed up."

I turn my head, tasting the salt on his lips and work my arms around his waist, melding my body against his. Despite the circumstances and his drugged condition, I feel his body's response, hear my own pulse in my ears.

"Rose," he whispers and leans into my kiss.

It is difficult to do anything functional, but I make my hand work into his and press the handcuff key hard into his palm. He tries to curl his swollen, cold hand around it. Despite his effort, the key slips to the floor with a tiny *clang*.

Without a word, Angola steps behind him and retrieves it. I lay my head against Tracey's chest, absorbing the thud of his heart as if it can somehow sustain us both.

"Enough," Angola says.

Reluctantly, I step back, my own chest heaving under the weight and ache of regret. I want to say more. There's so much more to say . . . but nothing that will make any difference.

Chapter Sixty

Just walking back to the cabin is exhausting. I scoop Amber into my arms and lie down again, defeated. I am so tired.

When I wake again, Jason is sitting on the bed. Like Tracey, his cheeks are stubbled, and his golden hair is windblown.

"I'm sorry, Rose."

"I'm thirsty."

He hands me a bottled water.

I struggle to a sitting position, careful not to disturb Amber, and narrow my eyes at it.

"This one's unopened. I promise."

This time I pay attention to the snap of the seal breaking, although I'm so thirsty, I might have drunk it, anyway. Oblivion might be a better way to face what's coming.

He waits while I drain half the bottle. "Rose, I am so sorry. This is not what I planned, not what I wanted."

"You have to do something."

He lifts his palms. "You don't understand."

"I understand Samuel plans to kill me and my baby. Are you going to just stand by while he does that?"

His gaze falls to the floor. "Samuel is head of House."

"I can't believe this," I say tightly.

"From the time I could walk, loyalty to House was everything."

"I thought you cared about me."

"I do. You can't imagine how painful this is. But even if I tried anything, he just would kill me too. It would be his right."

I want to throw something at him, but the only thing in reach is the water bottle, and I don't want to waste it. "Get out."

He does look miserable, but I don't care.

There are no more visitors until the moon rises. Although I want to, I don't linger in the shower. Why I want to be clean for the sharks, I have no idea. I leave the bathroom door open so I can keep an eye on Amber, less concerned about my modesty than the fear someone will try to snatch her. I tie my wet hair with a piece of ribbon I find in a bathroom drawer. I'm not surprised to find several toothbrushes still in their plastic containers, toothpaste, mouthwash and other necessities an unprepared female guest might require.

The remaining time we have, I spend nibbling on the mostly crumbled piece of toast from my pocket and caring for Amber. When she is not nursing or crying to be changed, I sit on the bed against the backboard, knees up and prop her against my thighs, talking to her. I tell her about her Great-Great Aunt Alice.

"You would like her. She makes the best tea with mint leaves right out of her garden, and her house is full of interesting things, each one with a story that I haven't had time to ask her about. She would love to tell them to you. And you have an Aunt Becca too. She's already bought you a dozen outfits and is dying to dress you in them and spoil you rotten. You have Tracey, your father, already wrapped around those tiny little fingers, and he hasn't even laid eyes on you."

She seems to try to focus on me, but her eyes cross with the effort. I think that's precocious considering she is only a day old—or is it two days?

A bubble of spit forms at the corner of her mouth, something I would have found disgusting days ago, but now think is adorable. I wipe it with the cotton pad I use to protect my shoulder when I burp her. I've seen enough movies to know I should do that after she eats.

I tell her a lot of things, including what I remember of my birth family. "You're named for my little sister, Amber. She would have loved you. You're House of Rose." To my surprise, I hear pride in my voice. "But you're more than that. You're also House of Iron and House of Stone—the *Y Tair,* maybe. I'm not sure what that means, exactly, but it's something important—something that could have changed the way things are and haven't been in a long, long time."

The sound of the key in the lock stops my prattling, and I pull her against me. *It's time.*

Angola enters. This time with Samuel behind him.

"Hello, my dear," Samuel says cheerfully. "You have given us quite a run."

He sounds as if he's talking to a treed fox, while his snarling hounds leap against the trunk, baying for blood.

I've never hated anyone more, with the possible exception of his brother, Theophalus.

"But, regretfully, it is time," he says. "I thought I would offer you the courtesy of not having to witness—well, why don't we let Angola take the child now and save the dramatics."

"Please," I say, losing all my dignity. "Don't kill her. Whatever you think she is, she is an innocent." I would be on my knees if I thought it would make a difference.

He gives a deep sigh. "Now, perhaps, but she has the blood of two Houses, and even if she doesn't, we can't risk her breeding one day with House of Iron or Stone."

I'm not about to argue that she is not Jason's child. Jason has claimed her as his, and that might be the only path to a strand of pity.

"She's your niece," I say. "She's family."

"Take the child," Samuel instructs Angola.

Angola steps forward.

I hold Amber tighter. "No."

"Very well." Impatience now stains Samuel's voice. "Come out on your own, or I will send two very muscular men to bring you."

I stand. For a moment, I don't think my legs will hold me, but they do. The world fills with surreal details—the blood-satin bedspread that matches the perfect roses; the sharp angle of Angola's chin; Samuel's clear-polished nails; the slow sink of plush carpet beneath my feet.

In a fog, I am up the metal stairs and onto the deck without knowing how I get there. Soft blue lighting rings the base of the stern deck, gleaming off the polished wood. Desperately, I reach for the living-green that scratches at me like pressure on a foot that has gone to sleep, but it eludes me. I want its comfort, a bulwark against the pain at leaving the world so soon, at losing my daughter, losing Tracey and Alice and Becca.

Chapter Sixty-One

Tracey is already on the aft deck, standing between two men, his hands still bound behind him. He sways, unsteady, his head bowed forward as if it is too much weight to hold upright. Have they given him more drugs?

I recognize one of the men holding him. Months ago, he had been in the cave when Theophalus Blackwell handcuffed me to the iron chair they call a throne and tortured me. I never knew his name, but I called him Jaws.

It was a long shot, trying to give Tracey the handcuff key. After the Ordeal, I swore I would never be handcuffed again without a key handy. It had taken hours of practice in handcuffs to get where I could manipulate the key into the tiny lock—a skill I took with me when I had to walk into Angola's lair once before, a skill that saved my life. To ask Tracey to manage that in his condition with his hands already swollen and numb from hours in the cuffs was too much. But I have another one that was taped to the back of my underwear. Yes, I am that paranoid. I've hidden it in Amber's blanket.

"Can I kiss Tracey goodbye?" I ask Samuel, who leans on the stern railing. Maybe I can work my last key into the lock for Tracey. He doesn't look like he could manage to do anything even if his hands were free, but he's a big guy and House of Stone, even without access to his power. I'm hoping it takes a lot of drugs to affect him.

"Too late for that," Samuel says, crushing my last hope.

Now what? After we are overboard, floundering in the heartless sea, I could release Amber and try to unlock Tracey's cuffs before he sinks like a rock. And then what? We would all still drown. The thought of water, which has always been my friend, closing around me like solid walls, seeping into my lungs, suffocating me, triggers my heart into a jagged rhythm.

Angola might shoot us out of mercy and . . . whatever it is he feels toward me. There is something there. I believe that—respect at the least. If there's more, I don't know what to call it. But if he shoots me, it would mean a mess to clean on the deck, and if he doesn't aim true . . . the sharks would come, possibly before we drown.

I expected the wind would be cold and biting, matching my fear, but it is strangely warm, the untimely kind of warm that stirs a brewing storm. But it's not the time of year for a hurricane. The sea is placid, the stars bright pinpricks in the dark bowl of sky opposite the moon. It's a full moon that's rising, latent with a creamy light that will soon blot out the stars.

Should I spend my last breaths keeping Amber's head above the water, or let her drown first, holding her close? My sweaty hands clinch at her blanket. Maybe I should have pulled it over her tiny mouth and nose. . . . I clutch her, and she squirms in my arms, giving a muffled cry of protest. I make myself relax. No point in frightening her.

At Samuel's signal, one of the burly men leaves Tracey's side and steps behind me, grasping my upper arms. From nowhere a wind stirs, rocking the deck.

I turn to Jason as my last resort. He stands near the railing to my left, as far away as possible from Samuel. "Jason!" I plead.

He won't meet my eyes. *Coward.*

Angola appears before me and holds out his arms for Amber.

"No!" I fight against the grip of the man behind me, who pulls my elbows back until I'm forced to release Amber or drop her.

Angola, his face chiseled stone, carries her in the crook of one arm to the railing a few feet from Samuel. He doesn't look at her. His gaze is fixed on Samuel, waiting for a signal to throw her overboard.

Choking on the fist that wedges in my throat and chest, I strain against the grip holding me, reaching desperately for the living-green and the power of Iron, ready to mix them with my fury and burn this boat and everyone on it to cinders. With all my being, I pull for them.

Nothing.

"Stop!"

It takes a moment to realize the shouted order came from Jason. He holds a small gun in his hand. It's not the gun from the guard. They must have taken that from him. Then I recall he wore an ankle holster in the hospital room. Jason points it, not at Angola, but at Samuel.

"Put the child down," Jason says, "or I shoot Samuel."

I catch my breath. Jason knows that Angola will not allow him to kill Samuel. Samuel walked into an enemy camp to rescue Angola. Samuel is head of House of Iron.

Everyone goes still. In the stretched silence, the slap of waves against the hull seems deafening.

"Jason," Samuel says with a low chuckle. "Spare us the heroics, nephew. Stand down. You still have a place in the House. When these last witches are gone, there'll be nothing distracting you."

"No, I will not stand down to you. Not ever again."

Then everything happens at once.

Angola takes a step toward Jason and bends forward as if to lay Amber on the deck. Instead, he lofts her in an underhanded pitch.

My heart stops. Terror stills time. At the apex of her flight, she hangs, suspended in the air against a backdrop of moonlit sea—*my vision!*

Jason, forced to catch her or let her fall, drops the gun to capture her in his arms.

Angola has snatched his own weapon from the back of his waist-band. He levels it at Jason . . . and my baby.

Amber is crying.

"No!" Adrenaline gushes through my veins, brushing aside pain, fear, and the carefully built acceptance of death.

Tracey lowers his head and bellows a deep roar. *His dragon awaking?* He throws his head back into his captor's jaw and wrenches from his grip. Jaws goes to his knees. Hands still cuffed behind him, Tracey stumbles forward, throwing himself at Angola.

That snaps something inside me. If Tracey, handcuffed and drugged, is not going down without a fight, neither am I.

I lift my foot and kick behind me onto my captor's shin as hard as I can, then rake my foot down it onto the top of his foot. The effect would have been better had Angola not confiscated my boots. But he cries out in pain and his grip loosens. Taking advantage of his distraction and hoping I'm doing it right—there will be no second chance—I bend my knees, dropping my weight, and shift to one side, lifting my arms to raise his and duck under them, a move practiced in jujitsu class. Before he can recover, I turn and step close, kneeing him hard in the bladder. He pitches forward, groaning.

"Jason!" I shout.

Jason, still holding Amber, kicks the gun, sending it spinning across the deck in my direction.

I dive for it, but I'm not the only one.

From his knees, Jaws does the same thing. We hit the deck flat out at the same time. His head is inches from mine, his longer arms reaching for the gun. Desperate, I jam my elbow into his closest eye.

With a scream, his hands contract to protect his injured eye, and he rolls away from me in agony. My fingers close around the gun. It's a snub-nose .38 revolver. That means I don't have to worry about chambering a round, only pulling the trigger. The greatest threat is Angola, but I don't have a shot because Tracey, his hands still cuffed behind him, has crashed into Angola and pinned him against the rail, trying to down him with a clumsy foot sweep.

Samuel steps behind Tracey. His solid cane lifts in an arc that will end at Tracey's temple. In police academy baton training, the temple is a forbidden strike zone because a hard hit is likely to cause brain damage or death. It's an area of thin bone and very little protective muscle, even for a man of Stone.

Stomach pressed against the deck, I shift my aim, squeezing the trigger. The blast of gunshot in my ears muffles everything, including Amber's cries.

Samuel opens his mouth without sound. He doubles over slowly, as if the air has clotted around him. *Is this real or a vision?* The cane falls from his hand, and sound reenters the world as it clatters to the deck.

The side of his normally jovial face, frozen in a fierce scowl, smacks the polished, gleaming wood, spittle landing just short of my outstretched arms. In the blue deck lights, the blood that seeps from his gaping mouth is black.

"Tracey, get down!" I shout.

Without hesitation, my partner drops and rolls to the side.

Angola's dark eyes lock on mine. Freed from the pin of Tracey's weight, he lifts his gun. I have looked down that barrel before.

I fire again, two shots. Blood blossoms from Angola's chest. Like Samuel's, it is dark in the moonlight and the blue glow of the deck lighting, as dark as the black roses he has left me. He too sinks slowly to his knees, his gaze still fixed on me, a slight smile on his face.

Caught in the adrenaline-induced hyper-focus of detail, something wrong registers—Angola's gun is aimed directly at me, but his forefinger lies flat along the barrel . . . *not on the trigger.*

And then he is down, his cheek against the deck, his body still, rocked by the passing swells.

Epilogue

Alice's living room shimmers with Christmas tinsel, lights, and a fat, fully decorated tree. For Becca, who is Jewish, a Chanukah menorah hosting nine candles sits on the windowsill. A banner hangs from the ceiling between the living room and kitchen printed with little pink roses and the words, "Welcome to the World, Amber!"

I sit on the sofa and sip my chilled fruit drink. Tracey stands nearby with a cup of hot spiced apple cider. My stomach does a flip-flop at the smell of cinnamon. *Angola is dead*, I have to remind myself.

Daniel and his little friend Kaleshia are playing a board game near the Christmas tree, watched over by Kaleshia's big brother, Devon Segal. Kaleshia is as oblivious of Daniel's scars as he is that her skin is a darker shade than his, or that she is bald from the cancer treatments. Becca is chatting away with Jamal. She's rocking Amber in the crook of her arm as if she has raised a dozen children.

Boo Boo and Charlie are batting at the tree decorations within their reach. Alexander, the schizophrenic black devil, is nowhere in sight, hiding crouched under something, I suspect, watching everything. I brought Angel over for a visit, and she has claimed my lap. She's still not sure about the status of the pink thing I brought home.

Alice emerges from the kitchen with a tray of cookies my nose informs me are chocolate chip, hopefully with pecans. My favorite. Hobart, sitting in a chair on the opposite side of the room, gives her a warm smile and she actually blushes.

I can't imagine living like that, but they seem delighted with each other. I will endeavor to be civil with Hobart, for Alice's sake, for Tracey's sake, and to give Amber the opportunity to have a grandfather.

I close my eyes and just relish being here. Being *safe*.

It has been a week, but it seems like forever ago that we waited onboard the *Iron Fist* for the US Coast Guard in the Gulf of Mexico. We had a lot of talking to do to explain two dead bodies. The FBI has the case since it happened outside coastal waters. Jaws and the other thug were arrested on federal charges. Birmingham's internal investigation is ongoing, even though everything happened off duty. There is no such thing as off duty for a cop. Not my first rodeo there. The only thing Tracey and I have withheld is Jason drugging me and the real reason Samuel wanted me and my baby dead—to kill off House of Rose. From their perspective, the kidnapping and planned murder was to prevent us from arresting Angola for the murder of Laurie Stokes and Doris Zane Jansen and the attempted murder of yours truly.

Jim Jacobson's fall and death will remain officially an accident, and Jessie Zane's overdose in the senior home, an open case. Neither can be explained without bringing House magic into play, something Tracey and I will never do.

Alice sits beside me on the sofa. "I want to tell you first," she whispers, her cheeks rosy.

"What?"

"My news."

"And what news is that?"

She smooths her skirt and sits straighter. "I'm expecting."

I glance at the door, wondering if she is having a premonition. My purse and gun are at my feet, and I'm sure Tracey is armed.

"Expecting who?"

A huge grin spreads across her round face, dimpling her cheeks. "Amber's cousin."

"What?" My gaze falls to her belly. "You're not—? You couldn't be."

"But I am, my dear, and I couldn't be more pleased."

I look from her to Hobart, who hasn't taken his eyes from her.

"Yes, indeed," she says.

"But, your . . . age?"

"Yes, isn't it marvelous?"

I'm staring at her.

Her smile broadens. "I do think there might be something to Orson's theories about fertility between the Houses and perhaps a tad of an old herb witch's magic."

"That's just not possible."

"A woman is born with all the eggs she will have, dear. One just has to take care of them."

I am trying to process this. "How?"

"Well, it has to do, I believe, with the quantum frequency, singing them the right music, so to speak—"

"—Does Hobart know?" I cut off her explanation before we go too far down the quantum path.

"Not yet, so don't go spilling the beans."

THE FOLLOWING DAY I ATTEND A SECOND PARTY, taking Amber to the Homicide Unit's Holiday celebration. Lieutenant Faraday made it into a surprise baby shower. And I am surprised. Guys from our old Burglary Unit, including cranky Lieutenant "Fish," have joined in. A heap of presents fill a nearby table.

Tracey watches from across the room. He has not acknowledged fatherhood, nor have I brought it up. The first thing that would happen would be a transfer out of the unit for at least one of us and neither of us want that.

While Amber is passed around, I drink punch from the non-spiked orange and pineapple juice bowl, since I am still nursing, and nibble at the plentiful goodies, curbing my normal tendency toward gluttony with the goal of shedding a few baby pounds before I have to return to work.

Detective Harper picks up a chocolate chip cookie, my contribution via Alice, to the party goodies. "Good news, sort of," he says around a mouthful.

"What's that?"

"Feds have backed off the zoo shooting. Couldn't find any evidence of terrorism from outside the US, and the state investigators cleared Tracey."

"Did you find a motivation?"

"Not one that made sense, but that's where you have to leave it sometimes. The suspect is dead, and we don't think anyone else was involved, so it's not like we have to build a case on anyone. It's officially closed. I'm sorry we didn't figure out what was going on in that young man's head. Just glad Tracey reacted so fast. He's a big guy, but turning that table over took some adrenaline rush."

"Adrenaline. Yeah."

"I've heard about wimpy guys lifting a car in an emergency."

"The body is an amazing thing." I pat my middle. "I should know."

"Ha!" He takes another cookie and drops it in a pocket. "These are good. Maybe you could whip up some more for the office while you're on R&R taking care of that baby."

R&R? Men are clueless. "I'll think about it."

He saunters off, and the last person I expect to see holding Amber approaches me with her cradled expertly in his arm. The other holds a cup of the pink stuff that only the supervisors pretend is lemonade.

"Finkman," I say.

He looks down at Amber and then at me. "You done good."

"Yeah, she turned out pretty fine."

"She did, but that's not what I meant."

My forehead knots in puzzlement.

"I was hard on you." He clears his throat. "Harder than I should have been."

I don't comment. Apologies do not come easily to Finkman's lips and that might be a vast understatement.

He shifts his weight. "What I'm trying to say is you saved Tracey. That's two po-lice who owe their lives to you."

He is referring to my shooting of a suspect last year to keep him from killing my ex-partner/lover, Paul Nix. I still see that young man's face at night, but I would do it again if I had to. I would kill Angola again to save those I love.

"I'm no hero. The suspect would have killed me too."

But would he? Was I really faster on the trigger or did Angola release himself from his obligation to Samuel and choose to die rather than continue to be a monster? I have come to believe he wanted me to hear him play his violin to know that what I saw was not the totality of his soul.

Finkman, unaware of the swirl of my thoughts, just nods his head. "That doesn't matter. I mean, you did what you had to, and that's what we all do." Reluctantly, he holds Amber out to me. "That's what makes our blood blue."

I smile and take Amber from him.

I LEAVE THE PARTY BEFORE IT'S OVER, wanting to get home and feed Amber. She gets cranky if I'm late with the milk goods. Though it is sixty-three degrees, I tuck her blanket around her. Technically, it's winter and tomorrow it's going down to thirty-two. Schizophrenic Alabama weather.

The parking lot is almost deserted, not surprising for a Saturday. Just before reaching my car, a familiar leap of my pulse stops me—a warlock alert. And not just any warlock.

"Rose?"

I jump at the voice behind me.

"Damn it, Jason, don't sneak up on me like that!"

"I did not intend to sneak, *amore*."

"And don't call me that."

"I must call you that." He shrugs. "But if it angers you—"

I take a deep breath and a step back from him. But I can only back up to my car, and the distance isn't enough to help much.

"What do you want?" I ask.

He smiles. "You mean besides taking you into my arms?"

"Yes, besides that, because that is not going to happen. You don't get to drug me, kidnap me, and then act like it doesn't mean anything."

"I only wanted to protect you."

"All the same, I don't trust you. I can never trust you."

He is silent for a long moment. "I understand."

"I can't—" I struggle for the words. "I understand what you're feeling. It's hard on me to be near you too." *Damn it, I will not be a pawn of this magic!* "But stay away from me and from Amber."

He looks stricken, but that will go away with enough distance and a few women. I'm certain there will be no lack of those. With Samuel dead, Jason is now head of House of Iron, and I imagine he will also have his hands full ferreting out all the webs of House power and intrigue spun across the globe.

Jason is not a bad person. I'm not pressing charges on him. When it came down to it, he made the choice to go against his own House. He saved my baby. I will always owe him for that.

"Very well," he says. "I respect your desires, though I do not understand them."

"Thank you."

"I am always at your service should you change your mind."

I stifle a guffaw at his choice of words, noting that he didn't offer to come if I needed him, only if I changed my mind about hopping into bed with him.

"I wish you and your child well."

"And I wish you well too, Jason," I say to his retreating back.

FOUR MONTHS LATER, TRACEY AND I sit on a bench in the April sun at the Vulcan Trail Park with double-chocolate ice-cream cones. Above us, the Big Man holds his spear up to the light, checking to make sure his hammer and forge are true. His silvery-gray "skin" shines in the spring sunlight. It's a color I always found slightly annoying since he is made of iron, but now I know it's the color of true iron, pure iron. I wonder if whoever decided on the color knew that, or if they just wanted him to shine in the moonlight.

Amber sits on the ground before us on a thick quilt surrounded by a few of her too-many toys. There is no sign that she is anything but a toddler intent on exploring her world, but the magics of three Houses exist in her. She is something the world has not seen for a long time.

For a moment, I hear Theophalus Blackwell's warning—*when the blood of the Houses mix, the powers are uncontrollable.* What will happen when my baby comes into her powers? I don't know. I would say that I can't see the future, but that's not exactly true. I just don't have any control over it—when I see it or how mutable it is. Blackwell was right in that sense. Was he right that my baby is dangerous? Did the iron chair "wake" her in some way?

Her chubby hand shakes a rattle, and she looks up at us, innocent and vulnerable, a dot of double-chocolate ice cream on her nose where she gummed my cone. Her eyes are now a steel blue. Alice says they may change again. No one can predict what color the *Y-Tair's* eyes will be, but I say it makes sense because she is a child of all the ores needed to make steel. Having them all in proximity is what made Birmingham a steel town and gave it the name "Magic City."

I look down over the trees of Red Mountain's north slope, laced with the off-white of blooming wild dogwoods, to the heart of the city we are both sworn to protect. Birmingham has changed from those days of mining ores and manufacturing steel. The rusted pipes of Sloss Furnaces in the valley below are now a museum. The Magic City is a medical-university complex and more. What the city will become is still unwritten, like Amber's eyes. Like our future.

Amber's bulging bag of stuff on the bench forces me close enough to Tracey to feel the warmth from his body. But I don't mind. It feels right to be here, to be with this man of Stone who loves me. My pulse will always jump if and when I encounter Jason Blackwell. But relationships are built on trust, not lust, especially magically induced lust. There would never be real, intimate trust between Jason Blackwell and me. I can't control the magic, Amber's latent powers, or the seductive magnetism between us. I can only make choices. One of those was to tell Jason to stay away from me and from Amber.

Tracey shifts, stretching his arm across the top of the bench. He is a good man in all the ways that matter—someone who will always have my back. The hard muscles of his arm press against my shoulders, and I think I want to see if that kiss in the engine room of the *Iron Fist* or the hour spent in conceiving Amber is replicable without the entanglement of desperation. What he stirs in me might be something purely human . . . but it is also a kind of magic.

"Lohan?"

"What?"

"How do you think you might be at diapers?"

Photo by Roger Thorne

T.K. Thorne's childhood passion for storytelling deepened when she became a police officer. "It was a crash course in life, in what motivated people and what mattered to them." She served more than two decades in the Birmingham police force where she worked in the patrol, detective, and administration bureaus, retiring as a precinct captain. Following that, she took on CAP (City Action Partnership), a downtown business improvement district that focused on safety, retiring after seventeen years to write full time. Her writings roam wherever her interests and imagination take her, from award-winning historical fiction to civil rights nonfiction and urban fantasy. She writes from her mountaintop home northeast of Birmingham, often with a dog and a cat vying for her lap.

www.ingramcontent.com/pod-product-compliance
Lightning Source LLC
Chambersburg PA
CBHW010737130726
47899CB00015B/3296